Wyoming Tryst

THE FRONT RANGE SERIES

CHARLENE WHITMAN

UBIQUITOUS **P**RESS

Morgan Hill, CA

WYOMING TRYST by Charlene Whitman
Copyright ©2018 Charlene Whitman

ISBN: 978-0986134784
LCCN: 2018939493

Cover and interior designed by Ellie Searl, Publishista®

UBIQUITOUS PRESS
Morgan Hill, CA

Be sure to join Charlene Whitman's readers' list to get free books, special offers, giveaways, and sneak peeks of chapters and covers.

When you join, you'll get a FREE copy of Wild Horses, Wild Hearts!

Sign up at www.Charlene Whitman.com

Praise for *COLORADO PROMISE*
Book 1 in The Front Range Series

"A fresh new voice in Historical Romance, Charlene Whitman captured me from the beginning with characters I won't soon forget, a sizzling-sweet romance, a love triangle, spiteful villains, heart-throbbing heroes, and a plot full of intrigue that kept me guessing. Ms. Whitman's magnificent research transported me to the Colorado plains and left me longing to join the characters amidst the wildflower-dotted fields, rushing rivers, and panoramic Rocky Mountains. Fans of Historical Western Romance will not soon forget *Colorado Promise*."

— MaryLu Tyndall, best-selling romance author

"An adequate writer of historical fiction will include minor bits and pieces about the setting of their story. A good writer will do a bit of research to make sure there are historical facts included in the pages of their novel. A superb writer will create characters that could have actually lived during the time in which the story takes place and allows them to act as people in that time period would have really acted. Charlene Whitman is a superb writer."

— Examiner.com

"Ms. Whitman's voice is honest and true to the times. Not only in the way her characters spoke but also in the narrative. I lost sleep because I wanted to know what happened next. It's one of those stories you become invested in the characters. Five stars and 3 'YEEHAWs' to Charlene Whitman and *Colorado Promise*!"

— author Su Barton

"I was so utterly thrilled to have a story hold my attention this completely. It is the second in The Front Range series, but the story was complete within itself. Monty's and Grace's faith in God was strong as they met with many disastrous situations. It was also a story of holding onto hope when there appeared to be no hope. To me, this is the perfect story to 'cocoon' yourself in to your favorite reading spot, and try not to come out 'til you're done."

— D. Coto

Praise for *COLORADO DREAM*
Book 3 in The Front Range Series

"A courageous protagonist in relentless pursuit of her dream hooked me from the first page of this wonderful novel. Whitman's "sweet romance" is just that and so much more — her characters are deep and thought provoking, the story well-paced. And her research is impeccable. I thoroughly enjoyed this book and will be reading the others in this series."

— bestselling author Ginny Yttrup

"This is my first book by Charlene Whitman but it will not be my last. Wonderful story of two hearts broken by their pasts and the abuses heaped upon them by others. The love they find in each other and the author's word pictures of a part of this great country made me believe I was watching from beside them. I could taste the dirt and smell the smoke and hear the music. If you enjoy learning more about the people who risked everything to open the frontier you won't find a better place to start. Beautiful!"

— P. M. Jones

"This is a story that fills your heart with love and a touch of warmth. If you love Wwesterns, sweet romance, a little history and characters you can relate to, then pick up a copy of this book and travel to Greeley, Colorado, with Angela and meet Brett."

—Gayle Pace

"I could not put this book down. Enjoyed every second of it. Charlene Whitman is a excellent story teller and all her books never fail to keep you sitting on edge of your chair. Wonderful book."

—Sue Mays

"Great story and the author has a wonderful imagination. I could not put it down until I finished reading it."

—Dionne Washington

Also in The Front Range Series by Charlene Whitman

Wild Horses, Wild Hearts
Colorado Promise
Colorado Hope
Wild Secret, Wild Longing
Colorado Dream

"From ancient grudge break to new mutiny . . .
where civil blood makes civil hands unclean."
— *Romeo and Juliet*, William Shakespeare

Chapter 1

November 5, 1878

"I DON'T CARE WHAT IT costs—get it done! Stop lollygagging and make Morrison sign that paper. Rohrbach has other offers, and he knows I'm chomping at the bit—"

Julia Carson cringed at the sound of something heavy smashing against the wall adjoining the sewing room, but a glance at her mother showed that Lester Carson's histrionics ruffled her not at all. *When did they ever?* But Julia knew that was the only way her mother could successfully navigate around her husband's outbursts.

Her mother, with her lustrous back hair piled atop her head in perfect fashion, pulled another straight pin from between her teeth and said, "Stop wiggling, Julia. How will I ever get this hem pinned if you keep swiveling about?"

Julia sighed, feeling the familiar constriction and barely telltale rattle in her chest. But thank the heavens autumn was here. A glance out the wide windows showed a bright, crisp morning, though menacing clouds were gathering in the distance. She wouldn't be surprised if the first snow fell later that day.

This summer had been the worst yet, and twice her parents had flown into a panic when Julia had awoken in the middle of the night unable to breathe. The tonics the doctor had given her did little else but make her woozy, and though Reverend Charnel urged her to give her burden to the Good Lord, it seemed He wasn't all that keen on lifting it from her shoulders. Predictions over the years said she'd never make it to her sixteenth birthday, but yet, here she was.

"—Get out! Just git!"

Her father's boorish directive followed on the heels of two short, fastidious men in three-piece suits making a hasty exit from her father's study. Upon noticing Julia standing on the round dais and her mother squatting with pins in her mouth, the solicitors nodded brusquely from the hallway and muttered their farewells, their hats clenched in hand.

Julia's mother muttered, "Heavens, your father is putting those poor men through the wringer." She shook her head and finished pinning the last section of hem of the elegant white satin party dress. Then she took a step back, her petticoats swishing under her toile skirt, and admired her handiwork.

Though her mother could easily afford to hire the finest dressmaker in Wyoming Territory, she made all of Julia's dresses and blouses, spending her quiet evenings, especially in the winter months when snow piled up the windows, bent over her tiny stitches. The sewing room in which they stood overflowed with bolts of lace and strings of seed pearls that her mother painstakingly added in beautiful detail to Julia's party dresses.

And this dress would be the most magnificent yet, for, as her mother kept reminding Julia, "No one must outshine you on your sixteenth birthday."

But there was more in her mother's eyes than admiration for her handiwork and pride in her only child—*her only living child*, Julia noted. Because, wasn't that at the heart of this celebration? That Julia was the only child of Danielle and Lester Carson to have survived into adulthood.

And that was what Julia read in her mother's eyes. Pain and loss. Three stillborn babies lay in the nearby family graveyard. Alongside the small coffin containing Julia's older brother, who'd succumbed to the influenza when he was four—two months before Julia was born.

Julia could never be free of her mother's loss, never be absolved. Her parents stifled and smothered her with love and protection and worry because, as her mother often lamented, "We couldn't ever bear to lose you. It would kill us both." Though her father never voiced such sentiments aloud.

And it was hard to interpret his heavy hand and unfair restrictions as fear of loss. No, her father's actions seemed anything but fearful, and his protection anything but loving and concerned.

But no matter. She would soon find a man to wed, and though she'd been so sheltered, hardly even permitted to say hello to any unhitched young man, even at church, she secretly hoped she'd get her chance at her party. A party that would make the high-society columns in papers all the way to the Mississippi, if her mother had her way. Her parents were sparing no expense for an event that would no doubt be hailed as the most extravagant gala Laramie City had ever seen.

Julia's throat tightened at the attention that would be heaped upon her that night, for crowds of people made her terribly claustrophobic, often exacerbating her asthma. Her rigorous protests for a small family gathering had been lost on unresponsive ears. Though, why was she surprised? This party really wasn't about her, or for her, for that matter. It was, in essence, a way for her father to show off his opulence and success as Laramie's foremost cattle rancher. *And to flaunt that success before the Morrisons, who, as a matter of course, were not invited and never would be.*

"Oh, you are such a beauty," her mother crooned. "Spin around and show me."

Julia dutifully spun, the layers of eyelet-lace-edge skirts whirling and fluttering like snowflakes on a breeze. Wearing such a gorgeous dress made Julia feel beautiful indeed. But she wondered if any dress could negate her flaws. Her pale complexion that freckled terribly in the sun. Her long lifeless hair the color of bark that constantly slipped out of her pins. And worst of all—her height. She stood over her mother by four inches. What man would want to look up to his wife? At five feet eight, she was taller than most of the ranch hands on the farm. Except Ty, her much-older cousin, who was like a brother to her. And, of course, her father, who towered a head above every man in town. The Carson men had always stood out prominently in a crowd—due to both height and propensity for bluster. But, unlike Julia's uncles, Lester Carson was more the quiet but intense type who believed in an economy of words. Except when someone sparked his anger.

Julia stepped down from the dais and turned so her mother could fuss with the button loop at Julia's neck. The spacious sewing room with its floor-to-ceiling windows spilled warm light across the thickly varnished oak floorboards that shone like glass. Dust motes danced on the air.

"Mother, why has Father been meeting with his lawyers so often? And what is he so crotchety about?"

Her mother's sigh blew warmth onto Julia's neck, making a shiver run down her spine. "It's nothing to concern yourself with. Another land deal. He wants to acquire the thousand-acre parcel to the northwest."

Julia shook her head. "But why? Doesn't he own enough land? Aren't fifty thousand acres sufficient for his purposes?"

"It's the water access. You know in late summer Dead Man's Creek is the only source of water for the cattle. That property has the only year-round spring for miles around."

"So? Father has always moved the herds north in the fall."

"And it appears he doesn't want to be bothered to do so any longer."

Julia fell silent. Once her father got a hankering in his craw, there was no pulling it free. But this was something different than his normal dealings. He'd been downright perturbed these last months, working himself into a frenzy, more apt to snap at Cousin Ty and Sheldon McManus, his ranch foreman, than ever before.

"Is . . . Father ill?"

Her mother turned Julia to face her. Julia saw close up the tired lines etching her mother's still-beautiful face. Dark splotches sagged under her eyes, and her mouth drew into a tight line.

"No," she said, then hesitated. "Though, I daresay if he keeps up like this"—she gestured to the now-closed door to the study, where Lester Carson was tromping across the floorboards so loudly, Julia feared he might bust through them—"his heart just might succumb from the aggravation."

But there was something her mother wasn't telling her. Something—Julia knew—whose source went way back, before

Julia was born. Something neither parent ever mentioned, but on occasion Julia caught a whiff of, like the scent of a moldering dead carcass carried on the wind. In the late hours Julia sometimes heard terse words spoken behind closed doors. Words that often included the name Morrison.

Her father hated Stephen Morrison. That was a fact everyone in Wyoming Territory knew well. And Morrison hated Julia's father. But no one seemed to know what had started the feud that had been going on between the two men—and that had dragged both families through the mud of hate and threats—for decades. Ty had once let slip words that hinted at a card game and someone cheating, but for all Julia knew, his words were little more than grist for the rumor mill in town.

And she'd heard her father tell his lawyers to make Morrison sign the papers. Did Stephen Morrison own that land her father coveted? If so, he had to know Morrison would never sell—not on his life.

Oh, all this land wrangling and vying for power made Julia more than weary. She felt like a prisoner in her own home. Her upcoming party was the only bright glimmer of hope on the horizon. If only it held the promise of escape. Would she ever be free of her father's heavy hand?

The door to the courtyard swung open, and Ty came in, a grin on his sun-baked face, his unruly wheat-straw hair splaying out from under his floppy hat. He touched the brim and said, "Ladies," then knocked on the door to the study. As Julia's mother gathered up her scissors and pins and spools of thread, Julia felt a sudden urge to change out of her fancy dress, throw on a riding skirt and blouse, and race across the range on Little Bit. The house seemed to be closing in on her, and the glorious late-autumn day was passing her by.

Her father opened the door and exchanged quiet but terse words with Ty. Then, without another word or a glance at his wife or daughter, he strode past the open doors of the sewing room and down the hallway, his footfalls echoing loudly.

Ty turned to Julia and her mother, his soft gray-green eyes thoughtful and intense. "I'm headin' to town with the wagon to pick up supplies at Harold's. Need anything at the mercantile?"

"Milkman Mary should have our order ready for pickup," her mother said. "I'd be obliged if you stopped in and picked up the milk and cream."

"May I go with you?" Julia asked. She'd rather stroll the shop windows than saddle up her mare and ride, alone, with no one to talk with. And Ty, always so funny and cheerful, was just the company she needed right now.

"Dressed like that?" He pointed at her. "You'd 'bout give every fella apoplexy if'n they saw you *saunterin' down the street*." He sashayed around the room, making Julia laugh, as he stroked the wiry goatee on his chin.

Though Ty was her cousin and fourteen years her senior, he had come under the wings of her parents when he was twelve due to a mudslide that had left him orphaned. The two of them had been raised like siblings, and Julia couldn't imagine having more affection for Ty if he'd been her brother. Or Ty having a fiercer sense of protectiveness for his younger relation.

"There'll be no town visit today," her mother said sternly.

"Why not — ?" Julia tried to keep the whine out of her voice. It wasn't fair.

"Because I said so."

Ty frowned. "I'd keep her safe, ma'am — you know that — "

"No, Ty. It would be highly imprudent . . . at this time. This discussion is over."

Ty promptly shut his mouth, as he was wont to do when her mother spoke in that tone.

Her mother hastily stuffed the remaining notions into her sewing box and latched the cover. She looked over at Julia. "Have Edna help you out of that dress, and hang it up in my parlor so I can hem it." Her tone brooked no argument or even a reply.

"Yes, Mother," Julia said anyway, keeping her tone even and respectful, though she held back what she really wanted to say. *I'm a grown woman. I can take care of myself. I'm not your sick little baby anymore. How will I ever live in the world if I'm sheltered from it?*

Ty stood and watched as Julia's mother exited the room, then turned to Julia, kneading his hat in his hands.

"She's only bein' protective."

Julia scoffed. "I know Laramie's a rough town, but surely—"

"You didn't hear the news? What happened last night?"

Julia shook her head as a chill settled on her neck. She'd seen the *Daily Sentinel* lying on the credenza in the dining room, but she hadn't glanced at the headlines. Fights and trouble plagued the streets of Laramie, always had. Most people—decent folk—knew to stay away from Front Street at night, where the brothels stretched for blocks and drunken men poured out of saloons to fight, cheered on by equally drunken crowds. And no decent woman would wander the streets of downtown past dark unchaperoned.

"Two fellas were shot, right in the middle of Grand Street. One o' the fellas had a woman on his arm, and in the brawl that ensued, she was . . . trampled to death."

Julia felt the blood leave her face. "Was . . . she someone I knew?" She swallowed at the reticence evident on Ty's face.

"Lola Peterson—"

"Mrs. Peterson? The school marm?" The young woman who'd taught Julia her letters and read her first primers with her had recently wed. Oh, Lord, it couldn't be . . .

Ty nodded. "Your ma hadn't told you." It was a statement, an observation. His lips quirked in an expression of empathy. "I'm so sorry. I know how much ya liked her. I did too."

Julia had a flash of memory—of Ty putting a frog on their tutor's chair and guffawing when she squealed in shock. A rock lodged painfully in her throat.

"And her husband?" Julia brought to mind the sweet-faced man with the thick black hair and beard who had a little gap between his front teeth—a grocer by trade.

Ty shook his head slowly. Julia's throat clenched, and she struggled to draw air into her stubborn lungs.

"Why doesn't that blasted sheriff bring order to this town? He and his hooligan deputies don't seem to do anything but drink and cause their own kind of trouble."

Ty's severe expression said it all.

If there was someone her father hated even more than Stephen Morrison—if that were possible—it was Sheriff Thomas Jefferson Carr. And it seemed the feeling was mutual. Julia had only met the beefy unpleasant sheriff on a couple of occasions, at public affairs that she'd been allowed to attend, such as the Christmas concert at the Grange Hall and the Fourth of July picnics in the park, where all the politicians and public figures made their appearances—especially on election years.

When Sheriff Carr was elected, he said he would "put fear in the hearts of evildoers," and he'd certainly made true on his claim. But from what Julia gleaned from overhearing the men on the ranch, the sheriff was a scoundrel and as corrupt as they came, always flanked by his posse of Irish thugs. Which

21

contributed to Laramie's reputation as the most lawless town in the West.

Julia's heart weighed heavy as her thoughts drifted back to Mrs. Peterson. The news sucked out her restlessness and filled her with melancholy. Now she just wanted to run up to her room and bury her face in her pillow.

"I reckon I should git goin'," Ty said quietly.

Julia nodded, glancing down at her white satin gown with the lyrical waves of shiny pearls and layers of lace. It felt so wrong to be standing there, wearing something so pristine and pretty, when the news couldn't be more gloomy and dark. She couldn't wait to get out of the dress. Maybe a long gallop across the prairie would do her some good. Maybe being unmarried wasn't so deplorable a condition.

How horrible to finally find a man to love and wed, only to lose him—and your own life—to such senseless violence. Like many women, Mrs. Peterson had come to Wyoming, and Laramie specifically, because of its radical views of equality for women. Not ten years ago, Laramie became the first town in the West—maybe in the whole country—to let women serve on a jury and vote in elections and hold jobs as court bailiffs and other county positions.

But, judging by the way Julia's father smothered his daughter with his overbearing protectiveness, you'd never know she lived in such a progressive community. Oh, she was so tired of being kept in a box.

"I'll bring ya back a licorice stick," Ty said with a wink, then slipped out the courtyard door, leaving Julia alone, silence filling in the space around her. She could hear the beating of her heart as she stood and looked out over the Front Range through the windows. A few flakes of snow swirled around the glass.

Someone had named Laramie "The Gem City of the Plains" because at night, when a person gazed down from atop the Black Hills to the east, the lights of the town looked like precious stones nestled in a black velvet jewel box.

Julia wondered if that person had ever walked the streets of Laramie at night, when the whoring and shooting and drunken brawls erupted. She doubted the person who penned that sublime description would be inclined to give her town such an appellation then.

Thinking about her lawless town made her thoughts settle back on her father and the never-ending feud between the Carsons and the Morrisons—a feud Julia neither wanted nor understood. Yet here she was, in the midst of it, her party just one more piece of wood to throw on the fire of contention. She hoped it wouldn't add to the blaze and worried that rather than enjoy her sixteenth year celebration, she would suffer the heat of her father's ire for Stephen Morrison, and it would leave her scorched.

Chapter 2

FLURRIES OF SNOW BATTERED ROBERT Morrison's eyes as he buttoned his coat and pulled the collar up to his chin.

He blew puffs of steamy warm air on his hands, cursing that he'd forgotten his gloves. Another thing he blamed on Rose Huffington. She was plaguing his mind, and there was naught for it.

Ellsworth elbowed him as they strode along the boardwalk, their heavy boots rattling the boards. Benjamin, Robert's boisterous shirttail cousin, trailed some steps behind, spinning like a child's top every time he caught a glimpse of a painted lady peeking out a window or leaning over an upper railing.

"Them gals are somethin' else," Benjamin said, squashing his hat down on the mess of unruly curls that fell over his face and ears, pointing to three "soiled doves" waving at him from an open saloon door and blowing kisses.

"Kid, you act like you never done seen a woman in your life," Ellsworth chided, rubbing his bearded chin that looked like an abandoned bird's nest and shaking his head.

"Well, I reckon none like them."

Ellsworth laughed, his ponderous gut jiggling, but Robert stopped and grabbed his cousin by the arm. The kid stiffened, and Robert regretted his foul mood had put a sharp edge to his temperament. "You don't want to mess with the likes of them. They'll steal your money and give you the Cupid's disease. You oughta hold out for the right gal, one pure and God-fearin'—"

Ellsworth chuckled. His narrow eyes squinched into slits, like cats' eyes. "Yeah, like the one that's roped your heart. Rose? Rose Huffington? Why, she—"

Robert punched his best friend's shoulder. "Hobble your lip, El."

"I'm just sayin'—"

"Don't." Robert gave Ellsworth his "I mean it" glare, which, as usual, hardly made a dent in his big, husky friend. Ellsworth reminded Robert of a buffalo, with his thick wild chestnut hair and beard, his bushy eyebrows, and a body as dense and lumbering as the beasts that once filled the rangeland. As hardheaded too.

"How you likin' Laramie so far?" Ellsworth asked Benjamin. He gestured at the wide street lined on both sides by newly built wood boardwalks elevated out of the mud and puddles and fronted by colorful clapboard businesses. Townsfolk on this Tuesday in early November were going about their business, buying and selling their wares, plenty already in the dozens of saloons, starting their drinking early.

Twenty-three saloons and but one church downtown. Robert's father wasn't a religious man, but his ma had raised Robert with his head buried in the Good Book. And while he'd never seen the inside of a church, he knew God in heaven couldn't be a mite pleased with what-all went on in Laramie City. It was as if once the railroad had cut a swath across the

Front Range and then moved on West it left behind the worst scoundrels and hooligans. Big Steve Long, the first sheriff, had marched some of those outlaws to the makeshift gallows set up on Front Street and hanged the men, then things quieted down some. That was before the Territorial Penitentiary was built. But since then . . .

Benjamin sighed. "I'd like it jus' fine, if'n I had two coins to rub together." He turned to Robert. "If'n your range boss here"— he gestured a thumb at Ellsworth—"didn't work me to death." Ellsworth guffawed and shook his head.

Robert, not in the mood for the kid's querulous yapping, said, "Everyone's expected to pull his own weight on the ranch. Just 'cuz you're some long-lost cousin who happened to blow into town lookin' for work, don't mean you get a free ride—"

"I ain't lookin' for no free—"

"There's cattle to herd and brand and sell at market, and it's no picnic. So if you'd rather work at some bank and wear fancy duds, get yerself properly edified—"

"Edi-what?"

Robert snorted. "I rest my case."

"What's that mean?"

Ellsworth pulled Benjamin along by the arm, seeing as his perplexity had brought him to a full stop. "And look at you—if'n you quit spending your pay on prettyin' yourself up, you'd save some—"

Robert stopped abruptly, causing Ellsworth to smack into his back.

"What in tarnation . . . ?" Ellsworth grumbled, righting his hat.

"What is it?" Benjamin said, sidling up to Robert and studying his face. His head turned to look down the street, where Robert's gaze had riveted.

A big rock plummeted into the pit of Robert's stomach.

"Now . . . take it easy, pal," Ellsworth said under his breath, gripping Robert's arm.

A long cold moment settled around Robert, as fat flakes of snow lighted on his hat and eyelashes.

"Who's that?" Benjamin whistled. "She looks like an angel with those big pouty lips and milky skin. And that hair—red as I ever did see."

"Come on," Ellsworth urged. "We got business at the bank. And I got those ledgers to finish before we ship out the cattle tomorrow." He yanked on Robert's arm.

Robert felt as if his boots had been nailed into the plank underfoot. He didn't know the fella Rose was talking to on the next block, his face just inches from hers as they stood in front of the haberdashery. It didn't take a genius to tell she was smitten. The fella looked to be some fancy-pants with that pinstriped suit and ridiculous scarf around his neck. Was he French? No one in Wyoming Territory would be caught dead wearing something like—

Rose turned, as if hearing his smoldering thoughts, and caught his eye. She threw him a smile—like tossing a bone to a starving dog. Blood pounded his ears. So that was why she'd been ignoring his affections as of late. He'd sent her letters and flowers over the last two weeks, his mother complaining that he was wearing a rut in the porch from his pacing and waiting on a reply. Ellsworth had warned him Rose was two-timing him. *But you didn't want to listen. All the signs were there.*

He didn't know which stung more—being jilted by a no-good heartless gal who'd led him on or realizing what a blind idiot he'd been. He thought he'd taken care to not let his passions get the best of him, knowing that marriage was a promise for a lifetime and wanting to wait for just the right gal. He thought

Rose was the one. It wasn't just her beauty—comely gals were plentiful in Laramie. But listening to Rose talk in her lilting way, those big blue eyes the color of lake ice sparkling as she bespoke her love for nature, a seasoning in her manner that few gals her age attained . . . He'd always held back, kept his heart locked in a corral. And now, when he'd finally thrown open the gate . . .

Last thing he wanted was to end up hitched to the wrong gal—he only had to look as far as his own parents to see the sorry results of marrying wrong. His ma, so sweet and fragile and deserving of tender affection, was wallowing in a loveless marriage. Robert tried hard to respect his pa, but it was dang hard to respect a fella that mistreated his wife. Not that his pa beat her, but words could be just as hurtful. And apathy even more so.

Another yank on his sleeve made Robert swivel back to Ellsworth. His friend cocked his head in the direction of the bank across the street. Benjamin opened his mouth to say something.

"Not another word, Cousin." Robert could hear the venom in his own voice. He was fit to punch his fist through a wall.

Benjamin pursed his lips and hung his head. Good thing too. Robert had come to the end of his patience with this young whippersnapper his mother had saddled him with.

He marched across the planks and into the street, heedless of the puddles and waste left behind in the wake of horses and dogs, his two companions following briskly behind. A wagon driver yelled at him as he pulled hard on the reins of his mule to stop before barreling into Robert, but Robert paid him no mind. He tromped up the steps to the bank and told Benjamin to cool his spurs outside while he and Ellsworth took care of their business.

Inside, he said little as the obsequious banker presented the papers to sign and he and Ellsworth made their marks. Robert didn't need to read the documents that sealed the contract for the sale of his next shipment of cattle to the stockyard in Missouri; it was standard procedure for all that he'd been taking care of for his pa going on six years now, since he turned twenty. *Since Cassidy died.*

The thought of his older brother's death caused a familiar stab in his gut, as if the knife that had ended Cassidy's life was lodged in Robert's flesh. Which only added to the lump of hurt and betrayal festering inside him, thanks to Rose Huffington.

As Robert put down the pen, and the banker stretched out his hand to shake Robert's, a movement out the window caught Robert's eye.

Ellsworth hissed, "Ty Lawson . . ."

Robert bristled, his palms itchy. Just what he needed—to run into Lester Carson's nephew—who'd been raised like a son to that snake and no doubt stood to inherit the elder's ranch and holdings. That no-good ruffian was the worst of the Carson bunch—with the exception of Lester himself.

Robert thought on what his pa had said last week—how Carson had the nerve to make an offer on that choice parcel north of town, the one Robert's father had bought from old Hennessy back in the sixties. Robert thought his pa was going to bust up the furniture, he was so spitting mad. He'd grown up hearing all the stories of what a cheat, liar, and greedy son of a snake Lester Carson was. *Someone oughta shoot Carson and put the town out of its misery.* Even the sheriff hated the Carsons and had more than once tried to force them to up and sell. But Lester would have none of it.

As Robert stomped to the door of the bank, he saw Ty up in Benjamin's scared face, a fist gripping the kid's shirt. *Confound it!*

Robert pushed open the door and lunged for Ty. "Take your hands off him, you piece of rubbish." After seeing Rose sidling up to that dandy, Robert was in no mood for civility. He welcomed the chance to throw a few punches Ty's way.

Ty turned his head, saw Robert, and heaved Benjamin to the boardwalk, who looked about ready to cry, though his fisted hands perched under his chin dared Ty to make his next move.

Ellsworth stood at Robert's side, and though Ty was taller, he was no match for the buffalo. And he knew it. The two had scuffled on more than one occasion—usually when both had been drinking—and though Ty was a vicious and skilled fighter, Ellsworth always had the advantage.

Except now.

Ty had pulled out his long-barrel Colt and had it trained on Ellsworth.

Ellsworth put his meaty hands on his hips, inches from his own pistols, which sat in a cross draw in his holsters. "You aim to shoot me—in broad daylight, in front of the bank?"

"I've a mind to," Ty said, not moving a muscle.

The gall of that fella! Robert was aware of the eyes upon them. All motion ceased in the street as the snow plummeted to earth, and a biting wind chewed at his cheeks and neck. A crowd began to gather—the vultures swooping in to wait for some carrion to feast upon.

"And why is that?" Ellsworth taunted. "What's got your underwear in a bunch now, you piece of—"

He took a step toward Ty, and Ty cocked the hammer back. The *click* sounded loud in Robert's ears. He grabbed Ellsworth's arm and pulled him back.

Ty hissed the words, teeth clenched. "My uncle wants that parcel of land, and the sooner you pond scum sign those papers, the better. He's running out of patience."

"My pa ain't selling," Robert said evenly, holding tight to Ellsworth's arm. Benjamin had gotten up from the ground and brushed himself off, keeping his distance, his eyes wide with alarm. Robert hoped his cousin wouldn't do something foolish . . . as he himself was about to do . . .

Ty never saw it coming. Robert's fist flew hard and fast, connecting with Ty's jaw and making the tall man spin on his heel and tumble off the boardwalk, sending his pistol flying into the street. Robert's hand stung, but it had sure felt good to land a blow on that hooligan's face.

People started yelling—some egging Ty on, urging him to hit back. Others, ladies mostly, squealed in alarm, and one yelled for the sheriff. Ellsworth stepped back and made room, knowing this was Robert's tussle. Though, Robert knew Ellsworth had his back. And Ty was outnumbered—what was the fool thinking?

Ty got to his feet and started swinging. Robert ducked the first two punches, but the third landed hard in his gut. Doubling over, he stuck out his leg and hooked Ty's knee, then pulled. Ty fell into Robert, who pummeled his grunting and cursing opponent as they rolled over the splintery planks.

Another blow rattled Robert's cheek, and pain streaked upside his head. Letting his rage and hurt propel him, he grabbed Ty's neck, ignoring the kicks and smacks to his body, and squeezed with all his might.

The gurgling sound coming from Ty's throat sent a wave of satisfaction through Robert's chest. He waited until Ty's eyes drained of anger and filled with fear before he let go and jumped back, a smile quirked on his face. That would teach that scoundrel to think twice before pulling his gun on him in the middle of town in the middle of the day. Did Ty really think such antics would scare him, make him whine to his pa with his tail atwixt his legs like some beaten dog? Force his pa to sell his land? Ty was a lame-brained sack of rocks.

Ty stumbled to his feet, steeling his face, ready to lunge at Robert. But just as he made to attack, a gunshot went off, followed by another—not more than ten feet from where they stood.

The crowd hushed as Robert planted his feet, blowing hard puffs of white breath and fixing his eye on Ty, who faced him, snorting like a racehorse.

"I shoulda known . . ."

Robert stiffened at the sheriff's voice.

Sheriff Carr pushed through the onlookers, his limp apparent, and stepped up onto the boardwalk, his rifle held aloft, giving Robert a cursory glance before resting his stern gaze on Ty Lawson, nephew of the man Carr hated with a vengeance. Robert pressed down his smirk, knowing Ty was about to be in a world of hurt once the sheriff learned he'd pulled his gun. Carr was as corrupt as they came, but for some reason, whenever there was a dispute between the Carsons and the Morrisons, he always landed on the side of Robert's family. Why, Robert had nary a clue, but he wasn't going to ask—Carr must've had his reasons. And, knowing Lester Carson as Robert did, no doubt Ty's uncle had done something egregious to the sheriff at some prior time. The vitriolic nature of his hatred indicated something personal, Robert concluded.

Carr pressed up into Ty's face, the scowl causing the wrinkles etched in his face to deepen. The sheriff's fat white eyebrows knitted, and he ran his thumbs along the thick moustache that trailed past his mouth to his flaccid scarred chin that sat above folds of neck skin resembling chicken flesh. "I'm plumb fed up with breaking up fights between your two families. This is—what? The third incident in as many months?" He sneered and leaned even closer to Ty, their noses almost touching. "I've lost count."

Ty clenched his jaw but said nothing. The sheriff took a quick look at Benjamin, then Ellsworth, lingering awhile on the ranch foreman's ruddy face. Sheriff Carr chewed his lip, his fingers of his right hand moving to tap on the heel of his rifle now resting at his side.

He turned to Robert and looked him over. Robert's head ached, but his hand hurt worse. Thomas Carr had a plastery hard look about him. A stray bullet had given him that slight limp, and his receding hairline exposed a long forehead riddled with worry lines over his small brown eyes that were as dull as pebbles. He had no qualms about throwing his weight around, and his two Irish deputies, who seemed to like little more than inflicting pain and watching a fella bleed to death, were nothing to scoff at. Robert didn't see them in the crowd, but he knew they were close at hand should the sheriff need their assistance.

No, Sheriff Carr was a force to be reckoned with, and at the moment Robert was glad that the man's ire was mostly directed at Lawson.

"I want you to get out of town—the lot o' you. Now." He turned and glowered at the crowd, which hurriedly dispersed, now that further altercations were unlikely to erupt.

None of the targets of his speech uttered a word. A squat Swedish man dangled Ty's Colt from his fingers as if it were a dead rat. The sheriff took it, then hesitated a moment before handing it, stock first, to Ty, who promptly holstered it, his eyes locked with the sheriff's in a fight of wills.

"You tell your uncle this: if I have to break up one more fight, I'm throwing y'all in jail and tossing the key into the Laramie River. You got that?"

Ty nodded, his thin lips pressed into a scowl. He gave Robert a cold glare, his eyes as dark as obsidian, then turned and walked west down the boardwalk.

The sheriff stepped off the planking and left them, crossing the street, which was now blanketed with a layer of soft snow. A few stubborn leaves clung to the big maples lining the street — the last gasp of autumn reluctant to give way to winter.

Ellsworth looked at Robert as Benjamin huffed and hurried to their side.

"Lordy," the kid said. "I haven't seen such excitement since Aunt Betty got her foot tangled in a rope and her mule dragged her halfway across the pasture." He stared after Ty, who eased up onto a sorrel with a Mexican saddle that had been tied at the post in front of the druggist's.

Robert set his sights across the street to where he'd seen Rose making eyes at that fella, and the pain started back up in his gut. She was gone. *Left with that dandy?* Robert reined in his speculations before they tormented him further.

"Head back to the ranch?" Ellsworth asked, his voice tinged with exasperation.

Robert's insides churned, mulling over Ty's threat. Stephen Morrison would never sell a wooden leg to Lester Carson, let alone a parcel of choice land. Whatever the scoundrel was up to, it wasn't going to work, and Robert feared more than fisticuffs were soon to follow.

"Naw," Robert said, studying his wide-eyed cousin as the snow petered out and a piece of sun peeked through the shredding clouds skittering above. The air smelled of damp sage and manure and fetid water. "I need a drink." He patted

Benjamin's shoulder, wondering if the kid had ever tasted good whiskey. "And I think my cousin could use one too, after our little scuffle."

Benjamin's eyes lit up like sparks in a fire. "Now you're talking." He added, chuckling, "That is, if'n you're buying."

Robert nodded, knowing not even the best whiskey in Laramie would wash away the sour feeling in his mouth or the ache of loneliness in his heart.

Chapter 3

JULIA CAREFULLY SHIMMIED OUT OF the dress as Edna helped, gathering up the long skirt so it wouldn't tangle in Julia's feet. She huffed, feeling the walls of her mother's chamber pressing in on her—the heavy damask curtains framing the tall windows and the dark patterned rugs from the Orient oppressive in this room of lacquered mahogany furnishings and flooring.

Her stomach grumbled and she called for Daisy, who Julia could hear pattering down the hallway.

"Yes, miss?" her young willowy maid said, her head peeking in through the door she'd just opened—a pretty face framed by raven-black hair.

"Would you bring lunch to my room, please?"

A fleeting look of surprise crossed Daisy's face before she composed herself and nodded. "Yes, miss."

Edna, with the dress draped across her arms, headed to the wardrobe and hung it on a padded hanger. "I dare say, you'll catch the eye of every gentleman at your party, Miss Julia."

"Oh, I'm sure not." Julia smiled at the stodgy old British woman who'd been her mother's maidservant since before Julia was born, before Danielle Millington, only daughter of railroad baron Rudolph Millington, had married Lester Carson. Edna oversaw the house servants with the eye of a hawk, and Julia sensed she did not care much for Daisy. But Julia enjoyed the gregarious girl's company and the way she helped liven the dull, long hours regaling her with her tales of her early years as a kitchen maid in the governor's mansion in Denver, Colorado. How that girl loved to gossip! But Julia saw little harm in it, since she had no one else, really, to tell her embellished stories to. And Daisy was a marvelous riding companion, having been raised on a horse ranch, with a father who cared for the stables and had broken many a wild mustang.

Julia changed back into her calico skirt and white high-collared blouse, glancing out the window at the steady fall of snow.

"Another early winter, it seems," Edna said, clucking her tongue. "Last year's snow has hardly melted from atop the mountains."

"I imagine it doesn't snow much in England," Julia said as Edna came over and fastened the last buttons on the back of Julia's skirt.

"No, indeed. A few flurries here and there, but nothing to compare with the blinding white winters of Wyoming."

"It's the moaning wind that gets to me. The way it races and shrieks across the open prairie, like a banshee."

Edna nodded. "Such has put the fear of God into more than one intrepid traveler."

Julia smiled. Edna came to face her and cocked her head as she studied Julia's face.

"The house will seem so empty when you're gone."

Julia's smile dropped. "Gone?"

"When you marry," Edna qualified with a knowing grin.

"Oh," Julia said, shaking her head wistfully. "But that I might marry—" She censored her next words before they could pop out of her mouth. Edna was as close as any friend Julia had ever had, but still, it would be wrong to voice her complaints regarding her father to her mother's maid.

Edna's expression shifted from gay to reserved.

"What is it?" Julia asked.

Edna drew in a long breath. "You've not been told . . ."

"Told what?" A chill crawled up Julia's spine.

Edna hesitated, but Julia's stern expression was not lost on the maid. "Your father, it seems, has been making arrangements . . ."

Her voice trailed, but Julia would have none of it. "What arrangements?"

"Concerning . . . a young Jarret Strickler . . ."

Julia's eyes narrowed, and an image of an imp of a boy yanking on her dress sash at a summer picnic in Cheyenne floated in her mind. She'd been perhaps ten at the time and found the boy precocious and annoying. Why was Edna mentioning his name . . . ?

Her eyes widened and Edna nodded.

"No . . ." Julia said on a breath that hardly made it out of her mouth. Her father would never . . .

"What does my mother say about this? Did she confide in you?"

Julia normally did not ask such pertinent questions of a servant, but she had to know. Had her father made some kind of deal regarding her—the way he bought and sold cattle? He wouldn't make a pact unless it helped to line his own pockets. And then she recalled that the Stricklers owned the Cheyenne

Cattle Company, the largest and oldest family-run ranch in Wyoming Territory.

Edna set to re-pinning Julia's long hair that had strayed from her head. "Your mother would never force a marriage on you—of that you can be certain."

But Julia wasn't so certain. Marrying her off to some rich young man in Cheyenne would remove her from the dangers of lawless Laramie—though Julia knew full well the streets of Cheyenne were hardly safer. If her parents were going to marry her off, why not arrange for her to meet someone from a well-to-do family back East, from Boston or Chicago? *And where would Father find such a family—by browsing the "Wife Wanted" ads in the* Sentinel?

"Nothing has been settled," Edna said reassuringly. "But the young man in question has been invited to your party, and no doubt your father will do all he can to give him a warm welcome." She added, "No reason you shouldn't grant him a dance or two. You may find he's to your liking."

"And if I don't?"

Edna shrugged and smoothed Julia's hair, finished with her pinning. "Then don't be rushed into anything. You've heard the words 'Go wisely and slowly; those who rush stumble and fall'? Marriage is for a lifetime."

"And I don't want to marry for money," Julia said with an emphatic wave of her hand. "I want to marry for love."

Edna chuckled. "Of course you do, my dear Julia." She sighed. "But love isn't always easy to find. And sometimes a gentleman can grow on your heart, over time—"

"Like a blemish? Or a wart?"

Edna threw her hands up with a huff and then gestured Julia to the door. "Just give the young man a chance. It's the very least you can do in gratitude for the splendid party your father is hosting."

Julia walked to the door and turned to Edna. "I suppose."

The smell of warm buttery bread wafted to Julia's nose, her stomach reminding her that she'd foregone lunch. She hurried to her room, where she'd intended to mope for being forbidden to accompany Ty to town. But she didn't feel like moping now.

As she walked down the long hallway, she tried to imagine what impish Jarret Strickler might look like now, six years later. Had that baby fat left his face? Was he handsome and dashing? Her pulse quickened at the thought of a man desiring her. But did Jarret Strickler hope to find a girl to love . . . *or does he want to marry me just to enlarge his financial holdings?*

Despite what he wanted—or what her father wanted—one thing was certain. When Julia Carson said "I do," it would be to a man who had captured her heart, not her purse. Of that she would brook no compromise.

When Robert pushed on the saloon doors a few hours later and stepped outside, he was greeted by a shimmering blue sky spread out like a lake overhead. He raised his face to the warmth and rubbed his scratchy chin that had gone a few days without a shave, wishing the whiskey had done a better job of numbing his heart. But it would take a barrel of whiskey and more to push those pictures of Rose flirting with that fancy-pants out of his head.

Ellsworth and Benjamin came stumbling out behind him, laughing over something, Benjamin tripping over his own feet—the buffalo and the bumbler now the best of friends.

"Whoa there," Ellsworth said, steadying Benjamin with his hand before the kid toppled off the boardwalk. But then Ellsworth's boot caught the edge of Robert's, and he nearly pulled Robert down to the planks as he flailed trying to grasp the hem of Robert's heavy wool coat.

"Criminy," Robert said, yanking the bear of a man to his feet with some effort. "I told you to quit after three glasses. You better hope my pa doesn't see the sorry state you're in when we get to the ranch." His pa tolerated no drunkenly behavior, and Ellsworth well knew it. But it wasn't like Ellsworth Akes to imbibe on a workday. He'd only done so at Robert's urging—and the Morrison ranch foreman couldn't very well decline the persuasive offer from his boss's son to work through a bottle of '64 Kentucky whiskey.

Ellsworth and Benjamin chuckled and fell into each as if pulled by magnets. Robert hoped the hour-long ride to the ranch would sober them up—if they could stay on their horses.

"Pal, you got a frown a mile wide," Ellsworth said as they trudged down the boardwalk toward the mercantile, where their horses were hitched. "Don't waste your love on a gal that doesn't value it." He stopped and pulled Robert around to face him. "We gonna have to do something about extricating that Rose Huffington from your heart."

"Extra . . . what?" Benjamin said. Ellsworth threw his head back and chortled.

"*Extricating*. Didn't your ma learn you your letters?" Ellsworth asked.

"Well, yeah, sure. I can read and write and do figures. But a fella doesn't need a slew of purty words to git by."

Ellsworth nodded, nearly tripping again as they stepped off the boardwalk and onto the muddy street. "I reckon you're right. You've elucidated the situation most adroitly."

"I . . . what?" Benjamin huffed.

Robert smirked as he went up to his gelding and patted the animal's neck. "Quit showin' off, El. I don't see how that hifalutin education you got in St. Louis does you a bit o' good in Laramie." Robert, too, had gotten a proper education—from his ma, who'd shoved books down his throat from the time he could crawl. Winifred Morrison, before marrying, had actually attended a college for women back in Illinois before meeting Robert's father, and had studied the classics and other "works of great literature," as she put it. Robert's repeated protests were ignored; he just wanted to ride his horse. But his ma believed even aspiring ranchers needed to read Hawthorne and Defoe. Robert hated to admit it—and he surely wasn't inclined to let on, especially to the cow punchers on the ranch—that he grew to love reading stories, especially dime novels. He'd spent many a long winter sitting by the blazing hearth with his nose in a good book. His pa would walk in, see Robert and his ma engrossed in reading, and huff and walk out. No one bothered a Morrison who had a book in hand.

"Maybe I'll run for territorial governor someday." Ellsworth somehow managed to tighten the girth on his horse and mount—and not fall out of the saddle.

"You do that," Robert said, feeling a grin rise on his face for the first time that day. The image of Ellsworth Akes sitting in some fancy office wearing a three-piece suit and smoking a fat cigar prompted a chuckle from his throat. He looked to see that Benjamin had found a way up onto his saddle, though Robert figured the kid could ride backward in his sleep drunker than a pig in a barley patch—he was, contrary to all appearances, one of the best horsemen Robert had ever seen. And that was saying a lot. If he didn't know better, he'd reckon the kid had been born on the back of a horse and had hardly hopped off it since.

Robert mounted and led the way north, heading out of town. Folks took little notice, going about their business, as the three walked their horses up Front Street at a good clip. A crisp breeze blew east, down off the foothills far in the distance, where Fort Fetterman sat, the air sparkling from the glistening patchwork of snow spread out across the prairie. The early dusting draped the land, a harbinger of the long, cold winter to come, and Robert dreaded it. Winter meant hard work, keeping the cattle safe from blizzards and drifts, your feet freezing in your boots, your face a block of ice, the days short and nights achingly long and lonely. He'd hoped his winter would have been full of warm nights by a crackling fire in a hearth, his arms around Rose, feeling her warm up against his chest, her soft skin under his fingertips, his lips on her moist ones . . .

"Well, this must be our lucky day," Ellsworth drawled. Robert sighed and looked over to him, noticing his eyebrows narrowed over his squinched eyes. "First Ty, now him."

"Who's that?" Benjamin asked as Ellsworth stopped and comically slid off his horse.

Robert reined in his gelding and watched Ellsworth tromp over to a scrawny kid no older than about ten. He recognized him too—Lester Carson's errand boy. He'd seen him on occasion in the wagon with Carson's feisty foreman, Sheldon McManus. And it appeared he was dutifully doing his job, a bulging canvas bag slung over his shoulder as he trudged up the steps to the post office.

Ellsworth stepped in front of the kid, blocking his passage into the building. By the time Robert joined him, the kid's freckled face was a sheen of sweat.

The kid nudged his hat back to look up at Robert, carrot-colored hair curling under the felt. "Pl-please, l-let me through," he said, glancing around, maybe hoping for someone to come to his rescue. But, presently, no one else was around.

Benjamin sat his horse, watching in amusement. Robert laid a hand on the kid's shoulder, and the youngster nearly jumped out of his britches.

"Whatcha got in that bag?" Robert asked, a big grin on his face. The kid looked about to wet hisself.

"J-Just some l-l-letters . . ."

"Let's see." Ellsworth yanked the bag off the kid's shoulder.

"Hey! G-Give that b-back!"

Robert held the kid's arm as Ellsworth reached into the bag and pulled out a handful of small white envelopes.

"Hmm," Ellsworth said, thumbing through a few. "Looks like someone's plannin' a party." He sniffed one and made a face, then pried open the wax-sealed flap.

"Hey, y-you can't d-do that!" The boy tried to grab the envelopes with his free hand, but Ellsworth swatted him away with a big paw and pulled out a folded white card. Pretty fancy-looking, from what Robert could tell. He wondered what the occasion was.

"'You are cordially invited to attend . . .'" Ellsworth mumbled the rest as he perused the invitation. Then he smiled wide and winked at Robert, wiggling the card in the air. "Seems Mr. Lester Carson is requesting the presence of"—he took a peek into that bulging bag—"practically all of Laramie, Wyoming, to attend the birthday celebration of his only daughter, Julia Carson."

"That so?" Robert asked. "Practically, meaning everyone but folks named Morrison, or who work for my pa."

"No doubt," Ellsworth said with a nod.

"Julia Carson." Robert thought hard through the foggy haze of his liquor-soaked mind. He knew Carson had a daughter, but he wasn't sure he'd ever seen her. Maybe from a distance. There were few times any Carsons came within spitting distance of a Morrison, but surely the girl came to town from time to time. He figured Carson kept her under lock and key. Now, wouldn't she be a prize—daughter of one of the richest men in Wyoming? And what a party this would prove to be. Not that Robert took a fancy to parties, but this one . . .

"When is this shindig?" he asked Ellsworth as the mortified kid stood waiting for Robert to let go of his arm.

"This Saturday."

"I bet rich folks from all over'll be showin' up to attend," Robert said.

"And there'll be a lot of fancy food and dancing and the like—"

"With Carson hopin' to impress all those important people—"

"And surely not wantin' the likes of us showin' up—"

"No indeed," Robert said with a grin. He let go of the kid's arm.

Ellsworth slid the card into the little envelope and tossed it back in the bag. He slipped the bag back onto the kid's shoulder and gave him a couple of pats on his head. The kid winced.

"Skedaddle," Ellsworth told him. "And you never saw us," he added with a glaring buffalo scowl. "Y'hear?"

"Y-Yessir." The kid gulped and, remembering he had legs, ran into the post office as if the entire Cherokee nation was hot on his tail.

Robert smirked, his heart feeling suddenly lightened of its burden. With all those guests pouring into the Carson ranch, why, he and Ellsworth would hardly be noticed. He'd always wanted to see the Carson spread; he'd heard about it all his life, and it wasn't but fifteen miles northeast of his own home.

He went up to Ellsworth as they stood before the post office, and a couple of old biddies approached. Robert opened the door for them and touched his hat in greeting, earning him two toothless smiles and a strong whiff of lavender water unmistakably tainted with au de whiskey. Or maybe laudanum.

In a quiet voice, Ellsworth said, "Wouldn't be hard to slip away on Saturday eve."

Robert cocked his head. "I hope you got somethin' appropriate to wear."

"O' course I do. Always have a suit on hand for funerals and weddings."

"The same suit?"

Ellsworth shrugged. "You seen it."

Robert chuckled. "I reckon I have." He added, "Be sure you bathe as well. You wouldn't want someone to mistake you for a stinky ol' buffalo and fill you full of buckshot."

"Speak for yourself." He leaned into Robert and exaggerated a whiff. "Phewy. You smell like a still."

"Well, plenty of hours atwixt now and Saturday to get gussied up. You want to bring the kid?" He swiveled and gestured at Benjamin, who was leaning over the pommel, his forehead against the horse's mane.

Ellsworth let out a laugh. "Well, don't that take the cake. The whiskey plumb knocked him out."

"Maybe we should leave the pup home," Robert suggested as he and Ellsworth walked over and mounted their horses. Then a thought soured in his mind. He looked over at his friend as he urged his horse to move. "You think . . . uh, Rose'll be at the party?"

"I reckon. But what do you care? I bet there'll be plenty of beauties there for you to lose your heart to."

Robert would have knocked his pal's hat off if he was closer. "I've had enough with the female sex for a while."

That detonated a loud laugh from the ranch foreman. "Oh, sure. Next thing ya tell me, you'll be joining the priesthood."

"I mean it. Rose mangled my heart. It'll be a cold day in hell when I set my sights on another gal. Mark my words." Robert hoped he sounded as convicted as he felt. For he truly wasn't in any rush to suffer such slings and arrows again. Women! Ellsworth had been courting a gal for months now—Elizabeth Brown, a quiet little mouse who loved nothing more than discussing ladies' fashions and sipping mint juleps—a teetotaler, go figure. There was no accounting for taste, Robert reminded himself. But Ellsworth seemed happy as a lark in Miss Brown's company. Robert hoped his pal didn't have plans to get hitched anytime soon, though. He well knew how a woman's persuasion could set a fella off on some wayward track, and Robert didn't want to lose his best friend.

Ellsworth laughed again, but Benjamin's head didn't rise up from where it bobbed against his horse's neck. Not even when they broke into a trot did the kid stir from his stupor. But he kept his seat, much to the amazement of the two cowboys, even when the prairie opened up under the pristine blue desert sky and they kicked their horses into a gallop, Benjamin's mare keeping stride behind them as they made for the ranch.

When they arrived at the barn and dismounted, Benjamin straightened, looked around, and wiped a trail of drool from his chin. A moan slipped from his lips as he slid off his horse, then stumbled over to a creosote bush and puked out the contents of his stomach.

"Best we leave the kid here on Saturday," Ellsworth said under his breath as he threw his stirrup over the saddle, uncinched his horse, and pulled the saddle into his arms.

Robert nodded, grinning. And while he felt a mite guilty for his cousin's current condition, he hadn't held a gun to the kid's head, forcing him to drink all that whiskey. And he'd duly warned him of the consequences of indulgence.

Ellsworth added, "We'll have to keep out of sight. Saturday the moon'll be full. If Ty Lawson spots you—"

"I'm sure there'll be plenty of trees to provide cover. I'm not hankering for a fight—not on Carson's ranch. He'd as soon hang us as chase us off."

"You sure ya want to go? If your pa finds out—"

When would he ever get the chance to snoop around the Carson spread? "He won't. Let's do it."

Ellsworth nodded.

"All right then." Robert unsaddled his gelding and walked him over to the pasture, where the grazing herd lifted heads and nickered at his arrival. Thoughts of Rose's face with those delectable lips and big inviting eyes sucked him down into a melancholy mood, and he knew it would take some time before he got over her. *Maybe Ellsworth is right. I need to find me a new gal—one true of heart, who won't break mine.* What better place to find one than that party?

Chapter 4

THE WHEELS OF THE TRAIN screeched, sounding like a long pent-up moan as if the conveyance were relieved to be coming to a stop at the Laramie station. Dr. Joseph Tuttle shared the sentiment. He held on to the seat in front of him as the carriage shook and jerked like a man in a seizure giving up his last breath. When he could finally declare "the patient" dead, he picked up his Lock & Co. Bowler hat from the seat—one of his few indulgent purchases—placed it on his head, then hefted the satchel at his feet and slung his heavy coat over his arm.

The stuffy, overly warm train car was packed on a Friday night—families and laborers and a few dressed in elegant attire. Some who looked like thugs out to stir up trouble, maybe trying to stay one step ahead of the law. Most had already been on the train, up from Denver, when Joseph had boarded in Greeley with a sadness in his heart, though he couldn't help but feel a stimulating mixture of excitement and dread over the work the Good Lord had in store for him. He'd thought he'd stay in Greeley indefinitely, practicing medicine as was his vocation, and after a year there in the quaint and peaceful little town, he'd settled in nicely, making friends and feeling a part of that community of fine, upstanding citizens.

But when he'd spotted the posting in the *Tribune* about the need for a physician at the Wyoming Territorial Penitentiary, he couldn't deny the stirring of the Spirit prompting him to inquire of the position. He'd had no interest in moving to Wyoming Territory, but the course of his life was not his to determine. That, he'd learned many years ago, when as a teen his family had all died within four days from dysentery. It was then God had put the fire in his heart to study medicine and seek ways of lessening the suffering of victims of all manner of disease.

His life then had taken many unexpected turns, full of surprises and new horizons, and now, as he allowed the other passengers to trudge along the narrow passageway to exit the car, he stood and looked out the windows facing west, the evening afterglow of a near-winter sunset thickening the sky with smears of vibrant peach colors, snow glinting in the shadows of the Rockies afar off. But though the expansive landscape was sublime and humbling, the jagged outline of the mountains against the sky was different from the one he'd gazed upon through the various seasons in Greeley, reminding him yet again that he was stepping into a new life, still without anyone by his side with whom to share his dreams and hopes. And lonely nights.

He stuffed the loneliness back into its little box in his heart and eased out from his seat. A sigh slipped from his mouth as he headed down the corridor behind a bedraggled heavy-set woman lugging a ponderous bag in one hand and supporting a toddler who lay sprawled asleep over her shoulder.

Joseph hurried to her. "Here, ma'am," he said, his hand out. "May I be of service?"

The woman turned, huffing from exertion and apparent exhaustion, gratitude in her eyes.

"I'm appreciative of your kindness," the woman said, letting Joseph take the bag from her hand. He nearly dropped it from the surprising weight. If he didn't know better, he'd have thought she'd recently emptied the Denver First National of its gold bullion.

She repositioned her child with a grunt, then trod through the train car and down the three metal steps to the wooden platform, Joseph at her heels.

The evening air felt cold and refreshing after his having been somewhat crushed like a sardine in a can for the last five hours, with only a brief respite in Cheyenne when he'd been able to exit and stretch his legs. Canada geese chuckled in a V overhead, and the scent of oil and river mud met his nostrils as he looked around the large depot and the back of the adjacent two-story hotel.

Joseph set the bag down at the woman's feet and watched as the porters began unloading the baggage car. He glanced around the platform that stretched for blocks and across to the wide street fronting the station, wondering if Mrs. Povey had arrived and was waiting for him. A few wagons and carriages were parked along the dirt roadway, but from where he stood, he couldn't see the occupants.

He knew little about Mrs. Cathryn Povey, but from the letters they'd exchanged, he deemed her to be serious-minded, dedicated, and efficient. She'd not only acted as the liaison to securing his employment; she'd found him lodging in what she declared was a safe part of town not far from the bridge that crossed the Laramie River over to the penitentiary.

Joseph found it fascinating—though somewhat disheartening—that Laramie was touted as such a progressive town while having the reputation of an equally lawless one. The first town in the entire nation to appoint women to serve on a jury and hold the position, and be allowed to vote, Laramie only recently opened the federal penitentiary to accommodate female prisoners. Which was what had prompted Mrs. Povey's interest in finding just the right physician after the former prison doctor refused to treat the women inmates and quit. Now, a local doctor visited the male inmates as needed, but the female prisoners had no one to treat their ailments.

Joseph spotted his two large brown suitcases, which contained all the earthly belongings he had left after selling his furnishings through a property agent in Greeley. He'd had a trunk shipped in advance that contained his medical books and instruments, and Mrs. Povey had confirmed arrival of the trunk by telegraph. Being a man of simple means and a lack of interest in material possessions made relocating a simple feat. He'd come into this world with far less and would leave empty-handed. It made little sense to hoard.

With bags in hand, he wended his way through the crowd of passengers gathering their luggage and walked to the street. Not a minute later, a woman in a dark-blue wool coat and matching hat stepped out the door of a nearby buggy, the driver of the two draft horses remaining wrapped in a buffalo robe on the bench. A glimpse of light-red hair could be seen framing her round face as her eyes lit upon Joseph. She walked with confident purpose toward him, a cheery smile lifting her rosy cheeks.

"Ah, Dr. Tuttle, I presume?" She inquired with a gloved hand extended.

"Why, yes," Joseph replied, glancing past her at the carriage. "Joseph Tuttle at your service. Mrs. Povey?"

"Indeed," she said, giving him a cursory look-over. She stood a good two inches taller than he, but that wasn't anything odd. He was often the shortest man in a room.

"Mr. Povey isn't accompanying you?" he asked, noting the door to her buggy remained closed. He thought it unusual for a married woman to be picking him up at the train station without her husband in attendance. But maybe customs were a bit different in this progressive town.

He thought he saw a cloud pass over her face. "Mr. Povey is not well," she said softly.

Joseph noted pain streak her eyes and wondered if the ailment her husband suffered was being treated by an able physician. But now was not the time or place to inquire. "I see," he said kindly. "Thank you for leaving his side to see to my affairs."

"Oh, it's no problem whatsoever. His condition is chronic and keeps him confined to bed most days."

"I'm sorry to hear that," Joseph said in all sincerity. This close, he noticed the delicate features of Cathryn Povey's face. She seemed close in age, perhaps early thirties, and though her face reflected the careworn aspect he had seen in many who spent long hours tending to a sick or incapacitated loved one, her simple beauty was enhanced by what Joseph sensed was her deep compassion for humanity. Her intrinsic goodness and charitable heart.

He had read an article she had written that was published in the Laramie newspaper, his interest in her work sparked by things she'd mentioned in their mutual correspondence. It spoke of the plight of women in the West and the dire need for those in government to protect women's rights, especially in the workplace. Joseph had been greatly impressed by the depth of her knowledge of law and her passion for ethical concerns, which he shared but restrained from voicing too explicitly in his letters for fear of overstepping. To be honest, he'd rarely had such discussions with anyone, let alone with a woman. Few seemed willing or eager to explore the disparities between sexes in modern society.

All told, though he was only now just meeting Cathryn Povey, he felt he knew her well, and he highly admired her. If only he could find a God-fearing woman of unmarried status who displayed such moral and emotional stature as this woman who now directed him over to her buggy.

The driver, an old man with a grizzled beard, made to jump down to help Joseph with his bags, but Joseph waved him off. "I can manage," he said, hefting the first bag, then the next, onto the rack behind the buggy. He then opened the buggy door for Mrs. Povey and climbed in after her. After they settled on the bench seats across from each other, she rapped on the roof, and the buggy began rolling along the street, the clap of the horses' hooves tapping a rhythm that joined with the jangling of the breeching and the drone of the big wheels turning.

Mrs. Povey sighed and laid her gloved hands on her lap. Joseph tried not to stare at this elegant woman as she told him of the recent developments in the penitentiary. The dozen or so female prisoners were being subjected to overly harsh treatment, she opined. The warden—a Mr. A. J. House—showed little regard to the necessary comforts the weaker sex required, and Mrs. Povey had voiced her complaints to both the warden and the territorial governor. But as the prison was a federal institution, she'd had to petition lawmakers in Washington, and, as she proceeded to explain, getting a timely response and subsequent assistance was not likely forthcoming.

"We lived for a time in the District of Columbia," she said. "My husband, Jacob, worked in a congressional office in the

Capitol. I'm very familiar with the workings of this great experiment in democracy, Dr. Tuttle. And one thing I know well is the wheels of this nation move very slowly. Too slowly, in my opinion, when injustices are perpetrated. Unless, of course, action results in money filtering into deep pockets." She shook her head, a hint of disgust and frustration evident on her face despite the scant light seeping in through the buggy's windows.

"Why did you move to Laramie, if I may be so bold as to ask?" Joseph said hesitantly, noticing the various shops and office buildings with their windows dark as they moved along the streets filled with cowboys and horses and laborers heading home or perhaps to a saloon — he didn't want to think about all the debauchery this notorious town had to offer. But Mrs. Povey seemed unoffended.

"When the War between the States broke out, Jacob felt it his duty to enlist."

The bitterness in her voice was unmistakable, though Joseph wondered if it was directed at her husband for enlisting or at the war itself — so many lives lost so needlessly. He himself had been too young to join up, though he, as had everyone east of the Mississippi, saw how the war had ravaged the country.

"When the war ended . . . the doctors suggested it be best for Jacob to move to a drier clime. Humidity greatly aggravates his lungs."

"I see," Joseph said, wondering when they would arrive at his lodgings. A wave of exhaustion sought to pull him under, and he could barely keep his eyes open.

She let out a soft laugh, and Joseph turned from his study of the town to look at her. Her cheeks flushed with dark pink, giving her a girlish aura. His heart beat a little too fast. It wasn't often that he found himself up this close to an attractive woman in such an intimate space. His head swam.

"I'm sorry—I'm talking too much. I can see I'm putting you to sleep."

"Oh, not at all," Joseph said, straightening and trying to brush the drowsy cobwebs from his head. "It has been a long day."

"Of course," she declared politely, dropping her gaze to her lap.

The buggy came to a stop in the middle of a block of simple cinderblock homes with large lawns and dormant shrubbery bordering the dwellings—a quiet neighborhood, it seemed. The moon, nearly full, peeked over the rooftops, splattering light onto the ground and giving Mrs. Povey's face an ethereal glow.

"Here we are," she said, motioning Joseph to exit the buggy. He stepped out and proffered his hand, which Mrs. Povey grasped as she descended from the buggy. Joseph retrieved his suitcases and followed her up the walk to the front porch. She procured a key from her coat pocket and unlocked the door, then handed him the key.

"I trust you'll find everything in order inside. There are stores in the kitchen, an ice box and some basics that will hold you until you can get to a grocer's."

"You needn't have gone to that much trouble—"

"No trouble at all," Mrs. Povey said, standing at the threshold and gesturing him inside. But Joseph remained where he stood.

"Well, then, I thank you kindly for your considerate preparations."

"It's the least I can do. Charles will bring the buggy round Monday morning and drive you over to the prison. Say, nine o'clock?"

Joseph nodded, feeling the weight of the key in his hand and wondering if crime was so rampant that he would be wise to lock his doors—something unheard of in Greeley.

Cathryn Povey's voice took a somber tone, and her hazel eyes searched his, unnerving him. "Dr. Tuttle, the women at the prison need our help and compassion. There have been instances of abuse, I fear." Her eyes grew misty. "Unconscionable abuse." She cleared the outrage from her throat. "I look forward to working with you to improve the deplorable conditions there and seeing that they receive the respect they deserve. They may be guilty of crimes against man or country, but they are fellow humans, no less worthy of our care and kindness than those living honorable lives."

"I heartily agree," Joseph said, suddenly feeling a great burden of responsibility thrust upon his shoulders. Was he up to this task? He tried to imagine the cold brick walls, the lack of proper heating, the misery and despair in the eyes of those incarcerated. And what about the hardened outlaws and their violent tempers and erratic behavior—inside and outside the walls of the territorial penitentiary? Would he be able to help them beyond tending to their physical needs? What about tending to their souls?

At that moment, standing in the doorway of an unfamiliar house in an unfamiliar and bleak town on the northern region of the Front Range that teetered on the edge of lawlessness, Joseph Tuttle felt small and unqualified and entirely vulnerable. But he would see this through, God willing.

Chapter 5

IN A NARROW WOOD SOME distance from the Carson manse, towering maples reached spindly leafless arms overhead as if supplicating the heavens. Robert leaned against the trunk of one massive tree, considering the gaily lit lanterns swaying on the chill evening breeze and wondering if he should send up a prayer. He chastised his griping heart, reminding himself of all his blessings, that he was rich, strong, and hale, and there were other gals in the world besides Rose — gals more deserving of his affections. But his heart was slammed shut and padlocked and wasn't listening. The sounds of chatter and laughter danced in the air, muffled, like tinkling bells, as the guests of Lester Carson sauntered in and out of the bank of French doors leading to the spacious porches enwrapping the Carson domicile. The festive mood only aggravated Robert's dour disposition.

Ellsworth rolled a cigarette, slumped against the tree beside Robert, his gloved hands struggling to manage the paper. His head lifted. "Smell that? Ahhh . . . I can taste that roasted pig all the way from here. My stomach's protesting."

"Then get you some of that food yonder," Robert said, thinking what a stupid idea it was to spend a Saturday night sneaking and snooping around the Carson ranch. He just knew Rose was inside, probably on the arm of that dandy. What was the point in torturing himself? "Where's Abel?"

Ellsworth, finally having managed to roll his cigarette and light it, sucked in a long drag and nodded to a copse of small pines to the north. "He's a-comin' now," he said.

Abel Pollack had been a cow puncher going on nigh twenty years on the Morrison ranch — a hardworking fella who Robert's pa trusted more than anyone else. Though, he might not if he knew some of the antics the Boston man perpetrated. A jokester of the highest order, Abel liked little more than to pull pranks on the unsuspecting. As such, Ellsworth had enlisted his company for this evening's agenda, perhaps thinking Abel's japery would squelch Robert's bad mood. But Robert knew exactly why Abel had come. A dog drooling over a bone fell short of describing the way Abel frothed over a dolled-up lady.

Abel was positively exuberant as he came alongside the two, his face shining with anticipation. Laramie City, with its two dozen brothels, was akin to St. Peter's courtyard inside the pearly gates for the likes of Abel Pollack.

"Lookit you!" Ellsworth exclaimed, gesturing at Abel's fancy three-piece custom-fit wool suit. "You're all spraddled out."

"Ya don't look so bad yourself, Cowboy," Abel replied, wiggling his brows.

Robert sighed, the ennui like a lead weight tugging his spirit to the frost-tinged grass. He didn't know why Rose had his heart in such a tangled mess. He'd spent the previous couple of days busying himself around the ranch, getting the last batch of cattle off by train before winter set in, perusing the entries in the journals—checking them twice. He'd even helped young Duane with his rope handling. He felt as if his skin were cankerous, fomenting some malaise for which there was nary a cure.

He wanted a wife something fierce. Simply put. But not just a wife. He truly wanted a gal to love with all his heart, and the loneliness that ate at him each day couldn't be ignored or drowned with whiskey. Or distracted by burying himself in work. There was just naught for it. Abel and Ellsworth might be perfectly content with flirtatious dalliances and fleeting brushes with romance, but that would never suit Robert. And that's why he'd always resisted in the past when the punchers tried to cajole him into joining them on their nights out on the town.

"Y'all ready?" Abel said gleefully, his smile lifting his thick waxed moustache that drifted down the sides of his mouth, blacker than tar, his eyes fixated on the flurry of swirling skirts over layers of petticoats as strains of lively music filled the night.

"What's the plan?" Ellsworth asked, drawing on his cigarette and removing his big hat to smooth down his unruly thick hair. They all looked like trussed ducks ready for the oven in their smart suit coats and pressed trousers. Ellsworth's silk vest strained the small pearl buttons at his ever-growing girth, and even in the cool night sweat speckled his forehead. Abel had the look of a riverboat gambler, with the quick wit and uppity posture of a high-rolling Easterner. Slicked-back hair, side whiskers perfectly trimmed—in contrast to the Wild Bill buffalo that stood beside him.

"Git us some grub . . . and git us some gals." Abel winked at Robert. Sure looked like a bit of drool gathering at the corners of Abel's mouth. Amazing how Abel could sound like a Wyoming cowboy one minute, then turn on the charm with a perfectly intoned Boston accent that bespoke upper class. Robert wondered about the life the puncher had left behind, which the fella never talked about and abruptly changed the subject when it was brought up. Like many, he no doubt had fled to the frontier to lose the trail to a sordid past. The two employees of the Morrison Ranch headed toward the house.

"Be careful," Robert said. "Someone might recognize you — even in those . . . uh, disguises."

Ellsworth stopped. "You ain't comin'?" Abel looked utterly incredulous.

"I can't risk being seen —you know that. Lester Carson would shoot me on sight. You two, well . . . I reckon, dressed as you are, you might go unnoticed. And if Carson does spot you, he may only beat you senseless." Robert grinned.

"Suit yourself." Ellsworth shrugged. "We'll bring you back some grub."

Robert watched his pals walk toward the elevated patio. A set of stairs trailed down both sides to the manicured lawn, and rows of privet hedges lined the walkway. The two parked themselves at the bottom of one of the staircases, no doubt planning their entry into the great room, where buffet tables laden with platters of food could be seen through the floor-to-ceiling picture windows. Lester Carson sure knew how to throw a party, and he probably had spared no expense.

After some minutes, Abel and Ellsworth slipped into the house, and from time to time Robert saw them mingling with the guests — of the female variety. At one point Robert saw Lester Carson, surrounded by businessmen Robert knew well — bankers, investors, land owners. A cigar sat in his mouth as he spoke, his thinning silver hair slicked back, his moustache like boar's whiskers, his beard trimmed to a point below his chin. The refined and elegant lady who sidled up to him, dressed in shimmering blue silk with her ebony hair wrapped in thick swales atop her head, Robert knew to be Danielle Carson, the rancher's wife. Though he'd never met her, he'd seen plenty of photographs of her in the papers, mostly in the society columns.

Robert pulled his heavy wool coat tight and turned up the collar as the cold bit at his neck. Restless, he wandered through the damp meadow, careful to stay in shadows, making his way over to the dark recesses of the house. Truth be told, he wanted to catch a glimpse of Rose. What if the man he'd seen her flirting with was just a friend? Or maybe even her brother? Had he read too much into the exchange? A tiny ember of hope flared in his chest, though he castigated himself for trying to fan it into flames. *They'll only burn you—you know that. If she was interested, she would'a replied to your letters.*

Still, he couldn't help craning to see through the plate glass into the crowded room, his gaze drifting over faces . . .

One of the doors to the patio above him flew open, and a young gal emerged, in a white dress so glistening and radiant he might have mistaken her for an angel, had he been drinking. She wore a thick fur wrap around her shoulders, and long white gloves rode up over her elbows. Robert slipped back into the dark space so he wouldn't be seen, as her voice carried to him.

"Please," she said, "I need some air," and at first Robert thought she was beseeching him, but then he dared peek his head out. A man barely into his twenties, his look declaring wealth and privilege, marched out behind her. Dressed in a charcoal three-piece suit and heavily starched white shirt, the man's narrow face and long prominent nose made his beady eyes seem like those of a crow. A smile that was hardly friendly pushed up his pale, bony cheeks. He had the softness and visage of a man who sat long hours and hardly ventured outdoors. A businessman, no doubt. And Robert didn't doubt the fella's keen interest in this young gal, who seemed teetering between adolescence and womanhood.

At first Robert was merely curious, listening to their discourse out of boredom, but the gal's sweet voice mesmerized him. Not only did she appear angelic in her dress stitched with hundreds of tiny pearls, the lanterns hanging from the porch rafters spilled a glow of ethereal light that made her delicate features seem like that of a porcelain doll. He could tell she had a head of thick brown hair that was presently twisted and pinned in elegant fashion beneath a lacy hat. He had a sudden urge to see that waterfall of hair tumble down her shoulders. The thought made his breath hitch in his throat.

The fella rambled on about some incident that had taken place in Cheyenne the week prior—something he thought amusing that involved some lost cowboys. The gal was only partially listening, and Robert guessed she was attempting to be polite but secretly wishing she was elsewhere.

Robert stiffened when the fella laid his hand on her arm and saw her flinch. Perhaps she was shy, but she surely wasn't being coy. The fella leaned in close and whispered something in her ear, and to Robert's—and the fella's—surprise, she slapped his cheek and stepped back.

Robert saw her swallow, her lashes fluttering over her bright hazel eyes as she composed herself, her teeth clenched. A hint of feistiness streaked across her face. The demure young lady had some spunk to her, Robert concluded with some amusement. He watched to see what the fella would try next. The man, his skin red-splotched, took the gal's wrist—tight, from the pained expression on her face—and pulled her to him. Robert's pulse quickened and his hands fisted. He would not hesitate in making short shrift of any fella that mishandled a gal.

But the French doors opened once more and the fella quickly released his grip, just as Danielle Carson stepped onto the stone patio, her eyes riveting on the young gal's in chastisement though she said not a word. The fella tipped his head to his hostess with an apologetic smirk and slunk back into the house. It didn't take the Pope to tell Robert who this angel was standing beside Carson's wife.

So that's the rancher's daughter. Julia. He wondered where she'd been hiding all these years. He was sure he'd never seen her about town on any occasion. He wouldn't forget a face like hers, no siree.

Worried that he might be recognized by the missus, Robert hung back, only catching a few words of the women's whispered exchange, but he could suss out the tone. The mother had expectations. The daughter expressed exasperation. Miz Carson urged Julia to go back inside, but Julia refused. Robert could only guess what they were at odds about, but if he had to wager, he'd say it might have something to do with that fella Julia'd slapped.

"I just want a few minutes alone, in the garden," she said, sounding as if she was having trouble breathing. She seemed to labor over each breath, from what he could hear in his hiding place. It had the same raspy sound his nana'd had.

Miz Carson acquiesced to her daughter's request and disappeared back inside the ranch house. A barely perceptible sigh slipped from Julia's lips, a wistful sound that resonated with his own melancholy. He imagined her as a beautiful caged bird that was brought out to amuse and delight the rancher's guests, then stuffed back in her cage and locked in a lonely room.

She sauntered over to the railing as the full moon lit her up, as if she were on a big empty stage. Robert stood below her, no more than ten feet away, sequestered in the shadows. When she began to pray, he felt suddenly awkward, as if trespassing—well, he was trespassing, he reminded himself—but his discomfort came from hearing her pleas to God that he should not have been privy to. Though his mind urged him to slip away and afford this young gal privacy, he feared any movement would startle her and his anonymity would be compromised. More than that, he felt drawn into her prayer, her soft entreaties to their Creator voicing the very words Robert would deign to pray, had he half the sublime gift of articulation that Julia Carson displayed.

She spoke from a conflicted heart, acknowledging her parents' love and adoration for her but yearning to leave home, feeling stifled and yet guilty for such sentiments. The more Robert listened—such a long and sincere prayer!—the more Julia's tender heart was revealed to him. It astonished him that such a delicate, gentle, and humble soul could have been spawned and raised by the likes of Lester Carson.

Something strange came over him. Like a gentle ripple of water lapping at his heart, his affection for this delicate flower swelled. Her words were like ropes pulling his deepest feelings up from the depths of his soul, as if she were a conjurer able to see into his darkest recesses where he hid from all but God. How was that possible? Blood pulsed in his ears as he reminded himself to breathe.

When she fell silent, Robert peeked a glance up to the porch railing. Julia Carson's head was tipped back, her creamy throat exposed to moonlight, her eyes closed, the thick lashes fluttering ever so slightly. Robert couldn't wrest his eyes from her—from her now-closed lips that were soft and enticing. Her countenance was ethereal as she stood there, gently swaying from side to side, as if hearing an angelic hymn whisper in her ears. He took in her slender shape, the silky dress hugging her slim hips and long legs. But his gaze drifted back to her porcelain throat and the hint of her swelling breasts at the lace of her bodice.

An unexpected ache throbbed in his chest as the yearning to pull her into his arms grew unbearable. It wasn't lust that sparked him but something akin to adoration. And perhaps awe. Though merely sixteen years, she was more woman than child. Her prayer had been no recitation or selfish pleading for God's benefaction; rather, she had spoken like a child to a trusted father with a maturity and frankness that Robert had never heard before. Certainly not from the lips of Rose Huffington. And not even from his ever-praying ma, who tended to ramble on to God in a perfunctory manner with a lot of *thees* and *thous*, reciting her memorized list of supplications and thanksgivings and the names of those she was interceding for.

Lively music started up again from inside the grand house, and when Julia's eyes opened, Robert stepped back out of sight, only to trip over his own feet like some love-struck cur. He cursed under his breath as he banged against the side of the stone retaining wall, aware that his presence had made itself known. *Just what I need—to get discovered by Lester Carson's daughter.*

There was only one thing for it. He didn't have to tell himself twice. *Run!*

Chapter 6

"WAIT!" JULIA CALLED OUT. THE man in the shadows stumbled away, only to freeze up at her command.

Had he been eavesdropping as she prayed? What was he doing under the porch, hiding like some Peeping Tom? First, Jarret Strickler and his ill manners, and now this ... this scalawag? How dare he? All her hopes for a promising party, for a chance of escape from this prison of a life, fled, leaving her with raw emotion and an unbearable desire to hasten to her room and lock the door until every last guest left the Carson ranch.

But, of course, she didn't dare do such a thing. She was the guest of honor, and this was her birthday party. A five-tiered iced cake sat on the buffet table. She huffed, at the end of her patience.

"Show yourself," she said in no uncertain voice. She stared at the man's back. He wore a long heavy black coat, shiny black boots, and a wide-brimmed hat, and from what she could tell, he was tall and broad-shouldered. Was he someone she knew?

Then he turned to face her, standing no more than ten feet from the porch. The bright moon lit up a face that was wholly unfamiliar to her. He had a handsome visage and a clean-shaven jaw, a neatly trimmed moustache, and his green-brown eyes studied her with an intensity that took her aback. His posture and demeanor bespoke a man of confidence, if not arrogance. He gave no hint of apology for his actions; rather, a smile played at the corners of his mouth, and the warmth and lack of guile befuddled her further. Did she know him? She thought not. Yet, the way he looked at her seemed to indicate he knew her well. Odd indeed.

Her previous ire melted in the wake of her curiosity. And, she had to admit, attraction.

"Do I know you, sir?" She guessed him to be in his midtwenties. Had her parents invited him to her party? She hadn't seen him earlier, but he was dressed appropriately. The cut of his suit revealed a man strong and used to hard labor. But his poise bespoke something other than a laborer.

"Well?" she pressed when he failed to answer. Now she detected a hint of embarrassment streak his face. Could such a poised man actually be shy?

He removed his hat, exposing a head of wavy brown hair, and the way he reached to tuck a wayward strand behind his ear laid bare a gentleness and respect that words would never have conveyed. She reminded herself that this fetching man had been hiding in the shadows mere feet from her and had failed to announce his presence.

"I believe we, uh, haven't had the pleasure of meeting each other's acquaintance, Miss Carson."

The corner of her mouth quirked, though she told herself smiling would be entirely inappropriate. Yet, she couldn't help herself. His words were so carefully articulated, without pretentious manner, and the way his eyes danced with mischief roused her curiosity.

"Perhaps not. Do you have a name?"

That smile again, full of mischief. He was holding a secret — one she suddenly wanted to be privy to.

"Oh, indeed. But what is in a name?"

Julia laughed, aware of the railing she leaned against, the man below her, as if she stood on Juliet's balcony, her Romeo below. Shakespeare's tragedy about the star-crossed lovers was one of her favorites, and she'd heard a traveling troupe would soon come to Laramie to perform the play.

As if he were reading her mind, he recited with exaggerated aplomb, "That which we call a rose by any other name would smell as sweet."

She cocked her head, impressed. How many young men could quote Shakespeare? "I perceive, sir, that you are not a simple ranch hand of my father's."

He pinched his lips and shook his head, then said, "Not likely. Not ever, Miss Carson."

"Whatever do you mean by that remark?" She wished he would come closer. But instead, he stepped back, glancing up at the house behind her. She inched closer to the patio's stone railing to get a better look, but her action prompted him to retreat back into shadow.

"I fear I truly am your Romeo," he said, pushing his hat down on his head so his eyes barely peeked out. "Or at least, well, would that I were . . ." His voice grew at once wistful and hard. And was he blushing? It appeared so, though it was hard to tell in the scant light.

For some reason, with each retreating step of his, Julia's heart pounded a little harder. A flutter of anxiety tickled her chest. His face held boyish impishness, yet with a stolid maturity underlying it.

"I'm afraid I must take your leave, Miss Carson. The hour is late —"

"And you'll be turned into a pumpkin?"

He stopped. "I'd what?"

Julia laughed again. "You are full of mystery, sir." A man familiar with the Bard but not with a common fairy tale. Where had he hailed from?

She dared look into those bottomless eyes and instantly regretted it. Those warm, sparking orbs pulled her down, down, into their depths. It took her breath away. The sounds of the party behind her drifted away.

"Please . . ." She could hardly get the word out. There was something so magical about this moment, about his attendance upon her. About this man standing below her. She wanted nothing more than to close her eyes and hear him speak to her.

"If . . . you won't tell me your name, would you tell me something about yourself?" Oh, she was acting so brashly, but she hated the thought of him slipping away —and having to return to the boisterous celebration inside, where her parents and their guests would be drinking champagne and whiskey and discussing politics. Here, under the moon, in the quiet of a November night, there seemed to be just the two of them, caught in time and place together like two drifting strangers who washed up onto a deserted isle, the last two people in the world. *My, we're awfully poetic this evening.*

"What would you like to know?" he said, his voice teasing, but oh so gentle and unpretentious.

She thought a moment. What would she like to know about this mystery man? "What would you rather be doing right now, if you weren't standing below me in the cold moonlight?"

He answered without hesitation. "Ahh . . ." He shook his head, ever so thoughtfully, his smile now exposing gleaming teeth and dimples at the corners of his lips. She swallowed, drawn to his mouth.

"At this moment, I can't imagine wanting to be anywhere else or doing anything other than looking into your angelic face."

She was dumbfounded. Such words coming from any other man would have made her bristle. Hadn't Jarret Strickler expressed a similar sentiment to her not many minutes ago? But the way this stranger said these words—with such simple sincerity and a surge of need—made her heart race.

"Sir," she forced out past her tight throat. "I fear I—"

"The name's Robert."

He looked pained as he waited for her response. Robert? Just . . . Robert? She was about to press him for his family name, when it came rushing at her. His furtiveness, his manner, his mention of Romeo . . .

Lines from the play surfaced in her mind. *"My name is hateful to myself, because it is an enemy to me."*

"Robert *Morrison*?" She looked at him aghast. But his dour expression told all. "What are you doing here? If my father catches you—"

He nodded, serious-faced, but the mirth still danced in his eyes.

Another line from the play slipped into her mind. *"'Tis but thy name that is my enemy."* But why would she feel one way or another toward the son of her father's nemesis? She knew little more about Stephen Morrison's son than he helped run the Morrison Ranch. She was so sheltered from the outside world, she hardly knew anyone in Laramie. She'd been taught to despise the Morrison name, though she'd never been told why. Was Robert in the same trap as she?

A voice called out behind her as the patio door opened and let loose a glitter of musical notes into the air from inside the great hall. *Mother.*

"Julia. To whom are you speaking?"

She spun around, catching a glimpse of Robert Morrison slipping into darkness along the side of the house. A horrible sudden sense of desperation grabbed hold of her. Would he now leave, and would she never cast eyes on him again? Why she felt so flustered and unhinged befuddled her. She knew nothing of this man, yet . . . some part of her knew all she needed to know. It was as if she'd been struck with Cupid's arrow, and the tip prodding her heart spawned such an ache, she thought she'd be sick.

Her mother strode over to her, searched the moonlit yard, then, seemingly satisfied no one was about, studied Julia's face.

"My dear, you look pale and wan. Has something happened?" Her mother's mouth tightened in concern.

Oh yes, Mother. Something happened. Something wonderful and magical and distressing. She dared to look into the shadows where Robert had vanished. But he was gone. How would she ever see him again? The thought that she'd imagined their exchange knotted her stomach.

"Come inside, my dear. Too much cold air might cause your asthma to act up. It's time for cake, and Mr. Strickler has been asking for you, expecting the first dance." Her mother held out her hand, her face uncompromising.

At the mention of Jarret Strickler's name, Julia's heart sank. The question she had asked of Robert flitted into her head, taunting her. *"What would you rather be doing right now . . . ?"*

As she forced a smile onto her face and let her mother take her by the arm and lead her back into the house, she knew the answer to that question. She pictured those strong arms encircling hers, and those mesmerizing, sweet lips coming close for a kiss, his sparkling eyes filled with adoration and mischief taking her breath away.

Chapter 7

THE LUMINOUS MOON SHOWERED LIGHT across the meadow. Robert's boots crunched hoarfrost that crusted the fescue as temperatures dropped. His hands stuffed in his pockets, he strode toward the stand of white pines a stone's long throw from the patio where he'd left Julia Carson.

Julia . . . He whispered her name, tasting it on his tongue, thinking of her angelic face and the way her eyes with their flecks of gold and green had searched deeply into his. He'd thought she meant to chastise him for eavesdropping, never expecting instead to surrender his heart so willingly and completely as she'd teased him, delighting in her banter with a mortal enemy of her family.

What would his own pa think, if he heard his son was smitten with a Carson? And not just a Carson but the only daughter of Lester Carson? He'd be fit to strangle Robert. *But for an angel such as Julia . . . I would face not only my pa but a legion of angels in order to see her again. I must see her!*

He thought about the man who'd grabbed Julia's arm. Was he her intended? Had her parents already arranged to marry her off? The thought sent panic racing through his veins.

Get ahold of yourself. You barely know the gal! What's gotten into you? Maybe he was crazy, but there was no denying this feeling, this *certainty* that consumed him. Were they divinely met? Was this truly a case of star-crossed lovers, as Shakespeare had penned? If he pursued her affections, no doubt it would be. For there was no way any Carson or Morrison would allow such a match.

But he was jumping the gun. A few words exchanged, a few glances. Just as with Rose, he was expecting too much. The women he knew found him fetching enough—though he was hardly an educated judge of what women saw in the opposite sex. But he wanted more than to be admired for any features he might possess. Was that all a gal saw in him—a handsome face, a desirable body . . . heir to a thousand head of cattle? Some gals only wanted the wealth and status his Morrison name carried, and he could sense those gold-diggers a mile away. But Julia Carson wouldn't care about his money. But would she care about *him*? What could he offer someone like Julia?

That was the question that burned in his soul, previously ignited by Rose's petered interest. For he feared he would be found lacking should any gal look too long or deep into his soul.

He knew he was hypercritical of himself. That came from too many years of his pa pounding him with criticism, and it seemed that no matter how hard he worked, how much he tried to prove his worthiness, his pa expressed doubts, held back responsibilities, often relegating them to Ellsworth, or to Abel. Here he was, midtwenties, and often treated more like a hired hand than the only son of Stephen Morrison. Why, he could run the ranch in his sleep, and he'd assumed someday he would.

Though, his doubts over his pa's intentions were growing daily. All because of Cassidy.

Six years. Robert knew his pa still blamed him for Cassidy's death—as if the knife that had been thrust into his brother's gut had been wielded by his own hand. His pa had yet to forgive him—and the Good Lord knew that Robert could scarcely forgive himself. Cassidy had jumped into the fray to protect his younger brother from Irish thugs down by the loading platform at the railway station. They'd held Robert up at gunpoint, then two of them restrained his arms while the third turned his face into raw meat. Cassidy had gone inside the station office to pick up transit papers for a shipment of cattle, and by the time he'd come out, Robert was nearly incoherent with pain.

Robert knew he shouldn't have made that snide remark to the lug-headed leader of their gang. He knew, as well, that he shouldn't have wandered over to where they congregated across the street, in front of the Front Street market, on that rainy, windy day. When they taunted him, he shouldn't have answered. But he did—all those things, despite the many warnings Cassidy had given his hotheaded, cocky brother.

After Cassidy fell to the rain-drenched and muddy ground, after the thugs had fled, after the life seeped out of his brother, Robert had knelt beside the lifeless body, rain pelting him in judgement. Robert's cockiness was buried six feet underground with Cassidy, and from that day on, his pa had drifted from him—whether purposefully or unawares, Robert didn't know. Didn't matter. His ma had found it in her heart to forgive him, and she told him over and over that it wasn't his fault, that *these things happen*. Some consolation. And though she'd forgiven him, the pain of Cassidy's death evident in her slumped shoulders and countless hours of seclusion was not lost on Robert.

Arguing voices pulled Robert from his rancid reverie just as he stepped under the boughs of the pines, whose crystalized needles glinted in the moonlight like a million stars that had been ejected from heaven. North of the manse, he made out Abel and Ellsworth facing off someone he would recognize in a blizzard from atop Laramie Peak.

Ty Lawson! Robert eased his way closer, under the darkness of tree branches, in case he was needed to step in. He hadn't brought his Colt, but he came prepared—always did. He'd be a fool not to, living in Laramie. He reached for the small Derringer strapped to his ankle and extracted it from its sheath.

The voices carried in the quiet of the night.

". . . gotta lot of nerve . . . but I don't want to make a scene . . . special night for the family . . ."

Ty's voice was mean and threatening, but he kept it low.

Ellsworth flapped his hands and backed off. "We're leaving . . . 'preciate the kind hospitality . . ."

The sneer in his words was palpable, even at this distance. Abel then said something that riled Ty, but before Carson's nephew could throw a punch, Ellsworth yanked Abel back and spun him around. As the two marched off across the field, toward a horse pasture, Ty stood like a sentinel, hands on hips, watching, soon joined by three others—their posture indicating they were probably ranch hands—that took up a vigil beside him.

Robert fell back behind a lodgepole pine, thinking to join his pals and ride back with them. Surely they'd be waiting— antsy and probably halfway to drunk—with the horses until he came over. But not a minute after Ty and his pals retreated back to the house, Robert caught sight of a swish of white fabric.

Like a dream, or maybe a cloud gone rogue, forsaking her heavenly realm and choosing to live among mortals, a shadow moved through the wide-open prairie as if floating a foot above the ground.

Robert gaped. He'd never seen the like. Moonlight splashing radiance on her dress, making it shimmer, the grass at her feet glowing as if a beam of light shone on her alone in a bleak and smudged world, her features sharp in contrast, but soft, as if drawn with pastels.

He could see every detail: the shine in her eyes, the tiny pearls of her gown glistening, her slender fingers reaching out as if imploring, as she watched Abel and Ellsworth get swallowed up into the night beyond the pasture fences that ran for miles north and east.

She was breathing hard, laboring over each intake of air, her body collapsing in on itself, like a deflating balloon. Before he fully realized she was in trouble, he was upon her, and even as she fell into his waiting arms, she was graceful in her surrender, and had it been under other circumstances he would have gathered her to his body and pressed her to him, letting his lips find her the way they so desperately ached to do so at this very moment, the need welling up so powerfully it took his breath away as well.

But a close attendance upon her stricken face shook him free of his yearning and instead stirred worry into an eddy of panic. He'd watched his nana suffer asthma attacks frequently over the years, and he knew the dangers they posed.

She threw her head back, that lovely mouth open but not for him, not beseeching him to kiss her but to help her find air that was denied entry into her pleading throat.

"Hey, hey, look at me," he said, trying to rein in her wild eyes. He'd seen eyes like hers plenty of times. Spooked horses, lightning-struck cattle. She wouldn't breathe until the panic subsided.

He gathered she was no stranger to this predicament. She quickly met his eyes, locking on as if clutching a rope, dangling from a cliff, a thousand-foot crevasse below.

"Breathe with me," he instructed, steady, softly, tenderly. His heart pounded as he drew in a slow, measured breath, watching her neck loosen, the air rattle as it found ingress into her lungs. The wild eyes lost some of their fear, and Julia blinked, then swallowed. He had her cradled in his arms, like a baby, and her hands kneaded the skirt of the dress, wrinkling the satin, knuckles white. He was sitting on his heels, hunkered down, his gaze never leaving her face as they breathed together, in unison, the simple behavior something he never before considered but now saw keenly as something so precious it needed guarding and cherishing.

Robert lost all sense of time. When he saw the color return to her face and heard the air gliding softly in and out of her partly opened mouth, he imagined an hour had passed. But when she straightened and extricated herself from his unwilling arms, then smoothed out her dress and hair, formerly ghostly cheeks flushing crimson, he knew only a minute or two had played out since he'd run to her.

She was tall for a gal but not lanky or boyish. No, she had all the curves in the right places, though he imagined as she grew into full womanhood, those curves would fill out and enhance her beauty even more. He stood and faced her, afraid to touch her even though she had nestled in his arms just seconds before, wholly surrendered to his care. But he had no claims on her, and any physical contact at this juncture would be highly indecorous, though his desire for her raged as hot as a metalsmith's foundry. A desire that sought to immolate him if he didn't put distance between them. He could barely breathe, so close to her, her scent soaked deep into his skin like a permeating dye.

He took a step back—a matter of survival.

"How're you feeling now?" he asked.

She swallowed, nodded. "Better." Her face still flushed in embarrassment. "Thank you for coming to my aid." She hesitated, looked away. "The cold night air . . . sometimes triggers an attack."

Now he nodded. She didn't need to explain. He knew he should accompany her back to her house, but after seeing the altercation between Ty Lawson and his friends, last thing he wanted was for someone to spot him with Julia. He was surprised he hadn't yet been discovered.

Julia turned and looked in the direction of the big house, though only the roofline could be seen through the thick vegetation. "I . . . I should be getting back. Before someone starts to worry about me."

"Why'd you come out here?" he asked, at once perplexed and entranced by the husky sweetness of her voice. What on earth had compelled her to run across the prairie in the cold air, in her party gown, risking her health? She'd seemed to be looking for someone when he noticed her out there, staring after Ellsworth . . .

Then it struck him, though he didn't believe it. Yet, when he turned and looked into her face, where a flush of red had leapt to her cheeks, the answer was written, plain to see. It hit him like a splash of ice water.

Time didn't just stop this time; it came crashing down around him like an avalanche, erasing the world and everything in it. Everything but him and Julia bathed in radiant moonlight.

Wordlessly, with a million unspoken words, he lifted a strand of her long bark-brown hair and tucked it behind her ear and felt her shudder through his fingertips. Her buttery soft skin was warm as he trailed a hesitant finger along her cheek, letting it come to rest at the edge of her mouth, which had dropped open once more.

He drank her in, and he could not get enough. His eyes absorbed the tiny details of her face, as if he were a sponge. He studied every eyelash, the way the bones lifted her cheeks, the shape of her face that curved to her small chin, the Milky Way of freckles streaking across her nose, his eyes fixating on that mouth and those moist lips, the steamy air now exhaling evenly, unhindered, as the blood pulsed in his ears in rhythm to the tiny pulse throbbing at her temples beneath wisps of gossamer hair.

Now that he had held her in his arms, feeling her strength rippling beneath her fragility, he felt as if a limb had been ripped away. Julia Carson was a stranger, and yet when he'd held her, it was as if he'd always known and loved and cared for her. But he couldn't say such crazy thoughts; she'd think him mad. And maybe he was. Maybe she had enwrapped him in a spell, and he had fallen under her enchantment, the way sailors were said to do upon encountering the sirens of the sea, who shipwrecked their vessels and dragged them to their watery graves.

He wrenched his gaze from her mouth—that delicious mouth that called out to him like a siren's song to join his to hers. Juliet was wrong, he thought, when she said parting was such sweet sorrow. There would be nothing sweet about saying good night to Julia Carson. It pained him to consider it, but he was risking more than his life by standing here, indulging his eyes in her beauty, undeniably love-struck.

He willed his feet to step back; they obeyed reluctantly. She wrapped his coat tightly around her torso. He was sure it was longing he read in her eyes. That was not a look easily mistaken for something other. She needed to leave, and so did he. But that was the last thing he wanted to do.

Her name drifted on the breeze, biting his ears. Her ma was calling for her, the tone frantic.

Julia's eyes widened, but not with panic this time. With urgency.

"I'll send word to you," she said. "By way of messenger." There was a hint of a question in her voice.

He couldn't stop staring at her face, as if he was leaving on a long journey and might never see her again. He couldn't help himself. He took her hands—her warm pliable hands that grasped his in return. He put them to his lips, almost as if he were praying with her.

"Tomorrow," he said, nearly begging. "Please?" The word came out as thin as paper, as ephemeral as hope.

She nodded emphatically. When her name was called again, she offered him a smile that lit up her face. He would have paid a thousand bars of gold for that smile. He grinned, hoping he didn't look as idiotic as he felt. But she merely smiled wider and repeated, "Tomorrow." Then she slipped the coat from her shoulders and handed it to him.

When she ran off, with the moonlight chasing her, he realized he'd been holding his breath. He imprinted the image of her in that white dress, running through the grass, in his mind and carried it with him and branded it in his heart, as he ran free and wild and out of his mind with love all the way across the pastures to where Ellsworth and Abel sat with the horses, waiting for him.

"Where were you?" her mother asked in a tight, almost seething tone, her frown fixed in disbelief and disapproval. "Your face is raw from the cold! Did you have an episode—?"

Julia caught her breath, startled at how easily it came into her throat. She laid her hand on her mother's gloved wrist. "I'm fine, Mother. I just took a walk in the pasture." Julia wondered if her mother had truly been worried over her health or was more anxious over the prospect of an asthma episode ruining her perfect party. She then chastised herself for her unkind thought. Robert Morrison had completely unhinged her, and socializing with guests was the last thing she wanted to be doing right now. But that was no reason to cast blame on her mother.

She closed her eyes, summoning the memory of how it felt resting in his arms—those strong and comforting arms. She had never felt so safe, so attended. The way his eyes had adored her made her tremble anew. His was a face that bespoke gentleness, tenderness, free of guile. But it had also revealed passion and desire, though held in check. He could have taken advantage of her, as men were wont to do with women. But he hadn't. He had been a perfect gentleman—though she was certain her father would have described the son of his enemy in much different terms. *And he saved your life.* If he hadn't been there to help her, she would have fainted . . . or worse.

She shuddered at the thought, then the realization pricked her. He couldn't have been there by happenstance. He must have been divinely sent to her rescue, a predestined meeting— an answer to her supplication to heaven. This thought sank into her bones, kindling her longing for him in unutterable words. *Tomorrow . . .* Could she even wait that long?

Her mother shook her headful of pinned curls. "A walk!" She huffed and leaned close. The cloying scent of her mother's perfume in the overly warm room gave Julia a headache. The strains of music and animated conversation around her swirled into a claustrophobic cacophony. Her attention flitted from person to table, then to her mother's stern yet curious face, as her limbs fell limp and weak.

"My dear, what has come over you?"

Julia's head spun, as if she'd landed in Wonderland and nothing around her looked familiar or made sense.

"Let's get you some punch. Your father is eager to give his speech, and the guests are ready for dessert." She took Julia's arm and practically marched her over to the festooned table covered with a starched white linen cloth on which sat the opulent crystal bowl full of juices and chopped ice.

The rest of the evening passed in a colorful blur of sounds and smells and tastes. But Julia hardly smelled, heard, or tasted anything, for she was like a specter haunting the great hall, barely substantial, attached to nothing, caring not at all who spoke to her or who danced with her. Not even when Jarret Strickler coaxed her onto the dance floor and waltzed with her, his arm a little too tight around her waist, did she mind.

The perpetual smile gracing her face no doubt gave the Cheyenne banking heir the wrong impression, but she didn't care. She knew who her smile was for, and when she saw Robert Morrison—*oh, when would she see him again?*—it would be his. That, and so much more . . .

Chapter 8

LARAMIE COUNTY SHERIFF THOMAS JEFFERSON Carr did not suffer fools. Or at least he didn't any more than he had to. While some might say Lester Carson was hardly a fool, Carr couldn't think of a better appellation for the rich rancher. Why on God's green earth would Carson try to broker a deal with his hated enemy Stephen Morrison? Something surely stank in Wyoming Territory, and it wasn't the fish-processing plant on the Laramie River he could see out the wall-to-wall windows two blocks to the east.

While he paced in his Laramie office at the back of the courthouse building, he checked his watch for the third time in the last few minutes. Asa House was rarely late—a man of impeccable punctuality, and one who had even less patience for fools—or even outlaws. Though Carr had the reputation of "putting fear in the hearts of evildoers," it was Asa who had long been the wellspring of Carr's passion for justice.

When Carr had first come to Wyoming Territory, the name A. J. House was on the lips of scoundrel and saint alike. As the first sheriff, he alone had the courage to take on Big Steve Long—the self-appointed marshal—and those snakes, his half-brothers Ace and Con Moyer.

Carr had heard how Asa organized the "Vigilance Committee," right about when Long and his brothers opened a saloon called the Bucket of Blood and began forcing settlers into signing away their property. Any who refused were killed, more times than not.

By October of '68, Long had killed thirteen men in gunfights, but when he'd attempted to rob Rollie "Hard Luck" Harrison, a well-liked prospector, Harrison produced a pistol and shot Long. Harrison was shot in turn and died as a result of his wounds—with no one as witness. But Long confessed to his fiancée, and she in turn told Asa, who stormed into Long's saloon and took him into custody. Asa lynched Long and his half-brothers by hanging them from the rafters in the sight of astonished onlookers.

Carr recalled how the town settled down after that, and how eager Asa had been to accept the appointment as warden at the newly opened territorial penitentiary. Carr couldn't've picked a better man for the job.

But as evil as Long had been, no one stirred Asa House's contempt and launched him into a vitriolic tirade as much as Lester Carson. Yet, even though Carr and Asa shared a close acquaintanceship, the story of that hatred had yet to be revealed. Many a night over many a shot of rye, Carr had tried to pry loose that story, but to no avail.

Asa was a man who considered his words and kept his cards close to his chest, especially when it came to his own past. What Carr knew about Asa before he became sheriff ten years back he could count on the fingers of one hand. Back in the day, he'd owned the biggest and most productive cattle ranch in

Wyoming, he'd heard some tell. But he'd lost it, overnight, and that had been the fuel for his righteous rampage against the lawless of the West.

Carr couldn't help feeling it had something to do with Lester Carson.

A knock sounded on the door, pulling Carr from the bank of windows. Asa marched in. Not a tall man, but imposing in his no-nonsense demeanor. His big nose and ears dominated his head, and his bushy silver eyebrows spread into his side whiskers. Carr noticed the warden was keeping his beard longer these days, nearly to his collarbone, the hair wiry and unruly, in contrast to the rest of him—a picture of fastidiousness in clothing and manner alike. How a fella managed to keep his boots spit-polish-clean like that after riding across town and tromping through the muddy, wet streets of Laramie, Carr couldn't say.

"Thomas," Asa said, his tone signaling Carr that his dander was up—way up. His face was a knot of anger, but his eyes glinted with what Carr suspected was mischief. "A little birdie told me a curious story."

Carr motioned him to sit in the upholstered burgundy leather chair facing his cherrywood desk. The small hearth in the corner with its cheery blaze baked the chill out of the air, and Carr was glad for it. He opened the box of cigars and offered one to Asa. The warden took one and withheld speaking until Carr had snipped the end of their cigars and lit them. If it hadn't been just after nine on a Monday morning, Carr would've offered him a glass of whiskey.

Asa sucked on his cigar, then blew out a plume of smoke, tilting his head back and studying the molding around the perimeter of the high plastered ceiling.

With another exhale of smoke, Asa looked at Carr. "Seems Lester Carson is hankerin' to buy old Hennessey's thousand acres."

"The thousand acres Angus Morrison bought a while back," Carr added. Asa nodded, then leaned over and carefully flicked ash into the tin tray on Carr's desk. Carr stood, leaning his leg against the wall, trying to ignore the throbbing that always beset him on cold mornings. Some days he woke to feeling the bullet still lodged in his thigh.

"You know Morrison will never sell."

"Don't I know it? But I'm bound an' determined to see to it the deal doesn't go through."

Carr knew better than to ask why. Questions like that would be met with a glare and a warning. Carr had learned that long ago.

"So what do you want from me?" Carr puffed on his cigar, letting the smoke swirl around his mouth, calming his agitation. Asa rarely asked for favors, but Carr sensed a request coming out the chute.

Asa set the cigar in the tray and stood, facing Carr. He chewed his lip thoughtfully. "I was jes thinkin' 'bout how you cleaned up the county, back when Charlie Stanley had that bawdy house on Ferguson Street in Cheyenne."

Carr half-consciously rubbed his ear where Stanley had shot him with his Derringer. Fortunately it only nicked the lobe, but Stanley hadn't fared as well. Carr had wrenched the gun from Stanley's hand and slammed him in the head with it. Then he carted him off to jail.

Carr looked at Asa, who seemed to be coming to a conclusion.

After some moments had passed, Asa said, "I think it's time for another cleansin'—this time in Laramie. Carson has run roughshod over this town, an' while I heard about the warning you gave that Lawson fella last week, warnings like that run like water over a duck's head. An' if too much water gathers, next thing we know, Laramie will be swept away in a flood." Asa puffed thoughtfully on his cigar.

Carr waited.

"So, we need to be more diligent."

Carr waited again, drawing on his cigar, the smoke lingering in the air around both men.

"Here's the upshot of the situation. It'd be best if you could find some way to ensure that land deal doesn't go through. If it does, Carson will own more land than any other rancher in the territory."

A body might argue that America was a free country. That a man who so desired could work toward his dreams and reach them. That if he wanted to own more land and cattle than anyone else in the West, he had the God-given right.

But Lester Carson—according to A. J. House—wasn't just any body. He didn't deserve the rights and privileges other men enjoyed. And who was he, Thomas Jefferson Carr, to make a case against the warden, who'd been his inspiration and model of righteousness all these years? It wasn't a big thing he was asking. And not an unlawful one. Carr disliked Carson as much as the next man. He'd heard plenty, though Carr had yet to catch the man in illegal activity. He imagined, if he dug a little harder, if he called in his markers with men who moved in close circles with Carson, he'd uncover some dirty dealings.

Besides, if there was one fella he really didn't want to rile, that was the man who was presently sitting in his chair, smoking one of his cigars.

Carr nodded. Asa got to his feet, then yanked on his vest to straighten it. The cigar lay smoldering in the tray.

"Join me for breakfast?" Carr suggested. The usual rabble hadn't woken from their drunken stupor to start rabbling, and only a couple of drunks were drying out in the jail cells.

"Some other time, Thomas. The new doctor is due to arrive at the prison shortly. I want to show him around, get a feel for the measure of the man. I hear he's an honorable God-fearin' fella—"

"That woman, Povey—she found him for you?"

"She did." Asa started for the door, then turned, his face looking like he'd tasted something rancid. "That pesky woman is a thorn in my flesh. But at least she's seen to this matter." He smoothed out his vest and ran a hand over his beard. "Let's hope this doc sticks around longer than the last. I'm up to my neck in problems, and last thing I need is to have Hoyt rainin' hellfire down on me for travesties in the prison."

With that, he doffed his big hat and bade Carr good day, leaving the sheriff of Laramie to finish smoking his cigar in the comfort of his leather upholstered chair positioned before the blazing hearth.

Carr recalled how John Wesley Hoyt, newly appointed territorial governor, had personally shown up at the penitentiary after one of the female prisoners had nearly died in what was, according to the male inmates who'd witnessed her tumble down the hard metal stairs, an "unfortunate accident." How that had happened in full sight of the guards, Asa couldn't say. Hoyt had given Asa a stern warning—he'd better not hear of any more accidents involving the female prisoners. While few in number, having women in the same prison as men—though the arrangement had been going on now for over a year—infuriated Asa.

After that incident, he subjected—and rightly so, thought Carr—the females of the prison population to the same strict adherences and routine as the males. Which, in turn, infuriated the most powerful and vocal woman of Laramie: Cathryn Povey. Truth be told, all this uproar over women and their rights started with Campbell—the first governor. He had the foolish idea that women should be given the right to vote, and that they should be allowed to own property and serve on juries. Why, Wyoming Territory was the only place in the whole country that gave women full suffrage rights. The stupidity of it all made Carr's head swim, and more than once he considered moving to the South—now that the war was over and things had properly settled down—where his forebears originally came from. A place where women knew their place and didn't stir up such trouble. Maybe moving there would get his wife to quit nagging him so much. Maybe some of those Southern manners would rub off on Berta, but he wouldn't bet on it.

Carr snuffed out his cigar with a sneer. Maybe that was why it was called "suffrage." For it was the men who truly suffered from such nonsense.

Joseph Tuttle stepped out of the carriage, holding on to his hat in the brisk wind and gazing up at the three-story gray quarried limestone structure before him. As he stood in the open yard, he looked around at the various drab buildings of brick construction, hearing the faint noise of machinery and, in the distance, railcar brakes easing on the tracks to the east. The Union Pacific station was hardly a mile away, across the river, but the site of the penitentiary seemed isolated and lonely. Tuttle wondered, for the hundredth time, why he'd agreed to take this position. Pausing there, all his fears and self-doubt pulling him under, he prayed with more fervor than usual, asking for the

Good Lord to impart to him an extra measure of strength, only to be jarred out of his concentration by three harsh metallic bell rings from inside the intimidating building.

He drew in a deep breath and approached the deep-set reinforced iron doors that rested on huge hand-forged brass hinges. Above him, the seven windows trimmed in red sandstone looked menacing, like eyes scowling out on the land in judgment. He rang the brass bell to the right of the door as he stood on the porch under the portico that allowed room for three, at most.

The sound of heavy footsteps on concrete preceded a key turning in a lock and the opening of one door. The man before him must have weighed over three hundred pounds, and when Joseph announced his name, he was led without a word into a cold, dank entry corridor with doors on all sides.

"The warden's expectin' ya," the man said in a strong Texan accent. After hanging a brass key on a hook on the wall, he knocked twice on the door to their right, and it opened to an armed sentry in a gray uniform, who looked ready to shoot on command without compunction. In the gloomy filtered light, Joseph made out a gun case on the wall full of revolvers and Winchester rifles. A chill settled on his neck.

"Mr. Tuttle," a loud and animated voice announced. "Welcome to the federal penitentiary." A man Joseph presumed was the warden marched toward him from behind a neatly appointed desk arrayed with numerous stacks of papers and a large inkwell from which protruded what looked like an eagle feather. The room in which he stood was akin to a cell block, to Joseph's chagrin, making him feel as if he too were incarcerated along with the prisoners he hoped to care for.

Joseph had prior seen a grainy picture of the man A. J. House, and he'd read up on every newspaper article he could find, to prepare him to meet and work with this man. Though

Joseph had been a doctor for going on five years now, he'd never had an employer, and he felt as he had the first day of medical school, lingering, self-conscious and trembling, in the back of the crowded classroom, back in Ohio, a bit awestruck at the authority radiating from the professor at the podium.

The warden was no less flummoxing. A big head, with overlarge ears and nose, yet a strangely small set of eyes, made his face seem cartoonish—though, heaven forbid Joseph should show any sign of amusement. One look told him Mr. House was a force to be reckoned with on the scale of a tropical typhoon or buffalo stampede.

House proffered his hand, and Joseph shook it. The man's strong grip brooked no hesitation on Joseph's part, giving Joseph an even stronger sense that he was in over his head. He wondered briefly if he had allowed his impression of the persuasive and articulate Cathryn Povey to corrupt his good judgement regarding this posting.

After both men properly introduced themselves and House gave a somewhat hearty yet reserved welcome—the man seemed preoccupied and eager to move on to other matters—he took Joseph on a tour of the prison, accompanied by the tall brooding sentry that had stood at the warden's door. They exited the room back into the hallway, then entered through the door to the right. House passed a key through an opening in the wall to a "rounder"—the term for the prison guards who rotated positions within the cell block.

House scrutinized Joseph with an abrading look that felt every bit as rough as sandpaper. "You'll not be given a key, but the rounder will admit you and allow you to leave," House instructed. "It's for security reasons, as you might infer. We have a lot of outlaws here lookin' for every possible opportunity to break out."

Before they entered into the belly of the prison, House thumbed at the other remaining door adjoining the hallway. "Through there is the processin' room. That's where new prisoners are assigned a number, issued their uniform, and told the prison rules and punishments for disobeyin' them. It also serves as a waitin' room for visitors. Most of our prisoners come from Cheyenne, but this being the only federal facility, anyone committin' an imprisonin' offense in the territory will land here."

Joseph merely nodded, and House continued to lead him through the many sections of the prison, including the dining hall, the guards' quarters, and the prison armory. He learned that the cell block had forty-two cells, fourteen on each of the three levels. Each level had a bathroom cell with a bathtub, toilet, and water basin, though each cell had its own chamber pot. The cells were tiny—to Joseph's horror—six by six by eight feet. He couldn't imagine a man having to spend endless hours pacing in a cage that not even a lion in a circus could tolerate. He imagined many men—and women—lost their minds in this kind of incarceration. The thought of those iron bars clanging and shutting him inside sent another chill racing across his neck. His feet itched to run out, but he reminded himself of why he was here.

The large open areas were freezing even though a system of heat had been mortared into the floors—venting slots of an inch wide every foot or so allowed warm air from the kitchen to drift into the cells. After fifteen minutes, Joseph could hardly feel his fingers. None of the prisoners were in their cells—the warden explained they were at work in one of the outbuildings. Most of the prisoners made brooms and whisks and brushes. They formed an assembly line—twenty to twenty-five prisoners per shift—and produced nearly four hundred brooms a day, which were sold throughout the country and even shipped overseas. In the spring they cut ice blocks for the railroad. They even rolled cigars.

Inside each brick-walled cell, accessed through an iron-strapped door, were a straw mattress, a bucket, and a nightstand. Sparse quarters indeed.

After the warden showed him around the cell block, Joseph asked, "Where are the women housed?" He imagined they had their own building someplace close, but to his astonishment, House said, "Right here, among the men."

"Here?" Joseph questioned, a little too harshly.

The warden narrowed his eyes. "We get few women prisoners—though, there're plans to build another cell block for them. Usually they're put in the last cells on each level."

"But that hardly gives them any privacy—"

"Mr. Tuttle," House said, with pointed exasperation. "The women who enter the penitentiary are guilty of crimes and have been charged in a court of law. Like any other prisoner, they forfeited their basic rights of freedom when they broke the law. We show women certain ... considerations, as they are the weaker sex. While they work the same hours as the men, they are granted longer breaks and are spared the hard labor the men are assigned to, such as quarrying stone and cutting ice blocks. At present, there are eleven women all told, and most work in the kitchen, preparing meals." He chuckled, as if there was something amusing in all this. "Not much different from what any respectable woman might be doing in her own home, for her own family."

Joseph fell quiet at the derogatory tone in the warden's voice. House led him to the infirmary, on the second floor, where Joseph took stock of the adequate facilities and supplies. The infirmary consisted of two small examination rooms, both with large windows facing the stairwell. One room contained two cots that were neatly made up with white sheets, a wool blanket, and a pillow at the head. Joseph noted with gratitude a small woodstove—not presently lit—in the corner of one room. Joseph learned that a local doctor, one William Harris, was entrusted with treating the male prisoners, in a different infirmary on the east side of cell block #1. Joseph was glad he didn't have that daunting task, which he was certain included suturing injuries due to the inevitable violent fights that might occasionally break out. The thought of being in close proximity to heartless murderers and other outlaws of the worst sort sent a frisson of fear through his limbs, and he wondered if Harris was paid more than the one dollar a day that Joseph was.

"When you arrive, ask the guard at the entrance to bring up firewood. We don't leave it lying around for someone to use as a weapon. This door is to remain locked at all times, even when you are inside. An assistant will be provided for you and a guard assigned during the time you are working in the infirmary.

"It's your job to examine all the new inmates. Every prisoner is written up in the book—with descriptions of all scars, moles, teeth. The prisoner must be stripped naked and stand before you, legs outspread—"

Joseph froze. "Surely, the women would not—"

"*All* prisoners, Dr. Tuttle."

Joseph gulped down his shock.

House waited while Joseph took this all in, then he headed to the stairwell and turned to face him. "We follow the Auburn Prison System used across the country—this goes for both male and female prisoners. The convicts' names are replaced with numbers, their uniforms are white with black stripes—so if they escape, they're easily spotted. We shave their heads upon admittance—yes, the women too. We don't brook any lice, and women might hide a small knife or other sharp object in their hair. Convicts are expected to do their own laundry, change their underclothing every Sunday, and keep their cells and clothes clean and in good repair.

"Prisoners are also required to walk in lockstep—that means each must place their outstretched arm on the shoulder of the man in front of him, head bowed, and maintain a rigid position. If not, they are punished. They are not permitted to speak while walkin', workin', or at meals. If any rules are broken, the prisoner is put in a dark cell, or solitary confinement, with only bread and water for five days. Any number of infractions can land you in a dark cell: talking, passin' notes, wastin' food, refusin' to work, possession of contraband, or assault on a fellow convict or guard."

Joseph's stomach knotted, hearing all this. He supposed the discipline was for their good—and for the protection of those who worked in the prison. But these policies were demeaning, dehumanizing. How might a woman suffer these indignities and, once released, be able to reclaim her dignity? Was it even possible?

"What about church services?" he asked.

"They're held every Sunday morning in the dining hall. My wife conducts the service, and the prisoners are given the rest of the day off. The hall is also used for holiday events."

Joseph was glad to hear that the prisoners were having the Word preached to them and wondered what the warden's wife was like. He was also pleased to hear she was a godly person of faith—though Joseph wondered if the same could be said for her husband.

"Guards quarters are upstairs on the south side of the cell block—"

A loud bell clanged, piercing the air and making Joseph throw his hands over his ears. The clamor of the ringing was joined by the sound of pounding footsteps echoing from all directions.

"Follow me," House instructed in a harsh voice, eyeing Joseph, then nodding at the guard beside him. The warden raced down the metal staircase to the bottom level, drawing his sidearm from its holster. Joseph hurried after him, his heart pounding in fear. What was happening?

Four other guards met up with them at the base of the stairs, their guns at the ready. Two of the guards had drawn pistols, but two others held rifles.

"Warden, the kitchen," a guard said breathlessly from across the cell block. Another pulled on a lever sticking out from the west wall, and a shudder of clanging ricocheted against the walls.

"Sir, we've locked down," another said, running over from the entrance doors.

No one was detailing the trouble, which made Joseph wonder if the prisoners were revolting. He could hear cries—a woman screaming?—and men yelling somewhere in the back of the building. It gave him a small measure of comfort knowing he was surrounded by armed guards. But he also knew the territory's worst outlaws were housed here—some, no doubt, convicted of brutal murders.

House strode across the building to the back, where the aroma of meat and bread wafted. Joseph hung back but didn't want to remain behind, alone, so he kept up with the warden as they entered into a large kitchen whose heavy door was being held open by another uniformed guard.

Joseph's eyes landed first on two women prisoners in their black-and-white-striped uniforms, who were slumped against a far wall, their arms held tightly by guards, immobilizing them. One had her face buried in her hands, and the other wept outright, her glazed eyes staring at nothing precise. Joseph sucked in a breath as commotion raged around him. Kitchen staff—cooks and food preparers—were questioned by two of House's guards as the warden was led into a dark space—perhaps a pantry—in the back behind stacks of vegetable crates.

Presently, the warden, his face red with either rage or shock, stepped back into the kitchen and gestured Joseph over.

Joseph gulped. The sight that met his eyes when he entered the small cold space full of shelving and cooking supplies and stores stabbed his heart. The young, thin woman's prison garb hung loosely from her limbs as she dangled from a thick gray metal pipe running across the tall ceiling of the storage room. What looked like a torn white sheet—or perhaps a cook's apron—knotted every foot or so, hung twisted around her neck. A turned-over chair told the sad story as her body gently swayed as if in a mild summer breeze, her bare feet mere inches from the solid ground that delineated the difference between life and death. But it was her eyes, devoid of not just life but hope, that threatened to break him.

"Get her down," House demanded, fury oozing from his words.

Guards worked quickly to cut through the cloth and carefully lower the body to the floor. The warden stared at the figure of the woman lying there, and Joseph was taken aback at his apparent seething, which stood in stead of the compassion Joseph expected.

"You'll need to pronounce her dead and fill out the requisite government forms," House told him. "Come to my office when you've finished your examination."

The warden marched out in the same resolute manner as shown by soldiers marching into battle. Maybe the prison was a type of battleground, Joseph thought with a heavy heart. *A battle for the salvation of lost souls.*

He knelt and, with a gentle touch, felt for a pulse at her still-warm carotid artery. Finding none, as expected, he closed the lids over her eyes and sent a prayer heavenward, for God to have mercy on her soul and welcome this lost sheep into His arms.

He stood, stepped back, and nodded to the guards, who lifted the dead woman by her arms and legs and removed her from the room. As they filed through the kitchen, past the crying prisoners and distraught kitchen staff, Joseph felt as if his blood slowed to a crawl in his limbs. He could hardly get his feet to move when the remaining guard indicated for him to exit the kitchen. He'd hardly been on the job more than an hour and already witnessed up close the horrors of prison life.

He hated to think what tomorrow would bring.

Chapter 9

I T HAD TAKEN A SIZABLE measure of cajoling to get her
mother to allow her to ride into town on this chilly Tuesday
morning with Ty. She knew her overprotective cousin
wouldn't let her out of his sight—with one exception. And that's
why she'd made the arrangement on Sunday.

She'd taken the good Reverend Elihu Charnel into her
confidence, after church services had ended, though without
going into much detail. She whispered her urgency to meet
privately, and though guilt had niggled at her heart at arranging
a secret tryst, the pressing need to see Robert again squelched
those distressing pangs. The reverend suggested she come this
morning and assured her that he would be beholden to
safekeeping her confidences.

Rev. Charnel and his wife, Lucille, were as close as
grandparents to her. Her mother had persuaded the kind couple
to relocate to Laramie from Cheyenne when Julia was six or
seven, and they'd founded the Methodist Episcopal Church in
'69, located on the southeast corner of 2nd Street—the first and

only established church in Laramie—much to the derision of many of the local citizenry. But the Charnels were, if anything, stalwart and unruffled by gossip and threats alike. Their devout faith carried many a parishioner through hard times, and that included her family—her mother in particular, at the tragic loss of her babies.

The good reverend had a soft spot in his heart for Julia, and she planned to use it to her advantage. But she also trusted his judgement as much as she distrusted her own. Did Rev. Charnel know Robert Morrison? What could he tell her about the man? Just the thought of mentioning a Morrison to anyone close to her family made her shudder with worry.

Thus, as she stood on the stoop of the brick church in the below-freezing temperature, blowing warm breath into her gloved hands while gazing up at the biblical scenes portrayed in the stained-glass windows—Ty had left, driving the horses pulling the supply wagon down the street to the mercantile—she wondered if she was making a grave mistake. Would the reverend, out of some sense of duty—or even fear of consequences—break his confidence with her? Worse was the thought that his report of Robert Morrison would shatter the hopeful promises she hid deep in her heart. She'd hardly slept or eaten since the night of her party—was it only mere hours ago? The hours dragged like years, and though she'd kept busy, avoiding her mother, who kept bringing up Jarret Strickler and his "admirable" character and "keen interest" in her, nothing she tried could hurry the minutes that ticked loudly from the grandfather clock in their foyer.

Thank the heavens Daisy—much to Julia's surprise—fancied a young ranch hand who worked seasonally at the Morrison ranch, though he was presently employed with a local farrier. When Julia had confided her need, Daisy had assured

Julia it would be no difficult matter to send a missive to Robert Morrison by way of her beau, for he would "do practically anything" for Daisy.

Julia had insisted her maid swear she would breathe not a word of this to anyone else, nor tell her young man who the message was from. Daisy was to impress upon him both urgency and secrecy, though, if the message proved to be intercepted or lost, it would hardly reveal anything untoward. All Julia had written, on a plain piece of vellum, was the name of the church and the words "appointment with Reverend Charnel, nine o'clock" and today's date. It was now a quarter to the appointed hour, but a hasty glance around the street showed no sign of Robert—only passersby taking no notice of her, their faces buried into the fur lining of their coats, hurrying about their business, and the occasional buckboard or supply cart drawn by horses or mules snorting frosty steam, their breeching jingling like Christmas bells.

Daisy's dark brows had risen in stunned silence when Julia had told her whom the missive was for, but they promptly dropped at Julia's fierce scowl. "Do not read into this more than it merits. It concerns the land deal Father is trying to broker with Stephen Morrison. I fear for Father's health." The lie, though sound, clearly did not assuage Daisy's curiosity, but Julia trusted her maid's affections and loyalty. She would not betray Julia.

Julia hated to lie—something she'd asked God for forgiveness later—but she couldn't have risked telling Daisy the truth.

And what was that truth? she asked herself. That she was being simply ridiculous to feel so infatuated with a man she just met. And the one man who was wholly off limits to her. She would only be tormenting herself to allow her feelings for him to grow. Like a wild thorny weed, the tendrils would end up strangling her as they cut into her, making her bleed. Yet . . . here she was, and her heart showed no appearance of heeding the warnings in her mind.

Julia steeled her jangling nerves and opened the heavy oak door and stepped inside. The candles lit along the base of the chancel at the end of the long aisle cast a comforting glow, and the scent of the melting beeswax soothed Julia like a warm blanket draped across her shoulders. Though the sanctuary was cold, being inside this place of refuge did much to dispel the chill in her limbs.

As she walked toward the pulpit, the reverend came out from the back, behind the heavy damask curtain, and greeted her. The wrinkles on his weathered face deepen as a smile showed his delight in seeing her. He reminded Julia of an overstuffed goose, for his feet naturally turned outward and he waddled as he walked. His cheeks were like St. Nick's—as round and crimson as apples.

Taking her hands in his warm ones, he said, "Julia, my sweet child, come, sit with me."

He started to lead her to the back room, but she stopped him. "I'm . . . I'm expecting someone else to arrive."

He turned back to face her, his face expressing his puzzlement.

"Is something the matter?" he asked, gesturing her to the front pew, where they would hear anyone entering the church.

She sat and placed her hands in her lap, trying to keep her throat from clenching. Her heart beat so hard, she feared it would trigger her asthma.

"No, no, Reverend. There is nothing the matter. I merely needed a place—one free of judgment and . . . prying eyes . . ." Her gaze wandered over to the front doors, and trepidation seized her. Why had she imagined Robert would come? He had everything to lose by meeting her. As did she. But his would be the greater punishment, for he was heir to his family ranch, as well as son to a man who purportedly meted harsh punishments on his enemies. Surely anyone defying him to sympathize with a Carson in any way would be considered the greatest of enemies. Julia didn't imagine Robert would be an exception.

She turned to face Rev. Charnel, whose patient eyes waited for her to elaborate. The need to confess her heart compelled her to speak against her better judgment.

"Reverend, are you familiar with Robert Morrison, the rancher's son?"

He cocked his head and rubbed a hand along one of his side whiskers, as he was wont to do when in deep thought. Julia was grateful he didn't cast a suspicious gaze toward her. "Only a mite. I've met the young man on occasion. But his father . . . Stephen Morrison I know well."

Julia noted his cautious tone.

He continued. "Morrison, the elder, is a troubled soul. His older son, Cassidy, died tragically some years back, and I fear the man has never gotten over it."

The news saddened Julia and prompted questions, but she knew better than to ask the reverend to reveal personal details.

"The younger son, I hear, is an honorable sort. He practically runs the ranch, as Morrison Sr. has been struggling with ill health, and Robert is hardworking and responsible. But as for his nature — that, I'm afraid I can't speak to. A truly honest man or a scoundrel at heart? Others would know better than I. But I will say this: the young man has a difficult path, dealing with a father who blames one son for the death of the other."

Robert, to blame? "What happened to . . . Cassidy?"

"Some Irish miscreants knifed him—by the railway station. Apparently coming to Robert's aid." He fell quiet, and Julia let the words sink in. How awful to watch your brother die in an attempt to protect your own life.

The cold air in the sanctuary felt heavy and oppressive. Why had her parents settled in such a lawless town? Every day, bodies were found, robbed of their belongings, in alleyways, in boxcars, behind buildings. Laramie was famous for its saloons and gaming houses, attracting all manner of outlaws and nefarious folk to its streets. How could such a small town of little more than a dozen blocks be filled with so much wickedness? It made her want to run away, to a proper town. Like Greeley, Colorado—where, she'd read, the entire town was God-fearing and prohibited drinking and brawling.

But how could she ever leave?

Her head swiveled at the sound of the heavy door opening at the nave of the church.

Julia's breath hitched at the sight of Robert easing into the sun-splattered sanctuary, and as he respectfully removed his hat, sunlight played on his silky brown hair and lit up his eyes. He took three steps inside, and when his attention landed on Julia, he froze.

Julia's hand rose to her throat, as if a sound were trapped in there—or more like a feeling, an overpowering need and longing that ached to escape. Robert wore a heavy sheepskin coat over dark trousers, the collar turned up, his face pinched pink by the cold morning breeze over the Laramie River. She thought she'd never seen a more handsome man. Or maybe her sentiments were spurred by the way he was looking at her, with an adoration she'd never experienced from a man before. She felt the way she often did during lightning storms—the hair on her skin electrified, her every nerve sparked and excited.

She heard the reverend clear his throat beside her. She turned to find a knowing look on his face.

"Ah ... I see ..." He shuffled over to Robert and introduced himself, and Julia kept back while they spoke in hushed tones, hardly able to control her excitement. He had gotten her message, and he'd come. But she did not want him to think her infantile. She would maintain her comportment and behave as befit a woman of her station and not a girl of her age. She didn't know how old Robert was, but surely he was years older, having long left the awkwardness of puberty behind him. Robert Morrison was every inch a man, and she yearned in this moment to be the woman he desired more than any other.

After an agonizing minute or two, Rev. Charnel led Robert to Julia's side and said in a tone laced with a subtle warning, "I'll leave you two to talk. I have next week's sermon to prepare. I trust"—he said this directly to Robert—"that you will respect the sanctity of God's house ..." He looked as if to speak further, then shook his head as a smile lifted the corners of his lips. "Well ... I need not say more." He shot Julia a brief look that she could only interpret as equal parts joy and sadness. Of all people, he knew how her father might react upon learning a Carson and a Morrison were meeting in secret.

"Of course," Robert said, and Julia bathed in the warmth of his husky voice and polite manner. Her body thrummed at his nearness, and when he turned to face her, after the reverend disappeared behind the chancel, her chest constricted painfully.

His chestnut-brown eyes searched hers as he took her hands in his. A crooked smile teased her. "Just breathe, Miss Carson."

A giggle tickled her throat. "I'm trying, Mr. Morrison."

"Why don't we sit and, uh, talk?" He gestured to the front pew, which Julia thought was wise. Her knees were about to buckle, and she wasn't sure she could bear much longer feeling his hands wrapped around hers. She told herself she should be aghast at his forwardness in touching her, but it was as if he'd heard her heart's cry, for she wanted nothing more than to feel his touch, his hands on her skin . . . his lips on her lips.

As she found the hard bench, her knees did give way, and he released her hands, much to her dismay. Instead of sitting beside her, though, he knelt before her. She questioned him with her eyes.

"My nana"—he gave her an embarrassed look—"My *grandmother* suffered from asthma. She lived with us for some years before she passed, and she would tell me family stories with her head bent over a steaming pot of water infused with eucalyptus and lavender and peppermint. She swore those 'steam baths' had saved her life on many occasions."

Julia nodded, immersing herself in listening to him speak. He was all cowboy, but clearly educated and articulate. She imagined he spoke differently to his ranch hands.

"I think, sir, that you may have saved my life as well," Julia said in all sincerity. But Robert brushed away the notion.

"Just happened to be in the right place at the right time."

She smiled, and an awkward silence hung around them like smoke from the candles by the altar. The attraction between them was thick enough to cut with a knife. Julia wanted to believe it was more than mere attraction. She felt a divine hand on her heart, pressing her toward him, and she wanted to believe it was destiny or fate that brought them together. But was that just wishful thinking? *Oh, Lord God in heaven, show me his nature—if it's true or false. Is he a man worthy of my love? Am I worthy of his? Don't let my years and my ignorance of such matters cloud my judgement.*

"I'd heard Lester Carson had a daughter, but why haven't we ever met?" Robert asked her.

She sighed, aware of the hard pounding of her heart. He stood and went to sit on the pew, facing her, looking more at ease than she felt. "My parents are overprotective. They hardly let me out of my cage."

At that, he laughed, shaking his head. She could soak in that laugh.

"But I knew they would allow me to visit with the reverend. He's been instructed to prepare me for matrimony—"

"For what?" Robert frowned. "Are you . . . I mean . . ." He stumbled over his words as his brows narrowed. "You're not hitched to that fella I saw—"

"Jarret Strickler?" She chuckled—more at Robert's somewhat stricken expression than at the thought of her agreeing to marry Jarret. "Heavens, no. Though . . . my parents wish I'd have found him suitable."

"But you didn't." He paused, considering his next words. "I saw how he treated you, how he grabbed your arm—not the behavior of a gentleman."

She looked at him from under her lashes. "And are you a gentleman, Mr. Morrison?"

He rubbed his clean-shaven jaw and gave her a sly grin. "I reckon you'll have to come to your own conclusions about that, Miss Carson. If you'll give me the chance."

Julia would have sworn she heard a quaver in his voice. And while his sweet smile reached his eyes, it also seemed to mask some uncertainty, or perhaps even worry. Did he care for her that much? He hardly knew her. But maybe he sensed a divine hand on his life as well. Maybe their fates were entwined in the stars. If so, was there hope their love could bloom in the midst of a decades-long feud? If her father caught wind of their meeting, he would tighten his noose around her, never let her out of his sight.

A flood of desperation surged through her. She must have paled because Robert leaned close, his breath warm on her cheeks, his eyes questioning her. She wished he would swoop her into his arms, the way he'd done three nights ago, so she could feel safely ensconced. She burned for his touch, like a moth driven to flirt with fire, heedless of the danger.

An anguished sound snuck out of her throat, and as if Robert somehow unraveled the meaning of her heart's cry, he complied with her deepest prayer and gently helped her to her feet. She lost herself in his eyes as he faced her and slipped his arms around her waist. She sucked in a breath, waiting, unblinking.

"This . . . this will never . . ."

"Shh," he said, unrelenting, keeping her gaze captive, like a calf he'd roped.

"We could never—"

"Shh."

"Our parents—"

Robert slowly shook his head. "Julia, Julia . . ." He pulled her closer—just close enough that she could feel his heartbeat against her chest. "You are like the sun risin' in the east, the bright ray of joy in my gloomy heart."

She fell speechless and wilted in his arms. How wrong it was for him to hold her thus. How forward and brash! How sacrilegious, to touch her in the house of God . . . yet, his holding her seemed almost sacred and holy, and his confession more a religious admission than an attempt at seducing her. She dared look once more into the beckoning depths of his eyes.

"Robert, you know as well as I that there is no safe place in Laramie for us to court. It is not possible." He began to speak, but she held up her hand. "Every effort would be thwarted. I would be sent away. You would never see me again. And we would be twice foolish to think we could hide such affections under a rug or . . . inside a church—"

"Marry me."

"What?" Her mind emptied of all thought.

He rested a hand on her cheek and cocked his head. "Marry me. Then we wouldn't have to hide. And once the deed is done, who could protest?"

Julia forced words out over her shock. "You speak like a man possessed."

"I am." Robert grinned, his eyes sparkling with joy. "And I'm glad for it."

Julia shook her head, but his words sank deep into her soul. She wanted to wed Robert—with every fiber of her being. But it just couldn't be. Their fate would be as disastrous as Romeo and Juliet's.

"We couldn't . . . we would have to leave Laramie," she said, her feet already eager to flee. She couldn't believe she was saying these things. And to a Morrison, no less!

He stroked her cheek, sending a ripple of hot desire through her limbs. She tried to ignore it and think clearly, but his touch was destroying her willpower.

"Julia, sweet Julia. Don't deny these feelings we have for each other. Let's get the reverend to marry us—here, now. What could our families do then?"

"Now?" Her head swam. "It's . . . too soon—"

"Then when?" he pleaded. "Why torment ourselves? Why risk gettin' found out? Why take the chance that our love might set afire this feud and cause an even bigger fire? Have you thought that maybe—just maybe—our getting hitched might end all this fightin'?"

She shook her head feverishly. "My father would never see it that way. He would consider my actions as a betrayal of the greatest order."

"And that's why we shouldn't wait. I've only just found you, Julia. I couldn't bear to lose you."

The fervor in his voice washed away all her reservations. Wasn't this what she'd prayed for—for a man to love her, heart and soul? A man to adore her, cherish her, be willing to risk all for her? Robert Morrison had everything to lose, and yet he was willing to leave it all behind, give it all up—for her.

He leaned in, tipping his head close, and Julia could already feel his soft, inviting lips on hers. But then, the door to the reverend's office opened, and Julia pulled back as Robert dropped his arms. A shiver ran up her spine as the absence of his strong arms around her set her adrift in a cold sea. It was precisely in that moment—that tiny instant of time—that she knew.

She loved Robert Morrison, and she needed to be in his arms forever, till the end of time. Losing him was unbearable to imagine. How they would manage, how they would make a life together, what their families and friends would say—none of that mattered—not a whit.

Chapter 10

ROBERT HELD JULIA'S HAND AND felt her tremble. He hoped the reverend's warning wouldn't scare her away.

But Charnel was right. It would take some doing to pull this off and get out of town before his and Julia's families discovered their tryst. They would have to leave everyone and everything behind. And while Robert could hardly care less, he didn't fancy the thought of hurting his ma. Yet, he knew in his heart of hearts that she loved him and wanted to see him happy. And what would make Robert happy was marrying Julia Carson.

He knew he was asking a lot of Julia, to trust a fella she just met, one she'd been taught to hate, more or less. But there was naught for it. He loved her — he had never been so sure of a thing as he was of this fact.

"So, Reverend, will you do it — will you marry us?" Robert asked, worry niggling at his neck.

Reverend Charnel studied the two of them, as if searching for an answer. Robert knew the man of the cloth was also putting himself at risk, for when — not if — Lester Carson learned how his own clergyman secretly performed the rites to legally wed Robert and Julia, well . . . that would detonate a world of hurt for the reverend.

Yet, Robert could tell Charnel had sympathy for their situation. Charnel had told them both, minutes earlier, that he'd been married some forty years now, and that with marriage came trouble and heartache. You had to be sure before you took that vow before God. But when God yoked two together, no man could tear such a union asunder. Robert knew all that and more. He knew he would never lose his love for Julia; it would only deepen with every sunrise. He had no doubt God had brought them together. Theirs would not be the loveless marriage of his folks.

"I'd like you to take some time to think this over. It's a big decision," the reverend said.

Robert looked at Julia, letting her answer. If she wanted time, he wouldn't press her. He'd already made a forceful plea. But he feared she'd change her mind. *If she really loves you, time won't matter*, he told himself. Last thing he wanted was to push her away.

Julia swallowed, her face flushed. Robert didn't want to take his eyes off her, but he dropped his gaze and counted nail heads in the floorboards, feeling as twitchy as if a mound of ants were crawling over his skin.

"My parents are pressing me to marry another man — one I don't love," she said, sadness lacing her words. She gave Robert a quick glance, then turned back to the reverend. "I don't want to wait too long. I'm afraid my feelings will become obvious to my parents."

Reverend Charnel nodded. "A week, then. Monday next? Will that give you enough time to make your plans?" He frowned. "And where will you live? Will you stay in Wyoming Territory?"

Robert shrugged. "If that's what Julia wants. But I'd like to settle someplace better'n Laramie. I know you came here to save sinners, Reverend, and that's mighty admirable. But I'd like to get as far away from 'em as I can, and give Julia a happy life — in a safe place."

"Well, that's admirable, son, as well. And while there are no perfect towns, surely you can find a place to settle that will provide both community and gainful employment. Though I'm sure your departure would cause a lot of grief."

Robert shrugged again. "I 's'pose we'll cross that river when it's time."

Julia said nothing. Robert squeezed her hand and looked at her. "You alright?"

She nodded, but Robert noted a glint of fear—or was it hesitation?—in her look. He thought she was being awfully brave to take a chance on him—and give up the life of comfort, however stifling, to which she was accustomed. He would make it up to her, he would! He would give her the moon and the stars if they were within reach. He wanted more than anything to kiss her, to feel her soft, yielding body up against his.

Just the thought enflamed his passion, and it took all his resolve to push away the enticing images that flooded his mind, ones hardly chaste, which had no place in this holy house of God.

Julia asked the reverend for the time, and he checked his timepiece and said, "Twenty after the hour." She frowned and looked at Robert, and he saw her glistening lips quivering, which made him ache anew to kiss her—an agonizing ache that racked his whole body.

"I better go wait outside. Ty will be by at half past to fetch me." Her eyes filled with warning, then she said to Charnel, "Thank you, Reverend, for your kindness and willingness to help us. I'm grateful beyond measure."

The old reverend smiled warmly and took her hands. Then he kissed her cheek and said, "I'll see you at church service next Sunday. If you need to talk further, let me know. Otherwise, I'll make the necessary arrangements for the ceremony—"

"What about a witness?" Robert asked.

"I'll speak to my wife, Lucille. I'm sure she'll volunteer." His words and confident, calm manner seemed to reassure Julia.

Then she turned to Robert, and with a gaze so loving he could hardly restrain himself, she whispered, "I'll be counting the minutes until next Monday."

"I'm sorry I can't give you the wedding you deserve," Robert said, thinking of what a beautiful bride she'd make, imagining the white satin gown with all those pearls she'd worn, which had made her look like an angel. He reckoned, under other circumstances, if she married a fella her parents approved of, she'd have a wedding so fancy, it'd be written up in the papers across the nation. But he would make it all up to her, give her everything she wanted and needed. He'd been frugal and saved up money for a day such as this.

"I don't need a big wedding or any pomp or fanfare. I only . . . I only need you, Robert. The two of us, with God as witness to our vows."

Robert's heart soared at her words.

"I'll bring my wagon and keep it ready at the back of the church. I'm afraid once we're wed, it won't be wise to stick around town. At least not for a bit. Best to lay low for a spell— until tempers cool."

Charnel nodded. "It'll be a short and sweet ceremony. Then off you go."

Robert had a sudden thought. "I know a fella—a good fella—in Fort Collins. He's in the freight business and has done some brokering for the ranch. Ships cattle all over the country. Name's Eli. Eli Banks. I'll send word to him to expect us, and I'm sure he'll put us up for a spell. Fort Collins is a nice town, Julia. I think you'd like it." He didn't add the next thought that came to him: *And I don't think anyone would look for us there.*

He took Julia's hands and pressed his lips to them, closing his eyes and praying the week would hurry by. But he knew the hours would drag, every one of them painful in their passing.

"Go," he said softly. "And just act like nothing's changed." He hoped she could hide her feelings better than she did now. Her emotions roiled like churning waves across her face. But he would pray and trust that they were fated to be together. He couldn't do much more than that . . . and wait.

Sheriff Thomas Carr strode down the puddle-pocked street, grumbling over his aggravated sleep—what little he'd had of it. With the weather turning colder, tempers were snapping. He couldn't remember a Monday night with more drunken brawls, fisticuffs, and guns waving wildly in the hands of the intoxicated and hapless, unlucky gamblers. Carr's shoulders were sore from hauling so many miscreants across the splintery planks of the boardwalk and tossing them, half-conscious—some bleeding—into the jail cells. By three in the morning, the drunk and disorderly were packed like sardines in a tin in the four barred cells.

He supposed he should be grateful no one had been shot, though he'd like to have shot the lot of them himself. What he would give for a full night of uninterrupted sleep. Not only did his wife, Berta, snore loud enough to raise the dead, his Russian wolfhound—all hundred pounds of him—splayed out on his bed and paddled his legs through his dreams like he was crossing the Atlantic. Nothing woke the cur—not even when Carr kicked him hard to make him stop.

Carr's plan for the morning was to rustle up some breakfast, drink a gallon of thick-as-mud coffee, and then, with his usual reluctance and fierce warning—which would fall on deaf ears— he'd release his prisoners to revel and wreak havoc another day in Laramie, Wyoming. He knew Miz Crout would whip him up a huge breakfast at the Frontier Hotel, and his stomach groused at the thought of flapjacks soaked in warm syrup. He hoped that would take the edge off this already bad day.

As he neared the corner of Grand and 2nd, his eyes narrowed at the sight of Ty Lawson, Carson's nephew, driving his buckboard wagon loaded with bags of grain and a couple of large crates. Carr stopped and watched as Lawson pulled the reins of the two horses and parked at the church. Curious. What business did he have with Rev. Charnel?

Carr made it his business to know everyone else's business in Laramie, and anything out of the ordinary caught his eye. He didn't particularly like or trust the reverend, who, on more than one occasion, bellyached about the job Carr was doing in cleaning up the town. Wasn't that the reverend's job—to turn sinners from their wrong ways? Carr reckoned Charnel was more to blame, since he was charged by a higher power to put the fear of God into the citizens of Laramie. Still, Carr trusted better results would be gotten from a rifle than a prayer nine times out of ten.

The church door opened, and out rushed a young woman. From where Carr stood, he was too far away to make out the gal, but it wouldn't take a genius to figure out she was Carson's teenage daughter. What on God's green earth was she doing in the church on a Tuesday morning? Some sins to confess? Did parishioners confess to a Methodist preacher like they did a Catholic priest? Curiouser.

Lawson helped the girl up onto the seat, then shook the reins and got the draft horses moving. Carr continued down the street, but then stopped again when the church door opened and a fella in a big sheepskin coat stepped out. What caught Carr's attention was the furtive way the fella looked around, as if he didn't want to be seen.

Carr realized, with astonishment, who he was looking at. *Well, would ya look at that?*

Robert Morrison. Son of Stephen Morrison — mortal enemy of Lester Carson. Cavorting in the church with Carson's daughter. *Don't that beat all?*

Wasn't it just a few days ago that Carr had busted up that fight between Ty Lawson and the Morrison kid?

And not two days past, Carr had walked by the farrier's and saw that chambermaid from Carson's ranch handing a letter to one of the Morrison ranch hands. One of his "little birdies" in town had followed the kid far enough up the Medicine Bow Road to determine he was indeed making a beeline for the ranch.

Something akin to a bright light clicked on in his mind and revealed a very puzzling conundrum. The daughter of Lester Carson and the son of Stephen Morrison . . . together, inside a church on a Tuesday morning.

Doing what?

Now, wasn't that the question of the day? Possibilities flitted through his head, but only one scenario made any sense to him. A secret tryst, aided by a colluding man of the cloth. Carr chuckled and shook his head in astonishment.

He continued toward the Frontier Hotel, watching Robert Morrison hurry down 2nd Street in the opposite direction.

He imagined what mayhem such news might cause, and who might pay dearly to hear of this. But for now, Carr intended to keep these cards facedown on the table. Until the right moment presented itself.

Then . . . an idea struck him. A brilliant idea. One that would cause Lester Carson all manner of grief. Grief that would surely sabotage that pending land deal between Carson and Morrison.

The day had started off badly, but now he had a lift in his step. It was promising to be a good day, after all.

Chapter 11

JULIA SPUN AROUND AT THE sound of a quiet knock at her bed chamber door, pushing in her armoire drawer with her legs. Her pulsed raced as she berated herself for trying to sort through and pack her most precious belongings in the middle of the day. After meeting with Robert and the reverend three days ago, she hadn't found the courage to begin packing, afraid she'd be caught. And now . . .

"Who is it?" she asked, hurrying to stuff her stack of blouses back into the open armoire.

"Daisy, miss."

"You may enter," Julia said, relieved it wasn't her mother. She'd been avoiding her parents these last two days, which wasn't all that hard, as her mother had been busy with her charity Christmas event planning, and her father infrequently came into the house other than to eat and sleep. Her father seemed particularly vexed and distracted, and Julia assumed it had to do with this land purchase he was obsessed with. What would her betrayal add to his aggravation?

She struggled with the thought of leaving a note, to explain why she left, that she loved Robert Morrison and married him, urging her parents to wish her joy in her new life. But try as she might, she could not find the words that might mollify them. There was no way to soften the blow—of that she was certain.

Her greatest fear was that her father would chase after her and somehow find her, then forcibly drag her back home. Or he and Robert would face off, and someone would get hurt. Most of all she worried about Ty, for he was so keenly protective of her, she didn't think he would listen to reason or the pleadings of her heart. She hated to hurt him, most of all. She loved him dearly. But she would just have to hope and trust he would understand her feelings and accept her decision . . . someday.

Daisy came to her side, concern streaking her features.

"What is it?" Julia asked.

"It's . . . Ty, miss. I-I was outside in the herb garden, gathering thyme and marjoram for the missus and . . ." She stopped talking and put her hand to her throat.

Julia's own throat tightened. "And what, Daisy?"

"The windows in the kitchen were open." She quickly added, "I weren't eavesdropping, miss—"

"It's quite all right. Just tell me."

Daisy swallowed. "He was speakin' to your mum, quiet-like, but agitated. It . . . it seems he found Dusty . . . and asked him some questions—"

"I don't understand," Julia said. "Where did he see Dusty?" She couldn't make sense of Daisy's words. Since Dusty—Daisy's beau—worked in town at the farrier's, it wasn't unexpected that Ty might see the young man in town, but would Ty even know him? Or know that the cow puncher worked at Morrison's ranch during the summers?

Daisy's face took on a stricken look. "He . . . um . . . Ty caught Dusty by the patio."

"Our patio, in the back? When? What was he doing there?" Julia was more confused than ever. Her patience was wearing thin, and she gave Daisy a look to make her cut to the chase.

The maid let out a tremulous sigh. "Just an hour ago, miss. He was bringing a letter." She paused. "For you. From Robert Morrison."

"What?"

Daisy nodded.

A letter. Robert dared send her a letter—and have it delivered to the house? What was he thinking?

Thoughts tumbled through her head—what might the letter say? Had Robert changed his mind? How could he have been so desperate *and careless* to try to contact her this way? Had something terrible happened?

Yet, of all the worrisome thoughts, the worst of them stared her in the face.

Did Ty now possess the letter, and had he shown it to her mother? Surely he had, and that's what Daisy had overheard— the heated discussion about its contents.

Even if the letter wasn't signed, knowing Ty's temper and overall protectiveness of her family's concerns, he would have squeezed information out of Dusty. She couldn't imagine anyone holding back in the face of Ty's threats.

Julia felt all the blood drain from her head, and she grabbed the top of her dresser to steady herself.

"Oh, Daisy, this is terrible, so terrible . . ." The familiar tightness worked its way into her chest, clenching her lungs.

"Here, miss, let's sit you down."

Julia allowed her maid to help her over to her bed, where she eased down on the coverlet, fear racing through her limbs.

What would happen now? Would her parents lock her forever in her room? Would her father go after Robert? Oh, what was happening? She fretted that she would never see him again and her heart would shatter.

Tears burst through Julia's resolve to hide her feelings—something she was never good at. As they streamed down her face, Daisy studied her, then said softly, "Ya love him, don't ya?"

Julia nodded, sniffling and wiping her eyes. Daisy pulled a handkerchief from her skirt pocket and handed it to Julia.

"Oh, miss . . . I'm so sorry."

"It's not your fault, Daisy."

"I should've told Dusty never to come here—"

Julia worked at pulling in air, managing to say, "You . . . you couldn't have known . . . he was just doing what he was told . . ."

Sobs erupted from her throat, making it even harder to breathe.

"Maybe I should get your mum—"

"No! I-I'll be all right . . . in a moment . . ."

Daisy fretted, standing next to her and wringing her hands.

When Julia was able to stem the flow of tears, she looked up at Daisy. "What else did you hear Ty tell my mother? Did he mention Robert's name?"

Daisy hesitated, then nodded. "The letter said something about how you and Mr. Morrison had met at the church on Tuesday—"

Julia stiffened. Robert would never be so careless as to mention that in a letter—would he? It didn't make sense. None of this made sense. But now . . . all her plans were ruined. And when her father heard about this letter—and her meeting with Robert—

Julia jumped up from the bed. She had to leave—now. There was no other way. She couldn't risk waiting until Monday. She had to see Robert. But how, where?

"Daisy," she said in a rushed whisper, "I must ask a big favor of you. And I know this is risky. You may even lose your job." Julia hurried to add, "But if you do, I will more than compensate. I'll . . . send for you, and you can come live with me—"

"I don't understand. Are you leaving?"

"I must," Julia said, looking around her room, thinking what she must take, what might fit in her saddlebags. Would she even have time to saddle up Little Bit with no one the wiser? Where was Ty right now? Her mother?

She felt trapped, the walls of her room closing in.

"Do you want me to go with you, miss?" Daisy's eyes implored her.

"No, but I need you to get a note to Robert Morrison. I must see to it that he gets it personally, and that it is not intercepted."

Daisy nodded, her eyes glistening with tears. "I'll take it directly to him, miss. I'll . . . get changed into some riding clothes. I know where the Morrison ranch is."

Julia guessed that everyone in Laramie knew that. Robert's ranch wasn't all that far away. It wouldn't take Daisy more than an hour to ride over there, so long as she wasn't unduly delayed.

Daisy hurried out of the room, and Julia pulled open her secretary drawer and extracted pen, ink, and paper. She had to meet Robert somewhere, but not the church. Someplace in town. Someplace her father wouldn't think to find her. What would the most unlikely place be . . . ?

She chewed the end of the quill, then it came to her. Lucille Charnel, the reverend's wife, had a sister in town, whom Julia had met on occasion at outings. A friendly woman named Molly

Brooks, who ran a boarding house. It was in the worst part of town, on Ivinson Street, sandwiched between a dozen or more brothels. Julia knew Molly would safeguard her until Robert showed up. And Molly could get word to her brother-in-law, the reverend, so that he could come to Molly's once Robert arrived and perform the marriage ceremony.

This was the best plan she could come up with on the spur of the moment. There was a stable behind the boarding house where she could put Little Bit. She'd have Daisy come fetch him once she was safely out of town.

The letter Robert had sent kept eroding her nerve. She desperately wanted to know what it said, but she couldn't stay to find out. She had to hope Robert would show up at Molly's without much delay—before someone caught sight of her and reported back to her father. She would have to disguise herself as best she could, not let anyone see her face. Not that anyone in that seedy, dangerous part of town would recognize her, but she couldn't take that risk.

Once sequestered inside the boarding house, she would lock her door and wait.

She wrote a brief note, telling Robert where she would be waiting for him, praying he would hasten to her side, then hurried to grab the few items she needed: a warm coat, a change of clothes and shoes, a hat with a veil that would cover her face, and, as an afterthought, her old Army Colt, which Ty had given her a few years back. She didn't like guns or the loud reports they made. But she knew how to put bullets in and to cock the trigger to rotate the cylinder. Ty had made her practice, insisting she learn in the event she'd have to defend herself from either man or beast.

She also retrieved a small change purse she kept in her lingerie drawer. It held a few coins and a handful of dollars. She hoped that would be enough to pay Molly for her room, though she imagined the woman would refuse payment. Still . . . Julia intended to pay. Who knew how long she'd have to stay there before Robert could slip away and join her?

Her nerves made her shaky as worry bloomed into near-panic. She had to remain calm and coolheaded. No time to think about her parents and how they would react upon learning she was gone. No time to wonder how long it would take Robert to come to her, if he even would. She had to believe. She had to trust. It was all she had. *Please, Lord, give me strength and protection. Show me the way. Keep Robert safe and bring him to me, dear Lord. I need him. I love him.*

Julia blew on the ink she'd used on the single piece of stationery, then, seeing it was dry, folded the page and slipped it into an envelope. After melting the wax and sealing it, she handed it to Daisy, who breezed into her room, now in a riding skirt and warm coat.

"Be careful," Julia warned her. So many things could go wrong.

"Don't you worry, miss," Daisy said, "there're still a few hours of daylight left. I'll be back before anyone's the wiser." She frowned then. "But . . . you'll be gone?"

Julia choked up. She hoped she would see Daisy again. Hoped that Daisy wouldn't be caught and punished. She didn't want Daisy to lie for her, but Julia's life and future depended on it.

"I'll make it up to you—I promise," Julia said. "I'll . . . send word soon, to Reverend Charnel, letting you know where we settle."

Daisy nodded. "God bless and keep you, miss." Tears splattered her cheeks, and Julia pulled her in for a hug, something she'd never done before. But Daisy was the closest thing Julia had to a friend, and she treasured the times they'd spent together, even though the class disparity had kept them from becoming close.

"Godspeed," Julia said. Daisy nodded and patted her skirt pocket, where the missive lay hidden.

Julia listened to Daisy's footsteps until they led out the back doors to the patio. She sat on the edge of her bed, feeling as if she were teetering on the sharp edge of the world. This was the moment of decision. She could change her mind and stay, give up her mad dream of a life with Robert. Or she could steam ahead, trusting God's leading and believing in Robert's faithfulness.

The decision was not an easy one, but the only one she could live with.

She stuffed her things into a pillowcase—she couldn't think what else to use, and she certainly couldn't stroll out of her house carrying a suitcase. She hoped all the ranch hands and cow punchers were out on the range, checking the lines, fixing fences. It would take but a few minutes to saddle up Little Bit. No time for a brushing, but they didn't have far to go.

What if she ran into Ty? He'd know what she was up to. Ty could read her like a simple primer. She couldn't face him. If he ever found out what she was doing . . .

Summoning up her resolve, she tiptoed down the stairs, listening for any tiny sound, hoping no one would see her. But her hopes were foolish wishes.

Her mother stood in the foyer, hands on hips, glaring at Julia, who stopped cold midway down the staircase.

"Where do you think you're going?" she asked, her tone as vitriolic as Julia had ever heard. "And where is Daisy off to?"

Julia fumbled for words, painfully aware of how suspicious she looked carrying her pillowcase.

She was about to tell her mother a truth: that she and Daisy were going riding. She didn't have to say they had two different destinations. But she didn't get the chance.

Her mother reached over to the credenza and picked up a beige envelope and wiggled it in the air, frowning. With her other hand, she gestured to her father's study.

"We have to talk, young lady."

Julia's heart plummeted like a stone off the side of a steep cliff.

She no longer had to agonize whether to stay or go. The decision had been made for her.

Chapter 12

AS FAT CLOUDS SKITTERED OVERHEAD, Robert clicked his teeth at the green mustang and gathered up the rope's slack. The animal had his ears flattened against his head, his eyes wild, letting his handler know he wasn't having any of it as he loped erratically in a circle in the pen.

But Robert wasn't paying all that much attention, working the horse through his paces as a matter of rote, his thoughts consumed with images of Julia—of her delicate features, her lovely figure, and her tender heart. How was it only Friday? He'd never make it to Monday without seeing her. He'd been so sullen and distracted, he'd hardly gotten half his chores done. Yesterday, he slipped away to town to send off a telegram to Eli Banks in Fort Collins, and along with the note he wired some money for Eli to hold for him. Robert hoped his pa wouldn't notice the cash withdrawal from the bank until after he'd skipped town.

Thankfully, Ellsworth had been with the herd over by the buttes these last few days, sussing out a pack of wolves that had taken a couple of yearlings. Ellsworth would take one long look at Robert and know Robert was hiding something. At some point Robert would have to tell him, but he hoped to put off the deed as long as possible. His best friend would not be happy, no siree, but he would hold to secrecy. He'd know that if the truth got out, there'd be hell to pay, and more. Robert hated being so secretive. And he couldn't stop worrying about Julia. Would she be able to sneak away? Would he be able to marry her and get her safely out of town before anyone discovered their tryst?

He pushed all his troubling thoughts from his mind and concentrated on the horse at the end of his rope. Maybe the animal was picking up on his fretting, and that's why he wasn't settling down yet. Robert spoke softly to him, met his gaze, played out the rope, and gave the horse more room to kick up the dust and work out his kinks. Presently the mustang's ears perked up, and he began working his mouth. A good sign. Robert wished it was this easy to get people to change their behavior.

The morning was warming, and sweat beaded on Robert's forehead. He hoped this shift in weather portended a dry week ahead. The road south to Fort Collins could be treacherous in a snowstorm, especially going through the pass just south of Laramie and crossing the Powder River. Years back, before the Union Pacific came to Laramie, his family would run the cattle over to Cheyenne for shipping to the Texas stockyards, which was a chore and then some to get through Evans Pass at more than eight thousand feet in elevation. But with the transcontinental railroad now cutting through Wyoming Territory, they no longer needed to move the herd over miles of open range to get them onto a train. He hadn't taken that road by horseback into Colorado in some years.

Robert slowed the horse to a trot and then a walk, his attention snagged by the sound of hooves pounding ground and the sight of kicked-up dirt a ways west of the ranch. He swiped a sleeve across his forehead and walked over to climb up on the fence rail. Two riders approaching.

It didn't take long for Robert to make out the lumbering shape of Ellsworth or his buckskin gelding. And there was his cousin Benjamin, keeping stride on that little mare he liked. Something was wrong, or they wouldn't be riding so hard.

By the time Robert deposited the mustang back into the pasture and hung up the halter and rope, the two punchers met up with him at the back of the main horse barn, their mounts heaving and lathered.

Benjamin said as he slid off his horse, "Ty Lawson's demanding ya meet him in town, all horns and rattles, three o'clock, behind the courthouse." His face was flushed and raw from the wind, his eyes crazy wild.

Ellsworth looked fit to strangle someone, sitting atop his horse, who pawed the dirt and threw his head up and down.

"I thought you two were up in the buttes," Robert said, trying not to let his imagination race off without him. Just because Ty was issuing a challenge, didn't mean it had anything to do with Julia. The snake probably just wanted to finish what he'd started last week in front of the bank. But the last thing Robert wanted right now was to deal with Julia's cousin.

"We were," Ellsworth said, nudging his hat back to look hard into Robert's eyes, "but Lawson sent a few of his boys to find us. Which seems a mite peculiar."

"Well, they surely wouldn't come to the ranch to fetch me. Someone must've seen you riding the line and reported it to Ty."

Ellsworth dismounted and came beside Robert. His windblown hair was all atangle, and he attempted to smooth it back off his face. "Doesn't make a lick o' sense. If Ty wants a fight, why not wait till you showed up in town? Ambush you."

A sour taste filled Robert's mouth. Ellsworth was right. Had Ty somehow figured out what Julia was planning? How? Did he pry it out of her? Julia knew full well how Ty might react. Not a chance she'd confide in him.

What if she was having cold feet? Were his worst fears coming true? Was Julia regretting her decision to marry him? Had he pushed her too hard, too fast? His mind flashed to seeing Rose with that dandy. How she'd smiled at Robert in that heartless way. He'd risked his heart, and she'd ripped it to shreds. Was Julia doing the same to him? Toying with him, now casting him off like some piece of rubbish?

He felt punched in the gut. Weak all over.

"Are ya gonna go?" Benjamin asked.

"Don't see why I should," Robert said, thinking of all the ways such a confrontation could go wrong. But a part of him hungered for a chance to shut Ty's mouth for good, even though he was as close as a brother to Julia. Still, he was a rock in the way. More like a boulder. The second Ty learned that Robert had left Laramie with Julia—had married her—he'd be after them. Robert had no doubt Lawson would try to kill him, to take Julia back.

Better to end this now than keep looking over his shoulder for years to come.

Of course, Robert had no intention of hurting the fella. But would Lawson be willing to listen to reason? If he truly cared about his cousin, he'd put her happiness above all else. Robert had to convince Ty that he loved Julia and would cherish her.

Ellsworth's expression mirrored Robert's thoughts. He looked like a horse snorting at the gate, ready to knock it down if a body didn't hurry and open it.

"I'm itching to fight that scoundrel," Ellsworth said. "He does all of Lester Carson's dirty work, no different from those Irish thugs the sheriff keeps in tow."

Robert nodded, the aggravation over all this feuding threatening to explode. In any other place and time, Robert could court Julia without a care.

He never hated his father more than at this moment. *This foolish feud is a bunch of nonsense. Whatever Lester Carson did years ago to offend my pa doesn't matter now. Whatever happened to letting bygones be bygones? And why would Carson—now, of all times—be pushing to force my pa to sell a parcel of land?* If Robert wasn't fixing to run away, he would give his pa a piece of his mind—and demand answers, for once.

"I should see to the horses," Ellsworth said. He narrowed his eyes at Robert. "Don't think 'bout facing Ty alone. I'm a-comin' with you. We left Abel to deal with the wolves." He grinned. "We got our own wolves to take down."

"I'm comin' too," Benjamin said. "I ain't missing this for the world."

"You shouldn't," Robert said to him.

"It's a free country," Benjamin retorted. "'Sides, you'll need witnesses—in case he tries some funny business."

Ellsworth quirked his mouth. "So long's you stay out of the way."

Benjamin threw up his hands. "I don't fancy getting' shot at."

"No one's gonna get shot," Robert said. "We're just gonna talk."

Ellsworth huffed. Then he took the reins from Benjamin and started leading the two spent horses into the barn to rub them down.

"I'll meet you back here at half past two," Robert said, the worry and fear roiling again in his gut. He decided he'd take a brisk walk down the road, so he could think, rather than head inside the house and chance running into his pa—who was, no doubt, in his study nipping from his hidden bottle of whiskey. *As if Ma couldn't tell how much he's been drinking of late.*

Robert just didn't understand. His pa was rich, had one of the biggest cattle ranches in the territory, had his health. *But he won't let go of Cassidy—or stop blaming you for his death.* How many years was it going to take for his pa to move on? Everyone lost someone at some time or other. Well, Robert wasn't willing to stick around and wait for that day to come. He had his own life to lead, and until he met Julia, he figured he'd spend the rest of his days running the Morrison ranch. How quickly his life had upended. And he was glad for it. He would always feel guilty about Cassidy—there was no way around it—but he couldn't spend his life wallowing.

He watched a flock of songbirds wheel in the sky, marveling at how they turned and dove as one, never bumping into one another. Snow frosted the humps of the buttes, glinting in the weak sunlight, and patches of ground fog hovered like ghosts, burying the sage brush. The stark beauty of late fall emptied his heart of malice and trepidation, leaving a sublime peace in the certainty of his love for Julia. He had been looking for her all his life. If he lost everything, it wouldn't matter—so long as he had her. He couldn't lose her. He couldn't. He would make a life with her, love her with every beat of his heart. And heaven help the fella, any fella, that stood in his way.

Robert walked until all he could see of the ranch house was the roofline through the thick pines on the ridge leading down to the pond. It felt good to walk, stretch his legs. Like most

135

cowboys, he spent most of his time on the back of a horse or up on the hard seat of a buckboard.

As he neared the pond, where a gaggle of geese were paddling and making ripples in the water, he saw another rider galloping up from the main road, heading toward his house. A gal—no mistaking. Young too. He stopped and watched her, a curious sight. He didn't often see a young gal riding around the Front Range alone. Why would she be coming here?

She almost passed him by, her head hunkered down over the horse's neck, riding hard as if someone was chasing her. But then, she caught a glimpse of him and drew in her reins and trotted directly to him.

Breathless, she asked, "Where might I find Robert Morrison?"

He studied her—her plain face offset by the blackest of hair, most of it still pinned under her brimmed hat, though some of the long strands had escaped to frame her pink-splotched cheeks. She couldn't have been more than eighteen.

"You're lookin' at him."

She quickly blushed and lowered her thick black eyelashes. It occurred to him she didn't expect the heir of the Morrison ranch to be aimlessly moseying around a pond and bird-watching.

"Miss Carson asked me to get this to you right away, sir," the gal said, her voice at once quiet and urgent. She reached into a skirt pocket and pulled out a pale-yellow envelope stamped with a red wax seal. Robert's heart hammered in his chest.

"Is . . . Julia . . . , uh, Miss Carson all right?" Who was this gal? One of Julia's friends? A family servant? He walked over and took the letter from her gloved hand as she sat on her winded bay gelding.

She struggled with coming up with an answer, then said, "I'm afeared not, Mr. Morrison. Your letter was intercepted—"

"My letter?" He stared at her in consternation.

She frowned. "Yes sir. The one you sent to her, by way of Dusty Anderson—"

Robert's blood turned to ice. "I didn't send any letter." And he hadn't seen that ranch hand Dusty since last Sunday afternoon.

"You . . . you didn't?"

Robert's head spun as he stood there, befuddled. "Why would she think I'd sent her a letter?"

"Because, sir . . . it was signed with your name."

His mouth hung open, but no words formed. Someone had written a letter in his name? Who in tarnation would do such a thing? The only person that knew about him and Julia was the reverend, and Charnel would never deign to do such an atrocious thing.

He suddenly froze.

"You said the letter had been intercepted . . . by who? Do you know what it said?" He knew his voice sounded harsh and gave her an apologetic look. "Please, tell me everything."

The gal breathlessly told the tale as she sat her horse, and the more Robert listened, the more his feet itched to run to Julia. He couldn't for the life of him figure out this madness. From what this maid, Daisy, had overheard, it seemed the fella that wrote the letter proclaimed his undying love for Julia and, in words too vulgar for Daisy to repeat, proposed performing unmentionable things upon her person. No wonder this gal seemed terrified to talk with him.

"I didn't write that obscene rubbish!" Robert said.

Robert's rage churned in his gut. Who could've done such a thing? It took little imagination to picture the reaction Julia's mother—and Ty Lawson—had upon reading such abominable words. But what could he do? Ride over to the Carson ranch and protest his innocence? Not likely he'd be believed—if they even let him get an inch onto their property before they shot him dead. No wonder Ty Lawson was searching for him, to give him what-for. *I'd do the same.*

His poor darling! What must Julia's family be thinking now? *And what did she say to them? She doesn't know my handwriting. She must think I wrote that letter . . . God help me.*

He ripped open the envelope, gritting his teeth. The message was brief:

> *Robert,*
>
> > *By now Daisy has told you about the letter that was sent to my house. I can't believe you would risk our chances by sending it. I'll be waiting for you at Molly Brooks's boarding house on Ivinson Street. No one will think to look for us there. Come quickly, and destroy this note upon reading it.*
> >
> > *Julia*

Robert blew out a hard breath and turned to Daisy. "You said she was gettin' ready to leave? She hadn't read the letter that Dusty delivered?"

"No, and . . . I . . . I couldn't bear to tell her what it said. I overheard the missus reading it aloud, with Ty standing there, his hands on his hips, fit to strangle someone—"

"That'd be me," Robert said grimly. The news gave him some consolation. Maybe Julia would never get to read the words in that letter. He hoped as much, but what little hope he had for their plans was slipping away quickly, like an unmoored boat plummeting over a waterfall.

He reread Julia's note. He couldn't tell what she was feeling. Did she truly believe Robert hadn't sent it, or was she recriminating him for sending it? He supposed he would find out when he saw her. Would she believe him?

He was about to tell Daisy where he'd be meeting Julia, then thought better of it. For all he knew, this gal could be to blame for having loose lips. Maybe Julia had confided in her, and then Daisy talked. Robert couldn't risk trusting anyone.

"If you see her," Robert said, "tell her I didn't write it. I didn't! I swear it on my brother's grave. And I'll meet her where she said."

"Yes sir. Though, I don't expect she'll be home when I get back."

Robert nodded, his gut now twisted in a giant knot. He had to meet up with Ty—there was naught for it. And somehow he had to get across the truth to the lunkhead. But would Ty listen? Would he care? Not a lick of a chance. Robert was trapped, every which way he turned.

Robert sent Julia's maid on her way. He watched her gallop along the road back to Laramie, her horse's hooves kicking up clods of dirt that settled into a dusty cloud. The light afternoon breeze whisked it away, leaving the rarified air crisp and clear.

He wished the breeze could clear the dirt and grit clogging his thoughts, but they only turned darker and heavier as he strode back to the ranch to saddle up and prepare to face Ty Lawson. Which he'd do as soon as he burned the note that was burning a hole in his heart.

Joseph fiddled with his napkin, avoiding making eye contact with those walking past him in and out of the café. Mrs. Povey had chosen this place inside the Holliday Building on the south end of town because, as her note stated quite plainly, "no lady ever goes to Front Street, and it's not advisable for even a gentleman to traverse the north side of town even in broad daylight—if he fancies keeping his billfolder." Would he ever feel safe in Laramie?

From where he sat at the long bank of windows, he watched the parade of men walking and riding, going about their day at this lunch hour. Across the street were a variety of novelty and furnishing shops, a grocer's, and a two-story office building. Few women strolled the muddy street that lacked a raised boardwalk, though two exited their parked carriages close to the doors of the shops they entered. The aroma of baked bread, juicy meats roasting, and the smoke from the oil lamps on the tables all mingled in his nostrils. His stomach growled, reminding him how little an appetite he'd had since the incident at the prison.

The warm sunlight radiating from the window pane did little to lighten Joseph's heart. Not even a week in Laramie, and he was considering abandoning all his high hopes of being a do-gooder in this lawless corner of the nation. After the tragic suicide by "inmate #13," he could hardly think straight, wandering the halls and staircases of the penitentiary in a daze, sequestering himself in the drab, disheartening infirmary, handling cases of croup and chest congestion with lackluster regard. Right now, even as he waited for Cathryn Povey, the cold and lifeless body of Bella Montague lay next door, in the funeral home that Joseph wryly guessed might be the most profitable business in town, what with all the pine caskets the owner built and sold for the sad victims of violence that erupted daily in Laramie.

140

Joseph had seen dead bodies. He'd worked on cadavers in college, studying their organs and skeletal frame and musculature. So it wasn't the shock of seeing the prisoner's corpse swinging from the pipe but the great sense of despair that was captive in her eyes. The same look he saw in the other women prisoners as they marched in lockstep to and from work stations and the dining hall. Mrs. Povey was right—this penitentiary was no place for the weaker sex. And as long as he lasted here, in his God-ordained position, he would work tirelessly, alongside the good woman, and do what he could to make life better for the female inmates, until the day came—if it ever did—that the prison would close its doors to them.

Joseph knew Mrs. Povey was doing all she could from the outside—beseeching the territorial governor, and, as she put it, "making myself a great nuisance, much to his annoyance," as well as badgering those in Congress who might hold sway over the politics of the territory. But, clearly, it was his job to effect change from the inside. How? Warden House was the not the sort of man to brook complaint or even polite suggestion on how to better run his facility. From what Joseph could tell, the warden was driven by a spirit of rage or some other underlying emotion simmering just under the surface of his carefully checked demeanor. He was the kind of man Joseph saw after the War between the States, wandering the roads, lost and bitter, hope tattered to shreds. Joseph wondered what wretched events had occurred to make the warden so possessed. He doubted it stemmed merely from an unhappy marriage or the pressure of his job.

He spotted Mrs. Povey's carriage pull up in front of the café, then stood and greeted her when she walked purposefully, grim-faced, to his table. He pulled out her chair for her, then sat, feeling his nerves tie in a knot over her presence. She looked

141

elegant yet stunning in her navy-blue blazer and wool skirt. A wide satin bow the color of clotted cream adorned the top of her high-collared pale-blue blouse, and, upon removing her stylish hat, her perfectly pinned blond-red hair shone in the streaks of sunlight falling upon her.

A young gal, hardly in her teens, came to their table with menus and asked what they'd like to drink. She lifted a brow at their request for hot tea, as if ordering anything but spirits with lunch was unheard of. Mrs. Povey suggested they have the minestrone soup—her favorite—and, with the order placed, the girl left them to talk.

Even though no other diners sat close by in the large dining area—most of the patrons were at the polished mahogany bar that spanned the length of the café, getting an early start on their liquor consumption—she spoke in a careful hushed tone.

"How are you faring, Dr. Tuttle? I can't tell you how upset I was upon hearing that Bella . . . passed." She drew in a long breath and straightened, as if trying to keep from allowing sentiment to seep into her voice. She was all business.

"It's been difficult," Joseph said, glad to have someone to talk with about this horrific tragedy. "The . . . mood in the prison is oppressive, and the women are . . . well, I can hardly think of how to describe such misery."

Mrs. Povey nodded. "Having one's identity stripped away in such an indignant way—from the moment they arrive and every waking second of their day—is a recipe for such despair."

"Do you"—Joseph paused, unsure what she wanted from him—"have any suggestions as to how I might make things better for the women?"

Her face showed she did, indeed. "Have you met them all yet?"

"Not personally. I've been introduced to them as a group—"

"Have you learned their names?"

"Their names?" What did she mean? The women were assigned numbers, as were the men, and he'd been instructed to refer to them by number only.

"Yes, Dr. Tuttle. These women have names." Her cheeks flushed, and Joseph worried that he was irritating her somehow.

"Viola Trout is serving two years. She was admitted seven months ago for kidnapping a baby. When she arrived at the prison, she'd been beaten and suffered three broken ribs, a broken wrist, and had two of her teeth knocked out. She was thrown directly into solitary for pleading to see a doctor." Mrs. Povey clenched her teeth in thought and kept silent when the serving girl brought their tea and soup.

Joseph offered Mrs. Povey milk and sugar, but she shook her head and let her tea steep. "Trudie Paddock, the only Negro woman incarcerated, shot a man at a dance in a fugue of morphine when he tried to drag her outside. Arminta Garrett poisoned her sister with a pie. Hassie Ethridge is serving six months for stealing clothing worth twenty-two dollars from a mercantile. She was freezing and broke, and no kind citizen was willing to give help to a woman in need, so she succumbed to desperate measures." She sipped her tea as Joseph poured milk in his. "These are but some of the women in your care, Dr. Tuttle. You may know them as 'prisoners numbers four through seven,' but they have names. And stories. Some have had their children put in foster homes in Denver. One woman served six months and paid a three-hundred-dollar fine for stealing a cow, which she did to get milk for her baby. Yes, some of the women are hardened and have little conscience. They feel little to no remorse for their crimes. Others are suffering an unfair and unjust fate in a system that has little compassion for circumstances of hardship and treats women unequally under the law. I'm presently urging the governor to institute a policy to release women early for good time served.

"But we also witness disparity in justice between rich and poor. However, that's a whole other problem, and one which I certainly don't have the time or strength to deal with at present."

Joseph ventured a smile. "You can't solve all the problems of the world."

Cathryn Povey actually returned the smile. "No, Dr. Tuttle, I cannot. But I can try. We must work within the system to buck the system," she said. "Return as much dignity to these women as possible."

Joseph nodded as he drank his tea, full of admiration for the woman sitting opposite him. The hot milky liquid thawed some of the chill from his chest.

"What I propose is that you schedule times to meet with each of the women, perhaps once a week. Under the auspices of a health examination, you can talk with them, draw them out. Use their names in conversing—"

"That's not allowed," Joseph protested.

Cathryn Povey gave a searing look that made Joseph wilt. "Each of these women is precious in the eyes of God, and He knows them by name. And it is the divine law we must heed, Dr. Tuttle—"

"Please—call me Joseph. I'd feel so much better if you did."

She cocked her head and studied him. "Fine. And you may call me Cathryn—at least in these circumstances. I, too, get tired of formalities. I had enough of them in the District of Columbia." She sighed. "But, surely . . . Joseph . . . you see we must do all we can to treat these women with dignity, as they are precious in the Lord's sight, and we are to obey God rather than man."

Joseph was flabbergasted by her show of passion in her faith. He'd never met a woman like her, and it took his breath away. And it wasn't just her passion in what she believed but her courage that moved him—and put him to shame. Never before had he seen himself so clearly. He felt like a puny worm, letting fear guide his hand and heart instead of the nature of God.

"You're absolutely right, Mrs. . . . uh, Cathryn." Her name sounded too intimate on his tongue, but it gave him a simple delight to speak it. "I will implement your suggestions immediately upon my return to the prison." Which would be later today. He would arrange appointments with all the women and make it his goal to elevate their spirits and even find ways to lighten their loads, if at all possible.

Having this goal branded on his heart lifted his own spirits immensely. Cathryn Povey had snuffed out his second thoughts about his calling, and it was humbling, to say the least, to have such a stark and revealing mirror held up to his heart. But it was exactly what he needed.

He was about to say as much to her, but he could tell by her expression that the matter was closed. As they ate their soup in companionable silence, he marveled at this woman across from him and felt a bit sorry, once again, that she was married.

Chapter 13

"WHAT WERE YOU THINKING—GETTING involved with Robert Morrison!"

Julia cringed as she slumped in the heavily brocaded chair in her father's study.

"Your father is going to go stark-raving mad when he hears about—"

"Why does he have to know?" Julia said, her anger tightening a noose around her throat. But she didn't care if she had a full-on asthma episode; she would not let her mother ruin her life and destroy her dreams. "And why won't you let me see that letter?"

Her mother had merely waved the envelope in Julia's face, anger blotching her mother's cheeks. Julia had rarely ever seen her this upset. What could Robert have said in that letter? She had to know.

"Because . . . no decent woman should ever read such words."

Julia grew even more confused. "Robert would never write anything indecent—"

"And how would you know?" Her mother fisted her hands on her hips. "Where did you meet him? Have long have you been sneaking off to see him?" Her tone brooked no excuses from Julia.

"You're only upset because he's a Morrison. Father's *dreaded enemy*. Well, Robert isn't Father's enemy—or yours. He's a kind, gentle, God-fearing man—"

Danielle Carson looked aghast. "*No* God-fearing man would write such obscenities—"

"Then Robert didn't write it." Julia was sure of it. Someone must have seen them together and wanted to destroy their love. Could it have been Ty? How could it? Ty hadn't seen her with Robert, and he only got upset once he caught Dusty. He wouldn't have sent the letter to Julia pretending to be Robert. That made no sense! Ty would have directly confronted her, and Robert, if he learned they were in love . . .

Julia's heart pounded wildly. *Ty stormed out once he told Mother. He's going after Robert* . . . Why hadn't she thought of that when she penned the note to him? *I should have warned him!* Julia prayed Robert had enough sense to steer clear of Ty. He had to know how protective and volatile her cousin was. Ty wouldn't hesitate to kill Robert.

Oh, this accursed feud! It will mean the end of everything I love. My family. My life. My home. Robert and I will be estranged from our families forevermore. For what reason?

She recalled that conversation she'd had a year or so back, when she overheard Ty talking with Sheldon, their foreman, who had known Julia's father from decades past. Something about a card game and a lost bet. Maybe it was time to get the whole story out about this feud, once and for all. She'd always been afraid to ask questions, for anytime she had in the past, her father reproached her with harsh words and threats of punishment. *But Father isn't here right now, and surely Mother knows the truth.*

"What is so wrong with marrying a Morrison, Mother? Why is Robert's family so hated by father?"

"You know better than to ask —"

"I'm not asking, Mother. I'm demanding." She stood from the chair and faced her mother, who was forced to look up at Julia. For once, her height emboldened rather than embarrassed her. "I think it's time I knew the truth. And if you won't tell me, I'll . . . ask Sheldon. Or find someone who knows why on God's green earth our family has been enemies of the Morrisons all these years."

Julia huffed, her heart racing, her throat tight. She'd never stood up to her mother like this. But she loved Robert, and no one, and *no feud*, was going to keep her from marrying him.

Her mother's fists uncurled, and her hands fell to her sides. "Julia, I can't tell you —"

"You can't or you won't?"

"I can't say, for I truly don't know what started all this." Her mother hesitated, and from the fearful look in her eyes, Julia knew her mother was holding back.

"But you . . . suspect?" Julia prodded.

Her mother began to pace the small study, her steps muffled by the thick Persian carpet beneath her shoes.

Julia softened her voice. "Just tell me what you know, Mother. Please. I'm not a child anymore. And I love Robert."

Her mother looked at Julia as if she were a stranger, someone she thought she knew but was mistaken. She swallowed, then closed her eyes. "I knew . . . Stephen. We grew up together. The three of us attended school together in Cheyenne."

"Three of you? You mean Stephen Morrison—Robert's father."

"And your father too. Our families lived on adjacent properties."

Julia was stunned. Why hadn't anyone ever told her this? She knew her mother had grown up in Cheyenne, and Julia had visited her maternal grandparents on many occasions. Her father's parents had passed away before Julia was born, from the influenza. Not a word was ever said about the Morrisons.

"Go on," Julia instructed. The room felt stifling without a window cracked. She ignored the familiar rattle building in her chest.

"When I was your age, Stephen doted on me. I knew he longed to court me, but . . . your father was more forward. He and Stephen were once close friends, but . . ." She shrugged and closed her mouth.

"You mean to say the feud is *about you*? Did they fight over you?"

"No. Well, good-naturedly. They'd joke about who would 'get me.' At the time, I wasn't thinking about marriage. Then, something happened."

"What?"

"I don't know. An incident. Perhaps they did fight over me. Your father would never tell me what happened. But suddenly Stephen moved away, left home and ended up here, in Laramie, and married Winifred. Found another ranch to work at—before he collected his inheritance and bought his own."

"Another ranch?"

Her mother rubbed her cheek, looking tired. "Yes. Stephen and your father worked as punchers for years in the same outfit in Cheyenne—Asa House's spread."

Julia frowned, trying to piece her mother's words together into a coherent picture. "The warden? He was a rancher?"

Her mother nodded. "Owned the biggest cattle ranch in Wyoming Territory. But then . . . it's said he lost it all, in one night. In a card game."

A card game? Was this the game Ty was talking about? What did it have to do with her father? A chill settled over her. "How did Father get our ranch?" Julia asked. She'd always assumed it had been in the family, that he'd inherited it from his father.

"He's never said," her mother finally answered.

"Have you never asked him?" Julia found that hard to believe.

"Of course I have." Curt words. Julia heard the anger underneath them. Not even her mother knew the secrets her own husband kept under lock and key.

What did a card game in which Warden House lost his ranch have to do with her father hating Stephen Morrison? Was there a connection? Her mother's answers were only serving to befuddle her even more.

"Julia, you mustn't ask your father—"

"Why not?"

"Because . . . just don't."

A thought came unbidden into Julia's mind. "Did you . . . love Stephen Morrison?"

Danielle Millington Carson didn't have to utter a word for Julia to get her answer. A lifetime of regret streaked across her face, and she turned away, but too late.

Julia saw it all in that moment. The hurt and sadness when Stephen left town. The regret at marrying Lester Carson, who had been left to properly court Danielle unhindered. If anyone could empathize with what Julia was feeling now for Robert, it would be her mother. Surely she understood what it meant to love a man and lose him. Julia wondered if her mother ever spoke to Stephen, or if her husband forbade it. What deep, dark secrets did her mother keep hidden? How peculiar that she had once loved Robert's father.

"What will you do?" Julia asked, imagining her mother wanted to ask the same of Julia. "Will you tell Father? Show him ... the letter?" She was still furious that her mother wouldn't show it to her. But it didn't matter. She would ask Robert, and he would tell her the truth. It didn't matter who was trying to prevent their union. It could be any number of people, with so many enemies on both sides. Laramie was a small town. Someone, no doubt, saw her and Robert together—in the church, speaking in the yard the night of the party. Perhaps even when Robert had saved her during her frightening bout of asthma, when she'd thought they were alone, under the stars. How foolish for her to think they'd been alone when her house was full of party guests.

Jarret Strickler! He might have followed her outside, watched her with Robert. Of course! If anyone would dare sabotage her tryst with Robert, it would be Jarret. She wouldn't put it past the scallywag to send a fake letter to her parents. *But how would he have known Dusty? Why not send the letter via the post?*

Julia looked at her mother, waiting for her to speak. She seemed torn.

"Please, Mother. Let me go to him." She swallowed past the hard rock trapped in her throat. "Please? I love him."

The words teetered before her, before crashing to the ground.

"I can't, Julia. It would be the death of your father. You must forget Robert—"

"The way you pushed his very father from your heart? I see what pain it's caused you."

"You know nothing," her mother said, her face tightening, her voice rough with emotion. "And there is more here at stake than you know. This land deal—"

Julia huffed and threw her hands in the air. "Land! It's always about land. Who cares about land—"

"Your father does."

"Well, I don't care about his land, or the Morrison land. Any land. I just care about Robert, and I want to marry him!"

"Heavens, Julia. Do you even know the man? How much time have you spent with him? I can't imagine it's been more than a few hours—"

"What are you going to do? Lock me in my room? Forever? You can't keep me here against my will!"

Her look said differently. Whatever tenderness or compassion or vulnerability her mother had just shown had vanished without a trace. "You aren't thinking this through. You're being selfish. And foolish. This is just a passing fancy, flirting with danger. You're only drawn to this boy because it's forbidden love."

"Oh, Mother, please!"

"Do you have any idea what will happen if you continue on this reckless course?"

Julia crossed her arms over her chest, wishing she could smother the rattle in her lungs. "Maybe it will end this feud, once and for all."

"Oh, no, you are mistaken, young lady. It will be like stepping into a rattler nest. Tempers will erupt, and people will get hurt. Mark my words."

"You talk as if you want this feud to continue."

"Of course I don't."

"Then do something about it." Julia stood her ground, facing off with her mother.

Her mother let out a long-held breath. "You will go to your room, and you will wait there until your father comes home. And then we'll sit down—the three of us—and discuss this."

Julia shook her head. "Discuss this? There will be no discussion, if Father learns about Robert. He'll hunt him down and shoot him. Or he'll send Ty in his stead."

"Julia! How could you say that?"

"Do you deny it's possible?" This conversation was over. "I'm leaving."

"I forbid you!"

Julia marched to the study door, then spun around. "How do you plan to stop me?"

Flustered, her mother spit out, "If you dare leave, don't think you can come back."

Julia's eyes went wide, feeling as if she'd been thunderstruck. Her mother was threatening her? Julia bit down hard on her lip. "Fine," she ground out. "Why would I want to come back to a loveless house full of judgment anyway?"

With that, she stormed out, then broke into a run as she made for the horse barn, tears streaking down her cheeks, a cold wind clawing her neck. She knew her mother wouldn't run after her. She'd just send Ty after her. *But he's not around, thank the heavens!* She would go directly to Molly's, then once Robert arrived, they'd send Molly to fetch the good reverend, to marry them right away. And then, when it seemed safe, they'd leave town.

How? She had no idea what Robert might be planning. They could take the stage or catch a train. Or ride their horses at first light in the morning. Whatever they chose, it would be risky, and Julia prayed Ty wouldn't find her—or Robert— before they left.

She would not think about the letter. She would trust in their love.

Her mother's cruel words gnawed at her stomach; they were hurtful and mean. Did her mother truly care more about appearances and appeasing her husband than she did about losing her only daughter? Why didn't her mother care more about Julia's happiness? Did she even love Julia? Her world was crashing down around her, and Robert was her only lifeline.

More tears fell as she saddled up Little Bit and tied her pillowcase behind the cantle. She smirked thinking of how little she was taking with her, leaving her life, her whole world behind. Sixteen years of home and hearth, burnt to the ground in a matter of days as if a wildfire had raged through the prairie. Would there be anything to return to, should she ever come back? Presently, she didn't know and didn't care.

Chapter 14

FLURRIES OF SNOW DUSTED ROBERT'S face and gloves as he sat his horse, Ellsworth and Benjamin flanking him on their mounts, at the back of the courthouse—a tall brick two-story building on East Grand Street with unusually tall windows. The place was deserted as black clouds amassed overhead, threatening to dump a load of snow any moment. What warmth he'd enjoyed earlier had been sucked up by the cold, which matched the chill in his heart.

"Where is the scoundrel?" Ellsworth muttered, blowing on his gloved hands, looking up and down the wide alley.

"Prob'ly chickened out," Benjamin said with a smug grin.

But that wasn't like Ty Lawson. More like he'd be coming with a small army, toting an arsenal, but Robert was ready. His pistol was at his side, the Winchester in the crook of his left arm. He didn't know if Benjamin had a sidearm, but he knew Ellsworth was packing his two Colts and probably that Bowie knife he liked to strap to his ankle.

Still, Robert clung to a small thread of hope that Ty could be reasoned with. If he truly cared for Julia, he'd put her happiness first. He was counting on Ty to at least hear him out, though Robert was unsure of what to say. He'd recited words as they rode to town, but it all sounded sappy to his ears. He was sure Ty would laugh first and shoot second.

The horses blew frosty steam into the air as more snow fell, in fat flakes that were starting to stick on the ground. Then, movement at the end of the block caught Robert's eye. It was Ty Lawson, and, to Robert's surprise, he was alone and on foot.

Robert, Ellsworth, and Benjamin dismounted as one, and Robert gathered up the reins of the three horses and handed them to Benjamin.

"Take 'em over yonder," Robert said, pointing to the post running on the west side of the courthouse, while never taking his eye off Ty. Who knew what that rapscallion had up his sleeve?

Out of the corner of his eye, he saw Ellsworth's hands resting on the butts of his cross-drawn pistols. Robert repositioned his hand on his rifle and let it hang at the ready.

Ben kept glancing back as he led the horses down the side street.

"You wanted to talk," Robert yelled to Ty. "So let's talk."

Ellsworth mumbled so Robert could barely hear him, "No one's here to talk."

Ty marched toward them, then stopped about twenty paces away. His arms hung loose at his side. His face was a mess of rage.

"How dare you cavort with my cousin," he said through clenched teeth.

Ellsworth huffed, looking flummoxed, but Robert spoke before his pal could open his mouth.

"No one's doin' any cavortin'."

"You stay away from Julia."

Robert felt Ellsworth's eyes upon him, questioning him.

"You're not her keeper. She can make her own decisions."

Ty took three steps closer. Robert saw Ty's fisted hands shake.

"I am her keeper, and no way will I let the likes of you get anywhere near her. If I even see you—"

"Aw, shut up," Ellsworth said. "You're a bag o' hot air. What's Robert got to do with a Carson? You outta your mind?"

"I saw that letter you sent to her—"

Robert shot back, "Nope, never sent a letter—"

"Ya did. I read it."

Robert shook his head. "Wasn't from me."

That stopped Ty a moment. His brows narrowed under his wide-brimmed hat. "You were at that church, Tuesday last. Meetin' with Julia."

Robert neither admitted nor denied it. He knew Ty hadn't seen him. If he had, he would have stormed inside and confronted Robert instead of riding back to his ranch with Julia. Robert had peeked out a window and saw the two of them head out of town.

Benjamin came back, stopped at the corner, and watched the exchange. Robert hoped he stayed put. The steady soft fall of snow muffled the sounds of the town.

Ty put his hands on his hips and glowered at him. "What're your intentions, Morrison?"

Robert considered his words. He could deny everything, buy time so he could slip away with Julia. Which wouldn't stop Ty from coming after him. Or he could try to reason with the fella, which had been his sorry plan all along. Not much hope for success, he thought, now that he faced Ty head-on.

"Truth be told, I intend to marry her."

"What?" Ty and Ellsworth said in the same breath.

"I said—"

"I heard ya," Ty said, taking a few steps closer, a mean spite in his eyes. "You got a death wish, Morrison? You ain't gettin' near Julia. Not if I can help it."

"Why don't you ask her what she wants?" Robert offered, fingering the trigger on his rifle.

"It don't matter what she wants," Ty retorted.

Robert shook his head, chuckling. "And here I thought you actually cared for your cousin. I see you don't. 'Cuz if you did, you'd want her to be happy."

Ty kicked at a rock, shook his head. "And you reckon she'd be happy marryin' you." He laughed hard, threw back his head.

"I do," Robert said evenly.

Ellsworth muttered beside him, "Criminy. I told ya to find a new gal, but I didn't mean her! Couldn't ya have picked someone else? Someone . . . less problematic? When did ya find time to court Julia Carson?"

Robert shrugged. "You left the party early."

Ellsworth mumbled something in that deep buffalo voice that sounded like a curse, but he didn't take his eyes off Lawson.

"I'm done talkin'," Ty said. "Let's settle this." He strode over, his face as hard as rock, and threw a punch at Robert's chin.

The impact knocked Robert backward. He reeled, righted himself, then handed his rifle to Ellsworth. Hate stirred in him, like a gush of blood.

"Don't," Ellsworth scolded.

Robert leapt at Ty, and the fists started flying. Robert smacked Ty upside the head, then pummeled his sides, letting his fury loose. But Ty squirmed away and managed to whack

Robert in the face, then punched his gut hard. Even through his thick coat, Robert felt ribs crack. The pain caused his knees to buckle.

Ellsworth lunged for Ty. "Why, you piece of — "

Robert, doubled over, saw a flash of metal. Gasping, he couldn't get the warning out in time. "El . . . knife . . ."

Through the haze of pain he heard Benjamin yell, "He's got a knife!"

Robert sank to the ground and watched in horror as Ty's arm rose up, long knife in his gloved hand, and swung down on Ellsworth's neck. Ellsworth was reaching for his own knife, had taken his eyes off Ty, when the blade plunged into his flesh. He cried in agony.

Robert stumbled to his feet, the splotches of black clearing from his vision. "No!"

He became dimly aware of footsteps and voices. As the snow fell, so did Ellsworth, the way a buffalo would fall when shot, slow and heavy to the ground. Ty crouched over Ellsworth, Robert's best pal in the world, gleefully holding the bloodied knife, the dark-red drops sprinkling the pristine snow-sprinkled street.

Robert wrenched his eyes from the sight of Ellsworth lifeless on the snow, blood gushing from his slit throat, fury igniting a firestorm in his soul. His rifle was crushed under his pal's bulky body, so Ty pulled out his six-shooter and took aim.

Ty, panting hard, met eyes with Robert, then laughed.

"Now what'cha gonna — "

Robert fired. Twice. Then again and again. He aimed for Ty's shoulders and legs. He didn't want to kill Ty. He'd never killed a fella. Any other fella, he wouldn't have cared. But he knew Julia loved her cousin like a brother. He couldn't do this to her. She might never forgive him.

Ty's body jerked as each bullet hit, piercing the heavy coat. He fell onto his back, letting loose a scream of agony.

"A crowd's comin'," Benjamin yelled, waving his arm, looking terrified.

Robert ignored him. Ignored Ty Lawson, who lay moaning and bleeding a few feet away. He hurried to Ellsworth's side, rolled him faceup, grimaced at the blood pumping out his pal's throat. Robert choked up, tears stinging his eyes, as he pressed his hands on Ellsworth's neck, trying to stem the flow of blood, but it was already too late. He could see that death had claimed him, quickly and without remorse.

"Ells . . . oh, God . . . oh, please, no . . ."

How had this happened? He should have told Ellsworth to stay at the ranch. This was not his war.

Feeling as if all the blood had drained from his own body, he weakly got to his feet, his gloves dripping with blood, as a crowd of people ran into the alley, yelling and raising a commotion. Robert trudged over to Benjamin, who stood in shock, his mouth agape, staring at the scene before him.

Robert's mind emptied, like someone had pulled a plug, as he draped the reins up and over his gelding's neck and swung up on the snow-speckled saddle. With a "Haw!" and a swift kick, he galloped down the alley, knowing the sheriff would be coming after him presently. He knew he'd put Julia in danger if he went to her now. Someone in the crowd would see where he went—most likely Carr's deputies, whose eyes were everywhere. And how could he face her, aggrieved over Ellsworth, enraged at Ty Lawson? But he hadn't mortally wounded Ty. Though, now, Robert wished he'd have killed him. The bastard deserved nothing less.

He knew he should stay. How could he leave Ellsworth like that? *But how would stayin' change anything? Ell is dead. Dead. And Ty Lawson murdered him.*

Robert felt nothing but rage and pulses of sharp pain in his chest. But as he rode hard and fast, like the Devil was after him, the rage melted into guilt. This was all his fault. Going to town, confronting Ty, hoping the fella might see reason . . . letting Ellsworth come along—all foolhardy choices. Ellsworth's death hung like an anvil around his neck.

He tried of think where to go, but no place would offer more than a temporary respite. His conscience railed at him; he had to somehow expiate his guilt, make amends. Without confession, his soul would burn with the eternal fire of judgment. But what could he do? Would Reverend Charnel help him?

When his pa got word about Ellsworth, he'd go on the scout for Ty, maybe even Julia's pa. The feud Robert had hoped to end would now flare into all-out war, and Robert feared the bloodbath to follow in its wake. He had to do something to prevent it. The only person he thought could help was his ma. She alone could handle Stephen Morrison. Robert prayed she'd understand . . . and forgive him. For, when Ty Lawson recovered, he'd want revenge. But so did Robert. Almost as much as he wanted Julia.

Julia . . . She was waiting for him at that boarding house. He had to go to her; she'd be worried. *And if she hears the news of what happened to Ty* . . .

His head felt woozy, and his gut ached and chest stabbed with pain with every breath. He had two, maybe three, broken ribs. Maybe even punctured a lung. He'd need to wash up, wrap his chest, pack his things, and get back to town, unseen and unhindered. He'd have to stall till dark. Julia would wait for him; she said she would.

Julia would be caught up in the middle of this conflagration. Robert needed to get her out of town, to safety, as soon as he could. So much for his hope that once they wed, their families would give up their hate. Now, he had no choice. They had to leave—for good.

Maybe, once they were in Colorado, they would be truly free. Though, Robert doubted he would ever be free of his guilt over Ellsworth.

"Out of my way!" Sheriff Carr pushed through the throng of gawkers and finally saw the bodies on the ground that was a mix of slushy snow and blood and dirt. It took a moment to recognize the big man with his throat cut. Carr knew Ellsworth Akes and that he worked on Morrison's ranch. Last time he saw the fella was when Carr broke up that fight, week last, with Ty Lawson.

And who should be hunkered over, groaning in pain, but the very scoundrel himself. Had he killed Akes? The bloody long-handled knife at his side seemed to tell that tale. Looked like Lawson had been shot. Carr glanced around but didn't see a weapon. Then he spotted the muzzle of a rifle sticking out from under Akes.

The sheriff addressed the crowd. "Who saw what happened?"

The crowd made a lot of noise, but no one was coming forward. Then Carr's eyes narrowed on the youngster holding the reins of two horses. Same kid that had been in front of the bank. The kid Lawson had been roughing up.

"You there!" he called out to the kid.

The youngster looked around, then realized Carr was talking to him. His eyes went scared and wide. "Come 'ere," he ordered. Then he scanned the crowd. "The lot of you — git lost. You" — he pointed at a concerned-looking old biddie — "go fetch a doctor. Be quick!"

As the crowd thinned, the wheels in Carr's head began rolling down a slick, fast track. His two deputies — McIntyre and O'Grady — came stomping over, their hawk eyes searching faces. O'Grady rubbed his bearded chin. "Who's that?" He pointed at Akes.

"Foreman that works at the Morrison ranch. You and Sean, haul him onto a cart and get him over to the morgue. Find Wilson if he's not there."

O'Grady chortled. "'Bout this time, he'll be chugging over at the Tivoli."

"Then pick him up on your way out."

McIntyre, the older of the two deputies, said, "What about that fella yonder?" He pointed to Lawson.

"Just get Akes to the morgue. The other fella's been shot. I sent for a doctor."

The two nodded and went about their business. Carr turned his attention to the scared kid holding the reins of a gelding and a small mare. No doubt the gelding belonged to Akes. The kid was frozen in his boots.

"Ya wanna tell me what happened?" he said to the kid, making it clear it wasn't a question.

The youngster gulped.

"What's your name?" Sheriff Carr asked, watching Lawson out of the corner of his eye. Someone had helped prop him up against the back of the Johnson Hotel and left him there, slumped over, maybe unconscious, Carr thought. *Perfect.*

Blood pounded his temples in excitement. Now was the ideal opportunity to hurt Carson where it counted. Asa House had told Carr to take care of the Carson problem once and for all, and now it seemed as if Lady Luck was smiling on him on this snowy, wintery day.

"Uh . . . Benjamin. Scranton. Sir."

The kid was positively shaking in his boots.

"You with the Morrison ranch?"

"Yes sir."

"Let's hear it."

"Well . . . uh . . . Ty Lawson—that fella over there"—he pointed across the alley—"he sent word to Robert. Morrison, that is. Said he . . . uh . . . wanted to meet."

"Morrison? He was here?"

The kid glanced around nervously, maybe considering lying. But Carr already figured out what went down here. "So, Morrison and you and Akes—you met Lawson here?"

The kid hesitated, then nodded. He went on to tell how Robert only wanted to talk. An argument ensued. Lawson knifed Akes, then Morrison shot Ty.

"You know what they were arguing about?" Carr asked him.

Again the kid hesitated, a worried look clouding his face.

"You're a material witness, Scranton. You may have to swear under oath in court and tell the truth. Best if you tell it now."

"Uh . . . somethin' about a letter Ty accused Robert of sendin'. But Robert didn't."

"A letter about . . . ?"

"'Bout Miss Carson. Julia. She and Robert were fixin' to marry."

Carr's brows rose. So his guess was on target. Wait until he told Asa House. The warden would be happier than a pig in a puddle. Carr's dirty deed of writing that letter and sending it along to the Morrison ranch accomplished all Carr had hoped—

and more. He'd found that ranch hand, Dusty Anderson, working at the farrier's mere hours after he'd seen Ty Lawson pick up his cousin at the church. Then, this morning, he'd paid a young boy a nickel to run over to Dusty and tell him to deliver the envelope, saying it was urgent. When Carr had realized Robert Morrison was secretly meeting with the Carson girl, well, he couldn't resist the temptation to throw a wasp nest into the fire.

Perfect! "I'm sure others can corroborate your story," he said, eyeing the kid. "You sure it happened like you said?"

"Oh, yes sir. Every word."

Carr believed him. The kid looked like he had the fear of God in him. And he was on the verge of crying. Clearly he'd liked the big lug that now lay dead.

Carr made it his business to know every little thing about everyone in town. One thing he knew for sure: Lester Carson had high regard for his nephew. Ty was like a son to him, and he'd raised him since Ty was about twelve. Anything happened to Ty, why, Carson would go on a rampage. Probably do all manner of crazy, lawless things, to pay back those who hurt his nephew.

From the looks of it, Lawson wasn't shot up all that bad. But the doctor had yet to arrive . . .

"All right, kid. Get a move-on."

Scranton looked over at Lawson. "Wh-what about him?"

"Don't you worry," Carr said, "he'll get tended to." *That he will.*

Scranton let out a shudder and frowned as he ponied the gelding to the strings of his mare's saddle. He then swung up onto his horse.

Carr tipped his hat, and the kid rode away, Akes's horse in tow, kicking into a gallop when he reached Front Street.

Snow was falling in great swaths, and the wind moaned through the alley, sounding like a gathering of ghosts. A careful look-see told him no one was watching. The bystanders had all retreated back into their shops and saloons—another day, another death.

But the day wasn't over yet.

Carr walked over to Ty Lawson, who lifted heavy lids and tried to focus on the face staring down at him.

"Sheriff . . . ?"

Lawson's face was a mess of pain. Carr counted four bullet wounds. Two in Lawson's left shoulder, one in his left thigh. Another in his left calf. *That's gotta hurt.*

The placement of the shots was clearly deliberate. Robert Morrison hadn't wanted to kill Ty Lawson. Why? Carr had no idea. Maybe because his beloved Julia might boil over if she heard he'd done the deed? Lawson's death might put a crimp in their romance, Carr thought, amused. A big crimp.

And anything that caused a Carson grief made Sheriff Thomas Jefferson Carr a happy man. *Maybe now the Carsons and Morrisons will have it out, once and for all. Maybe the whole lot of 'em will kill one another. Wouldn't that be nice?*

"Sheriff . . . help me . . . I'm bad hurt . . ."

Carr grinned, took another look around as the thick blanket of snow erased the hard edges of the buildings and covered Lawson like a shroud.

"Be glad to," Carr said. Then he slipped his pistol out of its holster, took aim at Lawson's chest, and fired.

Chapter 15

DESPITE THE HEAVY FALL OF snow, the revelers were out in numbers. Julia kept her head down, chin tucked into her thick wool-lined coat, a big cowboy hat stuffed low on her head. With only her boots peeking out from the hem of her long coat, she figured she could pass for a man—one minding his own business as he walked his horse at a steady clip down Ivinson Street.

Gunshots fired made her shudder. She could make out a group of drunks carousing in the middle of the next block, yelling up to the painted doves, who, despite the storm, hung over the railings and cajoled and teased potential customers. Julia dropped her gaze to her horse's neck, trying to become invisible as people skipped past her, horses trotted and bucked, and the stench of manure and sweat and whiskey drifted around her.

Music poured from saloons along with yelling and laughter, and Julia fought down her claustrophobia, thinking more and more what a bad idea this was. The snow had slowed her down, and twice she'd lost the road south from her home and wandered into deep drifts halfway to town. By the time she made out the imposing outline of the courthouse building, darkness had draped the streets.

Relief sparked when she spotted Molly Brooks's boarding house. The simple clapboard two-story looked squashed between the brothels, and only a small sign in the window, with "Molly's" written in block letters, provided identification. Two tiny windows glowed with light from within, though the sheer cotton curtains were drawn.

Julia looked about but couldn't see an alleyway. She knew the stable was directly behind the building, and the thought of having to go around the long block renewed her trepidation. She didn't dare leave Little Bit unattended; someone would surely steal him. Plenty of horses were tied to the hitching posts along the street, though, and her little gelding wasn't anything special. Maybe he wouldn't merit a thief's consideration.

A man in an old Army coat with a grizzled beard came up alongside her, waving something in his hand. "Hey, you there, young fella!" he called out in a drunken slur. "You lookin' for a good time?"

Julia realized the man was speaking to her. She shook her head in a frantic attempt to send him away, but he yanked on her boot. She had no recourse but to kick him.

"Leave me alone," she cried.

He looked up at her, pushing back his hat and squinting. Snow canted into his face. "Hey, you're a gal! Why're ya dressed like that?" He pawed at her arm. "Come on and dance with me, girlie!" he hissed through a gap where his two front teeth used to be, the whiskey breath washing over her with bits of spittle. Julia gagged.

The front door to Molly's swung open, and a woman in a simple calico housedress and slippers came barging out through the threshold.

Molly! Thank the Lord!

Molly Brooks wasted no time. She grabbed the man by the sleeve of his coat and yanked him away from Julia's horse. "Hey, now. What's goin' on?"

She stared up at Julia, and recognition lit up her face. "Julia Carson? Heavens! What on earth . . . ?"

She abruptly closed her mouth, then turned to the man, who was wobbling on his legs, looking about to fall over.

"Git goin', Fes. This gal's my guest. She ain't a saloon gal."

To Julia's surprise, Molly pulled the hat from his head and started whacking him with it. "Go on, git!" she said, as if she were talking to a stubborn mule.

The man gave her a doleful look, snatched his hat from Molly's hand, and muttered, "I'm goin'. I'm goin'." He slogged through the mounded snow covering the boardwalk, then picked up his pace when he spotted another rider getting off a horse in front of the adjacent brothel. He wasted no time in giving the man his pitch. Julia figured one of the brothels was paying him to drum up customers. She knew well what the citizens of Laramie were up to in these saloons and brothels, but being this close and seeing the raucous behavior made her sick all over.

Molly drew close to Julia and spoke in a hush. "What're ya doin' here, honey?"

Julia gulped. Would Molly turn her away? Maybe this was a bad idea. "I . . . I need a place to stay."

Molly studied her, then nodded, her face grim. "Trouble on yer tail?"

"In a manner of speaking," Julia replied.

"All right, then. Come on down," Molly told Julia. "I'll fetch Abraham to tend to yer horse. Don't worry your sweet li'l heart. He'll be nice and safe in his stall with my old Moses. My oh my, you sure picked a night to come to town!"

Molly held out her hand, and Julia slipped off Little Bit. After taking the pillowcase from the saddlebag, she gave her horse a few pats on the neck.

"Wait but a minute," Molly said. Julia looked nervously around as Molly ducked inside the boarding house and yelled for Abraham. Presently a lanky, tall elderly Negro dressed in baggy gray trousers held up with red suspenders came hurrying out. He tipped his hat at Julia and gave her a bright smile, the teeth shockingly white in contrast to his nearly black skin.

"This is Julia," Molly told him.

He nodded over and over, casting his eyes down. "Glad to make your 'quaintance, miss."

"I'm pleased to meet you, Abraham. This is Little Bit." Julia was glad Molly didn't mention her last name. She appreciated the woman's discretion.

Abraham grinned even wider. "Shore is. He's a little bit o' horse. But a right good size for a lady such as yorself."

She smiled back at him as he stroked her horse's forehead. "I'll take good care of him—don't you worry none."

Julia handed him the reins.

"I've got a hot pot of barley bean soup inside—and some biscuits 'bout to come out o' the oven," Molly said, gesturing Julia inside. "Jes shake the snow off and sit yerself down at the table, honey. This-a-way."

Julia was met with a warm blast from the kitchen as she followed the diminutive woman down the narrow hallway, passing a half-dozen doors on both sides.

"Those are the rooms I let," Molly explained, "but I got a nice li'l room upstairs next to my quarters that you c'n stay in." She led Julia into a tiny kitchen with a big cast-iron pot bubbling on the stove. The smell of the soup and powder biscuits set Julia's mouth watering. "Sit yonder," she said, waving at the small square table that had seen a lot of years of wear.

Now that she was safe inside the boarding house, the argument that Julia had pushed from her thoughts came barreling back. Pain gushed anew as she recalled her mother's words and the mean look in her eyes. Sixteen years of coddling and caring for Julia, and in one short argument, she thought nothing of discarding her. How could her mother be so cruel? And what would her father say and do once he learned what transpired?

Would he be angry at her mother? Or side with her? Would he scour the town looking for his renegade daughter? Julia's heart raced with worry. How long could she stay here before someone recognized her and word got back to her father?

"I was hoping you'd have a room I could rent—just for a night, maybe two."

"Honey, you c'n stay as long as ya need to." She opened the oven door and pulled out a steaming pan of biscuits. As she spooned soup into a big bowl, she said, "The boarders eat at six, in the dining room, but you look famished." She added, "Plus, I'm guessin' you came here 'cause you don't want to be seen."

Julia nodded. She certainly wasn't dressed for a night out on the town. She wondered how well Molly Brooks knew Julia's parents.

"So, I'd like to hear 'bout yer trouble, honey." Molly set a plate of three hot biscuits and the bowl of soup before Julia. "But first—eat somethin'."

"Thank you," Julia said, so grateful for the hospitality. Molly got up and filled a kettle while Julia wolfed down the soup, hardly ladylike. But she couldn't shake the fear and urgency gnawing at her.

When Molly finished fixing herself a cup of tea, she sat across from Julia and smiled warmly. "Nothin' ya tell me will leave this kitchen." She slathered butter on the biscuits and pushed them toward Julia. "Eat up, now. You're thin as a water reed."

Julia savored the delicious flavors of the sweet cream butter and powder biscuit. "Mmm, this is wonderful. You are so kind."

Molly waved away her compliment.

Julia wasn't sure what to say, but she needed Molly in her confidence. "Do you know the Morrisons?"

Molly cocked her head. "Course I do. An' I know your pa hates Stephen Morrison. It's a common fact. Carsons and Morrisons been enemies forever—since afore the railroad came to town."

Julia let out a breath. No use beating about the bush. "I'm going to marry Robert Morrison."

Molly almost dropped her teacup. "What's that ya said?"

"Robert and I love each other, and he's coming here—"

Molly looked up and said, "Oh Lordy. That there's a heap of trouble. No wonder ya came here."

Julia sighed. "When he gets here, we somehow need to get word to Reverend Charnel. He's agreed to marry us."

Molly shook her head and laughed. "He would." She looked hard at Julia. "You sure about this, honey? A whole lot of folks're gonna be mighty upset."

"I don't care. It's my life." Julia fell silent. Molly was right, though. Would her father—or Robert's—punish the reverend, or Molly, for aiding them?

"Maybe I'm asking too much," Julia said. "I don't want anyone to risk their life—"

"Don't be silly, honey. Love is stronger'n iron and hotter'n fire. If anythin' c'n melt hate, it's love. If you love this fella with all yer heart, then there's nothin' for it. Ya can't care a whit what others might think. Ya gotta do what's right fer you."

Molly's words, along with the warm food in her stomach, eased her jangled nerves. "Thank you, Molly." Without warning, the tears started falling. Julia tried to swallow them back, but her effort was to no avail.

Molly came over to her and slung an arm around Julia's shoulder, then handed her a crumpled handkerchief. Julia blew her nose and wiped her eyes, apologizing for her outburst.

"There, there, it's alright, it's alright, honey. Someday yer folks will unnerstand. They'll come 'round." She waited as Julia dabbed at her eyes and finally stopped the tears.

"Once you're hitched, where will ya go?"

Julia shrugged. "Robert... knows someone in Fort Collins..."

"Oh, that's a right nice town, from all accounts. Best for ya to git far from Laramie, find a purty place to settle down, raise some young'uns."

Molly finished her tea and asked, "You want some more? I got 'nough for a small army."

"No, thank you. I couldn't eat another bite."

"Well, then, let's get ya settled in yer room—"

A door slammed open in the back of the building. Molly walked into the hallway, Julia behind her.

Abraham came hobbling toward them, clearly upset, followed by a blast of wintery air.

"What is it, Abraham?" Molly asked, taking hold of the man's shaking hands.

His dark eyes shone with fear in the dim light of the hallway.

"There's been a shooting—behind the courthouse." He kept his eyes downcast. "Two dead, Miss Molly." He added, "I heard the commotion an' went over to Annie's, to see what she heard."

Molly's voice was little more than a whisper. "Who're they sayin' got shot?"

"Well. . . one fella wasn't shot—had his throat cut." He quickly turned to Julia. "Sorry, miss—"

"It's alright, Abraham. Go on," Molly urged gently.

"Not sure o' the fella's name, but he works at the Morrison ranch—"

Julia gasped, and her legs turned to jelly. "Robert!"

Molly quickly grabbed Julia's arm and steadied her. "Ya don't know that."

Abraham shook his head. "No, no, miss. They be saying it's someone named Akes."

"Akes?" Julia hadn't heard the name before. But a lot of people worked on the big ranches. Her father employed dozens, sometimes upwards of fifty during the fall roundup. Surely the same could be said for Stephen Morrison. She told herself not to panic, but her breath wasn't reaching her lungs.

"Sheriff's on the scout for the fella who shot t'other one."

"Who . . . who," she managed to eke out, "was the other man? The one who got shot?"

"Why, miss, that cowboy who he'ps run the Carson ranch."

Julia's head grew dizzy as she sucked in air that wouldn't come. She opened her mouth, but nothing went in or out.

"Who d'ya mean?" Molly asked him.

"The rancher's nephew—Lawson, I think's his name, Miss Molly."

"Ty Lawson?" Molly asked, her face stricken and suddenly pale.

She turned to Julia with a fearful expression. "Julia, honey. Are ya alright? You're not breathing . . ."

The spots dancing in Julia's eyes turned to big black splotches as her limbs melted like wax. She barely made sense of Abraham's next words as her vision went dark and she fell, tumbling down a black, cold shaft.

". . . An' they be sayin' Morrison's son killed him. Fella named Robert . . ."

Chapter 16

ROBERT COULDN'T VERY WELL LEAVE his hot, panting horse outside in the snowstorm while he went into the house. He hated delaying even a minute longer than necessary, but some things couldn't be neglected. All the ranch horses were in the big barn, out of the weather, and that's where Robert took his gelding, Sidewinder. The ranch dogs were hunkered down in the dry hay, and only Tike bothered to get up and greet him with a tail wag. The friendly face of his old dog sent a miserable shaft of regret through his heart. Never more would his home be a refuge of warmth and welcome. Not after what happened in the alley.

After removing the saddle and bridle, giving the horse a quick brush-down, and setting him loose, Robert saddled up Comanche, Cassidy's horse, then attached the saddlebags and strapped in his rifle. Robert tried to ride the big bay from time to time, knowing how much Cassidy had loved the animal. But the memories it pricked were painful. Tonight, though, Comanche was the best choice, for Robert needed to be at the ready for a long ride, should other options fail. He wondered about Julia, though. She'd told him she was a good rider, but the snow didn't look like it had any plans of letting up. He hoped she'd made it to the boarding house before dark.

Images of Ellsworth lying on the cold ground, his throat slit, kept badgering him, like wolves nipping at his heels. He let the anger drive him as he tightened Comanche's girth and, reins in hand, led the horse to the post by the big barn doors, his ribs stabbing him with pain, his shallow breathing hitching with each intake of air.

"Wait here," he told the animal as he tossed the reins over the post. "I won't be but a few minutes."

Robert could make out the fire blazing in the big stone hearth through the windows in his house across the field. Yellow light spilled over the shadowy mounds of snow, and darkness swallowed up the nearby woods. Snow piled on the eaves, and icicles were already dangling from the wood beams. The moon had yet to rise through the rips in the clouds. He squatted and rubbed snow on his blood-soaked gloves, but it did little to clean them. He started to pull them off, planning to hurl them into the sagebrush, then thought again.

The stain on his gloves, like the one on his heart, he would keep as a reminder, as a mark against him for all time.

He imagined his ma was fixing dinner, and his pa was probably in his study, morose and drunk. If Robert was lucky, he'd make it to his room without being noticed. He'd left Benjamin behind, in town, but Robert figured he'd be arriving presently. His cousin had seen the fight, and no doubt Robert's pa would grill him for every detail. He could only guess how shook up Benjamin was, and Robert hoped he got away from the obstreperous crowd without injury. The sooner Robert put miles between himself and his ranch, the better.

His heart so heavy he could barely lift his feet and walk up the steps into the house, Robert fixed his mind on Julia. On her sweet face. Her passionate voice. He tried to recall the words of her prayer as she stood on that patio, beseeching heaven, when Robert had silently joined with her, knowing in that moment they were fated to be together.

He grasped with all his resolve this shred of faith. It was the only thing he had left to cling to, his self-regard all but destroyed in the alley behind the courthouse. If Julia wasn't in danger, he'd have stayed in town, by Ellsworth's side, and let the sheriff haul him off to jail, where he imagined Ty Lawson was presently holed up, suffering mightily from the four bullets Robert had shot into him. Knowing Sheriff Carr's abhorrence for Lester Carson, it was doubtful he'd bother rendering any aid or sending for a doctor to tend to Lawson. At some point Carr would come to fetch Robert, and time allowing for his escape was slipping by quickly.

The pervasive pain chewed at Robert's ability to think straight. If he was going to wed Julia, then skip town—not knowing if they'd ever again step foot again in Wyoming Territory—there were some things Robert needed to take. Mementos, mostly. A watch passed on to him by his maternal grandpa. His Peacemaker and extra ammunition. A change of clothes, an extra pair of gloves. He wished he'd had time to buy a ring for Julia, but that—like so many other things he wanted to give her—would have to wait.

His head pounded with the pain pumping through his body as he stomped snow off his boots and pushed open the front door to a gust of hot air that instantly thawed his cheeks. He'd taken but a few steps when his ma came walking out of the kitchen, her hands and apron powdered with flour, the smile melting off her face quicker than snow tossed into a fire.

"Robert!" She rushed over. "You're covered in blood."

Robert cast his eyes down to his coat and saw why she was aghast. He hadn't noticed.

He raised his hands, feeling a need to ward off her concern, to infer his guilt and make known he was none the victim in this nightmare.

"Ma, Ma, it's not mine. I'm all right," he said over her fawning as he kept stepping back, keeping his distance, already feeling the natural affection between mother and son snapping, a wide and deep chasm opening up that they'd both fall into should they venture too close. How could he protect his ma's heart? She'd take Ellsworth's death badly, for she had great fondness for him.

He had to explain before others did the explaining for him.

He took off his hat, raked his hand through the thick matted hair. "Ty Lawson killed Ellsworth, Ma." He barely got the words out before he choked up and could say no more.

She lifted a hand to her mouth, eyes wide. "He's . . . dead?"

Robert stared at the floor, nodded. His ma sobbed. She took his hand, startling him. "Tell me what happened. All of it."

Somehow, he did. She stood there, pressed back against the pretty-papered wall, unblinking, unmoving, as it all came out, every bit. His words ran like warm treacle—he hardly made any sense to himself—as he told of how he'd met Julia and how much he loved her. About the mysterious letter he hadn't sent, and Lawson issuing a challenge. And then . . . the fight, the knife, the shooting . . .

His ma hung her head, the life snuffed out in her eyes. "Oh, Robert. Why?"

Why what? Why had he fallen in love with a Carson? Why had he gone to face Lawson? Why was he so stupid? Just that one word convicted him, nailed him to the cross that was now his and his alone to bear.

She looked at him, tears splashing her cheeks. Her voice was thick with feeling. "You better go. Before your pa—"

They both turned at the sound of a horse galloping and stopping at the front of the house. Robert's hand instinctively dropped to the butt of his pistol at his side. Benjamin Scranton blew in amid a swirl of snow, his face raw with both the freezing air and unmistakable grief.

"You're here!" Benjamin said, but Robert couldn't tell if the fact alarmed or relieved his cousin.

Benjamin shrugged off his coat and shook snow off his hat, aiming to dump it outside, but wind blew it back in.

"Shut the door," Robert told him.

Benjamin obeyed, then nodded at Robert's ma. "Ma'am," he said, then looked quizzically at Robert, as if unsure what was safe to say. Robert's chest grew even hotter with pain—he knew Benjamin had more bad news. But what could be worse than Ellsworth's death?

"She knows," Robert said, his eyes urging Benjamin to speak. He was itching to get shed of his bloody, sweaty clothes and be on his way. *Julia, please wait for me . . .*

When Benjamin stuttered, unable to speak his mind, Robert said matter-of-factly, "Spit it out."

"It's that Lawson fella." Benjamin rubbed his chin, shaking his head.

"What about Lawson?"

Robert stiffened at the loud voice behind him.

All eyes turned to Robert's pa, who'd eased into the foyer by way of the hall, his slippered feet silent on the waxed wood floor.

His pa's scowl stabbed like the knife that had killed Ellsworth. "I said, what about Lawson?" He stared down Benjamin, who tended to rankle his pa. But, then, just about everyone did these days.

Benjamin cleared his throat. "Well, sir . . . I-I don't know how to put it—"

"What about Lawson?" Stephen Morrison roared.

Robert's mother retreated two steps back, wilting into the dining room.

Benjamin's gaze flitted from Robert's to Robert's pa, then back to Robert. His words were as thin as willow bark. "He's . . . he's dead."

Robert's pa burst out in a drunken laugh that was more a sputter. "Lawson dead! Praise the good God in heaven—"

"Don't take the Lord's name in vain—" his ma started to say.

His pa spun to face her, spitting out his words. "I ain't even using His name, woman!" He laughed—the kind of belly laugh that made a body bob up and down like a marionette on strings. His mother paled.

Robert's breath felt like poison in his mouth. He stared at Benjamin. "H-how?" Had Lawson bled to death? *I know I didn't kill him. I couldn't've.*

Benjamin's face darkened in confusion. "Why, *you* shot him, Robert. I saw ya. Four shots—"

"All to wound him. Nary a one was fatal."

His pa glared at Robert, dropped a heavy hand on his shoulder. "You killed Lawson? *You?*" He started up laughing again, shaking his head, his cruel mouth in a twist. "You're joshin', right?"

"No sir." Benjamin looked uncertainly at Robert. "After, uh, the sheriff talked to me, I-I went and got a drink at one of the saloons. To calm my nerves." He gulped. "Then, everyone was sayin' it—Ty Lawson was dead. And that you kilt him."

"I didn't," Robert protested. Or was he mistaken? The numbing pain in his chest and his hammering headache made it hard to recollect. He'd seen where the shots hit. Close range. He was too good a shot to mess up that close.

"Don't matter if ya did or ya didn't. They believe ya did," Benjamin added. "Sheriff's deputies are comin'. I rode back hard as I could. You better git goin'."

"Goin'?" his pa mimicked. That blasted lawman will chase you to the ends of the earth." He laughed so hard, water pooled in his eyes.

Robert stared at him, slack-jawed. His pa was so drunk, he had no idea how bad this was for his family. For his ranch. For his only son.

Robert's ma started up crying, leaning on the table with one hand and sobbing into a handkerchief with the other.

"You need to go," Benjamin hissed. Robert didn't need reminding that he had precious few minutes left.

Robert looked over at his ma and mouthed, "I'm sorry, Ma. Sorry." Though, it didn't say by half what he felt.

He turned to head up the stairs, but his pa grabbed his arm and clenched it tight. The stench of whiskey smacked Robert in the face. "You're stayin' right here," his pa slurred. "Take yer medicine."

Robert forced his pa's hand off his arm and pushed him back. "You're pathetic. You're drunk—"

"And you're a coward an' an idiot! You pick a fight with them Irish, then let yer brother finish it for ya. Shoulda been you that died."

His pa's eyes were full of malice as he voiced the words Robert often heard in his own head. Knew his pa often thought himself.

Robert's stomach went queasy, and, whether due to exhaustion, pain, or fear finally catching up with him, he started to shake all over, about to be sick.

He wrenched away and stumbled up the stairs, his pa screaming after him in his slurred voice, "Go on, run! Run, ya coward! Ya killed Cassidy, and ya ran. Jus' keep on runnin'! They'll catch ya, and you'll pay. Yesiree, you'll pay!"

Robert heard his ma behind him, shushing his pa, and the door opened and Robert looked to see Benjamin stomping out.

The door slamming behind him was like the finality of a guillotine blade chopping into a block of wood—with his head on the block. He moved quickly, methodically, gathering his things, hardening into a rock, not letting himself feel a thing other than his profound exhaustion. He chucked his pa's words into a raging river of detachment, and not more than five minutes later he was on Cassidy's bay, the clouds now parted, the waning moon peeking up from the horizon as if unsure it was a good time to visit the Front Range. He'd warn it away, if he knew how.

Despite Comanche's smooth gait, with every pound of the horse's hooves, pain jabbed Robert's chest. The air was like a cloud of biting flies, attacking his face and what part of his neck was exposed, and the horse's mane was braided with threads of icicles. He rode Comanche hard, choosing a trail that went through the heavy pine woods east of the ranch, the trail barely dusted with snow under the heavy crisscrossing boughs. He didn't dare take the main road into town, knowing he'd be waylaid by Carr's deputies. The way was longer but safer by a long chalk.

He replayed the shots he fired, over and over, knowing in his gut as sure as he was alive that he hadn't killed Ty Lawson. Nor would his mortal enemy have bled to death, even if he'd been left unattended. Benjamin said the sheriff had questioned him. Carr had been there. He would've taken Lawson to a doctor, or, at the very least, the jail. Benjamin must've heard rumors that had no basis in truth. Gossip, which always spread through town like wildfire.

At any other time in Robert's life, he would've been glad for Lawson's death. He would've been proud to claim the kill. To bring down his enemy. To hurt Lester Carson at the very heart of him.

But now . . . hurting a Carson meant hurting Julia. Their best-laid plans had gone awry. Would Julia believe him? Forgive him? He urged Comanche into a faster gallop, swallowing down his worry, sorely vexed. He supposed he would find out when he got to town.

Chapter 17

JULIA GAGGED AT THE AWFUL acrid smell, opening her eyes to see Molly leaning over her with a small bottle of smelling salts in her hand. Panic surged into her heart as she sat up and looked around the bedroom she found herself in. She was lying on a single bed with a brass frame atop a white stitched coverlet. Tiny red roses clustered on the wallpaper around her. Julia's fogged head cleared, then she recalled what Abraham had said about Ty.

Ty's dead. It can't be true. It can't!

She tried to get to her feet, but Molly's hand stayed her.

"I have to go—" Julia insisted.

"Honey, it's best to wait. Ya don't know what's true and what's not."

"I must know . . . if Ty is . . . dead. If Robert . . ." The words strangled her throat tighter than any hands could manage.

She saw flickering light through the window and realized she was in an upstairs room that looked out over the street. Pushing aside Molly's protestations, Julia rushed to the window, where silvery shafts of moonlight sliced through the pane and streaked the floor. The agitated, undulating mob below her resembled a tumultuous sea, bodies crashing like waves into one another, into the sides of buildings, fists flying and the sounds of laughter and retching and squealing from man and beast alike creating a riotous tableau that seemed hardly real.

Julia stared in utter disbelief at the sight, feeling as if she'd been swept off the very planet and transported to some other, distant place that was nothing like that brave new world with such goodly creatures in it that astonished Miranda in *The Tempest*. Mankind, this night, was anything but beauteous. Stark in its base ugliness, humanity had never appeared so sinful, so beastly. And life never so hopeless.

"Oh, Robert." Her heart was clamped in a vise, and she could hardly gather her wits about her. The walls of the tiny room loomed over her, and the ceiling with its curls of peeling paint threatened to collapse on her head.

"I need . . . I need air," she squeezed out. Oh, why hadn't she thought to bring her medicine? Of all the things she needed . . .

Gulping air, Julia rushed from the room, Molly's words full of warning chasing her down the stairs. But Julia was frantic, the front door in her sights. She had to get out, now.

She stumbled down the carpeted hallway, her hands groping at her throat, tears dribbling down her cheeks and dropping off her chin. Her thoughts were a bramble of faces. Ty, with his sweet smile and sparkling eyes. Robert, adoring her, his look beseeching her. Her mother scowling, her father enraged. The faces blurred as she threw open the door and almost fell in a tumble off the front stoop and into the crowded street.

Here the noise was deafening, and she stumbled back in confusion, pressing against the side of the boarding house as revelers strode along the boardwalk, a crush of legs and torsos, swishing skirts and petticoats, bright tinkling laughter and the crash of bottle glass.

The brisk night air seeped into her lungs in meager measure, and soon the cold penetrated through her blouse, setting her teeth chattering. Once she was able to draw in long, deep breaths unhindered, she turned to go back inside Molly's, hoping to thaw out next to the woodstove in the kitchen.

A hand squeezed her arm.

"There ya'are!"

Julia twisted in the man's grasp and found herself staring into the small dark eyes of the drunk who had pawed at her earlier. Fes, Molly had called him.

His gray-streaked brown hair was greased down under his hat, smelling like lard. From the putrid stench, Julia guessed he hadn't bathed in weeks. His brown shirt was half-tucked into his baggy trousers, and the hand gripping her forearm was sticky like tar, the nails limned with dirt. Julia gagged and wrenched her head away, gasping for fresh air.

Fes yanked her close, like reeling in a fish, and she felt his slimy paws exploring her waist, fingers wiggling like worms.

"Get your paws off me!" With her free hand, she slapped his head, but it only made him burst out laughing.

"I like me a gal with spunk. Give me s'more o' that lip."

Before she could take a step, his squirming lips were on hers, like cold, wet worms. And then his tongue darted out like a snake's, thrusting into her mouth, probing her teeth, making Julia gag with nausea.

The more she struggled, the harder the cretin pushed himself on her, forcing her back against the building, ramming her into the cold brick, while, at the same time, forcing her, step by step, around the side of the building, out of the crush of the crowd and into darker shadows, where neither moonlight nor lamplight from the saloon windows fell.

The strangled cry never made it out of Julia's lips. Fear seized her, renewing its choke hold on her. She thrashed her body and tried to hit him with her arms, but with a force of uncanny strength, the vile attacker grabbed her arms and pinned them above her head, against the wall. There was hardly room for them both in the narrow slit between the boarding house and the adjacent brothel.

A couple of cowboys in tall hats stopped as they were passing and gaped, but when Julia tried to scream and wrest herself free, they cajoled and cheered Fes on, slapping their hands on their pants legs and shaking their heads.

Julia heard one say, "Atta boy, Fes. Ya picked yerself a live one fer a change!" The other, upon hearing those remarks, exploded in a paroxysm of laughter, then the two moved on out of sight. Their callous reaction intensified her horror. Would no one come to her rescue?

Fes's mouth was on hers again. Her chest heaved with choked tears and sobs as he slobbered over her with his sticky abominable tongue and laughed deliriously.

"Oh yes, oh yes, oh yes," he moaned and with a hard yank tore open her blouse, exposing her undergarments. Julia's gasp was smothered with that mouth, and her fear escalated when she felt his icy hands squeezing her breasts, eliciting stabs of pain she could find no escape from.

She sensed herself beginning to swoon, but when he pulled his face from hers and fumbled with his belt—first securing his hold on her arms with one fiercely firm hand that dug into her flesh—Julia sucked in a great breath. Her gaze dropped to see him clumsily unbuttoning his trousers, his manhood pulsing hard through his long johns.

Terror ignited Julia's limbs, and she somehow tore her arms from his grasp. As he yanked up her skirts and thrust his hand underneath, groping up her thigh and pushing the skirts up to expose her legs, she spit in his face, startling him.

He looked up and into her face, then slapped her hard, flinging her to the side.

Her cheek exploded with pain. She flailed her arms, striking at him, but her blows merely glanced off his rock-hard head. When she tried to knee him, he slammed her once more against the wall, this time his face a mess of rage and driving need.

"I've had enough o' yer games, now," he ground out, teeth clenched. "It's time ya gave me what I want."

His groin was up against hers, and he squirmed and grunted, again pulling up her skirts, but this time more forcefully, urgently. He slapped her face again, and she screamed, but the sound was buried in the revelries of the night around her. She could feel her eye swelling, and blood dripped from her lip where her teeth had cut it.

Pressed this hard against the bricks, she couldn't budge, her body limp and weak, despair pumping through her limbs, draining her of resolve, of strength. She did the only thing she could think to do. She leaned into his grunting face as he fumbled with his long johns, her skirts now bunched at her waist, the cretin poised to violate her in the worst way . . . and she bit his bottom lip as hard as she could, feeling teeth rip through flesh and the gush of warm metallic blood and the squishy lump of flesh float in her mouth, making her retch and spit the piece onto the dirt.

Fes fell back, screaming profanities at her, clutching his mouth with one hand and pulling out a gun from a hip holster.

Julia froze, then tried to run, her only chance to lose herself in the crowd, but he kicked out and tripped her, and she fell, landing painfully on her wrists, scraping her face on the slushy, gritty ground.

"I'll kill ya, I will!" he screamed with a lisp, flipping her over, his gun aimed inches from her face, his hand shaking hard, his face a knot of agony.

Blood gushed from his mutilated lip, through bloodied fingers trying to staunch the flow. His head jerked from side to side, like a crazy top about to topple off his neck.

He took his hand off his disfigured mouth and clenched her neck in a death grip. She fought the black swarm threatening to suck her under, and with all her might lunged forward and grabbed at his gun with both hands.

Her movement threw him off balance, and she hoped his drink-soaked mind and throbbing lip would give her the delay in his reflexes she needed. He fired off a wayward shot, cursing her as the bullet pinged against the building above her.

They fought for the pistol, Fes grunting and cursing and spitting blood as Julia finally wrenched it from his slippery grip. She cocked the hammer back, meaning only to threaten him, to force him to retreat, but, to her shock, he dove for her, straight at her, and she had no recourse but to pull the trigger, the loud report concussing her ears.

The drunken cretin named Fes recoiled when the bullet hit his chest, his eyes widening, his bloody mouth hung open, exposing a maw of brown and yellow teeth, the big gap in the center revealing an abyss of darkness behind it.

Sickened by him and shocked by her own actions, she collapsed to the dirt, still holding the pistol, watching as Fes fell onto his back, clutching his chest and groaning.

Julia couldn't move. She thought to go to him, to help him, which seemed so very odd after what he had just done to her. She mindlessly let her eyes drift to her ripped blouse and skirt splotched with grease and grime and blood and shakily pushed aside a swath of hair that had come unpinned in the attack.

Her heart pounded wildly, blood beating a rhythm in her ears, as first one man, then another, then two or three saloon gals, then more, surrounded her. She stared at the man lying, unmoving, before her and felt someone lift the pistol from her hand.

Words floated over her, like fog, like silk, but then someone pulled her to her feet roughly, and another forced her hands behind her back and tied them with rope.

Julia kept staring at the man as if in a dream, her head thick, her face and palms raw and throbbing, as someone grabbed her shoulders and pressed her to walk.

It was only then that she understood the words yelled around her. Disjointed words like *killed* and *whore* and *sheriff* and *hanged*. She was dragged out to the boardwalk, a crowd tight around her, yelling at her, waving hands and pointing fingers and shaking heads, mouths open.

A man with pale mottled skin and the reddest hair she'd ever seen came up to her and looked her over, from head to toe. A grin moved like a snake up his face.

"Why, if it ain't Carson's spawn." He put his hands on his hips and whistled, then looked at another man, older, also with a dark-red beard and side whiskers.

"Sure 'nough," the other said, chuckling. "Won't the sheriff be tickled when he finds out."

Joseph was still shaking the sleep from his head when the warden ushered him into the penitentiary. He'd been dozing peacefully by his hearth a half-hour prior, when a pounding on the door woke him. An incident at the prison, and he was needed.

Joseph was told no more, but he assumed it was a medical emergency with one of the female prisoners, and since all he might need in the way of supplies was in the infirmary, he shrugged on his coat, switched slippers for his boots, and trudged out to the waiting wagon, where the morose guard hopped up on the seat and told Joseph to climb up beside him.

Joseph had seen this guard but hadn't properly met him. He had to pry the man's name from him. Clearly, Charles Sweesy was not happy to be sent out in the snowy night to fetch the doctor. Truth be told, Joseph wasn't either. Not even a week had passed since his first fateful day on the job, and now—another crisis.

Warden House was in his usual foul mood, his face ruddy and strained. Joseph was merely told that prisoner #6 had been caught escaping and was scheduled for confinement, but first her "minor injuries" needed attention.

Joseph had a fire lit in the infirmary hearth, then paced restlessly behind the locked and guarded door nearly an hour before his patient's head appeared cresting the set of stairs, two guards holding her arms and dragging her.

Joseph gasped, horrified at the sight of the poor waifish woman with her shaved head a purplish mass of bruises—as if she'd been struck repeatedly with a blunt object—approach the infirmary. When the guard unlocked the door, the men flanking her pushed her into the room. It was then that Joseph nearly had apoplexy. One look at the woman's bare feet caused him to lose all decorum.

"Are you mad?" he yelled at the guards. "This woman has frostbite."

The guards didn't even flinch. The one named Pulchow shrugged.

"Did you make her walk all the way back?" Their insouciance was his answer, and it enraged him.

Joseph was about to boil over. He took the woman's arm and led her to one of the cots, then gently helped her sit. She was trembling, her eyes glazed, her face a mirror of emptiness, beyond hopelessness. In all his short days as a doctor, Joseph had never seen such frightening despair.

"You!" he shouted to the guard who had unlocked and stood sentry at the door. "Fill this bucket with snow and bring it to me. Quick!"

Joseph handed a pail to the guard, who nodded, unenthused but agreeable, and headed down the stairs.

"My poor woman," Joseph said under his breath, putting a scratchy wool blanket across her shoulders and noticing all the tears in her prison garb and scratches on her hands. He knew he should examine her more closely, check for more than scratches. If her head injuries were the result of guards beating her, who knew what else he might find? Yet, Cathryn Povey's words railed in his head, and Joseph wanted to spare this woman any indignities that were in his power to spare.

He glanced at the two guards outside the infirmary. They seemed to have no interest in what transpired behind the door. Joseph spoke softly.

"Can you tell me if anything else is hurting you — aside from your head and feet?"

He had water already heated on the hearth, and he poured some into a small bowl and added antiseptic.

His words elicited a barely perceptible shake of the head. The woman — Joseph searched his mind for her name, trying to match her face with the prison roll book—wouldn't meet his eyes.

"All right. Um . . . I am going to clean your head. This might hurt a little. I'll be gentle." He thought she'd resist, but as Joseph dabbed a rag soaked in the warm water solution, she sat stolid and unblinking. All the while, he was anxious for the guard to return with the pail of snow.

Upon finishing that first task and finding the bruising superficial, which squelched his fears over a concussion, he turned his attention to her feet.

Joseph had seen plenty of cases of frostbite. This woman's feet weren't badly affected, but the trauma of having to walk barefoot back to the prison and through the halls and up the stairs—he wanted to punch those guards for making her walk— turned her feet into a bloodied mess.

Thankfully, it was mostly her toes that were frostbitten. He didn't see much evidence of it having spread up her feet.

Finally the guard arrived with the bucket, then took his place outside the door. Three guards to restrain one feeble woman. Did they think she would try to sneak away again? She must have been desperate to make her escape on such a snowy day. Maybe it was the obscured visibility from the earlier storm that had tempted her with an opportunity she couldn't resist. Joseph could hardly blame her, what with the way this penitentiary was run. He was beginning to understand Cathryn Povey's passionate concern.

As he gently rubbed her feet with the snow, he tried to engage her in conversation, asking innocuous questions about her life, her family, but she wouldn't reply. Then it came to him: her name was Hassie Ethridge, and she was serving six months for stealing clothing from a mercantile.

"Hassie . . ." Joseph said, resting a hand on her shoulder as he squatted in front of her.

A flicker of recognition sparked in her eyes. Joseph wondered when the last time was that Hassie had been addressed by name.

"I'm here to help you," he said with much compassion.

She made a slight noise that reminded Joseph of a wounded animal. She wasn't much different from one, he noted. What she needed was what all creatures needed: affection, security, loving family. She would get none of that in the heartless penitentiary.

Little by little, by speaking softly and reassuring her with smiles and small talk, Joseph managed to get her to share some of her thoughts. Though she spoke few words, those words told volumes and held heavy pain and remorse. By the time he'd finished tending to her, he was confident that most of Hassie's circulation had returned to her feet and toes. He would keep an eye on them over the next forty-eight hours, hoping he wouldn't have to surgically remove any toes. For now, keeping her feet wrapped, warm, and dry was a priority. And that meant staying off them. He hoped the warden would not decline his request to allow Hassie to remain in the infirmary or even her cell until the full extent of the damage could be assessed.

He recalled Cathryn telling him how she was lobbying to allow prisoners to be released earlier for good time served. In this moment, seeing Hassie look at him, now with a glimmer of hope—or maybe it was a renewed will to live—he decided he would throw his all into the effort to help Mrs. Povey in her crusade.

Chapter 18

THE TOWN WAS A MADHOUSE. The trampled snow was a slush of mud that splattered Robert's pants legs as he trotted along Ivinson Street, pushing his horse through the wide thoroughfare clogged with drunken cowboys and laborers walking, atop horses, and driving buggies and buckboards, looking for the next drink or bit house gal to spend their wages on. The sky had cleared, leaving stars glistening across the sky, the moon on the rise.

He was cold, wet with sweat and snow, exhausted, and consumed with grief over Ellsworth. Remaining in Laramie a moment longer seemed imprudent. Instead of waiting for the reverend to marry them, Robert decided it was no longer safe — for Julia, for him, and perhaps even the reverend. He would find Julia, and they would ride out of town posthaste. He knew of an abandoned way station along the Fort Collins road, not twenty miles southeast of Laramie, where they could hole up for the night. A stack of wood and food stores were always kept on hand for travelers needing respite from their journey. With a fresh start in the morning, they'd make Fort Collins by the next evening, barring further inclement weather. Robert figured it wouldn't be hard for him and Julia to find a man of the cloth to marry them there.

When he reached the boarding house, he jumped off Comanche and threw the reins over the post. He scanned the riotous crowd of gunslingers and rabble-rousers, disgusted by the vulgarities that met his eyes and ears. Upon spotting a lad about ten years old, he made his way through the crush and told him he'd pay him a nickel to watch his horse. The kid eagerly grabbed the chance for some spending money.

That done, Robert pounded on the boarding house door, then, when no one answered, he tried the door latch and found it unlocked. He ran inside, calling Julia's name. When he looked in all the hallways and kitchen and sitting areas, he started banging on the doors to the bedrooms.

An old stooped man with rheumy eyes cracked open one of the doors and glared at him. "How's a body to sleep with all this ruckus?" he complained.

"Please," Robert begged," have you seen a gal—sixteen years of age, beautiful big eyes, brown hair—"

The old codger scowled. "You c'n find plenty of gals next door in Annie's Saloon! Yer bangin' is fit ta wake the dead." He started to shut his door, but Robert stopped it with his hand.

"No, I'm looking for a particular gal. She's staying here—"

"Well, she's not in my room!" The man slammed the door in Robert's face.

His anger boiling, Robert ran up the back staircase and searched the rooms there, which were not locked. He found no one and no evidence that Julia had arrived. He then went to the kitchen, spotted some warm biscuits, and wolfed down two, barely appeasing his ravenous hunger.

Where was Julia? And what about Molly, the owner of the boarding house? *Probably out with the carousers.* Was Julia out there too? Or had she yet to come to town?

As he stood in the sweltering kitchen, sour thoughts came unbidden to his mind. He wanted to ignore them, but they screamed for his attention. He'd pushed those thoughts away as he rode to their rendezvous, telling himself that Julia would be here, would believe him when he said he hadn't killed Ty.

Surely, by now, she'd heard the news. Ty was dead. *And she'd hear how you killed him.*

Robert went back outside and told the kid he'd return presently. Robert needed a drink something fierce. As he pushed through the throng of revelers to the saloon next door, a whore with a black coat draped across her shoulders, her long stockinged legs exposed under her layers of petticoats, smiled at him as she leaned against the side of the brothel smoking a cigarette.

"Hey, Cowboy, you lookin' for a good time?"

Robert went over to her. "What I'm looking for is a gal—sixteen, brown hair. She was supposed to meet me next door, at Molly's. Have you seen—"

The gal chuckled and said, "Honey, whad'ya want with a child? What ya need is a *woman* with the know-how to satisfy a grown man's urges." She stepped up to him and ran her hands through his hair, knocking off his hat.

He backed away and picked up his hat. She'd been drinking aplenty—that much was clear.

"Ain't been no *child* over at Molly's. I see everythin' from my room." She tipped her head to the bank of windows on the second floor.

She studied him with a pout, green eyes taking him in from his face to his boots. "Hey . . . don't I know ya?" Her eyes widened. "Why, you're that Morrison fella everyone's lookin' for. You killed Lester Carson's kin in the alley behind the courthouse!"

Before Robert could react, the gal yelled over to two cowboys about to enter the saloon. "Hey, Fergus! This here's that Morrison fella!" She turned to Robert, shaking her head with a smile that implied the trouble awaiting him. "The sheriff's on the scout for you, honey. If I were you, I'd leave right quick. Though . . . you could hide under my covers for a spell . . ." She sidled up to him, her fingers toying with the buttons of his coat.

Robert turned and ran back to the boarding house, noticing the two cowboys staring at him and conversing in a conspiratorial manner with another fella who stood outside the brothel whose gaze pierced Robert with recognition. The fella nodded, then said something to the two cowboys, who promptly headed down the street. Robert wondered if a bounty had been nailed to his head. He'd run out of time.

A bitter laugh burst from his mouth as he looked at the place he'd called home these twenty-six years. What a fool he was. The moment Julia learned that Ty had been shot and killed, his fate had been sealed. Ty was closer than a brother to Julia. Had been for most of her life. Why would she fee more loyal to Robert, a fella she just met, than to Ty Lawson?

Still, she could've kept her word and met him here, even if it meant giving him a piece of her mind and walking out on him. It was the least she could have done.

The fact of this truth hit him like a cold iron upside his head. He had let his love for Julia blind him. Why had he thought she was any different from Rose Huffington? Every gal he'd known was the same: frivolous, flippant, giving her heart then snatching it back. Cruel. Unwilling to hear him out.

He'd thought Julia was different. Sure, she was young, innocent, sheltered. But maybe what he'd read as love was only her desire to get out of her folks' clutches. Maybe all he was to her was a means to an end. Julia didn't truly love him. If she did, she'd have come to him. At very least left word for him, hear his side of things.

He thought about the letter she'd sent him. She'd sounded curt. *"I can't believe you sent that letter,"* it had said. She seemed all too eager to believe he was stupid and careless. She hadn't professed her love, her faith in him.

And when she heard you killed Lawson, that clinched it. He supposed, though, that he couldn't blame her.

Robert fished a nickel from his pocket and gave it to the kid watching Comanche. He stared at the boarding house, teeth clenched. Ellsworth's death had cracked his heart, but Julia's cold dismissal of him shattered it. There was nothing left for him here. Nothing.

He swung up on the horse, his broken ribs protesting, his many bad decisions railing at him inside his head. Cassidy's death, Ellsworth's death, Julia's desertion—they were all his fault. His pa was right. He was worthless. He should've died instead of Cassidy when those thugs beat him up six years ago.

Hearing his name yelled by angry voices across the street, Robert kicked Comanche into a gallop, practically running down the revelers as they jumped out of his way, waving their arms at him and screaming obscenities. But all their curses slid off his back as he rode hard and fast, turning south on 4th Street and leaving the ruckus behind him, the voices thinning into the night until the only sounds were Comanche's hooves pounding dirt and the rhythmic panting of the horse as they fled Laramie and made for the road to Colorado in the dark, hopeless night.

Hearing the more-than-usual commotion outside the jailhouse, Sheriff Carr set his cup of bitter coffee on his desk and strode to the door. The jail was situated on the west side of the courthouse on Grand Avenue, two blocks from the congested strip of brothels and saloons and private gaming houses. Carr dreaded Friday nights. Cowboys and laborers usually collected their week's wages on Fridays, and since the money burned holes in their pockets, they made a concerted effort to spend it as fast and frivolously as possible. And that meant Carr's jail cells would be packed full. Which they were at present.

"What now?" he inquired of O'Grady, who was breathless and stomping his big feet to fling off mud and snow from his boots on the stoop.

"You're not gonna believe it, Sheriff."

Carr looked past his deputy to the surging mass of bodies that moved his way. Like a school of sharks, he thought, surrounding their prey. He craned to make out faces, recognizing the usual rabble, but the level of agitation told Carr something out of the ordinary had captured their interest. Something bigger than the news of Ty Lawson's death.

Had Lester Carson come to town, to settle the score? That would be news indeed. Carr would like nothing more than to give the rich rancher what-for. Why, maybe he'd even taunt him, get him to reach for his gun. A mistake he might not live to regret.

Before O'Grady could say more, the crowd parted like the Red Sea—though a bit more unwieldy, he imagined—and McIntyre marched toward him, a pretty young gal in tow, her hands tied behind her.

The first things he noticed were her ripped and bloodied blouse, her bruised face with a black eye swelling, and her fear-stricken eyes—like those of a calf cornered by wolves.

The next thing he noticed was she was no soiled dove—practically a child. But a beauty, with a delicate kind of face. He didn't recognize her . . . though her features seemed familiar.

The gal's sullen face perked up upon seeing him. She struggled against McIntyre's hold on her arms.

"Let me go!" Her chest heaved as she gasped in long breaths of air.

"Sheriff, she kilt Fes Rollins. Shot him in the chest," O'Grady said, coming up alongside McIntyre.

"Did she now?" Carr couldn't have cared less about Rollins's death. One less piece of scum floating through Carr's streets. The fella'd had it coming for a time, Carr reckoned.

McIntyre smirked. "You don't know who this is?"

Carr narrowed his eyes and studied the gal, then shook his head. "Should I?"

"She's Carson's daughter."

The world felt like it stopped spinning with a jerk. "His daughter? She killed Rollins? Shot him?"

What in heaven's name is Carson's young daughter doing in town on a Friday night . . . ? It only took a few seconds for him to make the connection. Robert Morrison, not an hour earlier, had shot Ty Lawson behind the courthouse. *She came to find her sweetheart.* He chuckled. *But, sorry, darlin', he ran away with his tail atwixt his legs.*

Carr chuckled and got close to the gal's face, close enough to feel the heat coming off her cheeks. What a sweet prize this was—getting Carson's daughter in his clutches. And on a murder charge. He could barely contain his glee. *Wait till Asa hears this.*

"The vile man attacked me —"

"Aw, save it for the judge," O'Grady said with a sneer. He looked at Carr. "Witnesses saw her grab the gun and shoot 'im. Cut-and-dried case, I reckon."

"What do you mean?" she protested, squirming again, trying to get free. "He was about to shoot me!"

"Where d'ya want her?" McIntyre asked Carr.

"Where, indeed?" Carr replied. He could free up a cell for her. *Or throw her in with the drunken cowboys. They'll make short shrift of her.*

While he delighted in the idea of letting Carson's daughter be ravaged by a group of scalawags, there'd be hell to pay for his actions. If he locked her in the jail, Carson would find a way, with his money and influence in town, to force her release. *But he couldn't touch her if she was in the federal pen . . .*

The idea pieced swiftly together. It was no easy matter to release a prisoner of the penitentiary once admitted. It was a federal institution, the US marshal's jurisdiction, and Carson would have to jump through all kinds of hoops to get his little girl out . . . if she lasted long enough to be freed. Who knew what Asa would do with her, just to spite Carson.

"Bring the wagon 'round," he told O'Grady.

His deputy questioned him with his eyes but replied, "Sure thing, Sheriff."

McIntyre held fast to the irate gal.

"When my father finds out what happens, you'll . . . you'll . . ."

"I'll what?" Carr asked, touching her cheek. She squirmed harder, her eyes wild, her breath ragged as she tossed her head violently from side to side.

Bystanders cheered and jeered—a veritable circus. Carr laughed, relishing this moment, knowing how infuriated Carson would be when he heard the news.

Carson's daughter then spit in his face. Stunned, he slapped her cheek hard, eliciting a squeal from her.

"My, she's a feisty critter," McIntyre said. "Contrary to all appearances."

Bodies parted for the arrival of the wagon—a buckboard pulled by an old deaf draft horse who couldn't be flustered by the sounds of pistol shots or rowdy revelers. O'Grady brought the wagon up alongside the jail stoop and stopped.

Carr told McIntyre, "Load 'er up." He watched the gal fight with all she had, but his deputy manhandled her up into the flat bed of the wagon without getting kicked too hard in the shins. McIntyre pulled rope from his coat pocket and tied her ankles together, and she lay like a trussed pig—a purty one—on the splintery wood.

"Where are you taking me?" she demanded. Carr ignored her and climbed up on the bench to relieve O'Grady.

"Keep a watch on the jail, Sean. I'll be back presently—after I make my delivery."

A bowl of bright stars glittered above him as he drove the wagon west out of town, over the bridge, and onto the road leading to the penitentiary, which loomed in its solitary station in the acres of open rangeland. The air was frosty and damp, smelling of water reeds and mud. Bright lights shone from the prison buildings' windows, but he reckoned few brought to the prison found them a comforting sight.

He had no doubt that Carson's daughter would agree.

Julia stared up at the imposing gray-brick building. She knew exactly where the sheriff had taken her, and it stirred fear in her heart something fierce. Why had he brought her here?

Even if the sheriff thought she had committed a crime and deserved punishment, criminals first had to go to jail, be tried and convicted, then charged. This much she knew. But she also knew officials in towns as lawless and rough as Laramie didn't always follow the rules of law.

Her body hurt all over, and her cheek throbbed where the sheriff had slapped her. How dare he hit her? How dare his deputies drag her through town like she was a criminal?

When her father found out what happened to her—what they'd done to her—the sheriff and his cohorts would be arrested. She had no doubt. Whatever chicanery they were up to would be exposed, and they would be punished.

She simmered in her anger, for that was the only way to squelch the memory of shooting that man. She tried to console herself with reason. He'd attacked her. He was about to shoot her. She'd had no choice. She'd been defenseless.

The cold gnawed at her through her clothes, and her teeth chattered. The deputy had let her sit up against the wood slats of the wagon, never taking his lecherous eyes off her. Grievous thoughts of Ty pounded her head, and she prayed the news she'd heard was just a rumor or someone mishearing. Had Robert killed her dear cousin? What if Ty had waylaid him, and Robert shot in self-defense, just as she'd done with that drunken cretin? Could she forgive him?

The travesty of the feud between their families was never more heinous in her eyes than now, in this moment. What should have been a joyous night of wedlock and love had been poisoned by a senseless abiding hatred, the origin of which no one knew and probably no one cared about. But why would fate bring her and Robert together, only to wrest them apart so heartlessly?

The tears that dropped onto her cheeks felt like frozen bits of ice. She watched blankly as the sheriff strode up to the doors of the prison and rang a bell. He was ushered inside by a guard in a gray uniform, and long cold minutes passed before he came back out. With a wave of his hand, he indicated to the deputy sitting across from her to fetch her.

He yanked her to her feet, which sent shooting pains through her limbs, and practically dragged her out of the wagon and toward the front door. A man joined the sheriff and deputy who Julia presumed was the warden—Asa House was his name, and from what Ty had once told her, the man hated her father as much as the sheriff did. Julia didn't know why, but there was plenty of hate going around on all sides. She knew Lester Carson was a man sometimes feared for his wealth and power and influence and could think of many reasons a person might even hate him. Her father was brusque, arrogant, and demanding.

But he loved his only daughter, and Julia knew he would move heaven and earth to get her home safely. *Even if he is furious with me for falling in love with Robert Morrison.*

The thought of Robert renewed her angst. The throbbing ache in her heart was as palpable as the one in her head. The words the sheriff and the warden were exchanging were mere rustles of leaves in her ears. The day's trauma had worn her down to a nub, and she felt herself drifting.

But then, a prison guard took her arm and forcefully pulled her inside, into a dimly lit cold hallway with walls of rough-hewn stone. The sheriff and his deputy departed, and Julia was left facing the warden, whose face beamed with delight the way a child's might upon being given a dollar bill.

"Go fetch that doctor," the warden said to another guard standing by a nearby closed door. The guard nodded and rang a bell on a far wall, and a door was soon opened to him. Warden House glared at Julia, and his regard made her squeamish.

"Welcome, Miss Carson, to the Wyoming Federal Penitentiary. I know our accommodations here are a bit . . . sparse, compared to the luxury you're accustomed to in that fancy ranch house o' yours. But we'll see to it that you're comfortable enough." He chortled and ushered her into a small icy room that had only a desk and two chairs.

"What are you saying?" she asked, panic rising up her throat. She couldn't possibly be kept here, in the prison.

He gave her a grin that felt as cold as a block of ice.

"You can't lock me up!"

"I'm afraid I can do that very thing. If your father objects, he'll have to take it up with the territorial governor—"

"The governor! What about a trial? What about—"

"Miss Carson," he said, drawling her name in a tone dripping with condescension, "you shot an' killed a man. That's a felonious act. Sooner or later, you'd end up here, under my purview. May as well be sooner."

"Why, that's highly unlawful!"

Asa House merely snorted. Footsteps sounded down the hallway and grew louder upon approaching.

Warden House looked long and hard at Julia. "Be best for you if you cooperate. After the doctor examines you, you'll be issued a number and a uniform and be read the rules. Any infraction will land you in solitary confinement . . ."

Julia heard no more. Her mind clamored in denial. Confusion and a malaise of melancholy dragged her under. When her airway closed, she wondered why she even bothered to draw in air. She closed her eyes and prayed to die. She could think of no other remedy to her unbearable situation.

Chapter 19

EXHAUSTION TUGGING AT HIS EYELIDS, Joseph Tuttle sank into the thin mattress of the cot and sighed. Hassie Ethridge slept soundly in the adjacent examination room, with the help of a dose of laudanum. He imagined this night would perhaps afford the poor woman the soundest sleep she'd had in a long time. The thought of her having to resume her heartless prison schedule once her feet were on the mend distressed him greatly. He would enlist Cathryn Povey's help to see if Miss Ethridge could be released or given kinder lodgings in which to serve out the rest of her short sentence.

If only I had seen her on the street begging for alms. A few dollars may have made all the difference. Joseph knew he couldn't rescue everyone. *But you can help someone, anyone. And you should. The Good Book says those who give to the poor lend to the Lord, and He will repay them.* If only more people lived by that Scripture, fewer would end up in dire straits such as these, Joseph believed with all his heart.

He supposed he should gather his things and go home, then arrive early in the morning to check on Hassie. He would instruct the guard stationed outside the infirmary to keep an eye out for any movement on her part, but Joseph doubted she would wake anytime in the night.

As he forced himself to stand on his tired legs, thinking how hungry he was and that a sandwich would be first on his schedule upon being delivered back to his house, he spotted something on the tiny table beside the door. A piece of paper?

No, it was a letter, he realized, once he went over to investigate. A plain envelope, addressed to him care of the penitentiary, in neat script. The postmark was from Greeley.

Apprehension gripped him, and he supposed he was being morbid, though the circumstances he presently found himself in surely contributed to his mood. Was this more bad news? His first correspondence from his prior home — just the postmark detonated a wave of homesickness.

To his relief, his quick perusal of the missive assured him all those he loved were well. But how odd to get a letter from Sarah Banks, the Cheyenne medicine woman he'd briefly met at Logan Foster's ranch, where Brett Hendricks had worked for a time before starting his own ranch south of Evans — with Sarah's help. From the moment Joseph had met Sarah, he knew she had tremendous powers of insight and observation. Some called it Indian medicine. Those around her paid close attention to every word she uttered, and Brett had told him a remarkable story of how she'd given him a horse and then helped him in astonishing ways.

But why would Sarah send a letter to the penitentiary, to Joseph? Just to be friendly? He reread the brief letter. She made mention of her sons, Eli and LeRoy, noting that Eli was busy with his freight company in Fort Collins and that his wife,

209

Clare, was expecting, and then she said something rather enigmatic.

My good doctor, sometimes we are pressed to make a hard choice, indeed. The way through is a dark tunnel, but it is the only way through. When the time comes, be of courage and cling to your faith. For only when all secrets come into the light will true healing take place and long-ingrained weeds of hate can be uprooted and consumed by fire. See that you and those in your care escape unscathed. I will await word.

Joseph stared at the small inked letters for some time, puzzling over them. What in heaven's name was she talking about? Did she foresee a literal fire? In the prison? Whose hate was she speaking about? What secrets?

He let out a sigh. *I suppose I'll have my answers, in time. In the meantime* . . . He grunted at the strange truth of that word: mean time. The times here surely felt mean, and that was the God's honest truth.

Joseph startled at the sound of footsteps pounding the metal stairs. He turned to see a guard arriving at the landing and catching his attention through the window. He waved at Joseph to come out.

Joseph shrugged on his coat and slipped the letter into the inside pocket, thinking the guard had the wagon ready for Joseph's departure. But upon closing the infirmary door behind him, he was told he was needed downstairs to process a new female inmate.

"At this time of night?" Joseph asked as he hurried behind the man who tromped back down the stairs, ignoring the question.

This is highly irregular, Joseph thought, shaking his head and pulling his coat tighter as he descended to the ground floor. The hallway was as cold as a meat freezer. Once the key passed through the rounder's hands, Joseph was led through the door and into the processing room, where, to his utter shock, a young woman—hardly eighteen—was standing shivering, wearing a torn and bloodied blouse, a muddied skirt, and boots. Her hair was a disheveled mess, and her face was smeared with dirt and grime. A black eye was swelling, the tissue around it discolored. Yet, underneath it all, one glance told Joseph this was a young woman of some stature and means. She held herself with a bearing not usually seen in common folk, and, truth be told, Joseph knew the boots she wore cost a pretty penny. He would not be able to afford boots of such quality, which must have been imported from Europe.

"She's been entered into the book," the guard said. "Prisoner number thirty-seven." He gave Joseph a weary, stern look. "Be quick about your examination."

Befuddled, Joseph made to escort the girl out the door and upstairs, but the guard stayed him with his hand.

"No, do it here. She's to be put into her cell without delay. Here is her uniform." The guard nodded at the folded striped shirt and trousers sitting on the desk.

"Without delay? This is not procedure," Joseph said, thinking, *And not humane.* "This woman has injuries. She needs to be examined in the infirmary."

The guard chortled. "Take it up with the warden tomorrow." His eyes dared Joseph to do just that.

Joseph seethed, looking the girl over. She appeared to be teetering into shock, glazed and traumatized. *My poor girl, what has happened to you? Who are you?* Clearly this girl was underage. She had no business being thrown in a prison, any prison, let alone the federal penitentiary. Some serious shenanigans were taking place, and Joseph would waste no time informing Cathryn Povey.

The guard retreated to the corner, but the lurid look on his smug face sent a chill racing across Joseph's neck. It wasn't hard to imagine what the guard was anticipating, as if Joseph would deign to make the poor girl undress and change into her prison garb in front of the man. This was not a brothel show!

Joseph was beside himself with rage, but he forced himself to remain calm, praying for wisdom and a spirit of grace. There was nothing in the tiny room that he could use to clean her face. Perhaps in her cell she would have access to water and a towel. He would insist on that, but he doubted his instructions would be given any attention.

He went up to the girl and spoke quietly, hoping the guard couldn't make out his words.

"What's your name, my dear?"

The girl seemed to respond to the kindness in his voice. Her head turned ever so slightly in his direction, and her eyes found his. They were pools of sadness and despair. His heart went out to her.

He asked again, and she merely replied, "Julia."

He nodded and, after consideration, took off his coat and wrapped it around her shoulders. At very least he could try to warm her in this ice box.

"Hey, you're supposed to be examinin' her, gettin' her undressed," the guard said with a scowl.

"Get out!" Joseph yelled, at his wit's end. *So much for patience and grace.* "Now! I will not examine her with you lurking like a vulture on a tree."

Joseph gulped as the man strode to him, looming tall over him and glaring. But without another word, the guard left and slammed the door behind him. Thankfully, there were no windows through which he could watch. Joseph slumped in relief.

He turned and looked at Julia. "I'm so sorry for the way you've been treated. I will do all I can to help you. Would . . . would you tell me what happened to bring you here tonight?"

A long moment passed. Finally, she said, "I was waiting for my . . . the man I was to marry. Then I heard . . . I heard . . ." She choked up, and tears rushed to her eyes and streamed down her face, making muddy tracks along her cheeks. Joseph's heart went out to her.

"It's all right," he said. "You don't have to speak. Here, you should get into these clothes. At least they're clean." He thought about the warden's words as he handed her the uniform—how he was expected to strip her naked and note any moles or scars, for the record. Well, he was certainly not going to do that, and especially not in this cold room.

He turned his back to her after she'd taken the clothes and waited, hearing the sounds of her slow movements as she complied, wondering how extensive her injuries were.

He asked, staring at the brick wall before him, "How badly are you hurt? Are you in pain?"

To his surprise, she said, "What, pray tell, is your name, Doctor?"

Her voice was so gentle, like an angel's, he imagined. "It's Tuttle. Joseph Tuttle. I've recently arrived from Greeley, Colorado." His nervousness prompted him to ramble, but he reined in the urge to make small talk. This was hardly the place or the situation.

"You may turn around, Dr. Tuttle," she said.

He did. She looked altogether frumpy in the ridiculous striped shirt and pants, but an elegance shone through. He noticed she'd taken off her boots and stood in her stockings. She would be issued shoes.

He asked her some questions, including her shoe size, and noted her answers in the prison log book. She gave her full name as Julia Elizabeth Carson, for the record.

When he was done writing, he put down the quill pen and turned back to her. His voice was soft and entreating. "What happened to you?"

She let out a trembling sigh. "I . . . was attacked. By a drunken man, who tried to ravish me. When I resisted, he pulled out his gun . . ." She swallowed and stared at the floor. "I had no choice. He was going to shoot me. Somehow I . . . I got hold of the gun and . . . and . . ."

She said no more, and Joseph hardly needed her to. He grimaced, thinking how a claim of self-defense might mean little in a lawless town run by heartless and godless men.

"How old are you?" he asked.

"Sixteen."

The breath went out of him. "Oh, heavens," he said. "You have no business being here." He shook his head, trying to make sense out of a senseless situation.

"The sheriff hates my family," she offered, then smirked. "Apparently so does the warden."

"But this is wholly improper. Surely they cannot hold you here," he told her.

"Can you help me?" she pleaded, more tears threatening.

He laid a gentle hand on her shoulder, and she shuddered. "I'll do whatever it takes to get you out of this place," he said, thinking about Hassie and the hopelessness in her eyes. He would do anything to spare this girl such pain. "I'll speak to Mrs. Povey tomorrow. She's an advocate for the women in this prison. I know she'll help, without delay."

The guard banged on the door. "Are ya done in there yet?"

Joseph looked deeply into Julia's eyes. "Be strong. Don't despair." He felt a rush of hope fill him, as if the Spirit had lit his heart afire. "The Lord works in strange ways, my dear. Perhaps . . . perhaps there is a reason you are here, a plan beyond what we can see presently." He thought she'd laugh bitterly at that remark, but instead she regarded him thoughtfully, hope sparking in her eyes.

"I hope you are right, Dr. Tuttle. I do put my trust in God, and I believe meeting Robert was an answer to my heart's prayer. I have to believe He has a plan and will rescue me."

Joseph was encouraged by her profession of faith, but more so—he was entranced by the aura of peace that descended upon her. He would pray for her and seek the Lord's guidance in her case. *The Good Book says some have entertained angels unawares, and so we must show strangers kindness and hospitality. I wouldn't be surprised if this girl were an angel in disguise.*

When the banging resumed at the door, Joseph walked over and opened it. He shot Julia a brief glance, and she nodded. She may have found a measure of peace in her current circumstance, but fear streaked her eyes. What a brave mask she wore.

As the guard roughly grabbed her arm and practically hauled her off to cell block #1, Joseph was more determined than ever to be her champion and rescuer. How? He had no idea other than to enlist Cathryn's help. But, by God, he would help her.

Chapter 20

───────────────────────────

H AD IT REALLY ONLY BEEN two weeks since that night? The night he'd seen Julia on the patio, the festive music and tinkling laughter framing her against a moonlit canopy? The night he'd lost his heart to the gentle soul whose prayer had lifted not only his spirits but his countenance to heaven in awe and wonderment?

Robert had spent every minute since leaving Laramie trying to erase Julia's face from his mind, where it was etched deeply, so deeply that nothing he tried could erase it. His troubled dreams in the abandoned way station had followed him into the early morning clotted with brooding clouds, compounding his loneliness and conviction that he was destined to wander the world without love, without a home.

As he watched the soft edges of Fort Collins form out of the ground fog, he slowed the lathered horse, recalling that Eli Banks operated his freight company from an office on a street called Mulberry—he'd seen the address on the transport receipts. The buildings took on shape and muted color, and

Robert felt more than saw the sun radiating its weak rays above him east of town as the cold collared his damp neck. The abiding pain in his ribs had dulled to a steady ache, but he'd managed to ignore it. A few patches of snow glistened, attesting to a winter dusting that had fallen upon the town over the last few days. Shoppers and travelers plied the main street through the town, and he thought bitterly how he'd hoped to ride into Fort Collins with his bride, buoyed by the joyous prospects of a life with Julia in his arms, forever beside him, the future sparkling and full of promise.

What would he do now? He felt utterly unmoored, drifting, aimless. He needed time to think, to find his way. His entire life had been the Morrison Ranch, working alongside Ellsworth, in the comfort and company of his ma and her tutelage. He looked down at Comanche, thought about Cassidy. That's where it all started—Robert's demise. His was a house of cards stacked to the rafters, and someone had pulled out the bottom card. He had spent six years in a feeble attempt to restack them all, but without Cassidy they'd been precariously balanced at best. It was only inevitable that they had collapsed at the slightest whiff of disturbance.

Was Julia's rejection of him divine retribution for Cassidy's death? Why had he thought he'd ever deserve a stash of happiness?

He stopped Comanche in front of a druggist's and slid off the saddle, sore, achy, and not in the temperament to engage in discourse. He thought maybe he'd be better off securing a hotel room, taking a hot bath, getting a shave. Maybe cleaning up and looking half decent might improve his mood. Then he realized he'd wired money to Eli, and he had none on his person other than a scant few coins in his coat pocket.

He hoped he'd find Eli at his office on a Saturday morning. If not, it was either ask about for directions to his homestead or inquire of the local livery for temporary lodgings for Comanche on credit—though, he didn't dare mention his name, which would, under other circumstances, have assured him of such credit. But now? Robert figured he was a wanted man. Or at least he would be once the Colorado papers got wind of Ty Lawson's death—notwithstanding that the scoundrel had murdered Ellsworth first.

He patted Comanche's neck and checked him over, glad the horse was no worse for wear after galloping so many miles on the muddy rutted road. "I'll rustle you up some hay soon's I can." Then he asked the whereabouts of Eli's office from a couple of fellas coming out of the druggist's, who pointed him in the right direction.

When he spotted the sign in the window and caught a glimpse of Eli's back through the large glass panes, Robert regretted his ragged appearance. But there was naught for it. He swallowed down his pride—what was left of it—and tied his horse to the post outside the door.

Eli saw him through the window and went to open the door. Robert collected his renegade thoughts. His pal greeted him with a bright and cheery demeanor, and he was wearing his usual starched white collared shirt and black trousers—horse buster turned businessman.

"Why, if it ain't Robert Morrison. I got that telegram ya sent. Come in, come in." Eli ushered Robert inside and had him sit in a chair that fronted a small lacquered pine desk. Robert glanced around the tidy office with its stacks of papers and file drawers and paneled walls.

Eli looked Robert over and said, "I wasn't sure when you'd be comin'—ya didn't say." He raked a hand through his wheat-straw hair. Eli kept a neat moustache and side whiskers. "But I have to tell ya, ya look like someone's wrung ya through the ringer."

Robert sighed. He knew Eli wasn't prying; he was concerned. Robert imagined he looked near as bad as he felt.

"Lemme git ya some coffee," Eli said, his voice thoughtful. He went over to a compact woodstove in the corner that gave off waves of wonderful heat and poured coffee from a pot into a cup, then brought it over to Robert. The rich aroma failed to comfort him, and an abiding fatigue smacked him broadside.

"Thank you," Robert said. He hesitated, unsure what to tell this fella who Robert didn't know all that well but respected more than most. "I've gotten into a mess of trouble."

Eli pulled up a chair across from him and settled in to listen. Robert poured out his troubles, for he couldn't hold them back a moment longer. While it felt good to tell someone all he'd been through and how betrayed he felt, embarrassment washed his face with heat.

When he finished, he felt utterly spent. He'd shared with Eli Banks things he never thought he'd tell another fella, but Eli kindly nodded in understanding.

"That's a hard tale ta tell, but I'm glad ya came down here. I'm right sorry for yer troubles. I wish I could put ya up at our house, but Clare's with child, and she's like a banshee in the mornin's. You'd best stay elsewhere," he said with a chuckle. "But I'm sure she'll want ya over for dinner. Oh"—he went over to his desk and pulled open a drawer, then took out a fat envelope—"here's your money." He walked around his desk and handed the envelope to Robert.

"Thanks," Robert said. "I reckon I'll hole up at a hotel for a few days. I'd be glad to meet your wife." Another twinge of sorrow bit at his gut. He should have had Julia at his side, the two gals chatting happily, as wives were wont to do. He squashed the thought.

"I c'n use some help with a big order I'm puttin' together. Shipping goods to St. Louis from some manufacturers in town. That's if ya want somethin' to do to pass the time, maybe take your mind off'a things."

"I'd appreciate that. Glad to help." Weariness hung around his neck like a rope of rocks. Eli must've noticed.

"I'll ride over with ya to the Pioneer Hotel. It's not but a few blocks from here. We'll git ya situated—and your horse—and then mebbe I'll come by around three and take ya home for dinner. Clare'll be right glad for the company and the chance to cook. She practically raised her passel of siblings, bein' the oldest, and she misses cookin' for an army." Eli laughed.

He took a small wooden Closed sign off a shelf and hung it on the door. "Ya ready?" he asked.

Robert stood. "I s'pose." He suddenly missed Ellsworth terribly. He would never hear his pal's laugh or share a whiskey with him, ever again.

Eli patted him on the back. "Things have a way o' workin' out," he said, trying to be encouraging. Robert mustered a halfhearted smile—it was the least he could do in appreciation for Eli's efforts to cheer him.

Sheriff Thomas Jefferson Carr was in a good mood. In fact, he reckoned he hadn't been this happy in a long chalk. Not even his wife's usual nagging this morning had set his teeth on edge. He and Asa had breakfasted at Darla's Café—their regular Saturday morning engagement—where Carr had regaled the warden with the details of last night's arrest of one Julia Carson.

Asa reiterated how tickled he'd been seeing the girl's miserable countenance upon arrival at the penitentiary and being witness to her humiliation. How Lester Carson would boil over when he heard.

"There'll be hell to pay, and then some," he'd warned the warden.

Asa had chortled as he stuffed eggs into his mouth. "Oh yes, indeed."

Carr had wondered anew why Asa was so willing to risk his posting at the prison when there were already so many complaints about the inhumane conditions and treatment of prisoners. With that latest fiasco of that inmate hanging herself in the kitchen, Carr had assumed Asa would have entertained second thoughts about incarcerating the girl. But his desire to hurt Lester Carson apparently outweighed any concern over his employment. It was only then, as he sat watching Asa eating with such gusto, that Carr realized how possessed Asa was with Lester Carson. It smacked of nothing short of payback. But for what?

He'd pondered the matter through breakfast and as he walked back to the jail. He himself wouldn't be immune to the backlash that would be unleashed upon Asa House for imprisoning a minor so unlawfully. No doubt word had already gotten out, and the papers would headline the story. *And don't forget that suffragist—Povey. She'll go straight to the governor and demand he intervene.* Still, it would take time and slogging through the heap of bureaucracy to facilitate the girl's release. Weeks maybe. Weeks of misery for Carson, compounding the misery he had to be suffering over the death of his dearly beloved nephew.

As Carr stood in the doorway, looking out on the street, the agitation and excitement roiling in the citizens of Laramie was palpable. They cut a wide swath of the jail, casting curious and fearful looks at him when they dared glance his way. He reckoned some hated him more than ever, but others held him in higher esteem. The girl had committed murder, and his actions last night showed he was quick to apprehend the culprit, not dissuaded by the girl's name or family status in the town. Whether a body liked or hated Carson, all would have to agree their sheriff had done the right thing. In time, there'd be a trial of sorts. Minors were usually sent to a home for delinquents, and the nearest one that Carr knew of was in Denver. Whether she'd be acquitted or, when of age, sent to a local prison or even back to the penitentiary, that decision would be the purview of the courts.

Though he hadn't expected it so early in the day, Carr was hardly surprised by the arrival of an ornate buggy, driven by an older man in a dark suit who was obviously a servant of a rich man. Before the buggy had even come to a full stop in front of the jail, the carriage door flew open, and out leapt an irate and seething Lester Carson.

Carr straightened as the tall man marched over to him, his face blotched with rage, a long finger waggling at Carr's face. It had been a while since Carr had seen the rich rancher—probably a year, at the least—and never in such proximity. His drawn, lean face was etched deeply with lines that looked like cracks in rock, and Carr couldn't recall the man having such a receding hairline. His wiry gray moustache and goatee made up for the lack of hair atop his head, which was only partly concealed by his wide-brimmed hat.

His deputies promptly exited the jailhouse and flanked Carr, no doubt alerted by the sight of Carson's approach. A glance to their sides showed hands on the butts of their pistols, but Carr didn't expect the rancher to try to shoot him. The man was shrewd and discerning to a fault, and he'd know that shooting the sheriff might delay his effort in getting his daughter back. Carr had the upper hand, and they both knew it.

"Mornin', Lester," Carr said with a bit of joviality.

Carson's face turned a veritable crimson shade, as did his neck. "I heard you arrested my daughter. And you took her to the prison." Every word came out of his mouth laced with poison.

Carr turned to his deputies, whose fingers looked twitchy. He jerked his head toward the jail, indicating for them to go back inside. Though O'Grady questioned Carr with his eyes, he shrugged and complied.

"Did you hear me?" Carson demanded, either unconcerned about the advent of a curious crowd or planning on it. Carr wondered just where the loyalties lay in this crowd. How many of them hated Lester Carson? Carr couldn't say, though he knew that more people feared him than liked him.

"Your daughter shot and killed a man last night."

Carr studied Carson's face and got the impression the man had heard the tale but, up till now, didn't believe it. Maybe he still didn't.

"There were plenty o' witnesses," Carr added evenly.

"Is she over at the prison?"

"Yep."

Carson cursed under his breath. "I want you to get her out. Now!"

Carr shook his head. "Can't do that."

Carson lunged at Carr and clenched his hands around his throat. Carr stepped back, slapped the hands away.

"The upshot of the thing is this," Carr said, pretending to sound sympathetic while putting some distance between them, "the jail was chock-full last night. Hardly the place for a girl . . .

like yours to spend the night. I had no choice but to arrest her. You do understand that."

Carson snorted but kept his hands at his sides. Carr noticed the man's jaw working, teeth clenching.

"I suggest you take up the matter with Schnitger, the marshal—"

"He's all the hell the way over in Cheyenne—!"

"And he's the only one, 'sides the governor, who can get her moved to some other jail."

Carson cursed more, shaking his head so hard, Carr wondered if he'd shake loose his brains. Then he came close and spoke in a harsh whisper, his face strained and as wan as a cadaver's. "You and House—you're in this together. He put you up to this?"

"I don't know what you're implyin'. No one made your daughter shoot that man."

"And what about Morrison—is he in there?" Carson gestured at the jail.

"I'm afraid not. Seems he skipped town, accordin' to witnesses."

"For the love of—" Carson cursed even louder. A few ladies in the street looked shocked and hurried past. Others laughed. Carson turned his head, looking as if he had forgotten where he was, unaware folks were watching the spectacle, ever curious and eager for fresh news to gossip about.

"Are you tendering a reward for his capture?" Carson asked, barely reining in his explosive temper.

"The marshal's office in Cheyenne takes care of that. Do you want to offer a reward?"

Carson chewed on an answer, squinching his eyes. Then he said, "I want Morrison found and hung for what he did—"

"You'll have to take it up with the marshal—"

Carson threw his hat to the ground, veins popping in his neck. He muttered, giving Carr a death stare, "You're a dead man, Carr—you hear me? A dead man. You 'n' the warden both."

He faced off Carr for a long minute, then huffed, swooped up his hat from the boardwalk, and stormed back inside his carriage. Carr watched until the buggy turned the corner and vanished from his sight.

Getting death threats was a regular feature of his job, considering all the scoundrels he locked up in this town. Carson's words didn't ruffle him. But the rancher was rich, and he had a lot of influence. With his sway, Carr just might find himself out of a job. Which wouldn't be so bad, now that he thought about it. He'd more than had it with this town.

Still, he wouldn't put it past Carson to ambush him, or send others to do his dirty work. It might be a smart idea to put his deputies on high alert and pay his little birdies a little extra to keep an eye on Lester Carson. Just in case.

Chapter 21

J ULIA SAT ON HER COT in her tiny claustrophobic cell, her stockinged feet tucked under her to avoid any beetles or rats that might scurry across the rough concrete. She was vaguely aware that morning had broken somewhere on the eastern horizon. The darkness in the bitterly cold cell block had shifted to a gray pallor. Soon a guard would come and bring a bucket of ice-cold water and a hard bar of lye soap so she could wash; they didn't trust the prisoners not to drown themselves while unattended.

Though she'd been incarcerated for two days and three nights, no one had said a word to her other than the guards, and that was only to yell out orders. The prisoners were kept to silence at all times, though the handful of women, clustered together in line and in the dining hall, managed whispered conversations of short exchanges when the guards weren't within earshot. Julia didn't speak to any of them. Not just out of fear of punishment but due to the hardness in their faces. The gloom of imprisonment hung like a shroud over all the prisoners, and the air was charged with misery and a feral restlessness.

But Julia didn't mind the silence. In fact, she preferred it. She filled her waking hours with prayer, clinging to the thin thread of hope from which she dangled, trusting the good doctor to plead her cause and enlist his suffragist friend to prompt a speedy response from the governor. While she gave the appearance of bearing up under the indignity of it all, grateful Dr. Tuttle had managed to argue with the warden against shearing her hair—for the moment—she realized to her shame how cowardly she was. How terrified. This place, these prisoners who glared at her from out of the corner of their mean, hardened eyes, these men who murdered without qualms, godless and heartless . . . with whom she shared these lodgings . . .

She would rather remain locked in her cell, her cage, where she was at least safe from their lustful, leering gazes. Even the female prisoners glowered at her, mean spite in their expressions, as if she were responsible for their plight. Or being afforded special privilege because her hair hadn't been shorn. She would find no sympathy, no comradery here. Oh, how long would she be subjected to this horror? How long could she last? How had her parents reacted when they found out? She wondered wryly if her mother regretted voicing her ultimatum.

In the dark of night, her whimpers joined others'. All the women prisoners' cells were grouped together at the end of this long block, and while the guards strictly enforced silence, Julia could hear the men snickering and whispering, their lewd remarks drifting like demons cackling to her ears late in the night that smothered her in panic.

When she couldn't breathe that first night, trying to yell out for the doctor, one of the guards stood at the steel crosshatch grate that served as the door to her cell and derided her. "The doc's gone home, girlie. You'll git no pamperin' here, so shuddap!"

Somehow she'd managed to convince her throat to release its death grip, but she'd been wheezing ever since. Almost as if she could feel her lungs filling with moisture, she knew in short order she'd succumb to pneumonia, as she had when a child. Maybe it would be a blessing in disguise, for surely such illness would require she be moved into the infirmary and be treated under the doctor's watch-care. Or maybe she'd succumb to the illness and be put out of her misery altogether.

The clanging bell jolted her upright, once again nearly shattering her nerves as well as her eardrums. Six strikes at five thirty to wake the prisoners. Then three more at six, to announce breakfast. Minutes later, a guard brought her the pail of water, unlocked her cell, and set it inside. Her morning ritual was awkward at best as she tried to scrub off the sticky perspiration that her night sweats induced without the guard—who made no attempt to avert his gaze—seeing exposed flesh. She imagined that some of the female prisoners were anything but self-conscious about such things. And maybe, over time, one grew to care little about propriety and modesty.

As she soaked the rag in the icy water and rubbed it against the hard bar of soap, she wondered for the hundredth time why Robert hadn't come for her. She had no way of knowing the truth—had he indeed killed her dear Ty? Her anger simmered over her cousin, knowing how hotheaded and protective he was, which made her even angrier at her father. For it was he who had instilled the hatred for the name of Morrison into Ty's heart. If Robert had killed Ty, it had to have been in self-defense. Robert had no argument with Ty. He was the one who'd expressed hope that their marriage would end the interminable feud. Bring their families together. She laughed bitterly at the irony of it all.

Was Robert sitting in the jail at this moment? If he'd been arrested, would he be taken somewhere? To Cheyenne? Denver? Not knowing his fate was even more torturous than being locked up in this horrible place.

A guard called everyone to come out and get in line. Julia's knees wobbled as she stood. She'd hardly eaten since she'd arrived. The food was abhorrent, and the sight of cockroaches scuttling across the floors and tables in the dining hall turned her stomach.

Stepping out of her cell and following the guard's direction to slip into her place behind one of the other female prisoners, she thought how invisible she was. How her present situation was not all that much different from her previous one. She'd merely changed cages.

When Robert entered the railway office on Riverside Avenue, first thing on that crisp but dry Monday morning, he was ready to work, to take his mind off his troubles. He'd practically slept the whole weekend, succumbing to exhaustion and grief. Now his cracked ribs throbbed, a dull ache in his chest, never letting up, never giving him reprieve. He reckoned it would be years before he'd be free of the guilt and anger and hurt. He didn't want to wear his emotions on his sleeve for all to see, and the best way he knew to ignore them was to bury himself in hard labor. So he was grateful Eli was having him help load crates onto the flat bed of the train car.

But instead of leading him out into the train yard, Eli, upon seeing him walk through the station's door, took him aside, to one of the benches in the spacious waiting lounge. Eli's face was hard to read.

"Ya git enough rest?" Eli asked him as they sat.

Robert nodded, knowing he should try to be cordial. "I enjoyed meeting your wife. She makes a great Irish stew. Thank you. For everything."

Eli waved away the gratitude and said, "Listen, yesterday Clare and I had supper at my ma's—we do every Sunday, weather permittin'—and, well, she gave me somethin'." He reached into his coat pocket and pulled out a small glass jar sealed with a cork.

"What is it?"

Eli chuckled. "Heck if I know. Ma makes all kinds of potions and salves. Special Cheyenne medicine, she said."

"For me?" Robert couldn't figure why Eli was showing this to him. He looked closely at the contents of the bottle—a pale-green liquid, thick as honey or paste, filled to the top.

"No, for Doc Tuttle."

"Who's he?"

"Used to live in Greeley, but he moved to Laramie City. He's the new doc at the federal penitentiary up yonder."

Robert waited for more, but Eli seemed to be puzzling over something. "I don't know the fella," Robert said.

"No, ya probably wouldn't." He pursed his lips. "She wants me to take this jar to him. Personally deliver it, along with a letter she wrote."

Robert still didn't understand why Eli was telling him this. Did he want him to oversee his freight business until he got back? "Why doesn't she just send it by post to the doctor?"

"That's what I asked her. She told me I needed to personally deliver it to him at the prison. And, uh, that ya needed to come with me."

"Me? How does she know about me?" His friend's words baffled him.

Eli shrugged. "I've learned not to ask questions like that."

"I'm not going to Laramie. Not now, probably not ever." What a strange thing for Eli to tell him.

"Well, listen . . . ," Eli said, "it's like this. Ma has a way of *seein'*. She c'n sense things far and wide, and sometimes a body catches her attention. Don't have to be someone she knows. But she'll get a hankerin' to help 'em. It's jus' her Cheyenne way."

"I don't understand," Robert said, feeling a strange discomfort slip over him, like a cold silk sheet.

Eli smiled. "No, I reckon ya don't. But I've learned it's best to heed—"

"No way I'm going back to Laramie. No. Not a chance."

Eli shrugged. "Alright, then." He cleared his throat and put the jar back in his coat pocket. He dropped the matter, leaving Robert to wondering if Eli would go to Laramie anyways, without him.

"Let's git to work, then," Eli said, gesturing Robert to follow him across the waiting area and out to the rail yard—a much nicer, cleaner train depot than Laramie's. A train sat huffing steam on the closest track, facing south. The smell of water vapor tainted with oil and dust filled Robert's nostrils. Men worked on the tracks, loading freight cars, going about their business.

As Robert and Eli walked along the wide planked platform, they came upon a young boy waving a newspaper. Beside him sat bundles of papers neatly stacked. Robert made out the masthead of the *Fort Collins Courier*.

Eli started talking to Robert, but his words were raw noise in Robert's head as his eyes riveted on the headlines beneath the masthead. A pain like a knife stabbed his gut, and he nearly collapsed.

He felt a hand steady him, gripping his forearm. "You alright?" Eli asked, searching his face and then turning to read the headlines on the paper atop the stack beside them.

Robert took the newspaper from the kid's hand, and Eli handed the kid a coin as Robert sank onto a nearby bench, his brain having trouble understanding what he was seeing.

He read the headlines five times. But it wasn't until Eli uttered them aloud that Robert knew what they meant.

"Daughter of prominent Laramie rancher arrested for murder," Eli said, then craned to read the first paragraph as he sat beside him and pulled the paper closer. "Laramie sheriff Thomas Jefferson Carr took into custody Julia Carson, daughter of rancher Lester Carson, who shot and killed Laramie local Fester Rollins early Friday evening . . ." Robert felt Eli's eyes regarding him.

"Julia . . ." Robert's head began to throb. Arrested? It didn't make sense, not at all. Why would Julia have shot a man? Who?

Eli read the article in an undertone, then said, "This is your gal—the one ya thought had ditched ya?"

Robert nodded.

"But she hadn't. By the time ya got to town, seems she'd already been arrested . . . ," Eli said, his tone quiet and thoughtful.

Robert tried to think back to that evening. It felt like reaching back years. He couldn't recall.

"Says here she claimed the fella attacked her, that it was self-defense." He read further, then made a noise that caused Robert to turn and look at Eli.

"What?" Robert asked, not wanting to hear another word but desperately needing something to make sense. Had Julia been attacked on her way to the boarding house? Was that why no one had seen her? Was he wrong about her intentions? Was he? And then his heart berated him further. If he'd been there — if he'd gotten to her sooner . . . *If you hadn't run from the courthouse, gone directly to her, instead . . .*

Eli gave Robert a grave look. "She was taken to the prison."

"Prison? Not the jailhouse?"

Eli read, "Though Miss Carson is only sixteen, authorities admitted her into the Wyoming Territorial Penitentiary late Friday night, where she will await trial for murder." Eli whistled. "Them's some rotten fish. How c'n a local sheriff put a minor in a federal prison?"

Robert knew the answer. He said through gritted teeth, "Carr hates Julia's family. He'd do any slimy thing he could to ruin her pa. This is his doing."

He felt as if someone had grabbed his heart and squeezed the living daylights out of it. *Murder? Julia . . . this wouldn't'a happened if you'd gone straight to her after . . . after Ellsworth . . . Oh, I am fortune's fool!*

He couldn't believe how foolish he'd been. Running away, assuming Julia didn't love him. She did. She'd come to town to marry him. He knew that now, with all his heart. He'd been too quick to judge her. And now . . . she was sitting in a cold prison cell. Every nerve in his body flared as if set afire.

Eli sat in thought a long while, oblivious to the passersby and rail-yard workers coming and going, the clanking and hissing of train cars being coupled filling the rarified air. He then turned to Robert. "We need to ride to Laramie."

Robert started to protest, but then . . . a compulsion seized him. "We've got to get her out."

Eli held his hands up. "Whoa, I don't know 'bout that. Ya can't jus' walk into the federal prison and free her."

"You said you knew the doctor there."

Eli nodded, pondering.

"And that your ma told you to deliver that jar to him—at the prison. She didn't tell you to take it to his house?"

Eli nodded again. "Huh, you're right."

"Look," Robert said, "if I step foot in Laramie, I'll be arrested too. And if I'm in jail, I can't help Julia."

"Then we'll have to be sneaky. No one knows me in Laramie, 'cept you. I don't see why I can't knock on the front door of the federal pen and ask to speak to the good doctor."

Robert let out a long shaky breath. He didn't cotton to the idea of riding back to Laramie. Not without a good plan for saving Julia. It was madness. But Eli was adamant.

"It ain't a coincidence that my ma gave me that jar and the letter to take to Tuttle. I didn't say a word to her at supper 'bout you. But when she handed me that jar, she told me, 'Be sure you take that cowboy with you. The one from Laramie.' She also said somethin' else quite perplexin': 'Trust Tuttle. He'll know what to do.'" Eli shrugged. "My ma's never wrong 'bout things like this."

Robert's head spun. His heart felt ripped in half. He kept picturing Julia in a cold cell, alone, scared, confused. He flashed to the night she'd stopped breathing, when he'd first held her in his arms. She'd never last long in a cold prison cell, with her asthma. *Oh, Julia, what have I done to you?*

He looked at Eli, then at the train cars and the stack of crates waiting to be loaded.

"How soon could we leave?" he asked Eli. He never thought he'd want to go back to Laramie, ever. But now, his feet were itching to get into his stirrups. He yearned for nothing more than to ride hard and fast without delay, to do anything it took to come to Julia's aid.

"Inside of an hour, I reckon," Eli said. "Won't take me but a few minutes to rustle up some help to load them crates. Be right back."

Robert sat on the bench watching Eli stride back into the station, his former numbness replaced by a fierce urgency. What Eli Banks told him made no sense, his ma sending them to this doctor at the prison with a letter and a mysterious bottle. But Robert had no other ideas. All he knew was that Julia was in trouble — trouble because of him, because he'd failed her.

His heart ached so painfully, he could hardly breathe. Julia's dire situation tore at him. Going back to Laramie was madness, but there was naught for it. Julia needed him.

He would not fail her again.

Chapter 22

JOSEPH HAD THOUGHT THAT BY now he wouldn't feel so ruffled in Cathryn Povey's presence, seeing how this was their fourth meeting to date—if one counted the evening he'd arrived in Laramie. Yet, when she stepped down from her buggy and joined him in front of the steps to the courthouse, his breath hitched and his palms grew instantly sweaty.

He doffed his hat and wished her a good morning, and she politely returned the greeting. Though he barely knew her, he could tell she was greatly bothered by something, and Joseph, if he were a betting man—and he was most certainly not—would have laid heavy odds on the chance that her preoccupied mood was due to Julia Carson's unlawful incarceration. It was Cathryn who had summoned him—not the other way around—early Saturday afternoon, asking if he would meet her promptly at nine at the courthouse. Perhaps she needed his help, to attest to Julia's admittance into the penitentiary and her condition and subsequent treatment. Perhaps Cathryn planned to demand action of someone in this impressive two-story brick edifice.

Cathryn looked lovely, as usual, on this unseasonably mild Tuesday morning. Every lustrous red hair in place. A smart dark wool skirt that modestly accentuated her curves. A frilly-collared blouse peeking out from under the matching jacket. Rather than clutching a purse, she carried a large carpetbag. *No doubt full of legal papers.*

She wasted little time and began explaining her mission as they entered the drafty building that smelled of smoke soot and cleaning solution. An old man slumped over a mop as he swished the wet strings over the highly polished marble floor. Joseph's shoes clacked noisily as they traversed a long foyer with walls filled with survey maps in glass cases and stopped at a cherrywood desk manned by a portly uniformed officer.

Cathryn spoke briefly to the man, who then gestured them down the hallway. They passed two courtrooms, then stopped at a door that had written on the frosted glass panel "Judge Winston Chalmers."

"We've a few minutes yet," Cathryn said, motioning to a simple dark-stained pine bench set against the wall that Joseph only now noticed. He'd hardly been able to wrest his eyes from her appealing figure as she strode confidently ahead of him.

He cleared his throat and swallowed, sitting down and allowing room for her to join him as close or as far away as she chose. He was surprised that she sat mere inches from him, which detonated a bout of nervousness that prompted him to fidget with his fingers the way he used to in medical school while awaiting some professor to randomly call on him for an answer to a tricky question.

"When we meet with the judge, I will ask you to render an account of your time at the prison Friday last, regarding Miss Julia Carson's admittance." Cathryn did not try to mask the ire — no, it was surely outrage — in her voice. Cathryn searched his eyes. "I trust you examined her. Was she harmed in any way?"

Joseph drew in a long breath. "She'd been hit in the face, and had minor abrasions due to the ... scuffle with the man she'd shot—"

"My dear doctor, please do not say anything at all about her actions. Though it is no doubt common knowledge that Miss Carson shot a man in self-defense, we don't want to influence the judge prejudicially in any way."

Joseph blinked. He didn't realize he would need to censor his words. "I understand." He continued after a moment. "I did ask Miss Carson about her injuries, and she assured me they weren't serious."

"I'd like to hear everything she told you." Cathryn settled back against the gray brick wall, and Joseph recounted all he could remember. Her eyes began to glisten with encroaching tears as he told of Julia's courage and her inspiring faith.

Cathryn's shoulders slumped, but only momentarily. Joseph watched resolve brighten her countenance like the sudden flare of a flame igniting dry kindling. "I don't need to tell you what a travesty this is. We must get this judge to issue an immediate release of Miss Carson in this mistrial of justice. Short of that, to have her transferred to a safe women's facility this very day." She stiffened and stared up at the large looming windows letting in the hazy morning light. Joseph wasn't sure if she was thinking or praying. She turned her face to him.

"Being new to this town, I'm sure you're unaware of the prominence of Miss Carson's family. Lester Carson owns the largest cattle ranch in Wyoming Territory, and it's no secret that Sheriff Jefferson Carr holds vicious animosity toward Carson. No doubt this is why he deposited the daughter at the federal penitentiary—to aggrieve the child's father. And no doubt, Mr.

Carson will be pressing charges and attempt to force the sheriff's dismissal. But all that takes time."

Cathryn's brows knitted, her lips pinched. "Considering the current conditions at that deplorable place, I worry for the girl's safety and health. I understand she has severe asthma—did she mention that to you?"

Joseph shook his head.

"I want you to have her declared in ill health, in no condition to do manual labor. You must have her brought to you daily, to the infirmary—"

"I don't know if that will be—"

Cathyn's expression brooked no excuses. "We will ensure it will be included in the legal paperwork issued by Judge Chalmers, and if he refuses, I'll go directly to the federal district court in Cheyenne. And all medicines needed to care for her health in the interim will be amply provided without reservation. Though, I am hoping that my persuasive argument will facilitate her immediate release." She huffed in consternation, then the door opened and a rail-thin clerk with a complementary thin moustache gestured them inside.

"Judge Chalmers will see you now."

Cathryn whispered to Joseph. "Just follow my lead, answer any questions asked of you in a concise manner, and don't let the judge lure you off track." She added even quieter, "Which he is wont to do. Especially don't indulge him in his hunting stories. We are here to secure a helpless girl's release."

Joseph was inclined to salute but knew his attempt at humor would not be appreciated. He merely nodded and followed her into the judge's chambers, happy to let her take the lead in this and in all matters in this cause. She was—to put it simply—breathtakingly magnificent.

Two hours later, Joseph made his way to the diner catty-corner to the courthouse. Upon exiting the judge's chambers, Cathryn hurried off to other missions demanding her time. She'd kept her composure as the judge made sundry excuses regarding the requested release, eventually mollifying her with promises to set those big, heavy government wheels in motion. He'd have to discuss the matter with the marshal, he'd claimed. Joseph could tell Cathryn believed he was prevaricating, but, all charm and persuasion, she appealed to his sentiments as a father of three young daughters. Surely if his innocent and vulnerable girls were subjected to such atrocious treatment . . .

Joseph thought admirably on Cathryn's dogged determination to see justice done. He hardly recalled sitting in his chair at the diner or ordering his lunch. Only when harsh words with hard edges drifted to his ears did he pull out of his reverie over Mrs. Povey and listen.

It was the name of Carson that poked him, spoken by a man the next table over. Joseph threw a quick glance at the two men and then returned to his gazing out the window, sipping his black tea while waiting for his food.

He listened carefully, curious about the musings of this slipshod man with a grizzled beard and Irish accent. He kept his astonishment buried as he heard tell an intriguing account of a feud between Lester Carson and a man named Stephen Morrison. The way the Irishman slurred his words gave Joseph the distinct impression that the glass of beer the man drank from was hardly his first of the hour. The man across from him—an even older and crustier sort—chortled in spurts and gave fuel to the other man's storytelling with encouraging gestures and nods of the head. Joseph shifted so he could watch their exchange out of the corner of his eye.

"All because of a card game, I tell ya. House had lost his ranch, and rumor had it back then that Carson cheated. All that land"—he tsked and shook his head—"Poof, gone!"

"Ya don't say?" the other fella said, awestruck. "That's how Carson got so rich? He won the warden's ranch in a poker game?"

"Thasss right," the Irishman said, upending his beer and looking around for the waiter, waving the empty glass.

"No wonder the sheriff carted the gal off to the prison. Them two's in cahoots."

"Aye. 'Tis th' God's honest truth." The Irishman nodded emphatically, then finally got the waiter's attention, signaling for another beer.

Then he leaned in close to his pal. "Here's the thing not a body knows." He grinned at his secret. "Morrison was in that card game too. I was there. I seen it. 'Twas in the back room of Billy Bacon's saloon. 'Twas a Saturday night, deep into winter, snow pilin' up outside. Ever'one drunk, holed up till the weather passed. They'd been playin' cards for days, and tempers were testy. 'Twas back in the day afore I started workin' for Carson. When he and Morrison were House's punchers. I was bartendin' at Billy's, so's I saw what went on."

"Go on," the older man urged, soaking in the story the way hardpan soaked in the first winter rain.

"Morrison was dealin' the cards. Asa House had run out o' cash. He was drunk and festerin' over losin'. And Morrison had the look o' the Devil in him. It weren't no secret—Carson had stole his gal, and I heard tell not a week prior that they'd flipped a coin for her—"

The old man laughed uproariously. "Flipped a coin? Don't that beat all!"

"Aye. 'Tis th' God's honest truth. The whole game, Morrison was broodin', and you could see it—those wheels turnin' in his head. He had a smooth way with the cards—like one of those riverboat dealers." He leaned in close, as if to tell a great secret, but instead of whispering, he nearly bellowed in his friend's ear. "Carson kept proddin' House into goin' all in—the rancher an ace up and one in th' pocket—I snuck around to git me a glimpse—and Morrison, sittin' there all smug—he'd folded his hand right off—waitin' for House to make the next move, shufflin' the cards and keepin' his eye on House . . . well, it didn't git past me, no siree. Carson had a pair o' sixes, an' when he tossed out t' three cards, no one—that is, no one but meself— saw Morrison pull cards from the middle o' the deck. Mind ye, not the bottom, the way most chiselers fancy. Morrison was crafty, 'n' 'twere no surprise t' me when Carson, hardly able to contain his astonishment at his good luck, threw all his chips in. When House traded in his three, his eyes gave that quick little sparkle, for he reckoned his three aces had Carson beat. When Carson raised the bet, House didn't but hesitate a second afore puttin' up his ranch against the big ol' stack of chips Carson had."

"What did Carson have?" the other asked, so riveted by the tale, Joseph imagined not even a crowbar could pry the old man from his seat.

The Irishman chortled. Before the waiter could set down the new glass of beer, his customer swooped it out of his hand and took a long swallow, then wiped his foamy moustache with his sleeve. He scowled at the young man, waving him away with quick flicks of his hand, then turned back to his captivated listener. "Carson laid down 'is cards, nice 'n' slow, House scowlin' at first, as if he were confounded, then furious as he realized he'd been beaten by a full house — sixes over twos.

"House lunged across the table and grabbed Carson by the throat, all the while there's Morrison sittin' all calm and grinnin', mebbe hopin' House would kill Carson, for the rancher was sure Carson had hoodwinked 'im, and Carson was laughin', tellin' House what a fool he was to bet his ranch and sayin' how he'd better git 'im the deed afore the day was out, remindin' House that ever'one in the room was a witness to what had transpired."

The older man frowned. "You sayin' this was all Morrison's doin'? To git back at Carson for stealin' his gal?" He whistled and seemed to recall he, too, had a beer — nearly untouched — on the table. He took a long draw, all the while shaking his head and holding back his laughter. Finally, he spoke. "Well, don't that take all!"

The Irishman guffawed and slapped the table. "Aye, 'Twas Carson that took all! The puncher yanked the ranch right out from under the rancher!"

"No wonder House hates Carson so much." The older man's brows furrowed. "But why didn't Morrison cheat so's he'd get the ranch hisself?"

The Irishman flicked his hand again. "Morrison had family money — he didn't want House's ranch. He wanted Carson dead. Or, at the least, to make the fella's life miserable. Ever'one knew 'bout House's mean temper. Mebbe Morrison figgered 'twere jes a matter o' time afore House killed 'im. Truth be told, I'm s'prised he ain't done it yet."

"But now the warden has Carson's little bird locked up nice and tight, under his wing. Ooh boy, the lid's gonna fly off this pot."

"Aye. That's the God's honest truth, and then some."

Joseph startled when the waiter set down his sandwich and slaw—he'd been listening so hard, he'd forgotten why he was here. He nodded thanks to the waiter, then chewed his food thoughtfully, thinking about Julia sitting in a cold cell and Cathryn's urgent pressing of the judge to release her. If what the Irishman said was true, time was of the essence. With an enemy like Asa House determining her fate, her life could be in dire peril.

He gulped down his food, hardly tasting it, then after laying a few coins on the table, headed out the door to hail a buggy to take him over the bridge to the penitentiary posthaste. A cloud of doom swirled around his head, growing dark and ominous as a presentiment of danger of epic proportion gripped his gut. He was sure it was no coincidence he'd overheard that story; it was divine providence. The Good Lord had charged him with a task—a crusade, as it were—and he no longer wondered if he had done the right thing by taking this job in this lawless town.

Julia was in grave danger—this he knew in the depths of his soul—and it was up to him, with the Lord's help, to get her to safety. How? He had no idea. But one thing he did know to be true without a doubt—the Lord always made a way, and Joseph would rely not on his own wits and strength but the Lord's.

He just hoped it wouldn't involve guns and a lot of bloodshed and violence.

Chapter 23

THEY HAD JOURNEYED AT A steady pace so as not to tire out their horses. Eli had reasoned that it would be best to reach the prison after dark, when the chances of anyone spotting and recognizing Robert would be slim. Robert knew of a sandbank where they could cross the Laramie River miles before town so they wouldn't have to ride through the street fronting the train depot to get to the bridge that led to the prison. By the time they'd gotten to that shallow river bar by way of an old stage road due west through the foothills, the sun was setting on what Robert would have considered a glorious fall day at another time in his life. But not today. Today was a day full of worry and trepidation as they rode mostly in silence, Robert's thoughts only on Julia trapped in the prison and thinking how he'd abandoned her.

Determined not to let his guilt and despondency get the better of him, he kept a litany running through his head. *Hold on, Julia. I'm comin' for you. I love you, and I will get you out, come hell or high water.*

Robert didn't know what Julia would say to him when she saw him — and he was determined to find a way to see her, with the help of the doctor — but he held fast to his conviction that they were destined to be together. The kind of love that sparked between him and Julia just wasn't your ordinary type. They'd both recognized the hand of fate on their lives, with nary a doubt. How could he now deny it? He couldn't let the forces trying to tear them apart succeed. It would take a miracle — no two ways about it. So he prayed, putting the matter in the Lord's capable hands, realizing he had to truly surrender, for the situation was akin to the Israelites facing the Red Sea, hemmed in with waters in front and a pursuing army behind. His faith had never been so sorely tried, but he reckoned a body didn't know the depth of his faith until it was stretched to the limit.

These thoughts and more were churning in Robert's head as they forded the cold water that riffled around their horses' legs and clambered up the western bank. A deer trail cut through patches of quaking aspens that were still in full golden array, their leaves jangling like coins in the soft evening breeze. A peach-colored sky set the backdrop as they rode in single file, Robert leading, the pervading scent of river mud and damp grass tickling his nostrils. His ribs ached, but he hardly felt the pain anymore.

"We'd best hurry it up," Robert called back to Eli, aware the half-moon wouldn't rise till well after dark, and in the gloaming light they'd be struggling to make their way without misstep or wandering off on a side trail. Brush grew thick trailside, and the horses were tired and hungry, though Robert knew that they'd keep on without complaining. Not a few hours earlier, he and Eli had dismounted, stripped the horses' saddles, and let them graze in a grassy meadow for a spell.

Just when Robert thought he'd have to slip off Comanche and lead the way on foot, craning to see the path in the creeping shadows, the woods opened up to the expansive plains of the Front Range a mile south of the prison. In the faint light seeping from the town and the gleam of moon now peeking over the eastern horizon, the penitentiary cast a lonely, solitary figure rising from terrain flat and obscure and resembling some foreign land that had yet to be discovered.

Eli came up alongside Robert, and they sat their horses and looked across the bleak plains. Ground owls hooted in their hidey-holes, and the *shush* of the river to the east cast a peaceful net over the quiet night. It was in moments like this that Robert found the evil in the heart of men so incongruous. Not a mile away, scoundrels were cheating, fighting, and sinning in ways hard to reconcile with the stark and peaceful beauty of the natural world in harmony at this moment.

Robert sighed and turned to Eli. "What if the doctor isn't at the prison?" He didn't cotton to the idea of wandering the town looking for his house.

Eli shrugged, then after a moment of contemplation said, "Let's find out."

His heart pounding, Robert glanced about as they walked their horses to the outer walls of the prison buildings, then slipped from their saddles to the hard-packed ground.

"Best you wait over yonder," Eli said, pointing to a rickety outbuilding made of old wood planks in contrast to the sandstone brick of the prison.

Robert complied and stood at the ready, tucked back in the shadows, as Eli strode to the front door, leading his horse with a loose rein. Only a few seconds after Eli rang the bell, the door on the right opened. Robert couldn't hear more than the murmur of voices and see a partial silhouette of the portly guard blocking the entrance. When the guard retreated into the prison and Eli remained in his place, Robert guessed that Dr. Tuttle was indeed inside.

The thought filled Robert with equal parts of anxiety and hope. What if someone recognized him? He huffed, feeling like a rat marching into a roomful of hungry cats. Would he get to see Julia after all? It was the dream of his heart, yet . . . seeing her here, in this dreary, oppressive place . . . would his heart be able to take it? How would he manage to let her go, to leave her, once he had her in his arms again?

Again, he had to trust that all things would work out, that justice would prevail. He was more than ready and willing to face the consequences of his crimes, but he'd shot Ty after the scoundrel had killed Ellsworth. He'd had no intention of killing Ty Lawson. Still, he would willingly entrust his fate to a jury of his peers, if it came to that.

But in Julia's case . . . Robert could only imagine how the deck was stacked against her. Not just being a woman but being the daughter of Lester Carson, a man Sheriff Carr hated. She'd already been deprived of her rights, and justice had been perverted to an extreme degree. Would this doctor agree? Would he help? Robert got the impression that Eli held the fella in high regard. Eli's ma had said to trust Tuttle; he would know what to do. Robert was inclined to believe those words, but would the good doctor muster up the courage that might be needed when the time came? Would he be willing to risk his position, even break the law, should it come to that?

Robert reckoned he would find out.

A man exited the prison and walked over to Eli. Short in stature, wearing dark trousers and a long overcoat and bowler hat, he strode up to Eli and the two shook hands. Even from where Robert stood, the deep affection between them was apparent.

Eli stood, reins in his hand, as they talked in tones too quiet for Robert to hear. They then walked a ways from the prison, across the yard, where they stopped and signaled Robert to join them—no doubt wanting to speak in confidence without being overheard.

Nervously, Robert kept his head down, glad for the night's dark cover, and went over to them. Eli introduced Robert to Dr. Tuttle.

"Morrison?" Tuttle asked, his face suddenly clouding over. "You're Stephen Morrison's son?"

Robert nodded, a shiver of worry crawling up his spine. The doctor had probably heard the rumors saying how he'd killed Lawson.

But Tuttle then proffered his hand and shook it, studying him in all seriousness. The doctor had an honest face, sincere green eyes. It gave Robert a measure of hope.

Robert couldn't help himself. "How is she, Doc? Julia."

By Tuttle's reaction, Robert knew that the doctor had been apprised of Robert's feelings for Julia. Whether informed by Eli just now or by a confession from Julia, Robert didn't know, nor did it matter.

Tuttle's face was grim. "She's bearing up, but I fear the harsh conditions in the prison are taking a toll on her health. However," he added quickly, as if to reassure Robert, "I am championing her cause and ensuring she is withheld from hard labor. I am monitoring her health and keeping her asthma in check. In fact, she's in the infirmary at the present moment. I . . . insisted to the warden that if she succumbed to an attack at night and wasn't treated immediately, she could die, and her death would be on his hands." He cleared his throat and amended,

"Though, I did not say so in those exact words. I'd probably be out of a job if I had." He gave a forced smile, a clear attempt at softening the seriousness of the situation and adding a bit of levity.

His smile quickly retreated. "I don't know how long I can protect her in this manner. The warden conceded momentarily, but it's clear he is vindictive and has something diabolical up his sleeve." He looked at Eli with a puzzled expression.

"You said your mother sent you to see me." He blew out a breath. "That gives me great pause. Why, pray tell, did she do that? Does this have something to do with Julia? Does she know Julia?" He looked at Robert, who shrugged, then turned back to Eli.

"No sir," Eli replied. "At least, she didn't say nothin' 'bout any gal in the prison." He reached into his coat pocket and withdrew the sealed letter and the glass vial, then handed them to Tuttle, who took them, squinting in the scant light, brows furrowed.

"I have a bad feeling about this . . ." he mumbled, sweat pebbling his brow.

Eli's face showed an understanding and maybe even commiseration. Robert's gut churned. He felt exposed standing in the open field, and his feet were twitchy.

"C'n you take us inside?" Eli asked, tipping his head at the looming edifice.

"I . . . I don't rightly know," Tuttle said. "So long as you submit to a search and don't bring in any weapons, I imagine the guards would agree. Though . . . what explanation could I give them for your entry into the prison at such a late hour? You don't look as if you're on official business . . ."

"No, I reckon not," Eli said, taking stock of his attire. "How 'bout family matters? Tell 'em it's an emergency?"

Tuttle chewed his lip. "Well, there'd be truth in that tale."

"But wouldn't the warden just give ya leave—rather than allow your visitors to come inside?" Robert asked.

"I've already made it clear to the warden that I won't leave Julia Carson unattended. The guards know that." His strained expression relaxed. "Wait here. The guard that's on duty at the entrance is a reasonable sort. He might just comply without asking too many questions." Tuttle started to walk away, then turned and said directly to Robert, "When you write your name in the logbook, best you don't use the name Morrison."

Robert supposed that went without saying. He would use his mother's surname instead.

"May as well tie your horses to that hitching post"—Tuttle pointed to the rail just outside an adjacent building—"and leave your firearms and anything sharp you may have on your person."

Robert and Eli followed his instructions, then accompanied the doctor in through the door of the prison.

The damp, cold entryway sent a chill across Robert's neck. Closed doors met them on three sides, and a stale, acrid scent met Robert's nose. A lit oil lantern was cemented to the wall, casting a sickly yellow light on their faces and clothes. Eli glanced around, shaking his head. He said under his breath, "I hope I never end up in a place like this."

Robert couldn't agree more. His thoughts mired in his head as Tuttle spoke quietly with the guard, who proceeded to search the unexpected visitors—patting their clothes from collar to boot—then had them sign the large open book resting on a table in the claustrophobic space. To Robert's surprise, the prison was deathly quiet except for the barely perceptible groan of steam pipes somewhere in the building.

Robert thought it odd that the guard didn't ask them any questions. He merely looked them over with an appraising eye, then rang a bell next to one of the doors. The clanging jarred Robert's ears as the sharp sound ricocheted off the walls. He wondered if the noise would wake the prisoners or cause the warden to come out of his quarters.

To Robert's relief, something was slipped through a slot in the wall—a key, he saw—which the guard then inserted into the door's keyhole. With a click, the metal door opened, and Eli exchanged looks with Robert. The two fell in step behind the doctor and the guard as they traversed lamp-lit hallways and large open areas to arrive at a set of stairs.

A glance across the room showed the cell block in subdued haze. Robert made out the cells, which seemed unbearably small and were fronted by grated metal doors. The stench of men who rarely bathed and who sweat through their troubled dreams permeated the prison, and the sounds of their snores and grumblings and tossing on their cots unsettled Robert with a nightmare quality. Fear clutched his throat as he considered the prospect that he might very well end up in this godforsaken place. He imagined at any moment the warden would appear and grab him by the collar, exposing Robert's foolhardy decision to tempt fate by entering the rattlesnake's lair.

But it was too late to back out. He kept his head down, eyes forward, and arms clamped against his sides as he climbed the stairs, listening to the clacking of four pairs of boots on the metal steps. He kept reminding himself what was at stake, that this was worth the risk, if only he'd be granted a scant few minutes with his beloved.

"Wait out here," Tuttle instructed to Robert and Eli as the guard unlocked the door that read "Infirmary" at the top of the staircase and stepped to the side and positioned himself a few feet away, looking sleepy and bored.

The minute that passed felt like an hour to Robert, and he wished the heavy curtains weren't closed over the windows. Julia was only a few steps away, but in that long moment of waiting, she seemed unbearably out of reach—a galaxy away.

Eli stood quiet at his side, his eyes closed and his mouth moving, as if praying. Robert wondered if his half-breed pal prayed to the Christian God or to the Great Spirit of his Cheyenne ancestors—though Robert didn't know what the Cheyenne called the Creator. He imagined it didn't matter a lick, in the bigger scheme. He only hoped that the divine hand now upon him would show him favor and grant Robert his most fervent prayer—that he would somehow be united with Julia and she'd be set free. But standing here, inside the penitentiary with its impenetrable hard walls and metal doors, Robert knew it would take a miracle indeed.

Chapter 24

JULIA STARTLED AWAKE. WHEN SHE opened her eyes, she saw the doctor bent over her, whispering her name. He'd lit the lamp, and the light flickered across his features, but she couldn't tell if he was alarmed or if the light was casting imprecise shadows on his eyes.

"Julia, I'm sorry to wake you, but there is someone here to see you." He looked about the room, then fetched a white shirt of his from a drawer. "Here, put this on over your nightshirt."

"What's wrong?" She hadn't detected any panic in the doctor's voice, so she didn't imagine this was an emergency. She shook sleep from her head. Why would someone want to see her in the night? Her chest shuddered. The sheriff? Did he plan to steal her away under cover of darkness? Kill her? Fear clicked like a switch in her head, making her throat thicken and swell, narrowing the pathway for the precious air she needed.

She shrugged the shirt over her plaited hair, which lay mussed over her shoulders.

"I wish there was time to allow you to make yourself more presentable," the doctor said, urging her to her feet.

"Who is here?" she asked. "Please . . ." She implored the good doctor with her eyes, but he merely handed her her slippers and gave her a smile.

"Has my father come?" She worked to roll up the long sleeves that had swallowed her hands. Dr. Tuttle's expression caused hope to surge through her limbs and loosened the tightness in her chest. Maybe her father had used his money and influence to procure her release. Or maybe it was the woman the doctor had told her about—Cathryn someone.

Oh, would that it were true—that she could leave this horrible place. She clung to a thread of hope as the doctor went to the door and knocked for the guard to unlock it.

Julia stood, smoothing down her hair, feeling ridiculous in the doctor's shirt with shirttails that hung to her thighs but grateful for his concern regarding her modesty.

The key turned in the lock, and the door opened. Dr. Tuttle stepped aside and gestured someone to enter, then walked out of the infirmary. A man promptly entered.

Julia's knees melted to water. Her mouth dropped open, but nothing came out. It couldn't be. No . . . How . . . ?

"Robert . . . ?"

It was Robert! She stared at him—taking in his stature and bearing, his handsome features, his winsome smile. He stopped and froze, his gaze riveted on her face as if seeing an apparition.

"Julia. Oh, Julia . . ."

In the soft lamplight, the tears glistened as they filled his eyes and dribbled down his face. In a fraction of a second, she read everything on his face. His visage was a mix of despair, relief, joy, and apology. She knew all he was thinking, all he longed to say, all he yearned for, but not a word was spoken and none was needed. The love spilling from his eyes was fraught with fear of judgment, of rejection, of the need for her to forgive. The need to explain.

But Julia needed no explanation. Robert was here. He'd found a way to come to her. He hadn't abandoned her.

She flew into his arms—arms that gathered her up and enwrapped her in warmth and love and tenderness. Her own tears joined his as they held each other tight, so tight she knew he longed to never let her go.

And then his lips found hers. Julia swooned with joy as her love for him rushed like a roaring river, pouring into his soul, and he drank her in as if he could never be filled, never have enough of her. His lips, hot and wet, kissed hers over and over, across her cheeks, behind her ears, his tongue greedily exploring her mouth.

Their moans merged and swelled as they pressed tighter, Julia wishing their bodies could melt together in this soul's passionate fire, her body enflamed but wanting to burn in this delicious heat for eternity—not hell's fire but a paradise she never imagined she would know.

"Julia, Julia . . ." Robert groaned as he left searing kisses on her neck, her name a prayer on his lips that sank deep into her soul.

She felt utterly weak, glad he was holding her close, feeling like a fluttering bird falling wingless from a high tree. All her questions he smothered with his love—a love that comforted and reassured, filled with promises.

Julia pulled away, needing a deep breath. She was winded, as if she'd run miles across the prairie, and Robert's concern washed over her as he stroked her face and head.

He drank her in. "I thought I'd never see you again."

Ty's face intruded in her mind. "Tell me. What happened . . . that afternoon?"

She didn't have to elaborate. Robert's face was streaked with pain, for clearly the events of that fateful day had distressed him as much as they had Julia.

"I didn't kill your cousin, Julia." He raked a hand over his tear-filled eyes. "I swear it. He . . . he killed Ellsworth, my best friend. And I . . . I . . ." He hung his head, and his arms dropped to his sides. The sudden absence of his warmth sent a shock of emptiness across Julia's frame.

She took his hands in hers. "Ty was looking for trouble," she said, wishing once more that Ty hadn't been so hotheaded, so protective of her. But she couldn't blame him. Just as she couldn't blame Robert.

"I think Sheriff Carr killed Ty," Robert said. "He must've. My cousin Benjamin was there after I rode away, half out o' my mind with shock. He said Carr told him to go, that he'd take care o' Ty."

The sheriff killed her sweet cousin? She didn't doubt it, and the thought of his heartless cruelty burned like hot coals.

He shook his head sadly. "You know how much the sheriff hates your family . . ." He looked deep into her eyes, searching for something, she thought. Maybe for her to believe him. To trust him.

She nodded.

"I did shoot him," Robert said solemnly. "And I regret it, to my everlasting shame. But at the time, I thought I'd had no choice. He would'a shot me. I only wounded him. So I could get away . . . get to you . . ."

His voice choked, and Julia pulled him close. He rested his chin on her shoulder, his strong arms encircling her, great sobs racking his body.

"Oh, Robert. What are we going to do? Surely if anyone sees you, you'll be arrested."

"I'll have to lay low. But I'll get you out. Somehow, some way—"

The door opened, and Dr. Tuttle stepped inside. Julia's heart clenched at the sight of his stricken face.

Robert saw it too. "What's wrong, Doc?" He looked about to run. "Is there trouble comin'?"

Another man entered, and the door was locked behind him—the guard must have let them in, Julia reasoned. He also looked worried. Julia figured him about twenty-five—strong and muscular, boyish features and blond-brown hair, a tawny complexion.

"This here's Eli Banks," Robert said. "A friend from Fort Collins."

Eli gave her a nod of acknowledgment but said nothing, his face grim.

"There is a way to get you out, Julia," the doctor said, briefly glancing at Eli, as if he was the originator of the plan. He let out a long shaky breath, then swallowed.

"What way?" Robert asked, holding Julia tight, his arm around her shoulder, his free hand stroking her hair.

The doctor turned to Eli. "I don't like this. Not one bit." He pursed his lips and closed his eyes. After a moment, he sighed. "But I trust your mother. And if she says this is the only way, then . . ."

Julia looked at Eli. "Your mother?"

"She's a Cheyenne medicine woman," Eli said with a barely noticeable shrug.

Now Julia saw the Indian in him—in his cheekbones and forehead. She knew little about the Cheyenne—mostly that they'd ranged over all of Wyoming before being killed off or rounded up and sent off to Oklahoma. They weren't the Indian tribe that had killed General Custer at Little Big Horn in the summer.

"There's no time for long explanations," Dr. Tuttle said to Julia and Robert. "You're just going to have to trust me."

Julia did trust the doctor. He'd been looking out for her since the moment she arrived at the prison. She knew he was an honorable man. But would Robert trust him?

She looked up into Robert's face. He was listening intently, still stroking her hair, soothing her the way he had the night they'd met, when he held her in his arms for the first time. Oh, to stay in his arms like this . . .

"What do you need us to do?" Robert asked. His friend stood quietly, eyeing the door as if expecting the warden to burst in on them at any moment. Julia pushed down her worry. If Robert was caught in here . . .

"You know where the mortuary is on Front Street?" the doctor asked Robert, who nodded. "Tomorrow night, meet me there--come in the back entrance. At midnight. I'll bring Julia to you." He added, "Don't delay. And, for heaven's sake, find a place to hole up, outside of town, so no one sees you."

Robert nodded.

Julia hated to think of Robert leaving her. But . . . tomorrow? She could wait one day. One more day. It would be agony, but then . . . then she would be with Robert. Together, forever.

"I have to make preparations . . ." The doctor fretted and wrung his hands. "I'll need to get a wagon . . ." He spoke more to himself than to the others in the room. He straightened and looked at Eli.

"You should go. Both of you, now." He rapped on the door, and the guard unlocked it and opened it.

Julia's heart sank. Time was up. But Robert had come! He loved her, and he would never leave her. Never again. And she would never doubt his love ever again.

With a kiss too brief to linger on her lips, Robert said goodbye, then whispered in her ear. "Till tomorrow, my love. I'll move heaven and earth if I have to, to be there. Don't worry."

And then, with Eli, he departed. Julia listened to their footsteps as they made their way down the stairs until she could hear them no more. The clang of metal doors told her they'd exited the prison without delay, all the while she clutched her hands on the cot's frame, feeling elated and despondent both.

She turned to the doctor, who stood deep in thought, staring at the closed door.

"How do you plan to get me out?" she asked quietly, afraid of the answer and wondering how in the world Eli's mother was at the heart of Julia's escape.

Dr. Tuttle looked at her with the greatest compassion—a look that struck fear into her. It was the kind of look someone gave you when they had terrible news to deliver.

She swallowed and sat on the edge of the cot, not trusting her legs to hold her up. Then she straightened and looked the good doctor in the eye.

"Just tell me, Dr. Tuttle. If this is the only way I can be with Robert, then I am willing. Even if it means I have to die trying."

Dr. Tuttle startled, then huffed out a breath. "That's exactly what it means," he said.

When they arrived at the edge of the woods they'd emerged from not an hour prior, Robert and Eli dismounted and led their horses under the canopy of spindly branches along the deer

track. It would be a cold night, for he didn't dare make a fire—
not even a small one. A flicker of light could attract attention this
close to town. Eli had brought heavy blankets and hard tack.
Water was plentiful, as they set up camp not far from the
Laramie River in a level clearing where the horses could graze.
The half-moon was up now, splashing light on the trees and
spilling like streaks of paint across the grassy swale.

As Eli hobbled the horses, Robert listened to the night,
hoping whatever predators were close by might be repelled by
their human scents. As much as he longed to sleep to hasten the
hours until he reunited with Julia, he knew he wouldn't get in
hardly a wink. After so much riding, Robert wondered if his ribs
would ever heal. A persistent stabbing pain had plagued him
without letup, but he'd gritted his teeth and suffered through it
all the day long. Lying down would hardly provide respite from
the pain. Maybe Eli would catch some winks—*but not before I
get some answers.*

When his pal finished his chores and had the bedrolls set
out, he pulled a pouch from his saddlebag, which lay over his
saddle resting up against a thick-trunked aspen. He handed
Robert a chunk of white cheese and a block of hard tack, then
sat cross-legged facing him.

"What's the doc gonna do? How will he get Julia out?"
Robert asked Eli pointedly.

Eli took a bite from a wrinkled red apple. "I don't rightly
know," he said, making short shrift of the apple, then tossed the
core into the underbrush.

"You didn't read that letter your ma sent him?"

"Nope, and the doc didn't tell me what it said. Other'n he
weren't s'posed to tell anyone."

Robert snorted. "She couldn't'a meant you."

Eli merely shrugged.

Robert fell quiet, listening to the little rustlings that indicated birds and rodents settling down for the night and the horses snuffling as they cropped the grass. He sighed and said, "I s'pose I'll find out tomorrow . . . but why'd Tuttle say to meet at the mortuary? I don't like the sound of that."

"Maybe 'cause no one'd think to look there for a prison escapee?"

Eli chomped on his cheese, while Robert had taken only a few bites of his food. He could barely eat after seeing Julia in such a deplorable place and spending those precious few minutes with her. His mood was souring by the minute thinking of how helpless he was to free her and how dangerous it would be for her to try to escape the clutches of the warden and his guards.

"Whatever the doc plans to do, it better work," he told Eli. "I doubt he'll get a second chance." He picked at the piece of hard tack, then laid it down, grinding his teeth. "Do you . . . do you think what the doc is planning is risky? He was downright bothered—"

"Look," Eli said, his tone kind but firm. "You're gonna work yerself up into a tizzy frettin' 'bout this. Ain't nothin' ya can do. Nothin' but wait and trust."

He studied Robert's face, and Robert considered all the times Eli's ma must've said those very words to him over the years. "My ma saw the way out for Julia, and she sent us here to help open that door. So long's Tuttle does what she says, everythin'll work out fine." He gave Robert a smile meant to ease his fears.

Robert wanted to believe, but his mind kept conjuring all the myriad of things that could possibly go wrong. Tuttle surely couldn't walk out the prison doors with Julia in tow. Not even if she were in disguise. Would he try to sneak her out in some crate or container? How would he manage that? Then he thought about that small glass vial—some Cheyenne potion Eli's ma had concocted. Was he going to poison the guards? Robert couldn't feature the doctor doing something like that—he'd sworn an oath to do no harm, and he seemed an upright and God-fearing type of fella. And even if Tuttle were capable of poisoning a body, how would he manage it? Would he concoct a remedy for an ailment and give some harebrained reason the guards had to drink it, to prevent an outbreak? If the guards, why not the prisoners?

Robert sighed. Eli was right. He could gnaw this bone to the marrow and end up with nothing more than sore teeth.

Eli got into his bedroll and scooted down so only the tufts of his wavy hair showed. The sound of the horses shifting on their legs as they peacefully tugged at the grass with their mouths settled Robert into acquiescence, though he didn't bother to get under his blanket. Instead, he looked up at the blanket overhead pocked with glittering stars—those numberless worlds so far out of reach that drove home the truth of his puny powerlessness in the grand picture of eternity.

He'd made a mess of his life. He'd made foolhardy choices. His brashness and stupidity had gotten Cassidy killed and sent his pa to find solace at the bottom of a whisky bottle. And then there was Ellsworth . . .

His chest ached as he heaved a tremulous sigh. His future, the very salvation of his soul, balanced precariously on the edge of a knife. Tomorrow would determine which way he fell. It seemed as if the slightest bit of wind could topple him in either direction—toward redemption or damnation. And the choice was out of his hands.

Precarious, indeed.

First order of business: Joseph had to procure a wagon and a couple of horses or mules. He had to have the rig ready and waiting for him tomorrow night. Maybe Cathryn would know someone. Timing was everything. And who knew if the mortuary's back door was kept locked? Would he have to break in? The building's proprietor, in a town this lawless, would no doubt want to keep out thieves who might find the unoccupied mortuary ripe for the pickings. Though, Joseph imagined there wouldn't be much of interest in such a place to a thief. Still . . .

Joseph blew out a breath, pacing, clenching and unclenching his sweaty hands.

"Dr. Tuttle, you're working a rut into the floor," Julia said, sitting on the edge of the cot, combing out her long brown hair that hung limp over her shoulders. She was still wearing his shirt, and at any other time, the sight would have amused him. Julia's tender innocence and youth could hardly be buried beneath a man's tailored shirt.

He stopped and looked into a face fraught with fear. He'd wrestled with telling her the plan. He could just administer the potion, say it will help her sleep, but that wouldn't squelch her curious questions. And it wouldn't be fair or honest. She had every right to know the risks and refuse to be party to this madness.

Sarah had said the medicine was potentially deadly. Julia was to drink the entire contents of the vial on an empty stomach—no food or water for at least eight hours before ingesting the potion. His mind mulled over all the possible ingredients contained in the bottle that could achieve the results she detailed. *Aconitum*—wolf's bane. Mistletoe, germander, hawthorn, lobelia . . . any number of plant distillations. Enough to slow her heart to a near stop—and convince the warden she was dead.

And if Julia reacted adversely? What was to be done? What antidote, if any, could he prepare? There was no time to do the proper research, and not enough information—none at all, for that matter—to even point him in the right direction.

"Doctor," Julia said, her tone desperate and her eyes imploring him. "Do you believe in divine providence?"

Her words struck him at the center of his agitation. For, wasn't this the only question that mattered at this moment?

She didn't wait for his answer. "You see, ever since I met Robert, I knew the Lord had answered my prayers. Not just for a man to love. No—not even for a way to escape my father. For those things are the stuff of many a young girl's dreams. But, I've come to believe as I've sat these many lonely hours in my prison cell, that God wants us to know Him as more than a wish-granter." She paused, thoughtful. "The Bible tells us we are to share in Christ's sufferings and thus understand Him more deeply. That trials test and refine our faith, but more than that— they show us God loves us more than we can fathom."

Joseph gaped unabashed. Such wisdom from one so young, and a maturity that belied her years. Joseph knew few people, even of advanced age and experience, who demonstrated the kind of faith and discernment Julia showed. He felt almost ashamed of his meager faith, listening to her words.

"Yes, yes," he sputtered. Had the Lord sent this angel to minister to his own doubting heart?

"You see," Julia continued, now looking at the curtained window that blocked out the ugliness of the prison beyond it. "I believe God puts opportunities before us. And we are forced to make a choice. The night I met Robert, my parents had arranged for me to marry another man, someone handsome and rich and eager to wed. Yet, his true nature was exposed to me, and I knew that, should I have accepted his proposal, I would be exchanging one cage for another. I would be trapped in a miserable marriage in which I would wither away."

Joseph pulled over the chair and sat, engrossed in her tale, his worry dissipating into fascination.

"I went out on the patio the night of my birthday party, and there was Robert . . ." She smiled that sweet smile of a girl in love, and Joseph knew he had never come close to feeling such a deep and devoted love for someone. "Of all people. Of all the men who could have stolen my heart, the Lord sent Robert—the son of my father's enemy."

She searched Joseph's eyes, looking deep. "One might consider it irony. Or a fault of the stars, some mean trick of fate. But I knew it to be divine providence. We both thought perhaps that our love might bring about the end of the feud between our families. And though every sling and arrow has been hurled at us, our love remains true. I see now that, while it is a noble hope, I cannot control the thoughts and feelings of others. My actions can't change the condition of their heart. Yet, I cannot deny this conviction I hold that tells me all that has transpired is for some greater purpose." She let out a noise like a chuckle. "I know, it sounds presumptuous."

"No, not at all," Joseph said, rushing to her defense. "I believe that as well, with all my heart." *Though I could not have said it so eloquently.*

"And so, Dr. Tuttle, it cannot be mere coincidence that brought this man up from Fort Collins, with Robert, to deliver a message from his mother, an Indian medicine woman, in my hour of greatest need." Her eyes were suddenly shining, challenging him to refute her.

"No, it cannot," he conceded, the profundity of their conversation astonishing him, especially considering the setting in which they were holding such conversation. Something had caused a transformation in this girl who sat before him, dressed in his shirt, her feet in prison-issued slippers, the daughter of a wealthy rancher in the guise of a poor street waif. *Some have entertained angels unawares . . . indeed.*

Julia waited, composed now, resigned—but not with the previous flutter of panic. A spirit of peace enveloped her, and Joseph wished it would seep into his soul as well, for as he opened his mouth to speak, he was gripped by the enormity of the task that had been laid at his feet. He felt suddenly like the apothecary in Shakespeare's play as he pulled out the glass vial from his pocket and held it out to show Julia.

"What is it?" Julia asked, taking the bottle from him and studying it. The cork was tightly sealed with wax, the thick liquid a dull and gelatinous green under the lamp's light.

Joseph sighed. Julia was right—in perhaps more ways than she knew. Not only would she have to experience Christ's sufferings. She would, as the apostle Paul declared in the Good Book, have to be buried like Christ in order to be raised again from the dead.

The thought gave Joseph a rush of nausea as he held out his hand for the vial. He hoped that his role-playing of the apothecary would not tender the same tragic results as in *Romeo and Juliet.*

"This," he said wryly, "is your divine providence."

Chapter 25

"THAT WOMAN IS A POX on my life!"

Asa House slammed his fist so hard on the desk, Carr thought the old mahogany would splinter.

"Which woman do you mean?" Carr asked. He could think of three off the top of his head that might qualify as the culprit — Asa's irritable wife, for one.

The warden stomped to the floor-to-ceiling glass-door cabinet with shelves of perfectly ordered books, their spines aligned as if Asa had used a level to nudge them into place. He threw open the door and pulled down a crystal decanter and two shot glasses from the top shelf, then returned to face Carr.

"You know which woman! Povey. That meddlesome ex-congressman's wife."

"A congressman's wife?" Carr huffed. He knew the woman and her ailing husband had relocated from Washington, but he'd had no idea Povey had been in government. He clicked his teeth. "Just your luck, Asa."

"Don't provoke me today, Jeff. I'm in no mood."

"I can see that." Carr huffed. Last thing he needed was the warden bellyaching over troubles he had inflicted upon himself. If he spent more time watching over the prisoners and less locked in his office drinking and fuming, the governor might not be breathing fire down his neck.

Asa poured the whiskeys and motioned for Carr to sit.

"So what do you need from me?" Carr asked as he sat back in the chair. The whiskey went down his throat like liquid sunshine, taking the chill out of his bones that seeped in while riding across the bridge on such a blustery afternoon. Wind had been sluicing down from the Rockies and gusting in great spurts, knocking hats off heads and roofing off poorly constructed barns and sheds. The road leading up to the prison was littered with debris — branches, leaves, detritus from the rail yard. Black clouds were gathering out the window like angry gods about to let loose a quiver of lightning bolts.

Asa, still standing, leaned forward across the desk, glass in hand. "You got anythin' on her? Anythin' we can use to . . . muzzle her proper? What about Chalmers? Ain't he in your camp?"

Carr held up a hand. "Whoa, now." That fierce, wild look was back in his friend's eyes. This had to be about Lester Carson and her girl. Nothing else riled Asa this much. "I can only do so much with the judge. And he's already sent word to the marshal—"

"Don't I know it. That's why I sent for you."

Carr chewed his lip. He thought the warden would have rested on his victory laurels, for having infuriated Lester Carson by locking up his little girl. He'd gotten his pleasure in seeing the rancher boil over, but how long did Asa think he could keep up this dangerous game? He was breaking every law in the book, and if he didn't release the girl soon, he'd have his own book thrown at him. With Asa in such a volatile mood, though, Carr ditched the idea of mentioning that. Still, it needed to be said. He'd have to tread carefully.

"Look, I can't do a thing about the marshal. You know that. When he gets here, if Carson's girl is still in the prison—"

Asa slammed his fist again, rattling the decanter of whiskey he'd set on the desk. "And that new doctor. I heard tell he'd gone to see the judge with that Povey woman. She's workin' him. Gettin' him to do her biddin'. I shoulda never asked her help in findin' someone to fill that position."

Carr was about to say "What did you expect?" but he kept his thoughts to himself.

Asa looked as if the air had leaked out of him, as deflated as a balloon. He went around the desk and slumped in his chair, then upended his glass and poured himself another shot. He tapped his finger on the glass, studying the amber glow of the whiskey.

"I recall when Lester Carson worked as a puncher on my ranch—him and Morrison. I weren't but some eight or nine years older'n him. My daddy had passed suddenly, and the ranch was all mine." He had a faraway look in his eyes, his bushy brows scrunched. "Them two were my best punchers. Loyal, hardworkin', ambitious. And then ... I don't know what the dickens happened. The two were thick as thieves one minute, but one day, I rode out to check on the herd, and when I got to the camp, Carson was nursin' a shiner and a sprained wrist, and Morrison had ridden off to gather strays. My foreman said he'd had to pry the two apart, they'd nearly killed t'other." He stopped to take another gulp of whiskey. "Weren't long after, I lost my ranch to that scoundrel. I rue the day I ever hired Carson."

Carr stiffened, almost dropping his glass. *Well, there it is —
the truth I've been itching to get at for years.* He didn't dare say
a word, didn't even breathe. Just kept his gaze on the lacquered
surface of the desk.

But Asa said nothing further, spurring more questions in
Carr's head. Asa wasn't a gambler, but how else could he have
lost his ranch other than in a game of chance? A business deal
gone bad? Some trickery Asa couldn't prove?

What did it matter how it happened? Carr wondered why
Asa didn't kill Carson back then. Then figured he couldn't have
done so without everyone knowing. *Probably were witnesses —
and Asa couldn't'a gotten out of it.* Whatever went down, that
must've been the impetus for Asa running for sheriff and going
on the warpath against outlaws in the territory, back when the
railroad came to Laramie.

He looked up at Asa, considered his words. "Asa, that's all
water under the bridge. A long time ago. Maybe . . . it's time to
let it go —"

"No!" Asa snorted and narrowed his eyes. "If you're not
gonna help me —"

"I'm not sayin' that —"

"— then I'll take care of this myself —"

"Asa, don't do anything you'll regret later —"

Asa stood, pushed back his chair, and came around the desk
to face Carr. His face was as stormy as the weather churning in
the peaks of the Rockies.

"It's too late for that. I already used up all my 'regrets.'"

Carr felt the heat coming off Asa's face as he looked into the
eyes of a man he wasn't sure he knew half as much as he'd
thought. The kind of eyes Carr had seen plenty of times. Eyes of
a man intent on doing something unspeakable — and not caring
a whit about the consequences.

Now it was Julia's turn to wear a rut into the infirmary floor. She didn't know what time it was, but the glow of sunset softened the walls of the cell block that she could see through the window and into the hallway, and the clangor of the dinner bell had sounded not all that long ago. The doctor had been gone the whole day. She prayed he'd been able to accomplish all that was needed to ensure her escape. He told her she'd need to drink the contents of the vial at nine o'clock.

Her mouth felt like cotton batting, but she'd heeded his instructions and hadn't had anything to drink or eat all day. What she would give to have even a tiny sip to wet her mouth, but she didn't dare. She trained her thoughts on Robert, remembering how right it felt to be ensconced in his strong, protective arms. Her heart kept hurting over Ty, but the loss of her dearest companion served only to strengthen her resolve. She couldn't let Ty's death be in vain. He would want her to be happy. *If only he was still alive . . . if only he could have trusted me, given Robert a chance.* It was his own hotheadedness that had been his undoing. But that comforted her little. No, she refused to blame Ty. Or Robert. She blamed her father. Robert's father. For this cursed feud. None of this would have happened if those two men had let bygones be bygones, done what the Bible commanded and forgave each other, repented of their sins, whatever they were, whatever had caused offense.

Was all this really about her mother? Robert Morrison full of animosity over her father marrying her mother? And what about that card game? She'd been mulling her mother's words over for days. Had her father won the warden's ranch in a game of chance? Julia had assumed her father had family money, and that's how he'd come to own the biggest ranch in the territory. *But what if he'd cheated?*

How did any of this matter now? The past was a tangled skein of yarn, impossible to unravel. Best to cut the string and walk away, never look back. The prospect of never seeing her parents again pressed tears to her eyes, but she swallowed them down. This was no time to indulge in her misery. She had to tend to the matter at hand.

The medicine woman's letter didn't say what would happen when Julia drank the liquid, but Julia could guess. She was Juliet, about to feign death and tempt the spirits of darkness to whisk her away from this world, and despite her fervent prayers and trust that this was the Lord's doing, she was, to put it simply, afraid.

She chided herself. Of course she was afraid. Any person in their right mind would have misgivings undertaking such madness. Then she thought of Jesus, how agitated he was the night of his betrayal, so distressed that he sweat blood. Surely he was terrified—even the Son of God. Even knowing the glory that awaited Him. Being afraid didn't mean you were weak, she told herself. It meant you needed to throw yourself on God's mercy and draw strength from Him.

She spun around as footsteps approached from the stairwell. *Oh, thank you, Lord!* She rushed over as the door opened, then stepped back awkwardly as two guards marched in, their expressions harsh and accusatory. They each grabbed one of her arms, and she shrieked.

As they yanked her toward the door, she resisted, trying to get purchase with her feet, but the slippers slid on the smooth surface. "Where are you taking me? I'm not supposed to leave the infirmary—"

"Shut yer trap," the fat guard said, his girth nearly bursting the buttons on his uniform shirt and his face a mess of red blotches, probably from the exertion of climbing the stairs.

"I don't understand," she protested, dragging her feet, her pulse pounding in her ears. The skin on the tops of her feet burned as they pulled her out the door. The other guard—one she often saw standing outside the infirmary window—said nothing and wouldn't meet her eyes. She'd thought, of all the guards, that he held a spark of compassion for her predicament. *Where are they taking me? They can't take me! Oh, where is Dr. Tuttle?*

Julia squirmed and flailed, but their grips held fast. They lifted her as they marched down the stairs, as the pall of night blotted out the prairie outside the large barred windows. When they arrived at the base of the stairs, a man with thick graying hair, big ears, and a drooping mustache stood, his hands fisted at his hips, his visage one of unbridled rage.

Julia grew faint as the guards brought her face-to-face with the warden—the one who'd spoken so heartlessly to her the night she was brought to the prison. A man whose eyes roamed lecherously over her body, as if he could see through the coarse prison garb to her naked flesh. His cruel attendance upon her detonated her asthma so severely that as she fought to suck in air, her vision blurred.

The man's laughter ricocheted in her head as she squinched her eyes and tried to will her throat to open, but all she could manage was a constricted wheeze. Somehow she pushed out the words. "Please . . . help . . . my medicine . . ." The effort it took to speak drained her entirely. She sucked hard, throwing back her head, her mouth open like a fish panting on a riverbank. *Help, please, someone, help!* Oh, where was Dr. Tuttle?

She tried to focus on the man's leathery face in the shadowy light that made him look even more sinister. Precious molecules of air made their way into her lungs, but it wasn't enough. A dark shroud formed before her, erasing her surroundings as she grew too weak to struggle any longer.

Julia slumped, hearing garbled words like the distant rumbling of a train or a stampede of cattle—nonsensical noise. Her hazy awareness flashed warnings in her mind, and her escalating fear that she would never get out of prison, never see her beloved Robert again, severed the last bits of air from her throat.

Just as blackness engulfed her, she was vaguely aware of being dragged once more along the floor. A metal clang shuddered through her chest, and she was flung to the cold ground, then another clang set her adrift in a sea of darkness in which her stalwart hope sank like a discarded anchor to the miry bottom of a bottomless ocean.

When Joseph arrived at the infirmary door, his heart pounded like a sledge. All through the day, as he made his arrangements and his plans fell into place, he dreaded this moment. He'd struggled with misgivings, feeling like Jacob wrestling with the angel. Though, in his instance, it was his confidence he was grappling with. He knew he was backed into a corner. This was the only way out. He believed Sheriff Carr and Warden House wanted Julia dead. He trusted Sarah Banks and her Cheyenne wisdom.

He just didn't trust himself. The thought of watching Julia succumb to a deathlike state, then having to witness her being carted out of the prison like a bag of refuse—would the warden even allow it? Even if Joseph demanded vociferously?—and tossed into the back of his wagon sent a shudder through his chest . . .

Joseph hesitated, swallowed hard, then realized there were no guards at the infirmary door. Odd. Whenever a female inmate was inside the infirmary, one always stood outside at the ready, in case the woman needed help.

Perhaps the guards had been called to a meeting. Or a prisoner had tried to escape. He'd never heard of a prison that suffered so many attempts at escape. Either the guards were inept or careless. *Or just don't care if their prisoners wander off.* No wonder Hassie had thought it worth the risk to sneak off that night. Most of the prisoners who escaped were never caught.

But how would he get inside, to Julia? It wouldn't help to knock; she had no way of opening the door. He had to find a guard with a key.

He pulled his watch from his vest pocket. Half-past eight. Time was running out.

He trotted down the stairs and hurried along the long narrow corridor toward the entrance, where the rounder who'd let him in stood half-asleep at his station. Wind rattled the windows as the ominous storm Joseph had seen gathering earlier rumbled down the foothills and onto the prairie. Rain and sleet smacked the glass, making Joseph even more anxious to be done with this task and get Julia to safety. He feared the clouds could dump snow by the bucket-loads before too long, and then how would he manage the road and bridge to town?

"I need to get into the infirmary," he told the guard, who looked as bored as could be.

"I can't help ya," the man said. "Can't leave my post."

Joseph's face scrunched in frustration. "Well, what should I do?"

"Ask the guard assigned to the floor to open the door for ya."

"But no one's there."

The guard shrugged dismissively. "Sorry."

Joseph huffed out a shaky breath. He didn't have time for this. He ran back along the corridor and up the stairs. Still no sign of any guards. The cell block was dark; only a few of the wall lamps had been lit. He raced across the large high-ceilinged room, past the cells that held the prisoners, no doubt garnering the attention of curious eyes, but he couldn't see anything through the heavily grated doors. Finally, he spotted a guard at the end of the row of cells. The man eyed him suspiciously, and Joseph hoped he recognized him and didn't think he was an escapee. He trusted his three-piece tailored suit announced him readily enough. Joseph hurried over to him, barely able to catch his breath, his nerves rattling.

In a hushed voice, he asked, "Where is everyone? I need to get into the infirmary. Do you have a key?"

Joseph hadn't met this guard yet. He had a dark, ruddy complexion, huge side whiskers, and a strong overbite revealing big front teeth.

"Cain't help ya." The man looked past Joseph, as if watching the cell doors for any sign of disruption.

"Oh, for goodness' sake!" Joseph sputtered. "Am I supposed to break down the door?"

The man cocked his head and glared at Joseph. Maybe he shouldn't have said that, but he was getting desperate. "You c'n try, but the doors are solid steel." He laughed. "But have at it, if'n you got half a mind to."

Joseph's patience had played out. He could think of only one other option, and that was inquiring of the warden, which was the last thing he wanted to do. He didn't dare draw any attention to what Joseph needed to undertake in the upcoming hour. Besides, the warden might not even be in his house across the yard. Oh, what to do?

"If'n yer lookin' for that gal—the one with the hair—they took 'er."

"They?" Joseph's breath hitched. "Who is they? Took her where?" Oh no, this was bad, very bad.

"From the looks o' it, she's down in the dark cell."

"In solitary? Where?"

The man smirked.

"Where?" Joseph demanded. "I'll report you—"

The guard suddenly grabbed Joseph by his coat lapel. "Don't ya dare threaten me."

"Please," Joseph said, softening his tone and lowering his voice. "I'm sorry. I need to find her. She . . . isn't well."

The guard rolled his eyes. "First floor, end of the hallway. Over by the back entrance." He turned away, back to staring at the cells.

Joseph ran to the stairs, took two steps at a time, and raced down the ground floor corridor once more, this time passing the rounder and finally spotting the secluded cell to the left of the alcove leading to the prison's delivery entrance.

Two guards flanked the cell, and when Joseph approached, they closed ranks, blocking the door. Joseph couldn't see past them into the cell. One of the guards he recognized—Pulchow. The other he'd never seen before. The older man with the gray-and-black peppered beard sometimes rotated as the rounder. He stood a whole foot taller than his companion.

"What are you doing here?" Pulchow asked.

"Julia, Julia!" Joseph called through the cell door. When he received only silence as his answer, he glared at the men. "Is she in there? What did you do to her?"

The men shared grins but said nothing. Joseph restrained his hands from lunging for the closest guard's throat.

"I'm the doctor at this prison, and I'm responsible for the care of the female inmates. Now let me inside!"

The guards shook their heads. The older one said, "Can't do that. Warden's orders."

"Warden's . . ."

Now Joseph understood. It all came together in one clear picture in his head. The words of the men at the café, the warden losing his ranch to Lester Carson . . . Warden House wanting to hurt Carson any way he could . . . *What would hurt more than losing one's only child?*

Joseph had smashed into an impenetrable wall. Had they killed her? Why wasn't she answering? Desperation gripped Joseph with a panicky hand. And desperation called for desperate measures. *Oh, Lord. What can I do? How can I get to Julia?*

Joseph's gaze dropped to the pistols at the guards' sides. *Don't be foolhardy*, he told himself. *If you try to grab a gun, they'll shoot you.*

"Look," Joseph pleaded, "this girl's father is the richest rancher in town."

"So what?" Pulchow said. He had the look of a man who didn't care about anyone or anything.

"So . . . if you help me, so I can help her, I'll tell him what you did. I'm sure he'll reward you for your efforts."

The guards chuckled, but Joseph saw something in their eyes, something unmistakable: greed.

"In fact, if you let me in, I promise, I swear to the almighty God, I'll petition Mr. Carson for a goodly sum."

"How much?" the older guard demanded. "And how do we know you're tellin' us the truth?"

"I'm a God-fearing man, and I am not lying to you." He kept glancing at the cell door, fearful of what he'd find inside. "How much do you want?"

"One hundred," the older guard blurted without hesitation. "Each."

"I promise that's what you'll get, each of you . . . even if I have to come up with the money myself."

The two men exchanged looks, then the older one nodded. "All right. You c'n have five minutes. That's all."

Thank you, Lord. That's all I need. He was glad he had put the vial in his vest pocket, not willing to chance leaving it anywhere in the infirmary, where someone might have discovered it and asked questions. *Or broken it.*

He wiped his sweaty palms on his trousers as the older guard inserted the key into the lock and opened the door. Joseph ran inside, the cell almost too dark to see Julia slumped in the corner. He might have thought she was a sack of potatoes if he hadn't known better.

Joseph gasped and hurried to her side in the room that contained nothing at all—not even a chamber pot or bucket. Had they meant to leave her in here to die?

He checked her over. A weak pulse. Belabored breathing. She'd fainted, probably from an asthma episode. But, thankfully, falling unconscious had caused her throat to relax and her lungs to draw in air.

Her eyelids fluttered as Joseph knelt beside her and pulled her head and shoulders awkwardly into his lap.

"Julia, Julia." His heart ached to see her in such a state. And he worried that if he administered the potion to her, her weakened condition might put her in grave danger. But there was no other option. He'd come this far, and, clearly, if the warden intended for her to die, then he could put this off no longer. Not even a day.

Well, if Warden House wants her dead, then dead she'll be.

He furtively glanced back at the closed cell door, certain the guards could not see what he was doing. His hand, more sweaty than ever, fumbled in the tight vest pocket and pulled out the vial. *What am I doing? What madness is this?*

Julia's eyes opened. She blinked and squinted to see into his face.

"Doctor . . ." A smile barely lifted the corners of her mouth. "You . . . found me . . ."

"Shh," he said. "Save your strength." Her eyes dropped to the little bottle in his hand as he gently pried the cork out with trembling fingers, careful not to spill any of the contents.

He stopped and looked at her. She radiated that same ethereal calm he'd seen yesterday. A calm that could only come from a heart full of faith. The confidence radiating from her visage infused him with reassurance. There was no way to the other side but through. Julia had to walk through the fire to freedom and to the man she loved. But would she come out the other side unscathed?

He felt her cold hand on his wrist.

"It's the only way," she whispered on paper-thin breath. "Have faith, Doctor."

Joseph drew in a long breath and nodded. "It's time to defy the stars."

Julia smiled, this time like a beaming ray of joy. "You read Shakespeare . . . then . . . let me have this mortal drug, this cordial, good doctor."

He gave her the vial, and she drank the murky liquid, wincing at the taste. He then removed his coat and laid it on the hard, cold floor, then Julia lay down on her back, gave him one last smile, and closed her eyes. He knelt beside her, holding her clammy hand, watching her body loosen into sleep.

How long would it take for the potion to work its full measure? He had no idea.

The door swung open, and the older guard popped his head in. "Time's up. Git out."

Joseph had to stall. "Wait . . . she's not well. She needs medicine . . ."

"I said, time's up." The guard came inside and pulled on his sleeve. If Joseph was thrown out, he'd never be able to get in again, of that he was sure. He had to stay by Julia's side.

Joseph swatted the guard's hand and glowered at him.

"She's had a violent asthma attack, and I fear it's taken its toll on her—"

He pointed at Julia. "Then, jes let 'er sleep." He sneered and lowered his voice. "Now, go git our money."

Joseph turned back to Julia and put two fingers on her carotid artery. Her pulse was already dangerously weak, and though he knew this was to be expected, it still alarmed him, prompting his outburst.

"Something's wrong," Joseph said. "Her heart is failing." He didn't have to playact to conjure up a look of dire concern. "Please, I need help to get her to the infirmary. If she doesn't get the proper medicine—"

The guard yanked Joseph to his feet. "Then, go—git 'er the medicine."

"I won't leave her side."

The man threw up his hands. "Then I reckon she'll die—"

"And you won't get your money," Joseph ground out under his breath. The man's lack of compassion infuriated Joseph.

"Look," the guard said, clearly perturbed and tired of Joseph's drama, "what d'ya want me to do?"

Joseph sensed more than saw a change in Julia, and he leaned close to her face, which, even in the scant light, had the veneer of death. His heart nearly buckled in his chest. If he didn't know better . . .

He laid his cheek close to her mouth. No air came from her nostrils—at least none that he could feel on his skin. He checked her carotid again. He held back another gasp as he repositioned his fingers. Nothing.

The potion Sarah Banks had prepared worked expeditiously—quicker than Joseph imagined possible. *Oh, dear God, I hope I haven't truly killed her.*

"Quick—get the warden!" Joseph ordered, pointing his finger toward the door.

"Now, don't—"

"She's dead! Dead!"

The guard's face paled. "What?"

"You heard me, mister. This is your fault!"

"My fault?"

"She's had some sort of heart failure. You knew—the warden knew—that she had a medical condition—"

"Now, don't go blamin' me—"

"Get the warden. Maybe he wants her dead, but don't think for a minute that he won't hang her death on you."

The guard's eyes went wide and wild. He fled from the cell, and Joseph heard the footsteps of both guards tromping through the cell block toward the warden's office.

Three hours. Sarah had said in three hours' time, Julia would wake from her death sleep. He had to convince the warden not only that Julia was dead but that he had to take her to the mortuary. He'd have to convince the warden that it was in his best interests not to have this underage girl's body found by government authorities on his premises. It was one thing for an adult prisoner to die due to neglect. Another altogether for a girl who had no business being incarcerated in a federal penitentiary. And the daughter of one of the most prominent ranchers in the territory, no less.

Joseph held Julia's hand, trying desperately to keep his worry in check. What was done was done; there was no turning back. He had to concentrate with a clear head, finish what he started, trusting Sarah. But all this went against every fiber of his being. And it took more faith than he had to believe Julia wasn't dead, that he hadn't poisoned her.

What if the potion had become contaminated or overheated, and its molecular structure had been altered? How could Sarah have known the exact dosage? For that matter, how could she have "seen" Julia's predicament at all, when it hadn't even begun to come to fruition when she'd prepared the potion?

He clamped down on his torturous thoughts—they were only making him more agitated.

Not more than three minutes had passed, by Joseph's watch, when the march of heavy boots sounded the approach of heavy-footed men.

"What's all the commotion about?" The warden's voice boomed as he strode into the cell, his presence crowding the confining space.

Joseph leapt to his feet, mustering the courage to show his anger—though it hardly took any effort.

"Look what you've done—you've killed this innocent girl."

To Joseph's shock, the warden laughed. "Innocent? She shot a man—a drunk and harmless one, at that—in the middle of town. Hardly innocent."

What was wrong with this man? How could he have been entrusted to hold the reins of this prison? No wonder Cathryn Povey despised him. Joseph would do all he could to have Asa House removed from his posting as soon as possible.

"She's a child, only sixteen! For heaven's sake, man. Have you no heart at all?"

The warden pushed Joseph against the wall and glared down at him. "You are in no position to lecture me, Doctor." He gave Julia a mere glance before turning back to Joseph. "From what I can see, the child expired due to your dereliction of duty—"

"My what? She shouldn't have been in the prison in the first place—"

"You'd been instructed to monitor her health, and while you were . . . gallavantin'—"

"Gallivanting?"

"—around town all day, when she suffered an attack, why, her doctor was nowhere to be found." The warden smiled smugly, his arms now across his chest.

"She wouldn't have had an episode if *you* hadn't thrown her in solitary." Why was he standing here arguing with this cretin?

"Are you certain she's dead?" the warden asked, stooping and looking Julia over. He lifted her limp wrist, feeling for a pulse.

"Of course she is." He tried not to shake, though he wasn't sure if his trembling was due to anger or fear that Julia might suddenly begin to recover from her "death" too soon. He needed to move her, get her away from further close scrutiny.

He needed to transport her to the morgue.

"I'll fill out the paperwork," Joseph said evenly, not looking at House. He didn't dare meet the man's eyes and risk giving any indication that he was up to something. "And then I want to take her to the mortuary on Front Street."

"You will do no such thing," the warden commanded.

What? "Why not?" Joseph asked, taken aback at his refusal. He hadn't imagined the warden would insist on keeping Julia here. He explained how bad it might look for authorities to find the body of a girl in the prison, but House only frowned and fisted his hands on his hips.

"I'll determine when this body is moved and to where. In my own good time."

Joseph's heart sank. Now what was he going to do? *This is worse than bad!*

"Get out, Doctor." The warden gestured at the two guards, who had stood listening outside the open cell door. "Lock this door and keep watch. I don't want anyone"—he scowled at Joseph—"not *anyone*, allowed inside."

Joseph reluctantly exited the cell, and the warden marched off, not a look back. The older guard slammed the cell door shut and locked it with the key on his big brass ring of keys with a smug expression. Pulchow gave him a barely perceptible shrug. The loud clang punctuated the dark night with an exclamation of finality.

Joseph stepped back from the cell, at wit's end, staring at the locked door and the two guards who'd taken up position on both sides, their eyes pinned on him. He thought of the Bible story of the apostle Paul, who, along with Silas, was chained in prison. While they were singing praises to God, a great earthquake shook the foundation of the prison, and all the chains dropped from the prisoners' legs and arms and the prison doors flew open.

Lord, I could use a miracle like that about now, Joseph prayed. He'd done all he could. Now, only a miracle could save Julia.

Chapter 26

ROBERT PULLED HIS THICK COAT collar up over his chin as he slapped his gloved hands together, trying to beat the numbness out of them. The icy wind chomped at his face, and flurries of snow spun like dervishes as the mean sky clotted with charcoal-black clouds hovered overhead. He reckoned by midnight snow would have Laramie City half buried, and while that might make it easier for him and Julia to ride away without being seen—figuring most sensible folks would hole up in their homes or in the saloons—heavy snow would make the journey difficult.

Whatever Tuttle had up his sleeve, Robert sure hoped it worked. There were too many "iffy" factors for Robert's liking, and few—if any—he could control. He'd said his good-byes to Eli and expressed his deep gratitude for his help. If all went well, his pal would see him and Julia soon. Eli assured him a pot of Irish stew would be simmering on the stove for them when they rode into Fort Collins. Robert wished he could be as certain of the outcome of this night as was Eli Banks.

He longed for Julia. So much so, his chest hurt anew, like someone had punched his broken ribs with an iron fist. Squeezing his eyes to picture her better, he let his longing run roughshod over the image of her angelic face with the arc of tiny freckles splattered across. He recalled with a sweet agony the way her lips tasted and the unbridled desire that ran rampant like a dozen bolts of lightning through his limbs and groin as he pressed close to her body that was the embodiment of softness and warmth. He'd never felt such smooth, alluring skin as hers. Her neck, her cheeks, her shoulders. He could practically feel her skin under his fingers right now as he pictured letting those fingers explore the nether regions of her body with tenderness and passion to ignite a wildfire.

More than the longing to unbutton her dress and watch it slip to the floor was the longing to see the flame of love burning in her eyes. That was the redemption he needed from his avalanche of sins. Her gaze of love smoldered his shame to ashes, and without her, Robert knew he would wander lost, a marked man like Cain, without a home, without a place to lay his head and sleep in peace. But with Julia . . .

He hunkered down under the side eaves of a listing storage building at the south end of the railway station, Comanche's reins in his hand and the horse leaning up against the wood siding, eyes shut against the wind. Robert didn't know what time it was, but he knew the bank on the corner of Front Street and Kearny had a grandfather clock in the foyer, which could be seen through the street-side windows.

He didn't dare ride around town, where anyone might spot him. And he didn't want to get to the morgue too early. The door could be locked, and then he'd be stuck outside, waiting for Tuttle to arrive with Julia. What he needed to find was someplace warm and dry, and this large storage building seemed the best choice for him and his horse to wait in.

Snow fell heavier now, in a steady canted sheet buffeted by the wind howling across the Front Range. His horse looked miserable. Robert slipped his pearl-handled Colt from his holster and whacked the butt on the padlock until he'd broken it off. The structure had no windows, which suited Robert just fine, and he was glad to find the room only partially filled with railroad parts, allowing space for Comanche to stand without tripping over anything. It would suffice for a stall.

Robert knew he'd have to do something with Comanche. In this weather, he surely couldn't ride the horse all the way to Fort Collins, and not with Julia. He hoped the doctor had a plan to get him and Julia to a safe place, maybe to a train depot or a stage. Though, it'd have to be someplace far enough away from Laramie that no one would recognize them. *Or maybe we can hole up at the doc's house until the weather passed. Would anyone suspect him of harboring outlaws?* That's what he and Julia were, he realized wryly. She'd killed a man, and he was being framed for killing another one. *Maybe Fort Collins isn't far enough. Maybe we'll have to go west. Or south, to Mexico.*

Why was he worrying about where they'd live? He didn't even know if Tuttle would get Julia out of the prison. If they were caught trying to sneak out . . .

He was worrying himself sick, and that wasn't helping his spirits any.

Robert uncinched the horse, slipped the saddle and bridle off, and set them aside. Comanche's eyes blinked then closed as he hung his head, no doubt grateful for a reprieve from the inclement weather.

Once Robert felt sufficiently thawed and the wind's moaning sounded more like a faraway train whistle, he shook the cumbersome weight of weariness from his shoulders and braved the night.

Gusts of snow stung his face the moment he pushed open the door, swirling angrily into his eyes and assaulting his neck. He scrunched down in his coat, stuffed his gloved hands deep into his pockets, and waded a path through a foot of powdery snow that sifted like flour as his boots navigated along the wide road, not a soul out, as far as he could see—which wasn't more than a dozen yards in any direction. Lights twinkled through the staccato of flakes—tiny fireflies through the windows of the storefronts ahead. The snow muffled the strains of music and gaiety coming from the saloons three blocks north, where the shadowy shapes of horses tucked under eaves could barely be seen as more than specters shifting from one leg to another in an attempt to keep from freezing. The dry cold of the high desert made the wintery temperatures tolerable, but it was the arctic wind that cut like a paring knife, peeling through every layer of clothing to slice into skin.

Robert hugged the wall of the Ivinson First National Bank, grateful for the reprieve from the onslaught of snow tumbling down from the mountains. He was even more grateful when the snowfall stopped altogether, and the wind settled like a blanket over the street with a soft hush. A block up Front Street, he saw figures coming out of the Johnson Hotel, one voice so loud, it boomed like cannon fire in the air.

Robert stiffened, slunk back, and flattened himself against the wood siding of the bank—hoping to blend into the building and not be seen. For the man that was hollering an angry diatribe was none other than his pa, and even in the murky light Robert could make out Abel Pollack marching after Robert's pa, grabbing onto a sleeve, trying to pull him back. Two other ranch hands, Jeremy Riggins and Prentice Restmeyer followed.

Even from where Robert stood, a block away, he could tell his pa was dead drunk, stumbling and righting himself, swaying like a sailor on a boat in heaving seas. What in heaven's name was his pa doing out on a night like this? *Not hard to guess. Prob'ly celebrating Ty Lawson's death . . . and braggin' to all the town that I'd shot him . . .*

Robert rubbed the window next to him with his fist and peered into the lobby of the bank. The clock face showed 11:14. He glanced down the street, from where he'd come. The mortuary sat dark and undisturbed. Anxiety twisted his gut. Would Doc Tuttle be late? Robert hoped for a sign of a wagon or buggy indicating an early arrival at their clandestine meeting place, but nothing came his way. The doctor would have to cross the bridge and come down Front Street . . . unless he traveled along Clark some extra blocks to bypass the heart of the town. That's what Robert would do. *So, the doc and Julia might already be inside, slipped into the morgue from the back . . .*

Last thing Robert wanted was for his pa to spot him. For anyone to recognize him. He inched his way along the bank, about to head back to the shed where he'd left Comanche . . .

Too late.

Abel saw him. Robert froze, his heart in his mouth. Abel hid his surprise well, said something to Riggins, who steered Robert's pa back toward the saloon, then walked not toward Robert but instead turned on Garfield. He cocked his head in an exaggerated manner, indicating Robert to meet up with him.

Robert considered running back to the shed but knew his footprints in the snow would lead Abel to find him. And then he thought the better of hiding from the last true friend he had in this world. He would tell Abel his plans, knowing he could trust him not to divulge them to Robert's pa—or anyone else. Abel deserved to know the truth. Besides, Robert needed to make sure Comanche was returned safely to the ranch. Abel would see to that, and the thought gave Robert some small comfort. It was the least he could do to honor Cassidy.

Twice Joseph had gone outside to check on the two old mules hitched to the rickety wagon he'd procured earlier in the day from a miner that had spent his last penny at a saloon and was looking to spend what he didn't have. He'd parked the wagon along the back of the prison, by the delivery entrance, which, to Joseph's surprise, was not guarded. It only required a key to unlock, and Joseph had gone to the cook to inquire how he might use this back entrance. To his further surprise, the cook, who was up to his neck in washing and peeling potatoes, nodded at a metal ring hanging from a nail by the kitchen door. "Just hang it back up when you're done," he'd said to Joseph before turning his attention back to the giant burlap sack of potatoes on the table.

No wonder so many prisoners escape. It wouldn't take much at all to grab this key and make for the hills.

He wished the key unlocked the prison cells, but the cook had told him it only opened the one delivery door. *And even if you could open Julia's cell, there's the matter of the two armed guards.*

As Joseph came out of the blustery, snowy cold of the night and into the hallway via the back entrance, he stomped his feet and tried not to despair. He was running out of time. If Julia awoke, and the warden learned she was alive, no doubt he'd suspect foul play, and Joseph would lose his job—and any chance he had to help Julia ever get out alive. Or help any of the other female prisoners, for that matter.

He locked the door, about to head back to the kitchen to return the key, when he heard the latch clicking. Joseph turned and peered at the door. Someone was jimmying with the lock, and he wasn't using a key—unless, perhaps, his hand was so cold, he was having a time of it trying to insert the key into the lock.

He thought twice about opening the door for whoever was on the other side, for if someone didn't have a key, and they had no intention of knocking, they might have nefarious plans in mind. And the last thing Joseph needed was more delay and distraction.

Though . . . a distraction might be exactly what he needed . . .

I hope whoever is trying to break in doesn't plan to shoot his way in. Why would anyone want to break into a prison?

Joseph's curiosity got the better of him. And, frankly, he had no other plan to save Julia. He'd run out of ideas. He was no hero, and he'd only end up behind bars—or shot—if he tried to wrest the key ring from the guard. He considered offering an even larger bribe, but he doubted the guards would go against the warden's explicit instructions.

Before Joseph could reach the door, it opened a crack. A hand in a dark glove eased the door wider, cautiously, quietly, and then a face protruded into the hallway, quickly shifting from concentration to surprise.

The man was about to slam the door, but Joseph whispered in a rush of words. "Wait, don't go. I'm a doctor, and I need your help."

The dark-skinned man, with wide eyes and big black pupils, eyed Joseph suspiciously. Then he looked him over, the full measure of him, and slipped inside, closing the door with a gentle push. He wore a long black wool overcoat that had seen better days, a black flop hat, and, strangely, soft leather shoes that were hardly appropriate for a snowy night. Now, with a little more light—which spilled from the kitchen into the hallway—Joseph saw the man was a Negro, with a big head and wide nose that looked to have been broken at one time. A heavy-set man, but not much taller than Joseph.

The unexpected intruder put a finger to his prominent lips and said, "Shhh." Then he glanced furtively down the hallway. When he seemed assured that no one else was taking an interest in his visit, he said somewhat enigmatically, "There's not much time, Doc, so's I'd git out o' the prison, if I were you."

"Not much time?" Joseph asked, following after the man, who had begun tiptoeing down the hall. "Wait. There're two guards up ahead."

The man stopped, then gave Joseph a wide smile revealing big white teeth. "Well . . . not fer long."

Before Joseph could ask what the man meant, the prison bells sounded an alarm, clanging loud and riotously without letup. Then he smelled it.

Smoke.

He grabbed the man by the sleeve, and the Negro turned around. His eyes were shining in glee. "Name's Levi, by the way." He put out his hand for Joseph to shake.

Joseph mindlessly shook the man's hand, equally horrified and excited. Was this the answer to his prayer? "I'm . . . Joseph Tuttle. What on earth did you do? Are the prisoners in danger?" Joseph imagined the sandstone-brick penitentiary couldn't catch fire the way a wooden building might, but dozens of prisoners were locked in cells, and smoke inhalation was deadly.

"Don'cha fret, Doc. It's jes a little fire. 'Nuff to set the guards a'runnin'."

Joseph hurried to the end of the hallway. The guards were gone.

"See," Levi said as he ran up beside him, "they's gone. An' now, I gots to go—"

Joseph grabbed onto the man's wrist. "Please, I need to get a girl out of that cell." He pointed to the solitary cell Julia lay in.

Levi's brows knitted. "A gal's in there?"

Joseph nodded. The man pondered a few seconds, then reached into one of the big coat pockets. He pulled out what looked like a key, but Joseph could tell it wasn't metal. Then he realized it was made of wood.

"This'll open any cell. They's all the same."

As Levi went over to the cell and inserted the key, Joseph asked, "How do you know this?"

The locked clicked, and the door swung open. The Negro turned and with that beaming smile replied, "I, uh, did a little time here in the pen. But me'n another prisoner made an imprint of one o' the keys, using some mud from the brickyard." He chuckled and gestured Joseph into the cell as the smell of smoke wafted around them, causing Joseph's eyes to sting and water.

Julia lay on the floor, still on Joseph's coat, her face ashen. She hadn't moved a muscle.

"Why, this gal's dead!" Levi declared.

"Trust me—she's not. But I must get her into my wagon and flee this place before she wakes."

When Levi hesitated, Joseph said, "Please, I'll pay you. Anything—"

"Ain't no need fer that, Doc. That li'l gal got no business bein' in such a devilish place."

With the care of a mother lifting her infant from a cradle, Levi hefted Julia's torso with his meaty strong arms as if she weighed nothing. Joseph rushed to her legs and lifted those. Together, they managed to get her out of the cell, down the hallway, and outside, where snow flurries danced like fireflies in the light seeping through the kitchen windows.

The cold collared Joseph again, drying the sweat on his neck as they carefully laid Julia in the back of the wagon. Joseph covered her with the heavy buffalo robe he'd put in the flat bed behind the bench seat.

He turned to thank Levi, but the man had run back to the door and was about to slip inside.

"Hey," Joseph called out to him, "where are you going?" He couldn't understand why a prison escapee would return and take such dangerous risks.

"I promised my pal I'd git 'im out. When we escaped, he got caught tryin' to cause a ruckus so's I could git free."

And now Levi was doing the same favor in return. Joseph couldn't help but admire the man's loyalty, despite his unorthodox—and highly unlawful—way of showing it. "You're a true friend. I hope you don't get caught."

Levi saluted Joseph, then disappeared inside. Joseph wondered if the man had served in the Union Army back during the War between the States.

The bells kept clanging, and though the acrid aroma of smoke carried on the breeze, Joseph saw no sign of a fire—not until he urged the mules into a fast trot and rounded the prison to get onto the road that led to the bridge. A glance over his shoulder showed flames licking the lower windows, just to the right of the main entrance, where the warden's office was. One of the large glass panes had been shattered.

Men in uniform were stationed by a small wagon with a water tank, aiming their hoses at the flames and yelling. Whatever Levi had used to set the fire seemed hard to put out. The water caused eruptions of smoke and flame and, apparently, hysteria and consternation. Joseph did not see the warden anywhere about. He hoped the man was uninjured—for it would be uncharitable to feel otherwise—but Joseph wouldn't mind if the prison fire kept House too busy to pursue a fleeing doctor and a missing "dead" prisoner. *Just for a few hours . . .*

He suddenly recalled Sarah's letter. Something about the weeds of hate being burned in the fire. She'd also written "*See that you and those in your care escape unscathed.*" Had she foreseen this literal fire?

Joseph let out a chuckle of relief. His nerves were frazzled, and though he longed for a down-filled mattress and a hot meal, he knew his fleshly comforts would have to be put off a while longer. There lay more danger ahead, of this he was certain. Any number of things could still go wrong. And he wouldn't have his new guardian angel, Levi, to help him see this madness to its conclusion.

But he'd made it this far. He could just picture Cathryn Povey's astonished face when he told her how he smuggled Julia out of the Wyoming Territorial Penitentiary. That, in itself, gave Joseph a surge of determination and courage.

He pulled out his pocket watch and noted the time: 11:28. He should make it to the mortuary without delay, so long as the roads weren't choked with snow or gunslingers or other manner of scalawags that might impede his progress. He hadn't yet ventured out at night into the heart of Laramie City's revelry district, but there was little chance of avoiding it entirely.

He shook the reins and got the mules moving in their surefooted pace across the bridge, plowing through drifts and nearly giving Joseph a heart attack when the wagon skidded on a sheet of hidden ice and almost crashed into the flimsy wooden railing that separated his wagon from the rushing river below.

Drawing in a long shaky breath, Joseph steeled his nerves and set his sights on the road beyond the bridge. When he made it safely across, he slowed the panting mules and caught his own breath. Miraculously, he'd rescued Julia from the clutches of Warden House. The Lord had sent him an angel in the guise of a Negro named Levi. He may not have been the same angel that came to the apostle Paul's rescue all those centuries ago, but he'd held the key to freedom just as readily—albeit a wooden one. *The Lord surely works in inexplicable ways.*

Chapter 27

"WHERE'D YOU DISAPPEAR TO?" Abel asked, clasping Robert's shoulders and grinning. "When I heard what happened ..."—he cleared the emotion from his throat—"to Ellsworth, I-I just couldn't believe it. But Benjamin said you didn't kill Lawson."

Robert nodded, pushing down the memory of Ellsworth choking, the gash on his neck spewing blood. "I shot him, but none of those bullets could've killed him."

"Word is Lawson has a bullet lodged in his heart."

Robert shook his head spastically. "Not mine. Someone else must'a shot him after I left. Then told everyone I killed him."

Abel's murderous expression washed Robert with relief. "I'd'a left town too—and never looked back." He stomped the cold from his feet, pounding the snow-choked street with his boots.

"That was the plan."

Abel smoothed his moustache and looked down the empty street. "Is it true? All this blew up over Carson's girl?" His face told Robert he didn't believe a word of it.

But Robert's silence confirmed the truth of it.

Abel whistled and shook his head. "I figured Benjamin was spinning a yarn, but I never . . ."

How could Robert tell Abel how much he loved Julia? He'd sound like a fool.

"Listen," he told Abel, "I need to ask you a favor."

"Anything." Abel's eyes told Robert he knew this would be the last time—at least in a long while—the two of them would talk.

"I got Comanche inside a storage building yonder." He pointed down the street. "You'll find it easy enough. The padlock's broken."

Abel fiddled with his moustache, eyes downcast. "I'll take care of him."

"Wait till 'bout one o'clock. There's some things I still gotta do."

"I heard the girl's in the prison—it was in the paper." He narrowed his eyes and studied Robert's face. "You aren't thinkin' of tryin' to break her out, are ya?"

"I'm not that stupid." *No, I'm even more foolhardy, trusting a doctor to sneak her out of the prison without mishap.* The urgency of the hour pressed upon him. "Listen . . . I'll get word to you, soon's I can. Maybe this'll blow over. Somehow."

Abel gave Robert a commiserating look filled with words that didn't need to be said. Robert's throat hurt. He shook Abel's hand and walked away, not looking back, waves of regret crashing over him.

Joseph pulled the team of mules into the alley off Second Street and let out a sigh, easing the wagon as close to the mortuary's back door as possible. The building was flanked by two smaller structures—storage of some sort. A single row of large wooden barrels lined the back of one, but Joseph had no idea what might be in them. He could hardly see, though the clouds backlit by the moon cast enough light for him to avoid tripping on the uneven ground.

As he got down from the bench and glanced about, making sure no one was around, he wondered how many more laws he would break tonight. He'd always been a law-abiding citizen, ever careful not to transgress with even minor infractions. But tonight, he was quite the criminal, and that fact did not sit well with him. Especially since he was about to commit yet another crime.

But it was all in the name of justice, to right a grave wrong. Besides, when he was done here, he'd leave the key he'd pilfered earlier that day where he'd found it—on the table by the back door.

After unlocking the door and slipping inside, Joseph stopped and listened. The antiseptic smell was one familiar to him, bringing to mind his college days and the rooms where they'd cut open cadavers. It gave him an odd comfort. The windows were shuttered, which might help to discourage curious eyes. Thankfully, the mortuary sat blocks from the saloons and gaming houses—no reason for anyone to be strolling through a lonely alley on a freezing night like this.

He lit the hurricane lamp on the desk and assessed his surroundings as he had in the daytime, when he'd paid a friendly visit to acquaint himself with the local funeral home proprietor. No doubt, in a town like Laramie, the man made a good living.

Good—the wood cart was still there, parked beside the far wall, a conveyance not unlike the ones used in hospitals.

Joseph rolled the cart to the door and clumsily pushed it over the threshold. After securing the door open with a brick, he positioned the cart level with the back of the wagon, then climbed up into the bed to begin the tricky extrication.

Julia was dead weight, and he feared he might hurt her as he wiggled her from the wooden slats to the surface of the table. It brought to mind that sweltering summer afternoon he'd chanced upon Brett Hendricks, who'd been wandering the desert miles south of Greeley for days, nearly dead and severely dehydrated. He'd had a dickens of a time getting Brett up into the back of his wagon—and out, as well—the cowboy weighing quite a bit more than this slip of a girl.

Still, with chilled hands and fingers stiff inside his gloves, the effort tired him and unraveled his composure just that much more. He didn't dare waste a second, so he jimmied the cart, now loaded with its cargo, back inside, then shut the door before he dared check Julia's condition. He hoped all this jostling hadn't aggravated her tenuous hold on life.

Joseph removed his gloves and rubbed his hands. The dark-paneled room had rows of shelving jam-packed with jars and stacks of cloths and surgical instruments, along with the accoutrements seen backstage at a theater venue—namely powders and paints, which the mortuary proprietor would use to make cadavers look more lifelike.

With a prayer on his lips, Joseph pulled the buffalo robe off of Julia's face and upper torso, wanting to keep her body as warm as possible in the cold room. It took a fearfully long moment for Joseph to detect the thready pulse in her carotid artery, and only then did his heart stop pounding his ribs. Her face in the repose of death was both beatific and unsettling. It was hard to imagine Julia Carson waking from such a deep abyss of sleep.

His pocket watch showed him it was mere minutes before midnight. Yet, Julia's countenance had not changed. He imagined that, however powerful Cheyenne medicine was, it probably was not an exact science and he should be prepared to stay longer than he'd hoped. It might necessitate a hasty escape once Robert arrived. Joseph would just have to wait and see.

And it worried him that Robert was nowhere in sight. What if someone had recognized him after all? He could have been arrested, for all Joseph knew. Sitting in the jail while Julia lay here.

What if he doesn't show up? Joseph hadn't truly considered that. What to do then? Return Julia to her parents and let them sort it out with the sheriff and the marshal? The thought of the poor girl being convicted of murder and sent to jail *again* made Joseph bristle. In the short time he'd been in Wyoming Territory, he had seen enough to make him want to crawl back to the safe moral environs of Greeley, Colorado. A town that prohibited liquor, saloons, and carousing. A town where women were respected and honored. Not treated like a criminal for defending her life against a man that could easily overpower her.

He couldn't very well hide Julia in his house. That would be the first place the warden would look once her "body" was nowhere to be found. *Cathryn would help me. No doubt she'd scurry the girl off to a place of sanctuary. Maybe even disguise her and give her a new name so she could start an unfettered new life.*

Joseph shook the notion from his head. When had he started thinking like an outlaw? Was this town already rubbing off on him? How did Cathryn manage from day to day to stay incorruptible and unsullied from the rampant violence and lawlessness? His admiration for her grew to new proportions. For she and her ill husband could have relocated to any number of towns in the West, towns like Greeley. But Joseph was of the mind to believe she'd chosen Laramie for its unrest along with its progressive stance on women's rights. He'd bet his last dollar that, more than anything, Cathryn Povey liked a challenge.

He studied Julia's peaceful face, glad to look upon it, for it gave comfort to his soul. He hoped that one day she would feel as peaceful, living a happy life with the man she loved.

Who still hadn't arrived.

Joseph huffed, his impatience bubbling up again, as he went to the back door and peeked outside.

A gunshot ripped the quiet of the night. Then another, close. On the other side of the mortuary, on Front Street. Screams and yelling followed.

He shut the door and pushed his back up against it, breathing deeply as dizziness engulfed him. Was Robert in danger? What if the warden was out there, looking for Julia's body?

He fought his urge to lock the door and hide. But after hearing more gunshots and screaming, he couldn't keep from bolting out the door to see what trouble was brewing outside. He had to know if Julia was in danger, and if so, he had to get her back in the wagon and take her someplace safe. *And that would be a lot easier if she woke up, so I wouldn't have to heft her up into the flat bed yet again!* The thought of trying to transport her yet another time exhausted him.

He tucked the buffalo robe around Julia's shoulders, leaving her face exposed so she could breathe easily, and if she woke, she wouldn't be startled or scared. *Just stay asleep a little longer. I'll be back in a jiffy.*

He put a cork in the unsettling feelings of trepidation bubbling inside him and went back out into the night. When he slunk around the side of the building, what he saw surprised him. A group of angry men carrying torches and rifles gathered in the middle of the street. They faced three men, who stood their ground not a block away. One of the three held his pistol aloft, as if threatening to rain bullets. *What in heaven's name is going on?*

"I'm givin' you three minutes to leave," that man with the pistol shouted.

His threat didn't deter one of the men holding a torch. That man took steps forward, waving the rifle in his other hand.

"It's you that better leave, Sheriff. Afore I shoot you dead."

Joseph's eyes went wide. Why was the sheriff out in front of the mortuary? And who'd be daring enough to threaten the man? Could that be Lester Carson? Joseph recalled Julia saying the sheriff hated her father.

"It's your fault! All your fault," the tall man yelled at the sheriff, stopping mere yards from the subject of his rage. Even from where Joseph stood in the shadows, he could hear the anguish in the man's voice. "My daughter's dead—and you're gonna pay."

A gasp slipped out of Joseph's mouth. It *was* Julia's father. *Oh dear . . .* How in the world had Mr. Carson learned that Julia had died? *News travels fast in this town. And bad news the fastest.* Had one of the guards from the prison spread the word? Or the warden?

This was bad, very bad. And where was Robert? Joseph hoped he wasn't caught up with this crowd. Surely he wouldn't dare. He decided he'd better get back to Julia, see if Robert had snuck in.

Just as Joseph turned, a rifle blast startled him. A man screamed in pain.

Joseph spun back, hearing cursing and someone yelling for a doctor. How could he ignore the cries? The man Joseph presumed was Lester Carson had dropped to his knees. He cradled his right shoulder, the cowboys alongside him aiming their rifles at the sheriff.

Joseph took tentative steps into the street, close to where Carson's men flanked him—just to get a look. A glance showed the sheriff aiming his pistol at Carson, and Joseph worried he intended to fire again. Two Irish fellows, most likely the sheriff's deputies, had their rifles up at the ready.

One misstep and a bloodbath could ensue. And Joseph would be right smack-dab in the middle of it. *There's no time for this. Get back to Julia!*

"Hey, that's the doc from the prison."

Joseph cringed and tucked his head, but someone grabbed his arm. Joseph looked back, and the men surrounding Carson swiveled and glared at him.

"That true? You a doctor?" one of them asked.

He pushed words out of his tight throat. "Yes, I'm . . . I'm a doctor. Please, let me help." No way out now. He prayed Julia was still asleep. What if she woke and went out looking for him?

Lester Carson stopped moaning and glared at Joseph as he approached. Joseph guessed the man to be in his fifties, and he'd suffered harsh weather and hard years as evidenced by the deep creases and worry lines. A thick bushy white moustache dangled over his panting mouth. His face blanched, and sweat pebbled his forehead.

Joseph pried the man's hand away from his shoulder so he could get a look at the wound.

Carson, wincing, breathed out, "You . . . You're the doctor . . . at the prison? You saw my Julia . . . ?" Tears filled the bereft man's eyes and spilled onto his cheeks.

That's not a conversation I want to have right now. Joseph ripped open the blood-soaked sleeve as the men closed ranks around Carson. "Please, step back. Give him some room." Though, it was Joseph who was feeling as if he'd been stuffed in a closet of rank-smelling clothing that hadn't been washed in months. In the torchlight Joseph saw the bullet had gone clean through and out the back of the shoulder. Still, the wound needed tending, but someone else would have to treat him. A clock was ticking emphatically in his head.

Joseph stood. "It went clean through. You'll be fine. Just soak the wounds with alcohol." He added, looking at all the men's faces, "Maybe it'd be best to cooperate with the sheriff and depart."

The men cursed and scowled, dashing Joseph's hopes that the conflict would shortly conclude. He made a hasty retreat back toward the buildings, then another rifle fired.

Joseph ducked as bullets whizzed past, some hitting the post of the building in front of him, others breaking windows and ricocheting off the ground. Another bout of screaming and yelling erupted. Townsfolk ran pell-mell in all directions.

As Joseph squeezed into a crevice between the building and a metal water trough, he wondered if all hell wasn't about to break loose in the town. Was this another "divine" diversion to help him get Robert and Julia safely away?

If so, there was only one problem: how to get back to the mortuary in one piece.

When the shooting stopped and the angry voices got angrier, Joseph took tentative steps from his hiding place. But no sooner did he straighten than two men, smelling like a liquor factory, broke out in fisticuffs beside him. Joseph leaped back, but not in time. A wild swing of a fist met with his cheek.

As he stumbled backward, his face smarting, he cursed his bad luck and pathetic reflexes. The back of his foot banged into the metal trough, and Joseph tripped and tumbled into the empty trough, smacking the back of his head so hard, brown spots swam in his vision. And then the flickering lights of the torches around him snuffed out.

Chapter 28

IS THAT GUNSHOT? ROBERT SHOOK his head, saw that he was slumped up against a wall, Comanche mouthing Robert's hair with his lips. The horse hovered over him and nickered.

What? Where was he? It took but a few seconds to realize, to his horror, that he'd fallen asleep. How in the world could he have managed that? Last thing he remembered, he'd come back to check on Comanche, the warmth of the shed making him drowsy.

Julia! Was he too late? The doctor had told him to be at the mortuary at midnight sharp.

Robert chastised himself as he felt around the murky space for his hat. He squashed it on his head and leapt to his feet. Then gave Comanche a last pat with great sadness. "Wait here, fella. Abel'll come git ya."

The horse made a move to follow him out the door, but Robert held out his hand, then, when outside, secured the door behind him with a piece of wood.

The cold air sobered him up quickly.

Blam, blam!

Robert froze in his tracks. *Gunshot, again. Rifles and pistols, both.*

And close—too close. Who was shooting and why? Would he be able to get across the street and over to the mortuary without being spotted?

All it took was a quick glance around the corner of the shed to get his last question answered. A crowd of angry folks clogged the street. He couldn't see who was in the middle of the commotion, but he heard the voices. And one was unmistakable.

The sheriff.

Last thing Robert needed was to run into Carr. He'd have to slip along the tracks, take a long way around to the back of the mortuary. Shouldn't be too hard, but it would take more time than he had, of that Robert was certain.

Had the sheriff shot someone? By the ruckus, it sure sounded like it. But what did Robert care? If some drunken fellas needed the sheriff to break up their fight, all the better for Robert. He could use a distraction.

With his hat pulled down over his eyebrows and his chin tucked, Robert inched closer, working through the crush to hear better.

Another shock met Robert's eyes when he slipped out from behind a fat man and saw Lester Carson sitting on the ground, cradling his shoulder. He'd been shot! By the sheriff?

Robert's gut roiled, thinking how Carr must've killed Lawson. How much Carr hated Carson with a vengeance. *I wouldn't put it past the sheriff—nosiree.*

And Carson had every reason to kill Sheriff Carr—for throwing his sweet girl in prison unlawfully. *Was that what all this was about—vengeance? Gettin' back at someone for something?* And then he reminded himself: *The sheriff prob'ly told everyone I killed Ty. Was that so Carson would hate the Morrison name even more?* Seemed like Carr's objective was to pour gasoline on the feud to make it burn hotter. *What's in it for Carr? Something, that's for sure.*

Lester Carson struggled to get to his feet, aided by two punchers on either side. "You killed my daughter. Let's have it out. Now." He aimed his gun straight and true at the sheriff.

A knife went through Robert's heart.

No. He couldn't've heard right. Julia—dead? Please, God, no!

Rage swirled like dervishes before Robert's eyes. He pulled out his gun from its holster. If Lester Carson didn't kill Sheriff Carr, Robert would. He would fill him full of bullets and then some . . .

Then he heard a horse galloping and swiveled to look. Some fool was racing down Front Street right toward the heart of the crowd, yelling and waving a pistol.

Oh Lord, it's my pa!

Robert took a step toward the street, his mouth agape, watching as his pa kicked his horse to spur it even faster. Folks screamed and pushed one another aside, making way for the huffing animal before it ran them down.

"Wait, stop!" his pa cried out, still brandishing his pistol, firing shots into the air. And halfway down the block ran Abel, his arms flailing frantically, as he futilely chased after the madman on the horse.

Robert knew he should run, hurry to the mortuary, to see if Julia was there . . . if she was truly dead, but his shock glued his boots to the snowy ground. The doc had promised to get Julia out. Alive. It had to be a false rumor, just had to be.

The crowd broke apart enough for Robert to see a sight that stunned him to his core. His pa yanked on the reins—Robert saw now that he was riding his favorite horse, Black Star—and skidded to a stop, the animal nearly buckling as he slid on the slippery street.

Stephen Morrison jumped out of the saddle and onto the ground, fired three shots into the air, then spun around drunkenly, searching the crowd. What on God's green earth had possessed his pa to act this mad?

Robert saw Sheriff Carr take three steps toward Robert's pa, put his hands on his hips, and call out, "Morrison, put down that gun, or I'll be forced to shoot ya."

"No, no, you got it all wrong, all wrong, Sheriff."

It was only then that Robert realized his pa was weeping. Weeping!

Robert hadn't seen tears on his pa's face since the day they buried Cassidy. What in tarnation was going on?

Riveted, Robert listened, along with the crowd of onlookers who stood, astonished and perplexed at the scene playing out before them.

Abel caught up, his sides heaving, and grabbed Stephen Morrison's arm, but he was shook off so Robert's pa could march up to the sheriff and face him just feet away. The Colt dangled in his hand, but the sheriff made no attempt to grab it from him. Carr appeared curious to hear the story Robert's pa seemed anxious to tell.

"He's drunk," Abel protested, picking up Black Star's reins and trying to stand between the two men. "Let me jus' take 'im home—"

"No!" Stephen said, standing his ground. "I have a confession, and it has to be told, once'n for all." He glanced over at Carson, who stared in bewilderment at his mortal enemy.

Abel looked upon him, befuddled, and the crowd hushed, always eager for a good tale. Robert gaped, unblinking. What could his pa possibly want to confess?

Carr's nerves were like jolts of electricity. He held his pistol at his side, ready to shoot anyone who made a wrong move. His deputies trained their rifles on Carson and his ruffians. And Carson was aiming his gun at Morrison. Carr counted eight hotheaded fools pointing guns at one another. A recipe for disaster. How would he break this up without someone getting killed? *And me, in particular.*

Stephen Morrison stood between him and Carson, holding his hands out.

Just what was this drunken fool up to?

The crowd was like a surging river, swaying, jockeying to see the night's entertainment, heedless to the danger to their own selves. *Idiots, all o' them.*

"Is it true?" Morrison asked, blubbering like a girl. "Lester's daughter—she's dead?"

The noisy crowd confirmed it. Carr heard condemnation from more than a few, blaming him, siding with Carson. No way was he going to take the fall for this.

He yelled out, looking at the angry faces, "It's no fault o' mine! I took her to the prison for her own safety—"

"That's a pile of horse pucky, Sheriff!" Carson yelled back. "You wanted her dead!"

Carson tried to run toward him, but one of his ranch hands held him fast. He squirmed like a fish trying to get out of a bucket.

To Carr's shock, Morrison wobbled over to Lester Carson, then fell to his knees and looked up at him in a beseeching manner.

Carson went stiff, staring confused and disgusted at Morrison.

Carr clicked his tongue against his teeth. *Well, if that don't take all . . .*

"I cheated. It was me. I did it." His words slurred together like mush, but the meaning was clear.

Carson took a step back, scrunched his face, glowering at Morrison.

"What're you talking about?" Carson asked him.

"That card game . . ." Morrison sobbed with great heaves, his body shaking. "I was so mad, so mad . . . You took my gal, my sweet Danielle, mine . . ."

Understanding lit up Carson's face. "You mean . . . you mean you fixed it so I'd win? Why? Why would you do such a thing?"

Carr knew exactly what Morrison was talking about. *That card game — when Asa lost his ranch. But why would Morrison make it so Carson would win?*

"I never meant . . . I just wanted . . . I thought House would shoot you, then . . . then Danielle would be mine . . . I never . . ."

Morrison collapsed in a heap on the ground, the crowd mesmerized and hushed. Carson stared at his enemy, long and hard, but Carr couldn't have guessed in a million years what the rancher was thinking.

All this over a gal! And then he thought about Asa House and his hatred of the man who had taken everything from him. *All these years he's hated Lester Carson . . . and it was Morrison who'd done him wrong . . .* Morrison.

And all this time, Carr had been doing Asa's bidding for him, meting out vengeance for him. Mistakenly so.

He thought of Carson's girl, so young, so frightened. Caught in the middle of this feud, an innocent that had been used as a pawn in Asa House's game of revenge. It made him suddenly sick in his gut, thinking how he, too, had been played, been a pawn for the warden in his skullduggery, a man Carr had admired, had thought was his friend . . . Then he thought about the letter he'd written, full of ugly sentiments, that he'd signed Robert Morrison's name to. That letter had set all this in motion—the deadly confrontation by the courthouse, Carson's girl coming to town to meet her intended and ending up in the prison. *And my killing Ty Lawson.*

He looked down at Morrison, who was weeping and repentant, his face buried in his hands, the pistol on the ground by his foot.

Carr reached down to pick it up, but Morrison grabbed it and jumped to his feet. Tears streaking his face, he spun one way, then another, a crazed man, aiming his gun at Carr, then at random faces in the crowd.

He turned to Carson, raised his hands. "I'm sorry, so, so sorry. Just shoot me. I deserve it. My life for . . . for your girl's. . ."

Lester Carson stood, holding his shoulder and wincing in pain, watching Morrison with an incredulous look on his face.

And then a voice boomed to Carr's right, and the crowd parted.

"Git outta my way!" a man shouted. "Morrison!"

Asa House strode into the middle of the street, his arm outstretched, taut like an arrow, his long-muzzled pistol pointed at Morrison's head.

The crowd gasped and murmured. Carr froze, instinctively reached for his sidearm. Morrison stopped swiveling and faced the warden, the man he'd cheated all those years ago, from whom he finagled the biggest tract of ranch land in Wyoming Territory from out of his grasp—forcing House to give it to one of his punchers. Morrison's hated enemy.

O'Grady started to say something to Carr, then froze up as Asa stopped and made to squeeze the trigger. Morrison closed his eyes and outstretched his arms, waiting for the bullet that would take his life.

"You're a dead man," Asa told Morrison, seething with hatred.

Gunshot exploded and Carr startled. Asa's pistol slipped from his hand as his face collapsed in pain.

To Carr's surprise, Morrison didn't jerk and fall.

Asa House grunted and clutched his chest, then tumbled to the cold, hard ground. Morrison stepped back, his mouth open, staring at the warden. Slowly, his gaze lifted from the ground and found Lester Carson.

Carr looked on as Lester Carson lowered his hand with the smoking gun then slipped it into his holster. Utter confusion gripped the onlookers, and their mutterings sounded like a stormy sea. One by one, folks backed away, vacated the street, until only a handful of bystanders remained.

A strange hush enveloped those in the street as the persistent wind died and clouds parted. Moonlight lit up Lester Carson's anguished face—the face of a inconsolable man who grieved the loss of an only child.

Carr felt tears press the back of his eyes, but he made no attempt to stop them from spilling out. He didn't need to examine Asa House to know that the man who'd truly killed Julia Carson was dead. But he also knew he himself had played an unforgivable part in that poor girl's death, and that sobering truth stabbed him with guilt.

Carr stepped back, his deputies still at his side, speechless. A woman ran to Carson, threw her arms around him as he stood still, like a bronze statue, staring into the cold night. She wept on his shoulder, and Carson mindlessly slipped an arm around her waist.

Stephen Morrison looked vacantly at the weeping couple. Carr saw in him a man who'd lost his way, long ago. And had been suffering mightily for it. Morrison holstered his pistol, swiped his sleeve across his eyes, then turned and walked over to his horse.

The cowboy from Morrison's ranch slipped the reins over the gelding's neck, looked up at Morrison, and stepped back as the rancher swung around and headed up Front Street at a slow walk. Moonlight followed him like a spotlight, an actor on a lonely, empty stage making his exit at the final curtain.

Chapter 29

W hen the crowd thinned, Robert ducked behind a dark-windowed storefront and peeked out around the corner. Now that the clouds had skittered apart, the half-moon could be seen dangling over the eastern buttes, and its harsh light illuminated the scene performing on the street's stage. Abel stood with his back to the sheriff, watching Robert's pa, slumped on Black Star's back, head north on Front Street, a thick somber mood in the air.

Robert was too far back in the severe shadows of the building to see much other than silent figures moving in a slow dance. A body lay on the ground. Dead, from what Robert could determine, since no one was rushing to get the fella any help. Though more than a few cowboys and a couple of fellas in some sort of uniforms lingered nearby. He wondered if it was someone he knew, but right now his only concern was Julia. She couldn't be dead — she couldn't.

He'd heard a shot reverberate in the freezing night as he scurried, hunched over, along the backs of the hodgepodge of structures between Steele and Park Streets, torn between wanting to watch the drama that held answers to so many nagging questions Robert had and needing to get to Julia and whisk her to safety.

He made out Carson, Julia's pa, and guessed the woman kneeling with her arms around him was Julia's ma. Thank the Lord, the sheriff hadn't killed Carson. Robert knew it would utterly break Julia to lose her pa so soon after losing Ty. Only weeks ago he'd seen Miz Carson decked out in her party gown and jewels, eagerly hoping Julia would want to marry that fella from Cheyenne. How much had happened since then, changed all their lives. All because Robert'd had a notion to sneak into a party he hadn't been invited to.

If he hadn't gone, none of this would have happened. Ellsworth would still be alive. Julia would never have killed a man or been tossed into the penitentiary. *But then, you'd never have met her. She prob'ly would've married that rich fella from Cheyenne, and you'd'a been none the wiser.* Was it worth it? All this . . . so he and Julia could be together? He knew how he'd answer, but he couldn't speak for Julia. When all the dust settled, would she truly love him? She seemed to see the good intentions of his heart even when he couldn't see it himself. She erased his abiding pain and replaced it with hope. Hope that one day he'd be whole again instead of the pieces of the man he saw in the mirror.

Whatever had transpired, between all the yelling and screaming and shooting, seemed to have concluded—if not amicably, at least in some sort of truce. Which made Robert even more vulnerable, more easily spotted. He still had to cross Sheridan Street to get to the mortuary. One more block—he craned to see through the murkiness of shadow and made out the shape of a wagon and what looked like two mules hitched and standing idly in the alleyway. Hope sparked in his heart — that had to be the doc's wagon behind the mortuary. Which meant Julia was inside, waiting for him . . .

Oh, please, Lord, let it be so.

A man walked along the east side of Front Street, crossing Sheridan. For some reason he stopped, then turned.

Abel!

Robert longed to talk to his pal one last time, enlist his help. But he'd run out of time for talking, for explaining.

Abel stared curiously and watched as Robert ran, head down, across the street and over to the mortuary. When Abel started his way, Robert shook his head.

Abel hesitated, nodded, then backed away. Robert hoped Abel would look after his ma. Who knew what shape his pa was in? Maybe he was losing his mind. But Robert couldn't find a shred of empathy in his heart for the man who'd cut him out of his own heart. Would reconciliation ever be possible? Robert doubted it. *You gotta let the past go. Think on your future, on how much you love Julia.*

Robert rushed to the back door of the mortuary, passing a row of large barrels — black powder, he reckoned. He glanced about, and, seeing no one, tried the handle. The door creaked open. He stepped inside.

The room was cold. It smelled of antiseptic and dust and mold. Shelves full of jars lined the walls. A lamp on a sideboard cast light on a shape lying on a small table in the middle of the room. At first Robert thought it was an animal of some kind, but as he neared the thing, something punched a hole in his chest, grabbed hold of his heart, and squeezed the living daylights out of him.

He couldn't take his eyes off her face; he couldn't move. He didn't dare see if she was breathing. The pallor consuming

Julia's visage told him she was dead, but he didn't want to believe it.

Choked up, he tried to swallow, searched around with his eyes. Where was Doc Tuttle? Why wasn't he here? Had something happened to him? Everything was wrong, so wrong.

He took a tentative step toward her. Why had Tuttle wrapped her in a buffalo skin? To sneak her out of the prison? To keep her warm? Why would she need to be kept warm if she was dead?

Unless . . . unless she hadn't been dead when he carted her away from the prison. Had she died on the way? Had someone hurt her? She couldn't be dead. Just sleeping . . . just sleeping. *Oh, please, let her be fast asleep . . .*

Robert couldn't breathe. He now understood the torment Julia had so often suffered, for when he put his fingers to her throat, searching for a pulse, he couldn't find air to suck into his lungs. Convulsions seize him as he frantically pressed his fingers again, this time to her wrist, then to the other side of her neck. Nothing. *Oh, God, nothing. No heartbeat.*

He screamed in his head, shook all over, laid his head against her heart, willing it to beat. Begging it. A wail left his mouth—sounding like an animal keening, in mourning.

Robert's thoughts congealed, clogged his head until he couldn't think at all. His limbs went numb; his eyes glazed over.

What had he done? Why had he trusted that doctor—that fool doctor! *He must've made her drink that stuff in the bottle—that . . . poison Eli's Indian ma made. And it killed her.*

Rage simmered in his gut. Rage at Eli and his meddlesome ma. Rage at the doctor for taking such a crazy chance. Rage at the sheriff for putting Julia in the prison. Rage at his pa, and at Lester Carson, for the feud that caused all this in the first place.

The last tenuous strand of hope snapped in Robert's heart. There was nothing left for him. Nothing this life had to offer. Nothing he wanted. All he wanted was lying here, on this hard table in this cold room, this angel who was now in the Lord's arms instead of his own. Why? *Why?*

Something hardened inside him, turning him to stone, as if some witch had cast a magic spell over him. He touched Julia's cool cheek; the flesh felt foreign, not human. She was gone, and all that remained was an empty shell. He would never see her gentle smile or hear her sweet voice again. Not until he joined her on the other side, in death.

The sooner he joined her, the sooner he would behold her once more. Be with her forever. What was he waiting for?

He went over to the shelves, mindlessly, emotionless, already one foot in the afterlife, one lingering behind long enough to complete this final task, thoughts of Cassidy flitting through his head, a smile lifting on Robert's face at the notion of seeing his brother again. This life, so full of trouble and woe, was a ball and chain. He would cut that chain and be free, finally free . . .

The glass jars were labeled with scribblings that Robert didn't bother trying to read. He unscrewed the top of one jar after another, smelling and tasting the contents, settling on the most putrid, vile concoction he could find — one that displayed a skull and crossbones on the label. He hoped he wouldn't vomit it up.

Robert climbed up on the narrow table upon which Julia lay. There was hardly room for him, but he unwrapped her from the buffalo robe with trembling fingers and dropped it to the floor. Then he gathered her lifeless body into his arms, sitting up long enough to down the horrid liquid that burned his throat and made him gag. Somehow he drank it all, dropped the empty bottle onto the buffalo skin, pulled Julia tight to him, and lay his head down on the splintery wood.

His steamy breath rose before his eyes, smudged by his tears, like mist hovering over a placid lake, until his eyelids grew heavy and he closed them, closing out the world, bringing that curtain down upon his sorry life that he was all too ready to leave behind.

The first thing Joseph Tuttle saw when he opened his eyes was the muzzle and fat lips of a horse.

Joseph yelped and sat upright, spooking the horse, who, Joseph suddenly realized, was merely looking for a drink from the empty trough he was presently sitting in. The stray horse wandered off into the street, which was infused with a hazy glow from the moonlight and drifting ground fog.

Joseph felt the back of his head and found the lump that was the source of the throbbing pain. He rubbed it gingerly as he cautiously looked around. The street was empty but for a few townsfolk standing and talking, smoking cigarettes, and ambling toward the saloons.

Panic struck him, whisking away his breath. *How long have I been out? Oh Lord, what time is it?*

He stumbled out of the trough and located his pocket watch. He craned to read the time in the faint light. He gasped. It was nearly half-past midnight! *Oh heavens! Julia!*

He slipped and skidded on the slushy street, hurrying as fast as his legs could carry him to the back door to the mortuary.

It took a moment to fathom what he was seeing. Julia—still unconscious and lying on the cart. The buffalo robe on the floor.

And a man lying next to her, his arms loose around her neck and torso.

Joseph's gaze snagged on the man's limp wrist, the hand dangling off the side of the cart. His heart slammed against his chest.

"Robert. Robert!"

Joseph ran over to him, felt Robert's face and neck, found his artery. He barely had a pulse!

What in heaven's name happened? Why wasn't Julia awake by now? Oh, what to do?

Then something glinted at his feet. He reached down and picked up an empty glass jar, the top missing. He read the label. *Embalming fluid . . .*

Joseph was a devout man, and it wasn't in his nature to curse, but words came out of his mouth that had never been uttered before.

What a blasted fool! Why would Robert do such a thing? The methanol in the liquid could cause coma and death and blindness. But, of course, Robert had drunk it to kill himself. *I wish Shakespeare had never written that horrible play!* Joseph was certain that's where Robert got the idea of killing himself.

Well, I'm not going to let this drama end the way the Bard ended his tragedy. The Good Lord didn't lead me down this path just to see these two young lovers die.

He ran to the shelves and craned to read the labels. The words in Sarah's letter ran through his head; he'd memorized them and affixed them to his heart. *"My good doctor, sometimes we are pressed to make a hard choice, indeed. The way through is a dark tunnel, but it the only way through. When the time comes, be of courage and cling to your faith. . . . See that you and those in your care escape unscathed."*

Sarah had entrusted him with this dangerous task. But it was God who had led him here. *"Lord, help me save them!"*

Ah! He found exactly what he needed. Joseph took the jar, unscrewed the top, and propped Robert's head high enough to force the carapichea ipecacuanha down his throat. Ipecac syrup was a poison itself, though in small doses was a remedy for cough. But larger doses worked as an emetic, and Joseph watched anxiously for signs of Robert's stomach clenching.

There! *Thank you, God!*

Joseph hefted Robert to sitting, as best he could, and just in time. The contents of Robert's stomach violently ejected from his mouth and onto the floor, narrowly missing Joseph's trousers.

Robert gagged and heaved, his stomach convulsing. When Joseph ascertained that Robert was sitting up on his own, he found a towel, wet it with water from a pitcher, and came to Robert's side.

As he wiped Robert's face, relief buoyed Joseph and calmed his racing heart.

"Wha . . . where am I . . . ?" Robert's eyes opened, and his attendance fell upon Julia at his side. "Oh no!" He turned to Joseph and scowled. "What did you do? What did you do?"

Robert's countenance fell like a rock into a well. Grief-stricken, he gathered Julia up and pulled her to his chest, tears streaking his cheeks.

"She's not dead, Robert!" The stench of vomit filled Joseph's nostrils, making him gag. He tried to loosen Robert's death grip on Julia's torso. "Please, believe me. She is alive."

Robert's face loosened in confusion. "Alive? I . . . I don't understand . . ."

"Here," Joseph said, extending his hand, sweat dribbling down his neck, "come down from there. I'll show you."

With an incredulous and perplexed expression, Robert shakily got off the cart, steadying himself on the cart's edge. Just to ease his own mind, Joseph pressed his fingers against Julia's carotid artery. There it was—her pulse. But no longer thready, just weak.

Joseph searched the shelves until he found a small vial of smelling salts. He was grateful the proprietor of this mortuary had stocked the shelves with medicines. Perhaps he treated injuries and illnesses in his spare time. Joseph didn't know what he would have done if he hadn't found the ipecac. Or gotten back in time to save Robert's life.

He imagined what Julia might have done if she'd awoken and found Robert dead at her side. Yes, this was far too much like *Romeo and Juliet* for Joseph's liking.

Chapter 30

H E SAW IT! HER EYELASHES fluttered ever so slightly. Robert looked at the doctor, who had a smile on his face.

She was alive. Julia was alive! He could almost hear a heavenly choir of angels singing a hallelujah chorus.

Robert thought he would topple over with relief. Joy flooded his body in raucous waves.

Doc Tuttle stepped back and lowered the little glass bottle of smelling salts. Julia made a face, then her eyes opened. She squinted, put a hand to her head. The doctor steadied her so she wouldn't fall off. But Robert couldn't move a muscle, astonished at the sight of her living, breathing . . .

Dark spots danced in front of her eyes. A stabbing pain made her head feel as if someone had smacked her with a frying pan. She was cold, so cold.

Wrapping her arms around herself, she realized someone's hands were on her shoulders. Why was it so cold? Shafts of light sliced her vision into a kaleidoscope of washed-out colors. She made out dark walls, shelves, a door . . . the shape of a man in front of her.

Julia rummaged through her memory. A prison cell. The clang of a door. The laugh of a guard. Mean, dark eyes . . . *the warden*.

Julia jerked upright. Heard someone uttering her name, sounding as if coming from the bottom of a deep, dry well.

Dr. Tuttle. The vial he gave her to drink. The smell of smoke . . . Was she still in the prison? In the infirmary? A strong putrid stench registered in her brain mixed with the unmistakable odor of smelling salts.

It all came rushing back to her. The warden throwing her into solitary confinement. The good doctor finally arriving and giving her the Cheyenne medicine woman's potion . . . *Did it work? How long was I unconscious?*

Woozy, she sat up straighter, the hands propping her up. Finally, the spots dissipated and she could make out . . . Robert . . .

"Julia," he said, drinking her in and holding out his arms. The look on his face washed away every thought, every last shred of confusion, every vestige of worry.

"Oh, Robert—you're here!" Her throat was raw and her words scratchy. She had worried that she'd never look again into his beautiful face.

He came to her and lifted her into his arms, those wonderful strong arms she missed so very much. She buried her teary face into his chest as he stroked her and crooned her name over and over. She had so many questions to ask. So many things she wanted to say to him, but they all could wait. She wanted to linger in this moment forever, but a niggling fear rose in her chest.

Julia pulled back and looked around the strange room and found the doctor standing next to the table she'd lain upon. *Not a table*, she realized. Some kind of cart. What was this place, and were they safe? Then she recalled the doctor telling Robert to meet them at midnight at the mortuary. Dr. Tuttle sported a wide grin.

"Back from the dead—a little late. But better late than never," he said with a nervous laugh.

"Oh, Doctor. You did it! I don't know how you got me out, but I'm grateful. God bless you, my dear doctor!"

Dr. Tuttle's lips pinched. "Well, it wasn't without its excitement. And quite a tale to tell. But we shouldn't waste any time. Who knows if—"

Julia heard voices—muffled ones, coming from outside somewhere. The doctor's face grew alarmed. Robert gently set Julia onto her feet.

"Can you stand?" he whispered, his arms still around her.

She managed, though she was so weak. And thirsty.

Someone pounded on a door.

"Oh dear," Dr. Tuttle said.

"What is it? Who's there?" Julia asked.

"You'll have to stall 'em, Doc," Robert said, his tone anxious. Julia watched with curiosity as he ran over to the shelves and grabbed a bottle.

A man's deep voice bellowed. "Is anyone in there? I have to see her. I must see her."

Julia's heart leapt into her throat. *Father?* She spun to Robert. "I can't . . . I can't—"

"Go! Quick now!" the doctor said, pointing at the door. The doctor took steps into a dark hallway opposite.

Without hesitation, Robert scooped Julia up into his arms again. "Thanks, Doc. Listen—don't let him inside. Lead him away from the building—"

"What are you saying?" the doctor asked.

"Just, please, do what I ask. Get far away—"

"Robert," Julia said. "If my father finds us—"

"He won't. Trust me."

She did. They said hasty good-byes to the doctor, though Julia wished she had more time. How did her father know she was here? Had he come to take her home? Where was *here*?

Robert hurried with her out the door, where they entered an alley painted with moonlight. A wagon rigged with two mules sat just outside, the animals rousing from a nap and stomping their feet and huffing steam at their approach. The cold night air brushed away all the weariness from her bones. It had to be well past midnight, and she was somewhere in the middle of Laramie City, and snow had fallen—a great deal of it.

She listened for sounds, for her father's voice, but the town was quiet, which made her think they were far from the saloons and brothels. She didn't recognize the backs of these buildings, but why would she? She hardly ever came to town and never through the alleyways between the shops and offices.

Robert helped her up into the bench seat, then gathered up the reins and put them in Julia's hands. "Drive 'em down the alleyway, yonder." He pointed. "Don't stop; don't wait for me. Get at least three blocks before you stop. Don't attract any attention."

"What are you going to do? Why aren't you coming with me—?"

Robert held her cool hands in his warm ones. He pulled her head to his and gave her a tender kiss. "I'll be but a moment. There's somethin' needs doing. Trust me."

She did. She fell into those deep blue eyes and drowned in the depths of his love. Then she slapped the reins against the front of the wagon at the same time Robert smacked the rump of one of the mules. They broke into a startled trot, and she hurried them through the alley swallowed in shadow, keeping her head down in case someone should see her.

A patchwork of moonlight lit up drifts of snow as the wagon rolled along. She pushed down her fear and worry and sent a prayer heavenward, thanking God for her rescuers. How Dr. Tuttle had managed to get her out of that guarded cell, she just couldn't imagine. But he'd done it. Would she ever get the chance to thank him? She would—she'd make sure of it. She owed him her life. *And what about that warden? And the sheriff? Will they come after us? Will my father?*

She couldn't think about it—not now. Not until she was safely away with the man she adored and yearned to hold in her arms forever.

He'd considered it earlier, while the hours had dragged by, waiting for night and for the doctor to bring Julia to the mortuary. But when he saw the barrels of black powder in the alley, it cemented his plan. *That is, until you decided to kill yourself.*

He'd made a crazy decision that had almost been fatal. Thank the Lord Tuttle had found him. Seeing Julia dead drove him to madness. Another terrible mistake. But this time, fate had stayed his hand.

Robert worked quickly. With a rock, he pried off the lid of the closest barrel as he eyed Julia's progress down the alley, watching for signs of anyone coming around the corner of the building. Carefully, he drew the jar of nitroglycerin from his coat pocket and set it on top of the black powder, nestling it in an inch or two, right in the center of the barrel. *That should do it.*

He didn't cotton to the idea of destroying property, but he saw no other way. Julia's pa knew she was inside that mortuary. And Abel had seen Robert head that way. He hoped everyone would come to the logical conclusion . . .

Robert ran after Julia, but stopped after crossing the street. He knelt in shadow and took aim with his pistol at the jar that glinted in the moonlight. He hoped Tuttle had gotten Julia's father far enough away. He drew in a breath and let it out slowly, counting to ten.

This would bring everything to a close, this stormy tale of Robert and Julia, of their forbidden tryst. Folks would grieve because of one little bullet. One bullet that would pierce a lot of folks' hearts. *But it's all for the best. To ensure Julia's safety and happiness. And that's what matters most.*

He wished he didn't have to do this. He wished to spare his ma the pain he knew she would suffer. But the suffering hadn't started with him. It had started with a feud. He had no idea why the Morrisons and Carsons were mortal enemies. He wondered if the confession his pa meant to make had something to do with that. He'd never know.

But one thing he did know: it would end here.

He set a bead on that bottle and pulled the trigger.

"I'm fine," Mr. Carson said, not masking his irritation, flitting his hand at Joseph. Carson's wife walked beside him, fretting.

"Just let the doctor help you, dear," she whined.

Joseph kept nudging Lester Carson across the street, but it was like trying to push on a giant sow that had eyes only for the slop trough. Carson was determined to get into the mortuary to see Julia's body, to confirm she was truly dead, and Joseph had told him he'd best come back in the morning. Now was not a good time. *It most certainly isn't. But what will I say to him when he finds no body inside?* Joseph had no doubt the influential rancher would hunt him down and want answers. And Joseph would have to lie, and he hated—

A loud explosion shook the ground and assaulted Joseph's ears. He fell to the ground and threw his hands over his ears, noticing that the Carsons did the same. Mrs. Carson screamed, and townspeople came running. Pieces of wood and other debris rained down on him, and fiery ash spun in the smoke-filled air.

His ears ringing, Joseph glanced about, then turned to look back at the mortuary.

It was in flames! And much of the building had blown to pieces. *Julia! And Robert!*

What had Robert done? Surely he'd gotten to safety before committing this heinous act. How could he have done such a thing?

But then, Joseph understood. And it wasn't likely anyone would have been loitering in the alley this time of night—not in this uneventful part of town.

Joseph watched, his jaw dropped, as the flames consumed the mortuary. People ran, yelling, and soon a water wagon arrived, and men pumped water through the hoses to wet down the adjacent structures. But there was nothing to be done for the mortuary. The storage building to the right had caught fire, but it was doused before too much damage resulted.

Joseph turned and saw Lester Carson cradling his arm where he'd gotten shot. His wife huddled beside him. They looked equally shocked and miserable as they gaped at the flames.

Mrs. Carson wailed. "Julia. My sweet baby girl. . ."

It broke Joseph's heart to hear her. To see the deeply etched grief on Mr. Carson's face. It took all his resolve to not utter a word of condolence—for fear he might somehow reveal the truth, that their precious child was alive. Yet, he couldn't say a thing. He had to keep this terrible silence. *It's for Julia to decide if she will reappear in their lives. She deserves this chance with Robert. And I won't sabotage it. Not after all I've gone through. All she's gone through.* At least they thought she was dead and not that she had been alive when the mortuary exploded. *Lord, forgive me for my collusion of silence.*

The events of the night suddenly hit him like a blow to his gut. He was beyond exhausted. As he watched the flames lick the leaden sky, he wondered about that Negro, Levi. *That makes two fires tonight, two separate escapes.* Had the escapee been successful in freeing his friend? Oddly, he hoped so. He hoped Levi hadn't been caught. Though, perhaps if he had, he'd find some new opportunity to escape once more.

Joseph reasoned that Julia could be included in that long list of prison escapees, although it would never go on the books as such. Only he knew the truth, and he'd keep that truth hidden deep in his soul and take it to his grave. Though . . . maybe he'd regale Cathryn Povey with the tale someday. He hoped that opportunity would present itself. But for now, for all intents and purposes, Robert Morrison and Julia Carson were dead.

Joseph had done all he could to help the star-crossed lovers escape unscathed, as Sarah had admonished him. Like rising from the ashes, they would begin a new life in a new home. Would Robert go to Fort Collins, as he'd planned? Work with Eli? It wouldn't be hard to find out. Though, he knew Eli was a man of great honor and integrity, and he would never divulge a confidence. But Joseph also knew Eli said a lot in his silence.

He smiled as he ambled along Front Street, in the direction of his modest house. He guessed it was about a mile north, and though he'd been afraid to wander about in Laramie City at night, duly warned by Cathryn, he felt strangely safe, ensconced in the wonderful swirl of relief and joy. He'd pulled off something—with the Lord's help—that was, frankly, impossible. *With man, yes, impossible. "But with God, nothing shall be impossible."*

Never before had this truth been pounded home so mightily.

Chapter 31

HOW A WOMAN COULD LOOK beautiful and elegant in black mourning clothes, Joseph didn't know. But Cathryn Povey's milky complexion and the wisps of bronze hair tickling her forehead under the short lace of her smart hat gave her a radiant look on this Sunday afternoon, the last day of November. A month that would go down in Joseph's memory as one of his most trying and, yet, inspiring.

As she walked toward him across the cemetery fields, a breeze danced along Joseph's neck. He wrested his gaze from the sight of her graceful body and glanced past her. The families still gathered graveside in the distance, consoling one another, a weak winter sun coaxing the fog to break apart at their feet. In the distance, the Rockies glistened with snow, standing like silent sentinels in witness to this tragic scene—a scene that only Joseph, in all of Wyoming, knew was anything but a tragedy.

Joseph couldn't bring himself to attend the service. He was afraid he wouldn't be able to convince anyone—especially not Cathryn—that he was in mourning. It would require a poker face he'd never been able to muster. And how would he restrain himself from wanting to yell out "They're alive!" upon seeing the grieved expressions and knowing the pain roiling in their hearts?

No, it was better this way. He wanted to avoid close contact with any members of Julia's family for fear they would ask him questions about what had transpired in the prison. The official report stated that Julia had succumbed to respiratory distress due to complications resulting from her chronic asthma, and while A. J. House, the recently appointed warden of the Wyoming Federal Penitentiary was found to be fully to blame — for both her incarceration and subsequent demise — the man was dead, and so there was no need for further investigation of the matter. The territorial marshal had come to the prison the next day and questioned Joseph, among others — such as the guards who'd participated in placing Julia in solitary. The marshal also interrogated prison staff and prisoners regarding the bewildering escape of male inmate #17, which came on the heels of an inexplicable act of arson that had practically destroyed the warden's office. Joseph had committed yet another crime when he'd told the marshal he knew nothing of those incidents, all the while wondering where Levi was at the moment. Joseph pictured the loyal Negro and his friend enjoying life on the lam. And while he'd promised the guards he'd pay them one hundred dollars each for letting him in to see Julia, he figured they'd broken their end of the bargain when they barred him from reentering her cell that night. At least, that was how he justified the matter to himself.

Cathryn Povey came alongside Joseph, her eyes glistening with tears. She smiled sadly. "A beautiful service, Joseph. And it was truly astonishing to see those families standing together, putting their beloved children to rest in the Lord's arms.

Whatever past animosity they'd held had been quenched by the deaths of Robert and Julia." She fell quiet, and Joseph didn't know how to respond.

It truly was a sight—Stephen Morrison and his wife standing with bowed heads next to Lester Carson and his wife. The "deaths" of these star-crossed lovers had accomplished exactly the same result as Shakespeare's lovers. The feud had ended. All bitterness and desire for revenge had been buried in those empty caskets. A feud that had begun because of a flipped coin and a card game.

Joseph thought it odd one would go to the expense and trouble of a burial without any bodies, but he understood the need these families had to lay their children—and their hatred— to rest in such a ceremony. He truly hoped, though, that one day Julia and Robert would return—return from the dead—and let bygones be bygones. And what a joyous reunion that would be. Joseph believed that unless they forgave their parents and welcomed them back into their hearts, they would never be at peace in their hearts. *In their due time.*

"Shall we?" Cathryn asked.

Joseph nodded, and they began walking south along 4th Street to the café where Cathryn liked to have afternoon tea. They spoke little, each engrossed in their own thoughts. Joseph wondered what kind of life Robert and Julia would carve out for themselves in Fort Collins. Friday last, two days after that fateful night, after Joseph had fretted mightily over their escape, he'd received a telegram from Eli Banks stating enigmatically that "his package had arrived" and "my ma is pleased to have such a courageous and faithful friend like you." It had drenched him with relief, but it also filled him with longing to return to Greeley. If Warden House hadn't been killed, Joseph would have considered leaving his new post, despite the protests that

Cathryn would, no doubt, assail him with. The papers stated that House's death had been an accident—that someone's gun had misfired. But the word around town was that Lester Carson had killed House to prevent the warden from murdering Stephen Morrison. Would wonders never cease?

But now . . . he supposed he would stay and see what the new warden would be like. Cathryn had spared no barbs when speaking of Asa House and his horrific management of the prison, even though Joseph thought it a bit unkind to speak thusly about the dead.

"I received a letter from Governor Hoyt yesterday," Cathryn said as they walked into the heart of Laramie. The streets were quiet, as was usual for Sunday. Most of the shops were closed, but the hotels and their cafés remained open. Families dressed in their Sunday best, coming from the lone community church—the Methodist Episcopal Church on 2nd Street, which Joseph had begun attending—when he wasn't called to the prison for some emergency or other—tipped their hats and said hello as they passed.

"Regarding the prison?" Joseph asked.

Cathryn nodded. "He's putting forth measures to improve the conditions. There are plans for a female department—an area on the second floor for the women, where they can be housed apart from the men. Next to the large windows, to allow bright sunlight to cheer them. It's not much, but it's a start."

"And your other concerns? Did he address them?" They'd arrived at the café door, and Joseph stopped and regarded her. As usual, speaking about her causes brightened her countenance.

"He's taking under advisement my recommendation that the prisoners be given early release for time served with good behavior. He's assured me Hassie will be released without delay."

"That's wonderful news." It made Joseph's heart glad to hear that. The poor woman had gone through so much — insult added to injury to be thrown into prison for stealing a coat to keep from freezing.

Cathryn studied his face, and he tried not to squirm under her close scrutiny. "I imagine these first weeks of working in the prison have been emotionally taxing for you, my good doctor. But I must say, I am so proud of what you've done to help these women. And while there are sure to be big changes at the prison, what with a new warden and, one hopes, more serious and compassionate oversight, there will certainly continue to be challenges in your post. But I can't think of a better man to hold it. I do pray, Joseph, that you will stay the course."

His cheeks flushed with embarrassment. He wasn't accustomed to beautiful women praising him in such a way. *You mustn't let it go to your head. You do nothing on your own strength, and every gift you have was given to you from your Creator. Don't forget that.* Ah, the challenges of staying humble.

Joseph nodded his thanks, then opened the door for Cathryn. They went inside, a wonderful warm blast of heat greeting them from the hearth in the back, and sat at their usual table by the window. Well, they'd only come here twice, but it felt like a routine. One Joseph hoped would continue. He wasn't sure he was the most entertaining of companions, but Cathryn seemed to enjoy their little chats, and he wondered if she was lonely, seeing that her husband was so incapacitated. If he could brighten her life in some little way, he was glad for it. And she certainly brightened his. And inspired him. He'd come to Laramie with trepidation and uncertainty, but she had set a fire under him, to join her in her cause, and Joseph had found great purpose—for the first time in his life.

The waitress brought their tea and biscuits, and they sat in companionable silence as they sipped and ate. Then, a youngster rushed into the café, waving a newspaper.

"Did'ya hear? Did'ya hear? Sheriff's been arrested!"

The roomful of patrons swiveled to hear what the lad had to say. Joseph was all ears.

"Says here the sheriff killed Ty Lawson. A couple'a witnesses came forward."

Diners began talking heatedly, throwing questions at the youngster and asking to see the paper.

Joseph's first thought was about Robert. Word around town was that he'd killed Carson's nephew. But Julia had told Joseph Robert was innocent. That he'd merely wounded Ty, in self-defense. Joseph wondered if Julia doubted Robert's assertion, but if she did, this news would remove that doubt. Joseph hadn't met the sheriff, but he'd heard plenty of complaints about him and his Irish deputies. *Those surly men will probably leave town, if they weren't arrested along with the sheriff.* And it was the sheriff who'd brought Julia to the prison, which was why Carson had shown up that fateful night to kill him.

Joseph had heard tell what happened—after he had stupidly tripped and fallen into the water trough—*I hope Cathryn never hears that tale!*—how Stephen Morrison had confessed to cheating at cards and rigged the game so Carson would take the warden's ranch and provoke the rancher's wrath. *Just like that crusty old geezer had said that day in the restaurant.* In a way, he was sorry he'd missed all the excitement that had played out that night. And then he'd heard that Stephen Morrison handed over a deed to a parcel of land to Carson, telling him to take it, free of charge. It was the least he could do, Morrison told Carson, to make amends for his sins.

When the ruckus died down in the café, Cathryn shook her head and said to Joseph, "Another of my prayers answered. Now maybe we can get an honest and incorruptible sheriff to oversee this town. Perhaps we may finally see some progress toward becoming a civilized town. Maybe one day it will earn its name as the 'Gem City of the Plains.'"

"With your dedication and hard efforts, no doubt it will," he said.

She smiled briefly, but sadness swam in her eyes. As she sipped her tea and looked thoughtfully out the window, she said, "It's such a shame, such a shame. Julia was so young, and she had no business being in that place. I know you did all you could, Joseph . . ."

Cathryn turned and looked at him. He swallowed down all the words he wanted to say to her, words he dared not utter. Not now. He pinched his lips to keep from speaking, not trusting himself to keep his sworn confidence in the presence of this compelling woman.

"There's something you're not telling me, Joseph," she said evenly.

He couldn't meet her eyes. He fiddled with his teaspoon.

She made a slight noise in her throat, and he dared look at her.

She waited a long moment for him to speak, but when he wasn't forthcoming, she said with resignation, "It's not healthy to keep secrets." Then she smiled, and that smile sent his heart soaring, though his guilt came fast on the heels of his elation as he reminded himself she was a married woman. *Don't you start falling for her. Those are dangerous waters.*

Joseph cleared his throat, then sipped his tea. Finally, he said, "Someday, I'll tell you. But I, uh, can't right now. I'm afraid you'll just have to wait until the time is right."

"Hmm. I see," she said with a hint of playfulness. "I'm not a very patient woman, I'll have you know."

"I do know."

She raised her eyebrows at that, but before a retort could come out of her mouth, Joseph said, "That's what is so admirable about you. And what puts the fear of God into those who stand in your way. Sometimes a lack of patience is a virtue."

She cocked her head, considering his words. Or maybe considering him in a new light. "I suppose you're right. One should never be lax when it comes to the pursuit of justice."

"Amen," Joseph said, wondering if one day Cathryn Povey would be appointed the first female territorial governor. In a place where women were allowed to vote, to serve on juries, and hold offices only men held, Joseph didn't imagine such a thing was all that farfetched. But he didn't voice his thoughts. He didn't want to plant any ideas in her head . . . though, it was more than likely she was already considering running for office someday. And he would be her most ardent supporter.

"Well, I must be off. I have letters to write to Congress."

"Of course you do," Joseph said, a wide grin on his face. Cathryn chuckled. They stood, each setting coins on the table, without Joseph protesting—for Joseph had learned early on that she would always insist on paying her share—and he walked her outside. Cathryn turned to him. "I never did ask—were you there at the prison when that inmate had set fire to the warden's office and escaped?"

"Um . . . thankfully, no. I was . . . already on my way to the mortuary."

Cathryn grew quiet. "I see. Well, I'm so glad you were unharmed."

Something caught her eye in the window. She pointed.

"Oh, a traveling theater group is coming to Laramie. One I've seen perform before, in the District of Columbia. They are marvelous."

Joseph turned and looked at the notice. He grunted.

Cathryn said, "You don't like theater, Joseph?"

He fumbled for words. "I . . . I do. That is, sometimes. But . . . I'm not a fan of tragedies. I prefer something more . . . cheerful."

"I understand," she said, "considering all you've been through in recent weeks. But Shakespeare's *Romeo and Juliet* is such a wonderful story, however heartbreaking. Might I convince you into accompanying me?"

"Thank you, but I'm afraid I'll have to decline," he said a little hastily.

Again, she raised her brows and studied him. "I suppose the story is not all that different from Robert and Julia's, now that I think about it. Two families in a long-time feud. The star-crossed lovers' death ending the feud. Uncanny, wouldn't you say?"

Joseph managed a nod.

"If only that apothecary hadn't given Juliet the potion. Then the lovers might have lived happily ever after."

Joseph gulped and averted his eyes. He wished to forget last Wednesday night and what he'd had to do to get Julia out of prison.

"I suppose Shakespeare had the right to end his play however he liked. But, I agree, Joseph. The comedies are much more uplifting. Perhaps one day a troupe will present *A Comedy of Errors*, and you'll accompany me to see it."

Joseph smiled, a feeling of closure coming over him. The drama of this "play" was finally over. "With pleasure, Mrs. Povey. With pleasure."

Chapter 32

"I WISH YA WOULD RECONSIDER. Fort Collins is a mighty nice town," Clare Banks said in her adorable Irish brogue.

She stirred a pot of delicious-smelling stew with one hand and supported her bulging belly with the other.

Julia felt uneasy sitting at the table, not helping at all with supper, but Clare had insisted. "I know. I would love to live here, but it's just too close to Wyoming."

"It's not that close," Clare protested, stopping her stirring and giving Julia a pleading look. "Plus, ya can legally change your names. No one'll be looking for a Jenny Johnson, f'r instance —"

"Jenny Johnson?" Julia chuckled.

"Sure. It's a common-enough name. Robert c'n be Ralph." She flipped bright-red curls out of her face with the back of her hand.

"Ralph?" Julia shook her head. She just couldn't feature Robert as a Ralph.

"I told ya," Eli said, his face gazing lovingly at his very pregnant wife as he came through the front door with an armful of wood. "Clare's stubborn to a fault—"

His pretty wife made a quite unladylike snort.

Eli dropped his load in the wood box next to the large river-stone hearth and laughed. "—but that's why I love her so."

Julia smiled, tickled by the banter Eli and Clare so comfortably engaged in. *I hope our love grows deep like that*, Julia thought, though it was hard for her to imagine loving Robert more than she already did. Not a week in Fort Collins, and they'd had their whirlwind marriage ceremony with Eli and Clare as witnesses in a quaint church with the only others in attendance being the kind old pastor and a stray cur that had wandered in. For a wedding gift, Eli and Clare had put them up in a fancy hotel suite, where they'd stayed the next three days and nights, hardly leaving their room, buried under blankets of red-hot passion that, even beginning to think about it, made her blush.

Julia had often imagined what it might be like to give herself, body and soul, to the man she would one day love, but she never imagined the fathomless joy to be so intoxicating. Robert's attendance upon her was tender and sweet and fervent beyond measure, and his kisses and gentle touches sent her soaring. They'd both been so nervous that first night, and Robert's fumbling and awkwardness eased much of her fears of intimacy—especially after that horrid man had violated her so cruelly. But those frightening moments Robert had erased, one by one, with his sweet kisses—though Julia knew it would take much more time to erase all the other hurts.

At first her mother's rejection and harsh words had stung, but Julia knew in her heart that her parents loved her dearly.

And while guilt railed at her for putting them through the suffering of her "death," she and Robert both believed this time of mourning would be good for both their families. Though, it had been awfully unsettling to read about their funerals in the Colorado papers. Hoping to avoid recognition in Fort Collins, they'd mostly stayed indoors or at the Banks's homestead, but first thing in the morning, she and Robert would be getting on the train for Denver, where Eli had set Robert up to work with a freight company—with a man Eli did much business with and one he highly respected. *And then once we get settled, maybe I'll send for Daisy.* But how? She'd think of a way.

Yes, she and Robert would change their names—the Morrison name was known far and wide. *But, Jenny and Ralph Johnson?* Julia giggled.

As she sipped tea and listened to Robert chopping wood outside Eli and Clare's homestead, and watched the adorable couple tease each other—Clare trying to knead bread while Eli played with her hair, playfully irritating her—Julia wished they could stay here in Fort Collins. But it was too risky. Too easy for Stephen Morrison to track where Robert had wired the money—a clear path to Eli Banks. She and Robert had decided that if they did return to Laramie one day, or revealed to their families that they were alive and well, it would be on their terms and in their own due time.

Eli came over to the table and plopped into a chair across from Julia.

"I keep thinkin' 'bout your ordeal in the prison—what-all ya told us about how Doc Tuttle got ya out." He grunted and shook his head. "It sure took a lot of courage to trust him—to take that poison."

Clare waved a floury hand at Eli. "To trust yer ma. I can't imagine bein' give a potion by some Indian woman ya never met and told to drink it." Clare came over and studied Julia's face. "Did it taste awful? How'd it make ya feel? Did ya see any bright lights on t'other side?"

"Criminy, Clare. Ya don't have to grill the gal," Eli said.

Julia chuckled. "That's alright, Eli." She told Clare, "It just felt like a deep sleep, is all. Good thing, too. When I read in the paper that there'd been a prison outbreak and someone had set fire to the warden's office around the time Dr. Tuttle must've gotten me out, I about had apoplexy. I wonder if I'll ever learn the whole story." She hoped someday she would get to thank the doctor for what he did for her and Robert. Her gratitude knew no bounds. She would have to think of a gift to send him, by way of Eli.

"Sure ya will," Clare said. "One way or t'other." She gave Eli a sly look. "The doctor's friends with Eli. I'm sure my sweet husband can weasel out the story."

Eli gave her a swat on her rump. "Don't look to me to do any weaselin'. I promised Robert and Julia both I wouldn't give away their secret. An' you better not either."

"Course I won't."

"Well," he said, eyeing her as she went back to kneading bread, "I've a mind to keep ya locked up in this house, with a passel of kids, just to make sure you don't spill the beans."

"A passel o' kids, huh?" She patted her belly. "Guess we got a lot more lovin' to git to, then, once this one's born."

Julia blushed, but Eli broke out in laughter.

"What's so funny?" Robert said, coming inside and letting in another drift of cold air. He wiped sweat off his forehead, his face ruddy from the exertion of splitting wood. His blue chambray shirtsleeves were rolled up to the elbow, and Julia couldn't tear her eyes off his muscular torso evident under the cloth. A torso she now knew as well as the back of her hand. The thought of their recent lovemaking sent heat to the nether reaches of her body.

When his question detonated laughter all around, Robert shrugged and sidled up next to Julia, planting a big kiss on her lips. "I reckon I should wash up. I smell like a dead rat."

"Not that bad," Julia said, putting a hand on the back of his neck and drawing him into another kiss. "You're still kissable."

Clare guffawed. "More kissable than a rat, I'd say." She nodded at a large cast-iron pot on the stove. "Water's already hot, if'n ya want to take that pot into the bathin' room out yonder."

"Thanks, Clare," Robert said. He gave her a nod and looked at Eli. "You've both been so kind —"

"Don't mention it," Eli said. "It's the least we c'n do fer ya. You've been through some hard times — more'n ya deserve. But sometimes trials are f'r the best. And in the end, justice prevails."

"Like that warden bein' shot," Clare offered. "And yer sheriff gettin' arrested. That lets ya off the hook for Ty's murder," she said to Robert.

Eli added, a bit thoughtfully, "And while it ain't pleasant havin' to kill a fella, ya did what ya had to, Julia. Never doubt it. A gal's got a right to defend herself, and her honor. At least in the sight of God, if not accordin' to the laws of men."

Claire's brows raised as she looked at her husband. "Well, them's some deep thoughts, Mr. Banks. As my ma would say, 'You're waxin' poetic.'"

Eli swatted her again, but missed this time. He got a puff of flour in his face for the effort.

Robert picked up the heavy pot by the handle and carefully navigated it out of the kitchen. Julia got up from her chair and made to follow him, and Clare gave her a conspiratorial wink. "Take yer time, lovebirds. Supper won't be ready for, oh, nearly an hour. Plenty o' time for—"

"Hobble yer lip, Mrs. Banks," Eli warned her, perhaps suspecting she was about to make another "unladylike" remark.

Julia grinned all the way to the back room, where a ceramic tub sat in a pretty wood-paneled room smelling of cedar.

Robert set down the pot and worked the pump handle, and water began to fill the tub a few inches. He then poured the scalding water into the bath to give him a foot's height of water to bathe in.

"It may be a little cozy in there, but would ya like to join me?" Robert wiggled his brows. Now it was Julia's turn to swat him.

"It wouldn't be proper! I should be helping Clare with supper."

"I think she's got everything under control," he said with a smirk.

Robert started to pull his shirt over his head, but Julia stopped his hands. "Still, we shouldn't . . . dally too long." She took hold of his shirt and slipped it over his head, then ran her hands along his broad chest, tickling his chest hair. Then her fingers slipped down a few inches.

A moan escaped Robert's mouth. "Now . . . uh, don't ya start something you can't stop . . ."

She gave him an overtly coy look. "It's not about whether I can stop . . ." She worked at his trouser buttons, giggling all the while.

Robert threw back his head and laughed. "Come 'ere," he said, pulling her into his arms and pressing his taut body against hers. "You know how much I love you, Julia Morrison?"

"No," she muttered as he smothered her with kisses. "Tell me."

"You, Julia, are the sun rising in the east."

She tipped back her head so he could trail kisses down her neck. "Ah, quoting Shakespeare again, are we?"

"No," he whispered hot in her ear, sending shivers to her toes. "Just borrowing a few lines. We can write our own play of our lives, and this one will have a happy ending. Wherever we end up."

"I see," she said, letting him untie the knot of her skirt. Her body shuddered with desire as his hands slipped under her waistband and wandered south. She thought of Juliet's words: *"All my fortunes at thy foot I'll lay, and follow thee my lord throughout the world."* Julia didn't care where they would call home, so long as they were together. That was all that mattered.

Then her handsome husband gently lifted her blouse over her head. Julia said, "I'm thinking your bath can wait a bit."

All she got for an answer was a nod and a nibble on her neck.

"I suppose," she whispered in his ear, thinking back to the night she'd met Robert and he'd held her for the first time, under the cold stars, as she fought for breath, "we have defied the stars, my love."

"Yes, indeed," Robert said, as her skirt fell in a puddle around her feet. "Oh yes . . . indeed."

As Robert lifted her like a bird into his arms, she wrapped her legs around him and felt about to explode in joyous pleasure.

Yes, indeed.

The End

Note from the Author

I HOPE YOU'VE ENJOYED THIS new story in The Front Range Series! After visiting Laramie, I knew this would be a great town to bring to life in my series. Laramie has such a unique and fascinating history. Along with being the iconic "Wild West" town, rife with lawlessness, it earned the nickname "The Equality State" because, in 1869, the first territorial governor, John Allen Campbell, approved giving women the right to vote—a first in the US.

Women in Laramie City not only could vote; they served on a jury and held positions, such as bailiff, that only men in the US could hold. Women could own property for the first time. And women could be sent to the federal penitentiary to serve out criminal sentences.

I took liberty with the dates in my novel in order to keep a tight timeline with the other books in the series. The first female prisoner was incarcerated in 1880. A total of twenty-three women served time at the prison over the years. I did, however, try to accurately describe the way the prison was laid out and run. And there wasn't a doctor specifically assigned to the female population, as I showed. I created that circumstance for the sake of my plot. The doctor assigned to the prison was on call, and, as I noted, he was paid one dollar a day.

I was surprised to learn that nearly one-quarter of all prisoners escaped. Some just wandered off when working in the brickyard or cutting ice for the railroad. Others broke out in various ways, including an instance of fashioning a wooden key in order to unlock the doors (I just had to borrow that idea!). Others escaped through the roof that had been damaged in a previous fire and not yet been repaired. The Wyoming Territorial Penitentiary was the only facility that had Butch Cassidy as a prisoner (when I visited, they had a terrific exhibit about him). It's worth the visit to learn all the interesting history of the prison.

I tried to portray the town and prison as accurately as I could. Many of the names of the characters and businesses are historically correct, and my apologies to the legacy of A. J. House, warden, for turning him into such a bad guy. I found nothing about him in my research other than his name. Thomas Jefferson Carr was a sheriff who was truly said to "put fear in the hearts of evildoers," The names of Morrison and Carson were made up to provide a parallel to Montague and Capulet in *Romeo and Juliet.*

I kept a close parallel to the plot of Shakespeare's play (I hope you noticed, and I hope you'll be inspired to go read the play now). The sheriff is the Prince, Ellsworth is Mercutio, Benjamin is Benvolio, Ty Lawson is Tybalt. And, of course, Dr. Joseph Tuttle is the apothecary. Many other characters paralleled those from the play.

I had fun borrowing some verses and action from the Bard's play, but I couldn't end in tragedy. I'm guessing you are glad the lovers didn't die. I got the idea of doing a Western version of the play upon seeing The Ashland Shakespeare Festival (OSF) a few years ago doing a Western adaptation of *The Comedy of Errors*. It was the most hilarious and entertaining Shakespeare play I'd seen yet—hammed up to the max. Though I had no intention of writing a comedic romp like that, I do love the way the OSF often sets Shakespeare plays in different times and locales.

Watch for more installments in The Front Range Series set in Laramie, and if you haven't signed up for my mailing list, be sure to visit CharleneWhitman.com. You'll get the first book, *Wild Horses, Wild Hearts*, for free upon signing up.

Thank you for reading my novel. I hope you'll check out the other books in the series. I welcome your comments and ideas for future stories. I write for you!

~ Charlene Whitman, March 2018

About the Author

CHARLENE WHITMAN SPENT MANY YEARS living on Colorado's Front Range. She grew up riding and raising horses, and loves to read, write, and hike the mountains. She attended Colorado State University in Fort Collins as an English major. She has two daughters and is married to George "Dix" Whitman, her love of thirty years.

If you enjoyed this book . . . One of the nicest ways to say "thank you" to an author is to leave a favorable review online. I would be appreciative if you would take a moment to do so! Thanks so much!

Comments? Questions? I love hearing from my readers, so feel free to contact me via CharleneWhitman.com.

Be sure to join Charlene Whitman's readers' list to get free books, special offers, giveaways, and sneak peeks of chapters and covers.

When you join, you'll get a FREE copy of Wild Horses, Wild Hearts!

Sign up at www.Charlene Whitman.com.

Take a peek at the first chapter of *Colorado Hope* ...

Chapter 1

May 16, 1875

A FIERCE WIND WHIPPED GRACE Ann Cunningham's hair, yanking at the long strands and pulling them free from their pins. She squinted through the haze of the blustery day and stroked her bulging belly, trying to comfort her baby, who seemed just as agitated by the sudden storm. Her back ached from sitting on the hard buckboard bench all these miles—much less comfortable than the plush sleeper car they'd enjoyed last week on the train from Illinois to Cheyenne.

She frowned at the dark roiling clouds that had moved in and quickly blotted out the sun. What had been a pleasant uneventful morning was now turning into an ominous and unsettling afternoon on the open prairie.

Grace sucked in a breath as the baby again kicked her ribs in protest. Her sweet husband's sun-browned face tightened in concern as he caught her gesture. He pulled on the reins of the two draft horses—sturdy ones they'd bought yesterday in

Cheyenne. Surefooted, the seller had told them. And Monty knew his horses, so she trusted his purchase and assurance that they'd haul them without incident to Fort Collins. But looking at her husband's face now, seeing the subtle telltale signs indicating that he hadn't expected this squall nor felt at ease about it, gave her pause. And her normally talkative husband had been too quiet this last hour, eyeing the sky and listening to the roar of the nearby river, as if hearing their complaints and trying to suss out nature's intentions.

"The baby all right, darlin'?" He scooted over on the buckboard seat to look her over, then took her hands in his.

Warmth from his gentle grip comforted her, but not as much as the love streaming from his adoring gaze.

"I think so," she told him, then smiled as he laid his hand firmly on her belly.

Grace thanked the Lord in a silent prayer for this wonderful man who'd married her in a simple ceremony last September. All those years she'd lived with her doting aunt Eloisa in the boardinghouse back in Bloomington, she never imagined she'd be blessed with such happiness. When Montgomery Cunningham had first stepped into the parlor to take a room before starting college at Wesleyan University, she'd been a shy, giggling girl of ten. Neither of them foresaw the love that would spark six years later when he showed up again unexpectedly, about to head west to explore and survey lands unknown.

Monty closed his eyes, his hand still on the baby in her womb. She imagined him communing with their baby, speaking to it the way he spoke to rivers, to trees, to the land he traversed by boat and on horseback and on foot. Something had happened to him when he returned from the Hayden Yellowstone Expedition. He had changed from boy to man, yes—but it was more than that. He had fallen in love with the West, and with rivers in particular. Although he'd studied geology in college with John Powell, water captured his heart, and he sought out trips that had him navigating whitewater. Nothing made his eyes sparkle more than talking about the way water moved and sang as it cascaded and carved the face of mountains and spilled into waiting valleys. Well, except the way he looked at her.

Monty may have loved rivers, but Grace knew he loved her more. So much more, for he gladly gave up his exploring to settle down and marry and start a family. Although, Grace thought moving to the new town of Fort Collins, Colorado, was adventure enough. She hoped he'd come to see it that way as well and not be beset by a restless stirring to venture back out into the wild.

The West! Quite the change from her simple, comfortable life in Bloomington—if the lawless and untamed town of Cheyenne was any indication. She shuddered thinking of the seedy saloons and lecherous unwashed men they'd encountered as they sought purchase of their horses and wagon yesterday. If Monty hadn't assured her she'd live in the manner she'd been accustomed to—with the same stars twinkling overhead—she would never have considered moving west. Not that she fancied some ostentatious lifestyle; she'd lived in a modest home under her aunt's care. But she desired familiarity and the comfort of belonging to a community.

When he opened his eyes, she dared asked, "How much further?" They'd been traveling since dawn, making good time despite the roughness of the road and the boggy sections dotted with patches of melting snow. They'd been assured in Cheyenne that the fifty-mile road south through Colorado Territory was a bit rough but well traveled—but then, they'd also been given predictions of clear skies and gentle breezes the whole way to Fort Collins.

"Well," he said thoughtfully, glancing around as the unseasonably warm wind increased to a dull roar. "Not much further. The river is coming closer to the road now, and according to the map, that large bend in the road back there comes right before the northern ten-mile marker."

A finger of wind lifted the brim of his felt hat, showing eyes as stormy as the day, his one hazel eye catching a glint as a fork of lightning snapped out of the brooding clouds overhead. A second later the ground rattled with thunder.

Grace cried out as the horses reared and whinnied—then thumped down hard on hooves that pounded the ground in agitation.

Monty jumped down from the buckboard and calmed them, speaking words that the wind snatched from his mouth as he held fast the hat on his head. He took the closest horse's leather neck strap in hand and, cooing comforting sounds, got the frightened beast to take a step, then another. He shot Grace a look that set her heart racing. She could tell he was afraid, and that wasn't a look she'd often seen on Monty's face. He seemed to be searching for some shelter, but they were on wide-open land, with no trees in sight.

"We'd best turn back," he yelled to her over the snarling storm, leaning close to make sure she heard him. Dirt and debris swirled in the air around their heads, and Grace squinted as it pelted her cheeks. "Maybe head to that ranch we passed a couple o' hours ago."

Grace wrapped her shawl tighter around her body as the balmy air suddenly turned chilly and icy fingers of wind tickled her neck. Monty grumbled something under his breath as fat raindrops assaulted them.

Monty rushed back to the wagon and pulled out a canvas tarp from underneath their boxes and crates filled with their possessions. Another flash of lightning streaked the angry sky, followed by an even louder thwack of thunder that sounded as if it had rent the earth.

Grace blurted out a cry and buried her face in her hands as she listened to Monty wrestle with the tarp. Presently, she felt it fling over her head, and the rain pelted the thick cloth sheltering her in dull thuds. Monty slipped in beside her and huffed, his body heat instantly warming the space.

He turned to her, and in the stuffy enclosure that ensconced them both, he planted a gentle kiss on her lips, then pulled her closer and deepened the kiss, as if to drink in every bit of her. As if the rain and the river were not moisture enough for his soul. Her heart thumped hard against his chest and the baby kicked again, making him chuckle as he reluctantly ended their intimate moment.

"He's a strong one," Monty said, his face gleaming. "And already making sure he's not left out of the fun."

"He?" Grace teased. For some reason Monty was sure she was carrying a son. But she knew he would just as gladly welcome a girl into his arms. He grinned and gave her a look that made her pulse race. That lopsided smile on his strong, square jaw never failed to stir her passion.

He lowered his voice and whispered hot words in her ears. "I'm looking forward to a bath and then a sweet night in your arms in a clean, warm bed—with a soft feather-tick mattress." He rubbed her bulging belly mindlessly as he peeked out at the storm that now howled like a sick wolf. Grace ran a hand through his hair as thick and brown as molasses, which inclined to curl around his ears.

"Maybe we should just wait a bit?" she said, thinking how Colorado weather was known to change suddenly. Just as this squall had come upon them unawares, perhaps it would clear up just as quickly. Or so she hoped.

He chewed on that idea a moment, then shook his head. "We're too exposed out here. The storm has stalled overhead, which means we're a likely target for lightning to strike. We need to get moving, get somewhere safe . . ." He blew out a frustrated breath as rain seeped in under the tarp and soaked his hair. His eyes grew stormier with the weather, and water dribbled down his rough-shaved cheeks and under his shirt collar. Grace felt the weight of her soggy skirt hem pulling on her, and noticed her stockings were wet and leaking water into her shoes. Her teeth started to chatter.

"It's bad and getting worse," Monty mumbled as the horses began dancing in place, just as eager to get out of the rain and the open prairie, as if they sensed danger coming their way. He jiggled the reins and yelled out, "Haw!" to get the animals moving. With a lurch they trotted forward, throwing their heads in protest.

Grace now heard the river as the wind momentarily calmed. It was close, and raging. They'd been skirting the Cache la Poudre for miles now, admiring the wild waters bouncing over boulders in the narrow sluices carved in the canyon. Most of what they'd glimpsed showed a swollen wide river moving at a fast clip, but as they neared Fort Collins, the banks had risen more steeply, with evergreens growing clear to the water's edge, and steep cliffs sweeping up into canyon walls that thundered with the echo of whitewater. Grace wondered if Monty would feel safer and more in control right now if he were at the bow of a canoe instead of holding the reins of two skittish horses he'd barely made the acquaintance of.

"The bridge can't be that far off," Monty said, pulling her attention back to the dirt road that was starting to resemble a pond before them. Grace shuddered. "Maybe we should try to cross, and seek shelter on the other side." His voice sounded unsure, which unsettled Grace even more.

"Can you make out the road?" What she really wondered was if the horses would mire in all the mud. They were less upset though, now that Monty had them moving again. Moving was better than sitting still, out in the open, she reasoned. Although, from what she could make out up ahead through the sheets of rain obscuring the horizon, there was nothing but more open, flat land. She hadn't been paying attention these last few miles. She'd been nodding off in the cool spring afternoon, the weak sun hardly warming her shoulders. How long would it take them to get to the bridge? Would it be safe to cross? A jolt of fear coursed up her back, and her baby kicked hard.

"Shh, little one," she said, more to herself than to her baby, "it'll be all right; just sleep . . ."

She fingered the silver chain around her neck and found the small round pendant, then gripped it tightly in her fist. Monty had given this trinket to her when he came back from his exploration of Yellowstone. An Indian guide had gifted it to him, after he helped rescue the man who had toppled overboard in some strong rapids. Etched into the flat silver disk was an eight-pointed star—an Indian symbol of hope, he was told.

She choked back tears as she huddled close to Monty, shivering and wet, listening to the rain beat on them, as if trying to drown out her dreams. She fussed with the tarp, trying to keep it draped overhead, as the wind grabbed at it, wrenching it from her grasp. Monty's full attention was on the road and the horses reluctantly pulling the wagon.

Would they make it to Fort Collins? She pushed down her panic as the wind attacked anew. The horses now fought Monty's attempt to urge them forward, and once more he jumped down and took hold of the long side strap and tried to coax them along the flooded road. Grace saw their hooves sink into mud with every step, which made them prance in agitation and throw their heads against the headstalls and blinders as if trying to get free.

Another crack of lightning exploded in the sky and set the horses into a near panic. Grace stiffened and clung to the side panel of the buckboard, shifting her feet but unable to get better purchase on the slippery wet wood.

Monty offered his hand. "You better come down, Gracie. I can't predict how these horses will behave. They seem right ready to bolt."

Grace nodded, and trying not to show her fear, gave him an encouraging smile, assuring him it was all right, that she'd brave this trial alongside him. She wanted him to see she was stalwart—despite her pregnancy—that she could handle the rugged West. They hadn't much further to go, she consoled herself, and now, through the haze of mist and wind and rain she could make out what looked like a sturdy wood bridge— unlike like others they had crossed, which had been constructed from old metal railroad cars—spanning the Poudre River just a ways ahead. The roar of the river gave her more shivers, for it sounded altogether monstrous.

But if anyone could assess a river and its dangers, Monty could. She trusted him to get them safely across to the other side. Although, even from here she could see the dark water roiling and churning and overflowing its banks, splashing the underside of the bridge with fury.

She gulped, let out a tense breath, then eased carefully down from the seat, Monty holding tightly to her hand and wrapping his other strong arm securely around her back to help lift her down and onto the saturated ground. Her nice new leather traveling shoes sank into sticky mud, but she would clean them later. Once they made it to the hotel in Fort Collins.

She steeled her nerves and took a deep breath. A surveying job was awaiting Monty's arrival—in their new western town. They'd head to the land office tomorrow and file a homestead claim. They had plenty of money from the sale of her aunt's property, plus the savings Monty had accumulated from his jobs as surveyor, cartographer, and river guide on the various expeditions he'd gone on over the last few years. They would spend the summer building a cabin and planting a garden and getting ready for the birth of their child—the first of many to come. They would make a home in the West, in the small but growing town of Fort Collins, presently to double in size with the advent of the railroad, assuring plenty of surveying work for Monty for years to come. The Indians no longer a threat, the West was becoming tamed, and towns like Fort Collins promised church, community, and hope for a bright future to those who dared to dream. Next year the nation would celebrate its centennial, and Colorado was slated to be admitted as the thirty-eighth state in the union. Yes, the country embraced hopeful prospects.

Grace consoled herself with these positive visions of her future, a way of fanning the flames of her hope against the attempts of the Front Range storm to snuff it out. With Monty's arm holding her close as he urged the horses forward, Grace settled into that hope and reminded herself she was safe. Monty would make sure they made it. He'd had many close calls on his wilderness expeditions, but he was careful and strong and knew how to keep calm and level-headed in danger—and he'd faced plenty of situations more dangerous than a little rain and lightning.

She managed a chuckle, thinking of how silly she was being. They weren't out in the wilderness. They were on an well-traveled road, and they'd passed not a few people riding north only two hours prior. She owed it to Monty to encourage him and show her trust in him.

But just as she turned to say something to him, the ground slipped out from under her feet. She screamed as a loud explosion erupted around her, and her world turned upside down.

Although the antique mirror was cracked and silver flecks of paint curled and distorted her image, Lenora Dutton could still see enough of her reflection in the glass to assess she was ready for the big day—a day she'd been long awaiting, yesiree. A quick glance out the window of the second-story room in the Drop Dead Saloon told her a nasty storm was brewing, but it only brought a pleased smirk to her face. God's judgment was about to descend upon the evil remnants of the Dutton Gang. Namely, her snake of a husband, Hank, and the last two beef-headed scalawags that had faithfully and blindly followed their boss everywhere he led them—which, much to her delight, included the last stop on their bank-robbing journey: the Denver City Jail.

The hanging had been scheduled for high noon, but due to the inclement weather—more likely the lazy men assigned to erect the gallows—it was now set for three p.m. Lenora figured it was approaching noon, but she had no timepiece. Her head was a little woozy after imbibing a bit too much whiskey last night. She craned her neck closer to the mirror and scrutinized the bags under her eyes, then reached for her powder puff and minimized the damage.

Last she remembered, she'd been sidling up to some such feisty card chisler whose name she couldn't recall—and didn't care to—and had no memory of being helped up the stairs and into her bed. Thankfully, when she awoke this morning, she still had her clothes on. Which made her wonder if the kindly but seedy saloon keeper had escorted her upstairs. The first thing she did upon waking was feel under the mattress for her leather satchel, then made sure all the contents were still there.

A little giggle bubbled up as she thought of Hank swinging on the end of that rope, his legs kicking frantically, a black hood over his ugly, squat face. Thank God she would never have to stare into that mug ever again or hear his grating laughter. Good riddance! She'd bided her time and paid enough dues all these miserable years, pasting her smiles on and playing sweet on his every word. But it had been worth it. Because after today, the gold would be hers. All hers for the taking. And then she could head to San Francisco and start her new life—buy herself a big fancy mansion in the heart of the city, overlooking the ocean. Far from the dirt and grime and all uncouth manner of folks on the Front Range. She'd be the lady she was meant to be.

Lenora grinned. Hank was as mean a rogue as ever was, but today he'd be dead. He'd rough-handled her plenty, and she'd had many a black eye and a few broken bones to show for her loyalty. *But it was worth it, all worth it.* Because she had watched him hide the gold in that cabin north of Fort Collins, up in the Poudre River Canyon. And it was a heap of gold.

As she dabbed at a bit of beeswax from the unlit candle on the dresser with a spent match, she puckered her lips and turned her head from side to side. She was still young and attractive. And she'd learned all the tricks to snagging a man's attention and heart, getting him to do her bidding. With her money and looks, she could live that high society life waiting for her in California.

She tapped her foot as she thickened her long lashes with the wax, then adjusted the combs in her ebony hair. The traveling skirt and neat wool jacket she wore would keep her warm should that storm edge in. But she didn't care if she arrived at the cabin soaked to the bone. She hadn't been there in months—not since the time she'd finally had the opportunity to ride up there and move the gold before Hank got back from his latest escapade in Nebraska. She'd sweet-talked Clayton into letting her go "visit her poor, ailing mother" for a few hours. He never could say no to her, and he was sour at Hank anyways, since Hank chose to assign Clayton the task of babysitting her while the gang held up a stage heading to the armory.

After plying that dunderhead with enough whiskey to choke a buffalo, she took his horse and rode north, returning the next day, Clayton nursing a pounding headache and none the wiser that she'd been gone a lot longer than promised. It gave her a thrill to know she alone knew where the gold was hidden, and it wouldn't be easy to find, nosiree.

But upon returning, she realized what would happen if Hank looked for his stash and found it gone. He'd question her, and she wasn't sure she'd be able to lie with enough convincing. Which made her go through with the plan she'd had all along. Her next opportunity, she used her feminine wiles—and another bottle of whiskey—to loosen Clayton's tongue to learn where that week's robbery would take place. And once the gang rode out of town, in the dark of night, Lenora slipped an itty-bitty note under the sheriff's office door.

Imagine her surprise when news spread through town the next day that there had been a confrontation at a bank in

Colorado Springs, with a goodly number of outlaws shot—none other than members of the notorious Dutton Gang. Sadly, Hank hadn't been among the dead, but at least he'd been caught—along with Clayton "the Blade" Wymore and that simpering chucklehead Billy Hill Cloyd—who couldn't bear to hurt a flea, even though he was a better shot than Clayton and Hank combined.

Lenora checked her reflection one last time, figuring her wagon would be ready by now. She'd paid the boy triple the usual to make sure all her bags and boxes were neatly packed and ready for her departure. She'd be able to get as far as the turnoff to Coyote Gulch up the Poudre canyon, but from there she'd have to unhitch the horse and ride the last few miles to the cabin, which was situated up against a wall of rock above some of the biggest rapids on the river.

After pulling her satchel out from beneath the mattress, she stuffed her makeup and handkerchief in, then strode out of the room, her nose assaulted with the stale odor of cheap cigars and even cheaper perfume. Wind brushed branches against the cobwebbed windows that lined the walls near the long mahogany bar below the red plush-carpeted landing she marched across. She stepped over one drunk, who was lying facedown and blubbering something incoherent. She heard a loud snoring from the door on her right and lightly flounced down the staircase, eyeing the few patrons holing up inside the saloon on this stormy day. Most were nursing drinks and shuffling cards. Probably waiting to watch the hanging—along with everyone else in Denver City.

The varnish on the banister railing had been worn down by the thousands of grimy, greasy hands that had drunkenly gripped it over the years, which made Lenora look forward to gracing the proper, upstanding hotels of San Francisco. There she would pursue her dream to act on a stage—a real stage, not some rickety, termite-infested saloon platform. She was meant for the stage, and had talent. Oh, no one had told her such, but she'd fooled plenty of folks with the roles she'd played throughout her life. She had more acting experience than anyone on Broadway in New York City, she figured. She'd even chosen a stage name: Stella Twilight. Wasn't that just divine? It meant the stars in the sky—or something akin to that. She met a saloon gal once upon a time by that name and thought to use it someday. She would be that star on the stage, come hell or high water, yesiree.

A glance at the newspaper on a nearby poker table showed headlines announcing the hanging. Already a crowd was gathering outside, their excitement building just like the storm. She had chosen to stay the night in this saloon on Blake Street for its proximity to the square, the courthouse visible from the front door.

She positioned her shawl over her head, pulled on her long leather gloves, and ventured outside. Upon opening the saloon doors, she was hit with a blast of cold wind and a splatter of rain. Overhead, mean, thick black clouds hung, ready to dump their wrath upon the earth. A big smile lifted her cheeks. *Soon*, she told herself. *California, here I come!*

Suddenly, a loud explosion rocked the street. Rocks and rubble flew into the air the next block down—where the jail was. Shouting ensued, and then gunshots. Lenora ducked under the saloon's porch overhang, ready to bolt back inside, when she heard someone shouting and the rumble of horse hooves pounding down a nearby street.

"They've escaped!" a man yelled.

Lenora clutched her heart. Oh no! She prayed the man wasn't talking about Hank. How could they escape? She gritted her teeth. *Clayton's brother* . . . He wasn't a member of the gang, but he lived in Denver City, and he was a locksmith. He'd been useful when they needed to jimmy a lock. He owned some fast horses too. She hoped she was wrong and it was some other prisoner that had gotten out. She pursed her lips and grunted. Well, there was plenty of law around. Even if Hank got out, he wouldn't make it very far. He'd be caught before he hit the city limits.

At that moment, the boy from the livery rode up in her Schuttler & Studebaker spring wagon and jumped quickly down from the seat. He squatted alongside the wooden boardwalk, using the wagon for cover. More shots rang out in the air, and people screamed and ran as the bullets whined. Her horse reared up but didn't break from his harness. If only she could see what was happening. But no doubt she'd find out soon enough.

Lenora slipped behind a few of the men who'd run out from the saloon to see the commotion.

"What's happening?" one of them asked, his head darting from side to side, trying to make sense of the mayhem.

Lenora heard rather than saw more horses. This time they were racing down Blake Street, in front of the saloon. She counted the animals' legs—what she could make out through the crowd now huddled around her. Five or six horses, she figured. Then she caught a glimpse of the men riding like the Devil was on their tail.

She gasped. Hank! Followed by Clayton and Billy. She cursed under her breath. With clenched fists, she watched as more horses galloped past, kicking up dirt and grit that mixed in with the pellets of rain whirling in the air. She wiped her face and covered her eyes until the sound of hooves petered out, and the crowd erupted in animated talk.

The boy came up to her. "Miss, here's your wagon." His eyes caught hers, and she shook her head to sort what he was saying.

"Oh, yes. Here's somethin' for your trouble." She reached into her satchel and pressed a coin into his palm.

"Thank you, miss," he said, wide-eyed and craning to see down the street, where the outlaws had made a run for it. "I wonder if the sheriff will catch 'em."

She showed him a nervous smile. "I sure hope so. I'd hate to think of those horrid outlaws on the loose."

A nicely dressed man that oozed money next to her gave her a look-see and gazed approvingly. She saw the longing in his eyes and smiled demurely, a smile full of innocence and tinged with the appropriate amount of fear. "Perhaps you could find out . . . if it's safe for me to travel all alone . . . ?"

He gave a sweeping bow, removing his hat to reveal a large bald spot on the center of his head. Lenora hid a chuckle under her thick lashes. The moustache he sported must have borrowed all that hair from his scalp. "It would be my pleasure," he told her, giving his facial hair a twirl before walking purposefully down the street. She really didn't need his help, but she just couldn't resist watching another slobbering fool rush off to do her bidding.

Lenora climbed up with as much ladylike grace as possible onto the seat of her wagon and picked up the reins. Before she'd even said "giddap," she saw the sheriff and two deputies trotting back her way—with a man on horseback in tow.

She ducked her head under her shawl as Hank rode past, careful to not look up until they were long gone. She was glad she'd bought a new horse, for Hank would have surely recognized her piebald gelding. Not that he could do much about her being here.

She squelched the urge to ride over to the courthouse and watch the hanging—from the front row. Pictured giving Hank a sweet smile so he'd know just who put him in his predicament. But she didn't want to take the chance that someone, somehow, would recognize her and connect her to the Dutton Gang. She'd never joined in on any of their robberies, but she knew she could be considered an accessory of some kind. She'd been treated like one—that was for sure—Hank's accessory to wear on his arm and toss about when he lost interest. She knew he'd had other women on the side. He'd often come back to where they were laying low with his clothes reeking of another woman's perfume.

Through the shouting, running crowd, she'd determined they'd only caught him. And from what she could tell from the loud exchanges around her, two of the Dutton Gang had somehow given the sheriff the slip. A group of concerned citizens was gathering on the steps of the courthouse, but Hank was being hauled over to the gallows.

"They're not taking any more chances." The man she'd sent to suss out news ran up breathlessly to her, his eyes shining with longing. She knew he was more interested in her and what she could offer him than what fate awaited Hank Dutton, bank robber.

Lenora gave him a coy smile and demurely fluttered her lashes. "Whatever do you mean?" she asked.

He pointed. "Look, they're hanging him now, without any delay or last words."

"Oh my," she said breathlessly, imagining herself in the role of a helpless woman lost on the prairie. Her heart pounded hard, and she suppressed a cry of glee as she watched from the seat of her wagon as her husband, the long-sought-after brigand, was led up the pine-planked ramp to the gibbet sporting the waiting noose.

"But what about the others?" she asked innocently. "Weren't there more in the gang? Did they catch them?"

"They're assembling a posse. The men just . . . vanished." At her horrified look, he patted her hand reassuringly. "But don't you worry your pretty head about that, miss. I'm sure they won't get far. And then it's the noose for them."

A nervous tic attacked her gut, and she rubbed her gloved hands. She wouldn't be so quick to agree. Clayton had smarts when it came to disappearing. And there were plenty of places to hide in the bowels of the city. But she knew just where they were headed — of that she had no doubt. They'd beeline it to the cabin and look for the gold. Then, when they failed to find it, she knew exactly what they'd do next — look for her.

Perspiration broke out on her brow even though the day was cool. She pulled out a handkerchief from her jacket pocket and dabbed her forehead. She dared not take the chance of heading to the cabin. Not just yet. What she needed to do was find some place near it, where she could lay low and wait until word of their capture. And somehow not be anywhere obvious where they could find her. Surely not in Denver City.

She realized the man was speaking to her.

"Miss? I said, would you join me for lunch? I'm sure the events of the day have flustered you greatly. Let me help you down from that wagon —"

"Why, that's perfectly kind of you, sir," she said in a syrupy voice, using a gloved hand to gently push him back from the wagon, which he was leaning over to get close to her bulging bodice. "But, I'm afraid I have other plans. And I'm in a bit of a hurry."

More than a bit. If she didn't get far from Denver City quickly, she stood the chance of running into Clayton and Billy. And even though she had a Winchester rifle and a Colt pistol under her seat in a locked wooden box, she did not want to face "the Blade" anytime soon. If he had any inkling she was the reason for his recent appointment with the undertaker, she'd be carved like a side of beef. She'd seen some of his handiwork, and it wasn't pretty.

Without further ado, ignoring the rich suitor's protests, she swung her horse and wagon around to head north and slapped the reins to get the gelding trotting up the street. A bolt of lightning arced the sky, bright white against dark clouds, followed by a loud cheer erupting behind her, over by the jail. She didn't look to see her husband's fate, but she could see him in her mind's eye—swinging from the gallows. Relief washed through her as she smacked the reins harder and forced the horse into a run. The heavens opened up and dumped rain upon her, filling the streets with water and washing away her trail. There would be no trace of her now; she was leaving her loathsome life in Denver City—for good.

And one way or another, no matter how long it took, she would get the gold and head to San Francisco. The glamorous stage awaited her.

Want to read more? Get your copy of *Colorado Hope* on Amazon!